John B Dyson

Methodism in the Isle of Wight

Its origin and progress down to the present times

John B Dyson

Methodism in the Isle of Wight
Its origin and progress down to the present times

ISBN/EAN: 9783742845108

Manufactured in Europe, USA, Canada, Australia, Japa

Cover: Foto ©Andreas Hilbeck / pixelio.de

Manufactured and distributed by brebook publishing software
(www.brebook.com)

John B Dyson

Methodism in the Isle of Wight

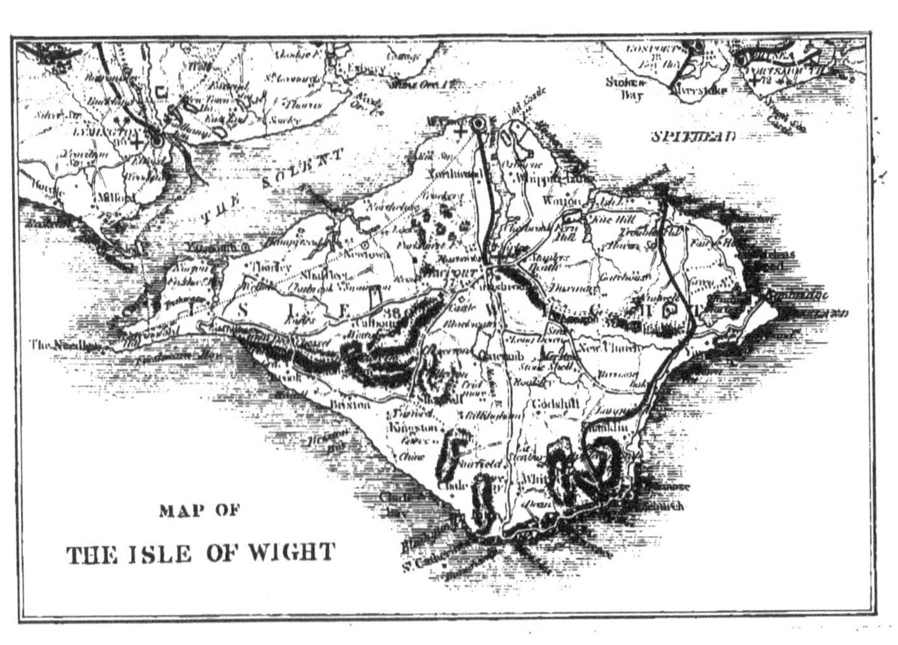

THE SOLENT
SPITHEAD
MAP OF
THE ISLE OF WIGHT

METHODISM

IN

THE ISLE OF WIGHT:

ITS ORIGIN AND PROGRESS DOWN TO THE PRESENT TIMES.

BY

JOHN B. DYSON.

VENTNOR, I.W.:

GEORGE M. BURT, HIGH STREET.

SOLD ALSO AT 66, PATERNOSTER ROW, LONDON.

1865.

PREFACE.

Few places are better known than the Isle of Wight. Visitors swarm to its shores, and crowd its thoroughfares during the summer; and invalids in great numbers avail themselves of its sheltered retreats and the amenity of its climate in winter. Lovers of science have explored its varied treasures, and given to the world the result of their labours in valuable works on Geology, Botany, History, &c. Nay, one might think that every nook and corner of this lovely spot had been photographed, illustrated, and described to repletion; but still—if we may judge from the multitude of new comers, new books published, the growing accommodation of rail, pier, and steam-boat—the interest is undiminished.

What other possible field of research can this little Isle present, which has escaped the notice of its many explorers? It happens that there is yet one left, which, although many would pass it by as unworthy of notice, and others would look upon it with sheer contempt, is nevertheless neither void of interest nor instruction : that field will be found in the Methodism of the Isle of Wight.

If we are not mistaken, Wesleyans—and, it may be, other Christians—will not be altogether indifferent to another slight tribute of historic facts, which may go towards the more perfect illustration of the important religious movement which will be for ever interwoven in the ecclesiastical history of the eighteenth century, and of which it will form so large an element.

We have endeavoured to discover and lay open the highway along which the great Revival advanced in these parts of the kingdom, that others may pursue it without the cost of time and labour which it required at our hands. At the same time the task was far from being uncongenial or unprofitable.

The author's thanks are due to the numerous friends who have most cheerfully rendered him valuable aid, two of whom it would be unpardonable not to name— the Rev. Dr. Etheridge and the Rev. William Moister.

NEWPORT, ISLE OF WIGHT,
March 4th, 1865.

CONTENTS.

CHAPTER I.

	Page
Origin of the name Wight	1
First settlers	2
Druidism	3
Introduction of Christianity	5
Saxon invasion	5
Wesley raised up	7

CHAPTER II.

The Wesleys detained at Cowes	8
Benjamin Ingham	9
Charles Wesley preaches at Cowes	10
Sail for America	11
The Moravians on board ship	12
Lady Margaret Hastings	12
Wesley's second visit to the Island	13
Spread of the revival	13
Reaches Portsmouth and Newport	16
The first Society in Newport	16
Carisbrook Castle	17
Origin of first Society	18
Wesley's second visit to Newport	19

CHAPTER III.

Mr. Hall	21
John Furz	24
Begins to preach	28
The Earl of Pembroke	30
An extraordinary sermon	32
Death of a persecutor	34
Charles Wesley in Dorset	35

CHAPTER IV.

	Page
The Shepherd of Salisbury Plain	38
His conversion	39
Christian labours and death	41
Salisbury made the head of Circuit	43
John Nelson	44
Wesley's third visit to the Island	44
Quarterly and Class Meetings	46

CHAPTER V.

Itinerants	51
Thomas Johnson	53
John Murlin	54
The Itinerant's horse	56
Item from Steward's book	57
Thomas Hanby	57
Robert Roberts	58
James Morgan	58
Departures from the work	59
Richard Henderson	60

CHAPTER VI.

The first Society in Portsmouth	62
John Mason	63
Alexander Mather	65
William Minethorpe	69
Alexander Coates	69
Preachers' Fund, and letter of Dr. Adam Clarke	70
Winchester	71
John Catermole	76

CHAPTER VII.

	Page
Elizabeth Bushell	77
Wiltshire divided	80
Whitefield's death	80
Francis Asbury	81
Richard Bourke and Wm. Eels	84
First Home Missionary to the Isle of Wight	85
Richard Rodda	87
Wesley's views of itinerancy	90
Richard Whatcoat—Wm. Green	90

CHAPTER VIII.

Extensive revival—Perfect love	95
The revival spreads	98
Captain Webb	103
Robert C. Brackenbury	104

CHAPTER IX.

First preaching place in Newport	106
New chapel	108
Opened by John Wesley	110
Jonathan Cousens	112
William Hoskins	115
George Story	116
Revival still in progress	117
Wesley on the Island	121

CHAPTER X.

Rookley—Thomas Whitewood	123
Revival—Robert Bull	127
Godshill	129
William Ashman	130
Sketch of Preachers	132

CHAPTER XI.

Merston—Mary Prangnell	134
Robert Wallbridge—Letters	138
Mary Ward	146
John Damp	147

CHAPTER XII.

	Page
Winchester new chapel	148
Mr. John Etheridge	151
Wesley and Coke at Yarmouth	153
The Mother of John A. James and the Methodists	154
Death of Charles Wesley—The Wesleyan Hymn-book	156
A Home Missionary resident in the Isle of Wight	157
Letters respecting him	158
The first chapel at Portsmouth	160

CHAPTER XIII.

Wesley's last visit to the Island	164
His death	166
Joseph Sutcliffe, M.A.	169
Jasper Winscom & Jos. Bradford	170
Wootton Bridge—Wm. Legg	171

CHAPTER XIV.

The Rev. James Crabb	177
Appointed to Portsmouth Circuit	178
Wearisome journeys and hard fare	179
His health fails	183
His character	184
Effects of war	185
Intolerance at Southampton	186

CHAPTER XV.

The Dairyman's Daughter	189
Birthplace and early life	190
Awakened under Mr. Crabb at Southampton	193
Her conversion of the New Testament type	195
Her letters	196
Returns home	204
Letters to her sister	205
Her self-denial, benevolence, &c.	207

CHAPTER XVI. *Page*

Dairyman's Daughter becomes known to Legh Richmond . 209
His error respecting her . . 210
Legh Richmond's letters to her . 213
Unfinished narrative . . . 217
Her Will 219
Rev. S. Marsden 222
The Dairyman 224
Narrowmindedness . . . 226

CHAPTER XVII.

Rev. Legh Richmond's relation to Methodism 227
His clerk and housekeeper were Methodists 228
Bembridge 231
John Wheeler 232
Legh Richmond visits the Island 234
His silence respecting Methodism 237
Robert Smith and John Burdsall 238

CHAPTER XVIII.

Civil and religious state of the Island 240
Smuggling 241
Wreckers 242
East Cowes—Osborne . . . 244
West Cowes—first chapel . . 246
New chapel at Newport . . 248
Ryde of recent growth . . 249
Methodism feeble in its origin . 251
New chapel 252
Discouragement 253
Revival 254
Visit of a band of Missionaries . 254
Chapel relieved of debt . . 256
Sea View 257
John Matthews 257
Rev. David M'Nicol . . . 259

CHAPTER XIX. *Page*

A Sabbath School opened in Newport 260
Home Mission work . . . 263
Haven Street New Chapel . . 264
Sandown 265
A noble Convert 267
The Island made a Circuit . . 268
Wesleyan Literature . . . 269
Circuit Income 271
Mr. R. Bull 271
Mr. R. Yelf 277
Revds. J. Rigg and E. B. Lloyd . 279
Shalfleet 280

CHAPTER XX.

Cause confined to Newport . . 282
State of the roads . . . 283
Yarmouth 283
Mary Coward 285
George Arnold 285
New chapel 287
Revival 288
Freshwater 289
Mrs. Mitchell 290
Methodism introduced . . 292
New chapel 293
Chale 294
Blackgang 294
Landslips 295
Mr. Russell opens his house for preaching 296
An interesting incident . . 297
The Bryanites 298

CHAPTER XXI.

Ministerial Staff in 1825 . . 300
A fishing adventure . . . 303
Dissent in Hampshire in 1827 . 306
New chapel at West Cowes . 307

	Page
First Wesleyan Missionary Society in the Isle of Wight	308
Bishop of Winchester	308
Noke Common	309
Rookley	310
Melancholy end of a persecutor	311
Rev. B. Carvosso	312
Captain John Matthews	313

CHAPTER XXII.

	Page
Ventnor	315
Beauty of its scenery	315
Rapid growth	316
Methodism introduced	317
New chapel	318
Future prospects	319
Rev. Zephaniah Job	319
Dr. Cole	321
New chapel, Godshill	322
Earl of Yarborough	322
New chapel, Wootton-bridge	323
Miss E. Roach, a seal of Mr. Dawson's ministry	323
Mr. and Mrs. Groves	324
Blackwater	324
New chapel, Merston	325
Red Hill	326
New chapel, Niton	327
Shorwell	327
A sun-set scene	328
Carisbrook	331
Rev. Calvert Spensley	331
Rev. Joseph T. Milner	333
Newport chapel debt	334
Juvenile Home and Foreign Missionary Society	335
Missionary Jubilee	335
Her R. Highness Princess Alice	336
Progress in the Ryde Circuit	337
Renovation of Newport Chapel	337
Scheme for extinction of Chapel Debts in Newport Circuit	338
Projected Day School at West Cowes	339
Conclusion	339
Schedule of Chapels, Local Preachers, Leaders, and Stewards, in Newport Circuit	340
Schedule of Chapels, &c., in the Ryde Circuit	341
List of Ministers who have travelled in the Isle of Wight	342

METHODISM IN THE ISLE OF WIGHT.

CHAPTER I.

" I love thee, O my native isle !
   .   .   .   .   .   .
——When I trace thy tale
To the dim point where records fail,
Thy deeds of old renown inspire
My bosom with our fathers' fire :
A proud inheritance I claim
In all their sufferings, in all their fame."

VARIOUS are the conjectures of Historians and Etymologists as to the origin of the name "Wight," by which this Island is now known. The most probable is, that it is derived from " Guith " (British), or, anglicised from the Roman "Vectis" (divorced). The Island forms the southern extremity of the county of Hampshire, and is divided from it by the Solent sea. Its length is 22 miles 5 furlongs, its breadth is 13¾ miles, and possesses a super- ficial area of 98,320 acres, having a population of about 60,000. Its principal river is the Medina, which, as its name imports, runs through the Island, and divides it into two nearly equal parts. The soil yields a varied and luxuriant produce, its climate is highly salubrious, its scenery beautiful—often unique—and its inhabitants are remarkable "for health high circling mantled in their cheek," and for longevity.

To see the Isle of Wight to advantage, it should be traversed leisurely on foot, having time to peer into its caves, nooks, and corners—to climb its gangs and cliffs—to examine its cromlechs and numerous tumuli, with the subterraneous abodes of its aboriginal inhabitants; and to walk on its high downs, on a mossy sward soft as velvet, stretching as they do for miles, like vast ramparts along the sea shore, or sweeping inland to the very heart of the Island.   The highest points command extensive views, which stretch across the Solent far into the counties of Hants and Dorset on the north, Portland Bill to the west, and it is said that the coast of France has been seen from St. Catherines, which is the loftiest hill in the Island.

The frequent occurrence of tumuli, crowning the summits of the downs, and scattered along their sides, carries the mind irresistibly back to the dim and remote past. Imagination calls up the wandering tribes who first peopled these lands.   You picture to yourself the Island, when it was a vast impenetrable forest, where the wild beast crouched in his lair, and the venomous reptile gorged his prey, undisturbed by the presence of man.

No date can be given, or hardly conjectured, but time was when the white cliffs of Albion were descried for the first time from the opposite shores of ancient Gaul, and some bold spirits, prompted by curiosity, or the love of adventure, crossed the channel: or, it might be stress of weather, or pursuing foe, caused the first settlers to approach in their frail coracles, and seek shelter on these shores. The beauty and fertility of the newly-discovered country would soon be known in the old, and quickly the restless Celt swarms over and plants new colonies on the southern shores of Britain.

Meanwhile, kindred tribes may have sent adventurers, as tradition tells, across the "hazy sea," from the shores of what is now modern Germany and Denmark. New comers continually arrive, the interior is penetrated, and as in America and our colonies of this day, a process was going on by which the whole country was more or less peopled. And to what a marvellous extent has this process been conducted in these islands, as, age after age, migratory or conquering wave upon wave of human beings, differing in race, language, and religion, have swept over them—Cymri, Belgae, Roman, Saxon, Jute, Dane, and Norman—each contributing its part to form the Anglo-Saxon race: thus resembling the far-famed Corinthian metal, which was neither iron, nor copper, nor silver, nor gold, but was a fusion of all metals into one mass, in which the excellencies of each were combined.

The religion of the early inhabitants of these isles was Druidical. This form of religion—no doubt, originally pure and patriarchal—was brought by the wandering tribes who filed off from the plains of Shinar at the dispersion. It prevailed over the continent of Gaul, but it is admitted by ancient writers to have existed in its purest form in this country. This is certain, that the ancient Druids possessed a considerable amount of both religious and scientific knowledge, including music, and that they were not only priests to offer sacrifices for the people and conduct their worship, but also their instructors; while there is but the slenderest evidence to prove that their followers were the untutored, naked savages which they have been represented.

Believing it to be unlawful to build roofed temples, they worshipped in the open air, always choosing the shade of a majestic oak, situated, if possible, in a grove. This was inclosed by one or two circular rows of stone pillars, which were covered with horizontal stones; these were, in some instances—as may be still seen at Stonehenge, in the adjoining county—of enormous weight. Near to these temples they reared their cromlechs, or stone altars, for their sacrifices. It has been supposed that these sacred enclosures had some reference to Paradise, from which our first parents were driven in consequence of their sin. Be that as it may, it is remarkable that there is such a striking similarity between the practices of our British forefathers and those of the Hebrew Patriarchs. Of the " friend of God" it is said, " Abraham planted a grove in Beer-sheba, and called there on the name of the LORD, the everlasting God."— Gen. xxi., 33; see also Gen. xxxv., 8, Josh. xxiv., 26.

> " The groves were God's first temples, ere man learned
>   To hew the shaft and lay the architrave,
>   And spread the roof above them,—ere he framed
>   The lofty vault to gather and roll back
>   The sound of anthems. In the darkling wood,
>   Amidst the cool and silence, he knelt down
>   And offered to Thee solemn thanks
>   And supplication."

Like the religion of other ancient nations, however pure

in its origin, Druidism became corrupt and perished. It is well known that it was an object of the bitterest hate of the Romans, who, shortly after their conquest of this country, pursued it to its last refuge in the Isle of Anglesea, and there inflicted so severe a blow that the Druid could never again raise his head.

During the Roman occupation, Christianity was introduced into England, and, in a comparatively short time, became the prevailing religion of the country. During the period that elapsed between the first and second invasion of Britain, an event took place which, for importance, finds no parallel in the history of our world—the birth of our Lord and Saviour Jesus Christ, whose atoning death is the only foundation of the sinner's hope, and whose coming was announced by angels as " glad tidings of great joy to all people." That Gospel was early proclaimed in these remote islands, but by whom it would be hard to say. Some contend that the embassy of God's mercy was brought to our fatherland by St. Peter, others say by St. James, or Joseph of Arimathea; while many claim the honor for St. Paul, who, it is said, preached the Gospel in the " Western parts"—that he brought salvation to " the islands that lie in the ocean," and that, in preaching the Gospel, he went to " the utmost bounds of the West."

Soon, however, there came a night of sorrows. In the fifth century, the roving Saxon cast a covetous eye upon the lovely valleys of Britain, and resolved upon its conquest. Fierce and bloody was the conflict, but the Celt, and with him the Christian religion, was compelled to retire and seek a retreat amid the mountains of Wales and the obscure isles of the sea; and the fair fields of Christianity, full of the promise of a rich fruitage, were overrun with the desolations of pagan superstition, and the grim Odin and Thor became the ruling deities.

In the year 495, Cerdic, with his son Henric, established the kingdom of West Saxon. They conquered the Isle of Wight, slew the inhabitants, and replaced them with Jutes and Saxons.* This night of weeping was turned into the morning of joy when, on the 10th of August, 597, Augustine and his band of evangelists landed on the shores of England. The darkness and immoralities of Saxon superstition gave place to the Gospel, and the light of Divine truth once more shone upon the nation. The Isle of Wight was the last place in the kingdom to receive the Christian faith. This happy event took place in 687, ninety years after the mission of Augustine.

The early ecclesiastical history of the Island furnishes no incidents worthy of note. Its isolated position, probably, preserved it from the sword of persecution, which fell so keenly on the church during the dark day of papal rule. The blood of the martyrs was not the seed of the church in Vectis, nor do its annals supply an illustrious name to grace their pages. Ireland has its St. Patrick, Iona its Columbia, Scotland its Knox, and England its Wickliffe and Wesley—names which will live when those of the proudest warriors have perished with the rust of time.

* The Jutes were a Teutonic or Scandinavian tribe who inhabited Jutland, or North Denmark ; Saxon (from "scax," a knife, sword, or dagger), a people who came from the North of Germany.

While this Island fell, with the rest of the nation under the iron yoke imposed by Popery during the dark ages, it also shared in the emancipation secured by the glorious Reformation. Still, while it is gratefully acknowledged that the struggles of the sixteenth century brought to our churches freedom from the doctrinal errors and superstitions of Rome, it cannot be denied that there was a great lack of experimental life. During the latter part of the seventeenth and the beginning of the eighteenth centuries, religion languished for want of spiritual strength to a degree that rendered it powerless for good. That want was supplied when God, in his abundant mercy, raised up the Wesleys, Whitefield, and others, who with a tongue of fire proclaimed the Gospel from Land's End to John O'Groats, with a power which neither the keen sarcasm of the sceptic, the popular fury of murderous mobs, the polished shafts of the learned, shot from the strong bow of bigotry, nor the cold formality of a dead religious profession, could withstand.

And in this there lies a marked difference between the two greatest of Reformers: Luther struggled to recover lost truth, and he restored to the world the Word of God, —Wesley laboured to recover lost life, and, with the blessing of God, he restored experimental religion to the Church.

The results of the labours of these men are matters of history, and are to be found this day in the hundreds of thousands of Methodists who are scattered over the face of the whole earth. To trace the rise and progress of this work of God in this Island, and adjacent places, will be the object of the following pages.

CHAPTER II.

(1735—1753.)

" Bear me on, thou restless ocean,
Let the winds my canvass swell—
Heaves my breast with warm emotion,
While I go far hence to dwell :
Glad I bid thee
Native land—farewell, farewell !"

THE length of time—now more than one hundred and ten years—since Wesleyan Methodism secured a foundation in the Isle of Wight, makes it probable that we shall never know the exact circumstances under which the first stone was laid of the spiritual edifice which by the grace of God has been reared. Nearly twenty years before that even, John and Charles Wesley had been on the Island, and Charles had preached several times at Cowes. They were detained by stormy weather as they were on their way to America. Under date " Nov. 1, 1735," John Wesley says : " We came to St. Helen's harbour, and the next day into Cowes road. The wind was fair, but we waited for the man-of-war which was to sail with us. This was a happy opportunity of instructing our fellow-travellers. May He, whose seed we sow, give it the increase !"

" Thur. 20.—We fell down into Yarmouth road, but the next day we were forced back into Cowes. During our stay here there were several storms, in one of which two ships in Yarmouth road were lost.

"Sun. 23.—At night I was awoke by the tossing of the ship and roaring of the wind, and plainly showed I was unfit, for I was unwilling, to die.

"Tues., Dec. 2.—I had much satisfaction in conversing with one that was very ill and very serious. But in a few days she recovered from her sickness and her seriousness together.

"Wed. 10.—We sailed from Cowes, and in the afternoon passed the Needles. Here the ragged rocks, with the waves dashing and foaming at the feet of them, and the white side of the Island rising to such a height perpendicular from the beach, gave a strong idea of 'Him that spanneth the heavens, and holdeth the waters in the hollow of his hand!'"

From the Journal of Mr. Benjamin Ingham, who was one of the Oxford Methodists, and a fellow-voyager of the Wesleys, we are able to cull some additional facts. He says :—" Having now no further doubt but that I was intended by Providence to accompany Mr. Wesley, on Tuesday, 14th Oct., 1735, he, his brother Charles, myself, and Mr. Delamotte (son of a merchant in London, who had a mind to leave the world and give himself up entirely to God), being accompanied by Mr. Morgan, Mr. Burton (one of the trustees), and Mrs. James Hutton, took boat at Westminster for Gravesend, and went on board the 'Symmonds.' We had two cabins on the forecastle, I and Mr. Delamotte having the first, and Messrs. Wesley the other. Theirs was made pretty large, so that we could all meet and pray in it.

"17.—Mr. Wesley began to learn the German language,

in order to converse with the Moravians,—a good, devout, peaceable, and heavenly-minded people, who were persecuted by the Papists, and driven from their native country, upon account of their religion. They were received by Count Zinzindorf, of Hernhut, who sent them into Georgia.

" 19.—Mr. John Wesley began to preach without notes, expounding a portion of Scripture extempore, according to the ancient usage.

" Sun., Nov. 2.—We passed the fleet at Spithead, and came into Cowes road, off the Isle of Wight, where we lay till the 10th December. During our stay here, we had an excellent opportunity of promoting the work of God among our fellow-passengers. Mr. Charles Wesley being known to the minister at Cowes, preached several times in the Island, and read at a poor woman's house to a good number of people, and I believe they were not a little edified by his admonitions and exhortations.

" 3.—Took a walk into the Isle, where we agreed upon the following resolutions :—' In the name of God, Amen ! We, whose names are under-written, being fully convinced that it is impossible either to promote the work of God among the heathen, without an entire union among ourselves, or that such a union should subsist unless each one will give up his single judgment to that of the majority, do agree by the help of God : first, that none of us will undertake anything of importance without first proposing it to the other three; secondly, that whenever our judgments differ, any one shall give up his single judgment or inclination to the others; thirdly, that in case of an equality, after begging God's direction, the matter shall be decided by lot.—J. W., C. W., B. I., C. D.' "

Mr. Ingham enumerates several things which he regarded as providential reasons for their detention at Cowes. Those reasons were—the departure of a gentleman from the ship who scoffed at religion and was a snare to him; the removal of the second mate, who "was a very insolent and ill-natured fellow, who had abused many of the passengers, and also Mr. Wesley, and at last affronted Mr. Oglethorpe to his face;" and the reception of a young man on board who gave the following account of himself: "he had left his parents, he said, who were rich, though he was their only son, because they would not let him serve God as he had a mind. He used to spend a good part of the night in prayer, not having opportunity to do it by day. When he left home he did not know where he should go, having no clothes with him; but he did not seek for money or worldly enjoyment, he desired only to save his soul. When he was travelling, he had prayed that he might go to some place where he could have the advantage of public prayers and the holy sacraments. Several times he had thoughts of turning hermit; but Providence had brought him to us, and he was glad to meet with ministers with whom he could freely converse about spiritual things. This, I think," says Mr. Ingham, "was another reason for our delay. All love, all glory, be to thee, O Lord!"

"10.—Now, at length, it pleased our Heavenly Father to send us a fair wind. We left Cowes about nine in the morning. We made the best of our way, running between seven and eight miles an hour. Most of the passengers were now sick; I was so for about half-an-hour, Mr. John Wesley scarce at all."*

That ship bends her sails to the winds which are to waft her over the ocean. Amid the thousands which are continually leaving the shores of Britain, she is almost unobserved, and soon forgotten. But elements are at work in that little bark which, ere long, are to assume a form and concentrate a power which is destined, in the providence of God, to be felt not only in the mother country, but throughout the world, and to the end of time. Follow that ship, and look on board. There is the band of missionaries, consisting as we have seen, of John and Charles Wesley, and their two companions. Influenced by missionary zeal, John Wesley had refused to settle down in his father's quiet living at Epworth, and, with the approval of his noble-hearted mother, was on his way to convert the wild Indians of America,—but was soon to learn the humiliating fact,

---

* After Mr. Ingham's return from America, he married Lady Margaret Hastings, to whom his ministry, it is supposed, had been made useful. This event created no little surprise in the circles of fashion in which she had heretofore moved. "The Methodists," says the Countess of Hereford, "have had the honour to convert my Lord and Lady Huntingdon both to their doctrine and practice; and the town says that Lady Margaret Hastings is certainly to marry one of their preachers, whose name is Ingham."—"The news I hear from London," writes a witty lady from Rome, "is that the Lady Margaret Hastings has disposed of herself to a poor wandering Methodist preacher." This union, notwithstanding the scornful pity of the world, proved a happy one. Mr. Ingham was the means of raising many societies in Yorkshire, which were united with the Moravians. He died in 1772, four years after his wife, who departed this life in the ecstacy and triumph of faith.

that he himself was unconverted. Beside about one hundred other passengers, there are about twenty-six Moravians, the influence of whose conduct upon John Wesley, especially during a storm, was of so marked a character as to be justly regarded as the turning-point in his future history. Again, while in America, he seeks advice from one of these devoted men, and, like Nicodemus, was met with a startling reply: "My brother," said the Moravian, "I must first ask you one or two questions— have you the witness within yourself? does the Spirit of God bear witness with your spirit that you are a child of God?" Wesley, like the Jewish ruler, was surprised and confounded; but the impression made, and the work thus begun, by the searching questions of Spangenburg, was completed after his return by the further instruction which he received from Peter Bohler in London, when the day of Gospel light broke upon him, and—is it too much to say —upon the nation.

More than seventeen years elapsed ere Wesley made his second appearance on this Island. This event took place in 1753. During that time the great religious movement had spread to all parts of the kingdom. The churches had been shut against it, and Whitefield and the Wesleys had been driven into the "hedges and highways," where, thousands flocking to hear, signs and wonders had been wrought. Already, from one end of the kingdom to the other, the awakening blast of the Gospel-trumpet had been sounded, and Wesley had claimed the world as his parish. The corner-stone of the first Methodist chapel had long since been laid at Bristol, and the example followed by many others elsewhere. David Taylor had begun to preach in the neighbourhood of Donnington Park and Sheffield. Samuel Deacon, one of his first converts, was rearing churches in Leicestershire. John Bennett was on his *round* in Cheshire, Derbyshire, and Lancashire. Nelson was rousing his countrymen in Yorkshire; and John Furz was reaping the fruit of his toil in his native village in Wiltshire; while Lady Huntingdon had opened her house for preaching, that the rich might hear the Word of Life. The self-denying Grimshaw was prosecuting his successful career on the bleak moors of Howden, and exercising a vigilant oversight of the work throughout the North; while the venerable Peronett, from his snug retreat at Shoreham, was looking on with an approving smile, and giving sage counsel to the chief actors in these stirring scenes. John Fletcher had left his native home amid the Swiss mountains, and was being led by a way that he knew not into union with the Methodists, and was soon to enter upon his saintly labours at Madeley; while Berridge was still preaching his dry and powerless morality, "living," to use his own words, "proudly on faith and works," little dreaming of the marvellous power which was ere long to clothe his word, and fill his church at Everton with pente-costal scenes. Howell Harris had for years been traversing the principality from South to North, facing, with the courage of a lion, the fierce mobs by which his life was imperilled; while Rowlands, the "Welsh thunderer," was making the valleys of his native mountains echo with his alarming appeals to the consciences of the terror-stricken thousands, who were drawn together by the charm of his soul-stirring ministry. At the same time the work was taking deep root in Ireland. Nor was the press silent. In the hands of Wesley, this powerful engine had done good service to the rising cause. A stream of religious literature, in the shape of sermons, tracts, hymns, and volumes of divinity, was continually issuing from this fountain to refresh the newly-planted vineyard. Lay-preaching had become established, class-meetings formed—wherever the truth had taken effect—quarterly meetings introduced, and ten Conferences had already been held. At the last, which was held in Leeds, in the preceding May, there were twelve circuits, thirty-six preachers, and thousands of members in Church fellowship. Such were some of the direct results of Methodism, while the indirect effect was apparent in the improved moral aspect which the nation was even now beginning to exhibit.

The torpid church was aroused, and hopeful signs of returning life were visible in both the Establishment and among Dissenters. The downward course which had sunk the morals of the nation to the lowest ebb was arrested. A Churchman thus describes the effect: " The licentious habits of the vulgar were checked, and the immoralities of the middle-classes, with the carelessness of the clergy, abated."*

Thus far had this great work advanced, when Wesley renewed his visit to the Isle of Wight. After preaching morning and evening in London, he took horse and rode to Godalming, about 12 p.m. The next morning found him

* Colquhoun, p. 294.

in the saddle by half-past four, and about one he reached
Portsmouth.   Here some amount of ministerial labour had
been bestowed, but by whom does not appear.   This was
the first time Wesley had visited this important town, and
what he saw there did not afford him much satisfaction.
He complains, " I was surprised to find so little fruit here,
after so much preaching.   The accursed itch of disputing
had well nigh destroyed all the seed which had been sown.
And this ' vain jangling' they called ' contending for the
faith !'   I doubt the whole faith of these poor wretches is
but an opinion."

" After a little rest," he adds, " we took a walk round
the town, which is regularly fortified, and is, I suppose, the
only regular fortification in Great Britain or Ireland.
Gosport, Portsmouth, and the Common (which is now all
turned into streets), may probably contain half as many
people as Bristol, and so civil a people I never saw before
in any sea-port in England.   I preached at half-an-hour
after six, in an open part of the Common, adjoining the new
church.   The congregation was large and well-behaved,—
not one scoffer did I see, nor one trifler.   In the morning,
Tuesday 10th July, 1753, I went on board a ' hoy,' and in
three hours landed at Cowes, in the Isle of Wight,—as far
exceeding the Isle of Anglesea, both in pleasantness and
fruitfulness, as that exceeds the rocks of Scilly.

" We rode straight to Newport, the chief town in the
Isle, and found a little Society in tolerable order.   Several
of them had found peace with God.   One informed me it
was about eight years ago since she first knew her interest
in Christ, by means of one who called there on his way to

Pennsylvania; but, having none to speak to or advise with, she was long tormented with doubts and fears. After some years, she received a fresh manifestation of His love, and could not doubt or fear any more. She is now (and has been long) confined to her bed, and consuming away with pining sickness; but all is good to her, for she has learned in everything to give thanks.

" At half-an-hour after six I preached in the Market-place to a numerous congregation, but they were not so serious as those at Portsmouth. Many children made much noise, and many grown persons were talking aloud almost all the time I was preaching. It was quite otherwise at five in the morning. There was a large congregation again, and every person therein seemed to know this was the Word whereby God would judge them in the last day.

" In the afternoon, I walked to Carisbrook Castle, or rather the poor remains of it. It stands upon a solid rock on the top of a hill, and commands a beautiful prospect. There is a well in it, cut quite through the rock, said to be seventy-two yards deep, and another in the citadel near a hundred. They drew up the water by an ass, which they assured us was sixty years old. But all the stately apartments lie in ruins. Only just enough of them is left to show the chamber where poor King Charles was confined, and the window through which he attempted to escape.

" In the evening the congregation at Newport was more numerous and more serious than the night before. Only one drunken man made a little disturbance; but the Mayor ordered him to be taken away."

Early in the morning the evangelist was off to Bristol, opening a new preaching-house at Shaftesbury on his way.

How did this little society which Wesley found in Newport originate? Of whom was it composed? And who was the spiritual counsellor of this orderly band of Christians? Deeply interesting as these questions are, to none, save the first, can we supply an answer. From Wesley's "Short History of the People called Methodists," we glean the important fact that one of his preachers had been on the ground before him; and doubtless it was by the blessing of God upon his labours that the infant Church in Newport owed its existence. Having gathered a few sheaves in this new harvest field, he brings Wesley to share in his joy, and to aid with his powerful ministry the work thus auspiciously begun.

In the History alluded to, there is this statement:—
"July 10. *After one of our preachers had been there some time*, I crossed over into the Isle of Wight."

The question very naturally arises, Who was that preacher who came as the pioneer of Methodism into this Island, and into the adjacent coasts? Did he come from the East or the West? After the most careful enquiry, we are compelled to acknowledge that a thick mist hangs over this subject which we cannot dissipate, and we are therefore left to conjecture. If the light approached from the East, then it was brought, in all probability, by one of the London preachers, who had wandered westward until he had reached Portsmouth, where he tarried awhile, and then crossed over to the Island and drew together the little society which

Wesley met with there. If, on the other hand, the light came from the westward, then, doubtless, John Furz was the first evangelist to these parts. We are inclined to the former conjecture, as it is probable that John Furz had not as yet extended his labours beyond Salisbury and its vicinity.

Wesley seems to have been pleased with his visit to the Island, for in less than three months he returned, and stayed three days, and preached five sermons—four at Newport and one at Shorwell. After preaching in the New Forest, he came by way of Southampton and Cowes, and reached Newport before eleven in the morning of Wednesday, Oct. 3, 1753. "At five in the afternoon," he says, "I went to the Market-place. The congregation was large and deeply attentive. It was nearly the same at six in the morning, and all seemed to drink in the exhortation to 'present themselves a living sacrifice, holy, acceptable to God.'"

"A little before noon we set out for Shorwell, a village six miles south from Newport. I never saw a more fruitful, or a more pleasant country than the inland part of this Island. About one, I preached at Shorwell to, I suppose, all the poor and middling people of the town. I believe some of the rich also designed to come, but something of more importance—a dinner—came between.

"At five I preached again at Newport, to most of the town, and many who came from the neighbouring villages. Surely, if there was any here to preach the Word of God with power, a multitude would soon be obedient unto the faith.

"Fri. 5.—After preaching at six, I left this humane,

loving people, rode to Cowes, and crossed over to Portsmouth," where a different scene met his eye. "Here I found another kind of people, who had disputed themselves out of the power, and well-nigh the form, of religion. However, I laboured, and not altogether in vain, to soften and compose their jarring spirits, both this evening and the next day.

"On Sunday noon I preached in the street at Fareham. Many gave great attention, but seemed neither to feel nor understand anything. At five, I began on Portsmouth Common. I admired not so much the immense number of people, as the uncommon decency of behaviour which ran through the whole congregation. After sermon, I explained to them at large the nature and design of our societies, and desired that if any of them were willing to join therein they would call on me either that evening or in the morning. I made no account of that shadow of a society which was before—without classes, without order, or rules—having never seen, read, or heard the printed rules, which ought to have been given them at their very first meeting."

In the "Short History" before referred to, Wesley says, "In October I visited them again, and spent three or four days with much comfort, finding that those who had before professed to find peace had walked suitably to their profession."

CHAPTER III.

(1745.)

" He has the stamp and signature of heaven,
Truth, mercy, patience, holiness, and love.
He is a man of God, for the Lord
Has commissioned him to make known to men
His eternal counsels,—in his Master's name
To treat with them of everlasting things."

IT is now time to direct attention to the important fact, that while the seed of God was taking root in the Isle of Wight, and in Britannia's most famous naval port, it was at the same time producing blessed fruit in the adjoining county of Wilts, under the zealous ministry of John Furz, who had begun to preach there so early as 1745.

Nor must we omit to notice that some years previous to that even, the doctrines of Methodism had been preached —for a time at least—with effect, in the same locality, by Mr. Hall, a clergyman who had been one of John Wesley's pupils at Oxford. He married Martha, one of the sisters of the Wesleys, a woman of "fine and noble qualities," and so remarkably like her brother John in "stature, form, and countenance," that Dr. Clarke, who knew them both well, declared had they been dressed in similar attire he could not have distinguished the one from the other." Mr. Hall is said to have been "a man of agreeable manners, good education, competent means, and appeared to be deeply religious." In a letter from the Salisbury Circuit, inserted in the *Methodist Magazine* for the year 1836, there is this statement :—" About the year 1741, Mr. W. Hall came to Salisbury, and preached his first sermon on Harnham Hill, and the following Sabbath in the Butts, on the Old Sarum road. He then announced that he should preach on the next Lord's day in the coach-house and stables of the 'Green Dragon,' Fisherton, adjoining Salisbury. The floor of the stable was hastily removed, and the east part left for a gallery. In this place he laboured with great success, and people came from distant places to hear him. Several persons were converted, and, had he continued faithful, it is believed that his ministry would have been extensively useful,—but, alas, he fell from his steadfastness." This account of the origin of the cause in the ancient city of Salisbury is perfectly correct, with the exception of the date, which is placed too late by some two or three years. This will appear evident on comparing the dates given in Wesley's "Journal" and in Mr. Kirk's biography of the "Mother of the Wesleys." In the latter work the writer, when tracing the widowhood of that much-tried, but noble-minded woman, states that after spending some time with a daughter, and with her eldest son, she removed, in July, 1737, " to the pleasant little village of Wootton, Wiltshire, where her son-in-law—the afterwards notorious Hall, who had married her daughter Martha—was curate. Here she received the greatest possible kindness." He " had not yet entered upon those paths of licentious profligacy in which he afterwards wandered so far and so long. His ministry seems to have been gentle and tender, his conversation godly and pleasant, his conduct as becometh the gospel of Christ."*

* "The Mother of the Wesleys," p. 220.

In the course of a few months, Mr. and Mrs. Hall removed to Salisbury. Mrs. Wesley accompanied them, and remained until about April, 1739, when she removed to London, the place of her birth and death.

In Wesley's "Journal" there are, amongst others, the following entries referring to this unhappy man:—"Monday, July 20, 1746. I set out for Salisbury, where, to my utter amazement, on Wednesday, 22, Mr. Hall desired me to preach. Was his motive only to grace his own cause? or rather was it the last gasp of expiring love?" Again, "Tuesday, Dec. 1, 1747. We rode on comfortably to Salisbury. From the concurring account of many witnesses, who spake no more than they personally knew, I now learned as much as is hitherto brought to light concerning the fall of poor Mr. H. Twelve years ago he was, without all question, filled with faith and the love of God. He was a pattern of humility, meekness, seriousness, and, above all, of self-denial, so that in all England I knew not his fellow."

In the following January, after being turned out of Hall's house, Wesley says, "I met a little company, gathered up out of the wreck, both in the evening and at five in the morning, and exhorted them to go on in the Bible way, and not to be wise above that is written."

What became of this poor wretched wanderer, is a question which very naturally presents itself. After a life of crime, he awoke to a consciousness of his awful position, and was made to drink deeply of the wormwood and gall of repentance. "I came to Bristol," says Wesley, "just in time enough, not to see, but to bury, poor Mr. Hall, my brother-in-law, who died on Wednesday morning, Jan. 6th,

1776, I trust in peace, for God had given him deep repentance. Such another monument of Divine mercy, considering
how low he had fallen, and from what heights of holiness,
I have not seen, no, not in seventy years. I had designed
to visit him in the morning, but he did not stay for my
coming. It is enough if, after all his wanderings, we meet
again in Abraham's bosom."

Notwithstanding this heavy blow, which brought so
serious a reproach on the infant cause, and so staggered the
faith of some, that they followed their leader into the
world, yet the "little company which Wesley gathered out
of the wreck" held together, and met at a place called
Quidhampton. After that they took possession of a shop in
Greencroft-street, in Salisbury, and in 1759 they opened
their first chapel. The providence of God early found a
shepherd for these deserted and hungry sheep. John Furz,
who resided in the neighbouring village of Wilton, was
converted during the time Mr. Hall was preaching the
gospel with success, and, indeed, had derived benefit from
his ministry. Mr. Furz, who was one of the first race of
Methodist preachers, after exercising his ministry some time
in his native village, removed about 1753 to the city to take
charge of the shattered cause.

The conversion and successful ministry of John Furz,
who in the minutes of Conference for 1755 is classed with
the "half itinerants," supplies an instance in proof that,
while God was preparing the Wesleys and Whitefield in
London, as the leading evangelists in the great work which
He was about to accomplish, He was, at the same time,
raising up subordinate agents in various parts of the nation.

This godly, zealous man was born at Wilton, near Salisbury, in the year 1717. He was the subject of serious impressions at ten years of age, became a communicant at fifteen; then came a night of the deepest anguish and horror, during which, for two years, he was in despair. Sleepless and without appetite, his flesh wasted, and he became extremely weak. His mother took him, at his own request, to the Dissenting minister, who pronounced him to be melancholy, and prescribed " merry company." Such company he fell into, and their " merry jests" banished his gloom, but it was only like the " crackling of thorns under a pot," the illusion was soon over, and conviction returned with redoubled force. In amazement he exclaimed, "Lord, what have I been doing ?" and adds, "I dropped to the earth utterly senseless. About midnight my senses returned, and I found my mother weeping at my bed-side, attended by some of her kind neighbours."

Once again was he ensnared by his new companions, but a powerful voice awoke him from the delusive dream. The description, in his own words, is too characteristic of the times, and too interesting to be omitted :—" One Sunday morning, as I was in bed, it seemed to me as if one griped me by the arm. At the same moment, a voice went through my heart, saying, 'Go to the meeting.' I was much surprised, and felt much pain in my arm. However, it being early, I composed myself to sleep again; but I had not lain long, when I heard the same voice as before. I rose and walked in the garden, but still found something within me saying, 'Go to the meeting.' I knew not what to do. I had ever been a zealous member of the Established Church, and thought it not right to go to a Presbyterian meeting. I seemed resolved not to go, but the impression on my mind was such that I could have no rest unless I went. When I came in, the minister was in his sermon. I had no sooner sat down than he uttered these words, 'Remember the promise you made to God on a sick bed.' I thought he spoke to me. I remembered how earnestly I had prayed to God to spare me a little longer. I returned home in deep distress, thinking, I am still the same unhappy creature, lost to all sense of good. All my resolves are come to nought, my promises broken, and I am left a poor guilty sinner."

This deep distress was rendered more intense under a sermon preached by Mr. Hall, who seemed to point at him with his finger, while he " said vehemently, 'There are two witnesses that are dead and buried in the dust, that will rise in judgment against you.' He took up his Bible, and said, 'Here are the two witnesses, the Old Testament and the New.' I felt what was spoken; I remembered that my Bible was covered with dust, and that I had written my name with the point of my finger on the binding. Now, I thought, I had signed my own damnation on the back of the witnesses." The terrors of that night were beyond expression great. The spirit of prayer returned, but Satan assailed him at the very mercy-seat. He continues, "I went and kneeled down at the foot of my bed. Instantly I felt as if cold water ran through every vein. I started up, and ran into the garden, and thought, God will not suffer me to pray; He has driven me from the throne of grace; there is no mercy for me. I went a second time, but had no sooner kneeled down than I was surprised as before. I flew again. As soon as I came into the garden, I looked round, and said, 'Who will show me any good?' I walked weeping, till I saw a dead toad, and said, 'Oh that I had been a toad! then I should have had no soul to lose.' I then felt a fresh desire to pray. I went again into my chamber, and kneeled down. But I was more surprised than ever. I thought the earth moved under me. I leaped down stairs, and fell to the ground, but strong desire constrained me to ask, 'Are there no bowels of mercy for me?' Before I could utter it, I heard a small, still voice saying, 'Thy sins are forgiven thee.' What a change did I feel! My sorrow was turned into joy, my darkness into light. My soul was filled with love to God for His unspeakable mercies. Now I did indeed draw water out of the wells of salvation. My tongue could not express the feelings of my heart; I was lost in speechless rapture. I now knew what it was to believe. I now knew on whom I believed, even on Him that justifieth the ungodly. Being justified by faith, I was at peace with God through our Lord Jesus Christ."

The heart being made new by the quickening power of the Eternal Spirit, all nature seemed to have put on a gay attire, and the Bible became to this young convert "sweeter than honey." Day and night he had communion with God, and a longing desire filled his heart for all the world to share in the glorious salvation which he had found.

His conversation was now made useful to a young man, who, after passing through a "waste howling wilderness" of doubt and guilty fear entered into the Canaan of Gospel rest, and became his companion in the way to heaven, their hearts being "knit together" like those of David and Jonathan.

Constrained by the love of Christ, John began to exhort sinners to flee from the wrath to come, and soon had the happiness of uniting fourteen persons in society. The circumstances, as related by him, are so deeply interesting, and throw so much light on the character of the times, that we are induced to give the narrative at length, in nearly his own words. Speaking of himself and his first convert, he says, "Our hearts burned with desire that all men might know this love of Christ which passeth knowledge; but how to impart to others what we had received we knew not, nor which way to begin."

Hearing of a company of Dissenters who met at a private house on a Sabbath evening, they went. They found ten persons sitting round a table, with a bible, newspaper, and decanter and glasses. They began their evening exercises. "First, they ridiculed the Vicar, &c.; next they drank one to another, and offered the glass to us, but we did not drink. Then they related the faults of the church-wardens and the overseers of the poor; till one read part of the newspaper, which gave occasion to discourse on the state of the nation. At last one of them read a chapter in the Bible; another, looking at his watch, said, 'Bless me! it is time to go home; it is past ten o'clock!' 'But,' said one, 'We ought to go to prayer first.' But they were not agreed which of them should pray. At last one of them stood up against a back of a chair, spoke a few words, and concluded. My friend and I were kneeling together. I was weary with forbearing, and began earnestly to pray that God would awaken them, and by his goodness lead them to repentance, that they might know the things which belonged to their everlasting peace. They turned about and stared at me, as if I had been speaking Greek. However, they told us we should be welcome to come again the next Sunday evening."

Accordingly, they went, and found about a hundred people standing at the door, who all rushed in when the master of the house opened it. To these, his neighbours, thus brought together, did John Furz preach his first sermon, and not without effect. "Many wept," and the gentleman of the house was so favourably impressed that he procured a license for his house, that none might molest the preacher. John also preached in his own house, and "many," he says, "were convinced of their evil ways; and about fourteen converted to God, who met with me daily, to spend some time in prayer. We lived as brethren, being partakers together of the same grace of God."

This may be regarded as the second Methodist society formed in the neighbourhood of Salisbury; the first being raised by Mr. Hall, whose ministry has been already alluded to. And, although neither of these societies had at this time a direct connection with the parent fountain, yet they both sprang from it, and were shortly afterwards brought into permanent union with the broader stream of spiritual life which it sent forth.

Persecution now arose. "Mr. Conway, the vicar, sent his footman to me," says Mr. Furz, "with this message, 'My master bids me tell you, you have a soft place in your head.' I said, 'be pleased to tell your master, the sheep when diseased do not run after the shepherd, but the shepherd after the sheep. Your master passes by my door almost every day. I wish he would call in and search about my head, and find out what my disorder is, and prescribe a remedy.' About two hours after I saw him coming. I opened the door, and waited for him; but when he saw me he drew off, and shook his cane at me, and passed by. He went straight to the Earl of Pembroke's (the old Earl), and told him, 'There is a young fellow in the town who, under a pretence of preaching, makes three riots every week, and disturbs all the inhabitants of the town from one end to the other.' The Earl said, 'I will send for the young man, and talk with him myself.'

"But instead of sending for me, he sent for the Mayor, with whom he used to converse frequently. He had heard me preach himself. Afterwards I learned what had passed between the Earl and him. 'The old Priest has been here,' said the Earl; 'but I know not what he would have. He was at first a Dissenting Minister. But he came to me and said his conscience constrained him to conform to the church, and begged I would assist him to procure ordination. Then he begged me to give him a benefice that was vacant: I did so. To that was added a second, and a third, and now he comes to me with complaints about some young man that preaches. Pray do you know the man?' He said, 'My Lord, perfectly well: he lives but three doors from me.' His Lordship said, 'I said at first I would send for the man: but I have thought otherwise. Take Lord Herbert and your son, who has taken his degrees at Oxford, and all the Aldermen with you; and you will judge whether

it is the preacher who makes the riot, or they that come to
disturb him. Afterwards come all of you to dinner with
me, and give me your cool judgment.' I knew nothing of
their coming till they came; but according to my day so
was my strength." The sight of such a body of nobility
and civic dignitaries entering the humble preaching house,
caused the rabble of the town to rush to it, under the supposition that they were about to raze it to the ground. "I
was praying," continues the writer, "when they poured in
like a flood. They pushed down some that were upon their
knees, and trampled on them. Lord Herbert rose from his
seat, and said, 'I desire you will let me hear quietly.' But
instead of regarding it, some of the mob gave him a very
impertinent answer. The Mayor then rose up, and with a
loud voice commanded the King's peace. I then said, 'My
Lord and Gentlemen, I and those that meet with me are
members of the Established Church. We meet together
every Sunday, before and after divine service, to make
prayer and supplication with and for one another; and I
read a portion of Scripture and explain it as God enables
me.' I paused. His Lordship bowed his head, and I went
on,—'I will preach now, as well as I can in this confused
noise.' I then read, 'I certify you, brethren, that the
Gospel preached by me was not after man. For I neither
received of man, neither was I taught it, but by the revela-
tion of Jesus Christ.' When I had ended, high and low
went away, and I and my friends were left alone.

"When the Mayor and his brethren came to the Earl's
(I was informed in the evening), he asked if they had been
at the preaching; and when informed they had, he advised

the Mayor to read the Riot Act at the next preaching, which he did. The mob quickly shrunk back; but one of them cursed the Mayor, and said he was a Methodist too. He looked upon me, and said, 'John, you see I have got a bad character too.' I said, 'I wish it were true.' He said, 'So do I; it would be better for me.' From this time we had peace.

"This method not succeeding to his wish, the Vicar thought good to try another. He procured the Rev. Joseph Horler to preach before his Lordship. And he did preach as extraordinary a sermon as ever was heard at Wilton. His text was, 'Take heed, brethren, lest there be in any of you an evil heart of unbelief in departing from the living God,'—'that is,' said he, 'from the Church: for there is sprung up among us a new religion called 'Methodism.' It is like the plague; they that have it infect whole families. Now, in such a case, if one were to come and warn you to shut your door, and keep out the man and his distemper, would not you be thankful? I am now come to do you this kind office. I will describe the persons in three particulars. In the first place, they look just like toads that are crept out from under a faggot-pile. In the second place, they pretend to be led by the Spirit; and when they are 'under his guidance,' as they call it, they look like toads that are crept out of a dung-heap, and croak just like them. In the third place, they look just like toads that are dragged from land's-end to land's-end under a harrow.' I was curious to observe what notice his Lordship took of the preacher, who stood bowing at his side as he went out of church. He passed by him without making the least motion, or taking the least notice of him at all.   After he was got home, he sent a footman to tell the preacher, 'If you please, you may come and dine with his Lordship.' When he came, and was sat down, the Earl asked him his name.   He answered, 'My name is Joseph Horler.'   'Mr. Horlor, what have you been doing?'   'Preaching, my Lord.'   'What have you been preaching?'   'The Gospel, my Lord.'   'I deny that, Mr. Horlor: you have been preaching against the Government.'   'I ask your Lordship's pardon: I do not know that I have.'   'Nay,' said his Lordship, 'have not the King, Lords, and Commons all agreed that every Englishman shall worship God according to his own conscience?   And are there not licenses granted for that very purpose? But, pray, who are those toads who creep out of the dung-heap? I hope they are not your neighbours.   Let me hear of it, sir, no more.   I will hear no more of it.   I will send a note immediately to the Vicar, to let me know, when I am in the country, any day that you are to preach, and I will be sure not to be at the church that day.''

Sufficient notice has not been taken of the liberal principles referred to by the Earl, by which the House of Brunswick has been actuated in relation to religious freedom.   Who shall say how much we are indebted to that fact for the spread of Methodism?   The noble maxim laid down by George the First, that " during his reign there should be no persecution for conscience' sake," has been acted upon ever since, and has proved a boon to the nation which it would be black ingratitude to God not to acknowledge with devout thanksgiving.

Some time afterwards, John Haime came and preached at the house of John Furz. A mutual love sprung up between them, and they unitedly laboured to spread vital Christianity in the counties of Dorset, Wilts, and Hants. This, however, was not done without opposition. While John Furz was preaching on the Common at Wincanton, and while the people were still as night, giving heed to what was spoken, the minister of Brewham, with an attorney, and Mr. Ring, the town clerk, came to the outside of the congregation. Some then cried out, "Make way, make way!" But the people stood closer and closer together, till I desired them to open to the right and left, and let the gentlemen come forward. Mr. Ring then read the Riot Act. I said, "Sir, was there any appearance of a riot here till you came?" He looked me in the face, and said with the utmost vehemence, "Thou rascal!" Then the blood spouted out in a stream from both his nostrils. He dropped to the earth, crying aloud, "They will say this is a judgment." (No wonder if they did.) All possible means were used to stop the bleeding; but in vain. From that time he was a lunatic. He was carried to Bath, and died soon after. In about a fortnight, I was informed, the minister of Brewham died also.

The wife of this good man was amongst his persecutors, and, on one occasion, she struck him so violent a blow in the face as to force out one of his teeth. Stepping up to her, he meekly placed the tooth in her lap, and silently retired. She was seized with conviction, and in deep distress fled to the Saviour, and on the following day received the remission of her sins, and was renewed in the spirit of her mind. She now became a true help-meet—cheerfully submitted to part with him, taking the burden of their large family upon herself, when, at the call of Providence, he left home to devote himself fully to the work of a Methodist preacher.

To this work John Furz was ardently devoted, and he continued in it until he was worn out with age and infirmity. He was compelled to retire in 1782, when he came to reside at Salisbury, where, as strength served, he laboured amid the exciting scenes of his early ministry, until the year 1800, when he finished his pilgrimage in peace, in the 83rd year of his age.

Mrs. Barbara Hunt was one of the early members of the Salisbury Society. She gave herself to God and his people in 1750, when she was but fourteen. The misconduct of Mr. Hall was at this time severely felt by the little company of Christians, which consisted chiefly of old people, who were the "butts of derision and contempt to all the city, and were often obliged to fly from the ungodly rabble as with their lives in their hands." But all this was insufficient to intimidate this young disciple, who, feeling her need of Jesus, cheerfully went forth with him without the camp, bearing his reproach. Mrs. Hunt removed to Bradford, Wilts, in 1761, and, after adorning the doctrine of God her Saviour during the long period of 63 years, died exclaiming, " O how glad should I be to clap my glad wings and tower away!"

While this work of grace was in progress in Wiltshire, Charles Wesley was on a missionary tour through the adjoining county of Dorset, stopping not until he had reached its southern extremity, Portland, where, on the 6th of June, 1846, he preached to a "houseful of staring, loving people." Here, too, his fervid imagination found inspiration even in stones, for it was during his stay on this rocky island that he composed the hymn beginning :—

> "Come, O thou all-victorious Lord,
>   Thy power to us make known,
>   Strike with the hammer of thy Word,
>   And break these hearts of stone."

He remained several days with this simple-hearted people, and preached almost day and night, nor did he leave them until he had gathered a society of twenty members. Portland afterwards formed the South-Western extremity of the Wiltshire Circuit. It became a separate Circuit in 1857. It now has two ministers, with 451 members in society.

This would be hallowed ground to Charles Wesley. In Dorset was the cradle of his ancestors—the home of his forefathers. The name which was anciently written Westley, or Westleigh, indicates a Saxon origin, and was held for generations back by persons of note, both for birth and scholarship. The great-grandfather of the Wesleys— Bartholomew Westley, a puritan—was rector of Charmouth in 1640, and ten years after he was appointed to that of Catherston. After the Restoration, he lost both these livings, and had to fall back for support upon the practice of physic, of which he had a knowledge. John Wesley his son, and the grandfather of the founder of Methodism, was a member of "a particular church at Melcomb, in Dorset-shire," and, in 1658, he became the minister of Winterborn, in the same county. A decided Independent in his ecclesiastical principles, he had to bear his full share of the troubles which the Act of Uniformity brought upon the Nonconformists. During this time of trial, his son Samuel, the father of the Epworth family, was born. "Finally, he was called by a number of serious Christians at Poole to be their pastor, and in that relation he continued to the day of his death."

CHAPTER IV.

(1751—1758.)

ONE of the firstfruits of Methodism in these early times was seen in the conversion of a man in the humble walks of life, resident on the obscure borders of Salisbury Plain. But, although his position was lowly—and with a family of children which ran far into the teens, he found the battle of life a hard one—yet, by the grace of God, he well and long served his generation ere he fell asleep. His manly piety, shrewd wit, intimate knowledge of the Word of God, and his frank disposition, excited the admiration of Hannah More, who, with a masterly hand, portrayed and gave to the world his noble character in the well-known " Shepherd of Salisbury Plain." This beautiful tract has embalmed the excellencies of the godly shepherd in the hearts of tens of thousands, and given an interest to Salisbury Plain second only to that which attaches to the Isle of Wight, as the home of the still more widely-famed Dairyman's Daughter ;

and to Christian minds, at least, those bleak plains possess, on his account, a charm superior even to that which they derive from the grand old Stonehenge, the mute but perpetual witness of the departed glory of the ancient Druid.

The name of the shepherd was David Saunders. He was born at Littleton, a hamlet of West Lavington, in the county of Wilts. This event took place in his father's humble cottage, about the year 1726. In that cottage he afterwards lived, and reared his large family. He began his shepherd life in early youth, and by constant exposure his frame became hardened and "nerved to life's rough path." Like Jacob, he was subject, if not to the scorching heat of day, yet to the pinching cold of winter nights, by which his feet were so frost-bitten and crippled that he walked with a limp.

About the year 1751 David was brought into contact with the Methodists, and, through their instrumentality, was led to a knowledge of salvation by the remission of sins, when he at once united with this then despised and persecuted people.

Turning to the life of John Furz, we find this interesting statement :—" Some years before I was an itinerant minister, I was invited to preach on Salisbury Plain, near the New Inn. It being on a Sunday, a very great company was gathered together from the neighbouring villages, on both sides of the Plain. Here I was met by John Haime, with a few of our friends from Shaftesbury. As soon as I began to speak, a man came straight forward, and presented a gun at my face, swearing that he would blow my brains

out, if I spake another word. However, I persisted, and
he continued swearing, sometimes putting the muzzle of
the gun to my mouth, sometimes against my ear. While
we were singing the last hymn, he got behind me, fired the
gun, and burned off part of my hair. But he did not lose
his labour, for he was so soundly beaten that he kept his
bed for several weeks."

John Furz left home for the ministry in 1758; hence,
the "some years before" that event would carry us back to
the year 1751, about which time, it is supposed, the
shepherd was converted, and joined the Methodists. It is
highly probable that he was one of the "great company"
drawn from both sides of the plain, and that he heard that
sermon which was preached at the "muzzle" of a gun;
and it might have been under that very discourse that his
mind was enlightened to a discovery of his need of a
Saviour. Be that as it may, it is certain that it was about
that time when he was united with the society at Hind-
marsh, a hamlet adjoining the village of Seend, where a
chapel was erected in 1774. He evinced the decision of
his character, and his ardent love to the means of grace, by
walking on the Sabbath—and sometimes on a week-day,
after the day's work—a distance of six or eight miles, and
back, to hear the Word of God, or to enjoy the communion
of saints.

David opened his cottage for religious services, which
thus became a little sanctuary for the scattered population.
Here, with his neighbours around him, this humble but
sensible man read the Word of God, and in homely Saxon
conversed with them on the momentous subjects of eternity,

and then by fervent prayer commended them to the grace of God. Thus zealously did he endeavour to bring them to a personal knowledge of that blessed truth which had made him free. These Christian labours were extended to other villages, and hereby did the godly shepherd, though making no pretensions to the sacred office, prove himself to be a sort of evangelist, imitating his Divine master, who "went about doing good." At first, as a matter of course, he met with opposition, and was actually taken before a magistrate, charged with the crime of preaching in his own house. When questioned on the subject, he replied, "May it please your worship to hear what I have to say. I think it my duty to pray with my family, night and morning, and, if opportunity permit, to read a portion of God's Word to them. On Sunday morning we rise an hour or two before I go to my sheep, that we may spend a little more time than on other days in the worship of God. Some few of my neighbours frequently come in and join us. We first sing a psalm or hymn. I then read a chapter or two of the Bible, and sometimes endeavour in my poor way to explain their meaning, as far as I understand it myself. We then conclude our Sabbath morning's exercise with prayer to God. As for preaching, I never attempted any such thing, but leave it to those who are called to preach." The magistrate (to his honour be it said), a clergyman, severely reprimanded his accusers, and advised them to go and do likewise.

Beside these cottage services the shepherd opened an evening school for the young; nor did he toil in vain. A great religious reformation was effected in the neighbourhood, and some of the Christian churches in that locality trace their origin to the pious efforts of this good man, who could say, " There is not a house in the parish in which I have not engaged in prayer."

The shepherd was a consistent and useful member of the Methodist Society during a period of forty-five years. The more he was known, the higher was the esteem in which he was held both by rich and poor.* His end was sudden, but it found him ready. His last work was prayer and praise. A vast concourse of his friends and neighbours followed his remains to their last resting-place in West Lavington Churchyard, " and when the body was laid in the grave they sang hymns with the strongest expressions of grief and respect."

His grave-stone bears the following inscription :—

" Erected in the year 1829, to the memory of
DAVID SAUNDERS,
Known through every quarter of the Globe under
the appellation of
'The Pious Shepherd of Salisbury Plain,'
whose little history has now been read with admiration
by multitudes of Christians
in Europe, Asia, Africa, and America.
He was buried here by his sons, September 9th, 1796.   Aged 70."†

---

* Sir James (afterwards Baron) Stonehouse took great notice of the shepherd. He often rode on the downs, and conversed with him, and sometimes had him to dinner at the Rectory.

† See " Shepherd of Salisbury Plain," by Rev. R. T. Jones.

The work thus begun by John Furz in and around the city of Salisbury, and which was extended, as we have seen, by him and others into the adjoining neighbourhoods, continued to advance until he was called away in 1758 to join the ranks of the Itinerancy, when other preachers were sent to supply his place, and Salisbury was made the permanent head of a circuit.

At the Conference of 1748, the kingdom was divided into nine circuits—London, Bristol, Cornwall, Ireland, Wales, Staffordshire, Cheshire, Yorkshire, Newcastle. The London Circuit included: 1, London itself; 2, Kent and Surrey; 3, Essex; 4, Brentford; 5, Windsor; 6, Wycombe; 7, Oxford; 8, Reading; 9, Bluberry; 10, Salisbury. In the year following, according to the minutes of Conference preserved by the Rev. John Jones, Salisbury was transferred to Bristol; but, according to the regular but brief minutes of that Conference, Wiltshire was formed into a separate circuit. We are unable to reconcile this discrepancy, or to say which of these changes actually took place. If the latter, it is certain it was not lasting, as there is no mention of Wiltshire in the minutes of 1753, nor does it appear again until 1758. It is difficult to say what became of it during the interval; whether it merged again into the London Circuit, or was re-united to that of Bristol, it is impossible to say.

The powerful corps of lay evangelists, of whom John Furz was a zealous and successful member, had now become an established and effective auxiliary in the promotion of the Methodist revival. One of these, from his early union with the Wesleys, his gifts, zeal, steadfast refusal to violate his conscience, his sufferings in the cause, and his usefulness, has occasioned his being placed at the head of that body of pioneers of Methodism—John Nelson, the honoured name of one who will never fail to find a place amongst our chiefs. About 1745, this zealous man found his way down into the South. This was after his release from being pressed for a soldier. He spent four months in Somersetshire and Wilt-shire. "Several were awakened," he records in his journal, "at Poulton, Coleford, Shepton-Mallett, Road, and Bear-field. So God doth work and none can hinder; though the instruments be ever so weak, if he command it, a worm shall shake the earth." We must now return to the Isle of Wight.

On Thursday, the 5th Oct., 1758, we find Wesley occupying Whitefield's Tabernacle at Portsmouth, where he preached to a "small serious congregation." On the day following he starts for the Island.

"Friday, 6.—I designed to go in a wherry to the Isle of Wight, but the watermen were so extravagant in their demands that I changed my mind, and went in the hoy; and it was well I did, for the sea was so high it would not have been easy for a small boat to have kept above water. We landed at two, and walked on, five little miles, to Newport. The neighbouring camp had filled the town with soldiers, the most abandoned wretches I ever yet saw. Their whole glorying was in cursing, swearing, drunkenness, and lewdness. How gracious is God that He does not yet send these monsters to their own place!

"At five I preached in the Corn-market, and at six in the morning. A few even of the soldiers attended. One of these, Benjamin Lawrence, walked with us to Wootton-bridge, where we intended to take boat." What follows shows that the heart of a true British patriot beat in the breast of John Wesley. "He (Benjamin Lawrence) was in St. Philip's fort during the whole siege, concerning which I asked him many questions. He said: 1. 'Abundance of cattle was left in the fields, till the French (long expected) came and took them. 2. Abundance of wine was left in the town, even more than the French could use, and there was not enough in the castle even for the sick men. 3. A large, strong, stone house was left standing within a small distance of the fort. Behind this the French often formed themselves, particularly before the last assault. 4. This might be easily accounted for: we had few officers of any experience, and the Governor never came out of his house. 5. The French made two general assaults, and were repulsed, and many blown up by our mines. But the mines having never been looked after till just when we wanted them, most of them were utterly useless; so that only two, out of three score, did any execution. 6. In their third assault (which they were hardly persuaded to make), Captain ——, who commanded the guard of a hundred men at the sally-port, ran away before he was attacked, and his men, having none to command them, went after. I was left alone, till I retired also; and the French, having none to oppose them, came in. 7. In the morning our men were mad to drive them out, and would have done it in an hour, but that they were told the fort was given up, and ordered to cease firing. 8. We had, at the approach of the enemy, three thousand eight hundred and thirty-three effective men, and we had near as many when we surrendered, with plenty of provision and ammunition.'   Oh, human justice ! one great man is shot, and another is made a Lord !"

"We hired a small fisher-boat at Wootton-bridge, there being scarce any wind. But it increased more and more when we were on the sea, which was seven miles over. Our cock-boat danced on the waves, and must have sunk if one large wave had come over her; but God suffered it not. We landed in two hours, and walked away to Gosport.

"Sunday, 8.—The wind and rain drove us into the Tabernacle. In the afternoon I preached in the main street at Fareham. A wild multitude was present ; yet a few only mocked, the greater part were soon deeply attentive."

Important events in the history of Methodism transpired during the period now under review. These were the appointment of Assistants, the introduction of Quarterly Meetings and Class Meetings. The name "Assistant" had already appeared on the Minutes of Conference, but at the Conference of 1749 it was defined, and the responsibilities of the office enlarged. The duty of those who sustained this office, in addition to preaching daily, were, to visit the classes, write lists of members, regulate bands, give new tickets, keep watch-nights and love-feasts monthly, hold quarterly meetings, watch over the helpers to see that they behaved well and wanted nothing,* and to take care that the societies were well supplied with books. The chief qualification for all this was a "close walk with God."

* A rather difficult task, as the preachers at that time had no regular stipend. Four years afterwards, they were allowed £12 per annum.

Quarterly meetings seem to have originated with John Bennet, in Yorkshire. The Rev. W. Grimshaw acted as the first Circuit Steward. At this same Conference it was enacted that they should be held in every circuit, Bennet being desired (1) to send up his plan, (2) to go himself as soon as may be to Newcastle and Wednesbury, and teach them the nature and method of these meetings.*

Next to the Conference and the annual district meeting, these quarterly gatherings of travelling and local preachers, leaders and stewards, are become the most important meetings in Methodism.

Class-meetings—which Wesley regarded as providential means of grace—were for years peculiar to Methodism, and greatly helped to conserve and mature the piety of its members. The multitudes of persons who were brought into union with the societies, especially in the larger towns, rendered it impossible for Wesley to afford them that personal oversight which he deemed necessary for their welfare. The subject was beginning to occasion him considerable uneasiness, when the providence of God supplied the need in a most unexpected, but effectual manner. His own words on the subject are : "But as much as we endeavoured to watch over each other, we soon found some who did not live the Gospel." Some grew cold, gave way to besetting sin, and caused the truth to be evil spoken of. "We groaned," he says, "under these inconveniences long before a remedy could be found. At length, when we were thinking of quite another thing, we struck upon a method

---

* Minutes, i., 709.

for which we have cause to bless God ever since. I was talking with several of the Society at Bristol concerning the means of paying the debts there, when one stood up and said, 'Let every member of the Society give a penny a week, till all are paid.' Another then answered, 'But many are poor, and cannot afford to do it.' 'Then,' said he, 'put eleven of the poorest with me, and if they cannot give anything, well; I will call on them weekly, and if they can give nothing I will give for them as well as for myself. And each of you call upon eleven of your neighbours weekly, receive what they give, and make up what is wanting.' It was done. In a while, some of these informed me they found such and such a one did not live as he ought. It struck me immediately, 'This is the thing, the very thing we have wanted so long.' I called together all the leaders of the classes (so we used to term them and their companies), and desired that each would make a particular inquiry into the behaviour of those whom he saw weekly. They did so. Many disorderly walkers were detected. Some turned from the evil of their ways. Some were put away from us. Many saw it with fear, and rejoiced unto God with reverence.

"As soon as possible, the same method was used in London and all other places." Ever since that period, the class-meeting has been an essential part of the Methodist economy. It invariably follows the introduction of successful preaching into any new place. Sympathy yields comfort, and in union there is strength. Wesley's long experience, and knowledge of the value of these means of grace, led him to declare that they were the "sinews of Methodism."

We were struck with an observation which was made by Dr. Newton, after preaching in the city of Philadelphia, on the very spot on which Whitefield had preached a hundred years before:—"It is remarkable," he says, "that not an orphan-house, a church, or a society, founded by Whitefield, remains; while the Wesleyans number between seven and eight hundred thousand members, and upwards of three thousand ministers. But Whitefield *did not* institute class-meetings, and Wesley did. There are now (1840) seventeen Wesleyan churches in this city, with two hundred thousand inhabitants."*

Scarcely less interesting is the entry which the devoted Richard Williams makes on the subject of class-meetings, in his Journal, when he was famishing on the inhospitable shores of Patagonia. "It is this coming to the vital matters," he writes, "and urging on the soul an immediate consideration of the truth as it is in Jesus; pressing home the conviction, at the same time carrying help to the stricken penitent, encouraging him to seek, and helping him to find, according to God's promise, a present salvation,—it is this which makes such a material difference betwixt our Methodistic mode of procedure and that of many other denominations of Christians. Many brands are thus plucked from the burning, who, according to a more formal mode of administering the things of God, might never have been saved." With true catholicity of spirit, Doctor Hamilton, the accomplished writer of the affecting narrative, remarks:

* Newton's Life, p. 197.

E

"It is not wonderful that reminiscences of love-feasts and class-meetings should have mingled with his adopted churchmanship," and "the personal urgency which Mr. Williams justly claims as a distinction of Wesleyan Methodism, is a lesson to all churches" (p. 171, 172).

CHAPTER V.

(1758—1762.)

" Their preaching much, but more their practice wrought,
(A living sermon of the truths they taught),
For this by rules severe their lives they squared,
That all might see the doctrine which they heard."

DURING the next twenty years, the weft and woof of fact and incident are scant and broken, so as to render it difficult to weave a continuous web of history. The Isle of Wight was united with Salisbury, called, according to the custom of the time, Wiltshire. Three preachers were sent to the Circuit, but where they took up their abode it would be difficult to say. The Assistant would most likely take possession of the house at Salisbury, just vacated by John Furz, while the other two, being young men, might have no fixed home. Their names were—Thomas Johnson, Richard Cornish, and John Murlin.

A short sketch of the more prominent of these memorable men who laboured in these parts will be given from time to time. The first and second race of Methodist preachers have long since gone to their reward, and they gradually recede into the dim and shadowy past. They have been eloquently described as "men of no ordinary stamp. They were taken, for the most part, from a humble walk of life, and were destitute of early educational advantages. But, besides possessing vigorous health and great muscular power, they were generally endowed with a more than average share of native intelligence and shrewdness, were distinguished for common sense and knowledge of human nature, and for a frank and hearty cheerfulness, which peculiarly fitted them for intercourse with those classes of society among whom they chiefly laboured. Above all, there was an emphatic decision, and a most contagious fervour about their religious sentiments and character. The doctrines of spiritual religion were almost forgotten, and the notion of conscious divine enjoyment was derided as a madman's dream, at the time of their conversion. No wonder, then, that the renewing and saving process was, in all its stages, sharply defined to their perceptions, and associated with the most intense emotion. Truly in those days 'the light shined in darkness.' These men had, many of them, been wrapped in the deepest gloom of spiritual ignorance, and for them, in most instances, there was no gentle daybreak, no gradually unfolding morn. Suddenly—'like the sun at mid-day'—the full blaze of divine truth burst upon them, revealing their hidden iniquities, and disclosing the yawning gulf at their feet. 'The sorrows of death compassed them, the pains of hell gat hold upon them.' And the transition into the 'joy and peace in believing' was equally sudden and remarkable. With singular uniformity do these facts appear in the biographies of these memorable men, and they give uncommon vividness to their spiritual perceptions, and depth and intensity to their feelings. Fired with an all but unexampled ardour, burning with the love of Christ, they began at once to tell their fellows of the things which they had 'felt and seen.' In homely, nervous Saxon speech they proclaimed 'the terrors of the Lord' and the consolations of the Gospel. They had been anointed with 'an unction from the Holy One,' and they displayed a pathos and a power such as had not been witnessed for ages. The results which followed their preaching are matters of history; and all competent and candid men admit that the only Christian age that will bear a comparison with that which these burning and shining lights illuminated, was the age of Apostolic triumph. The scenes of their greatest success were the high places of wickedness. Brutal and unruly mobs were subdued, outcasts and reprobates reclaimed in astonishing numbers, and a religious and moral reformation was begun, and has now reached an extent, which it is impossible accurately to measure, and the value and importance of which it is equally impossible to exaggerate." *

Of some of these worthies, who were as remarkable for originality and variety of character as for their ministerial success, we will now take a hasty glance. Our notices will be confined to those chiefly who were on this ground. We begin with Thomas Johnson, who stands at the head of our list of preachers. He was a Yorkshireman, born in Wakefield, converted in 1748, and began his itinerant labours in 1752. He continued to travel thirty-two years, and was acceptable and useful in all his circuits. In 1784 he

* London Review, No. xix., 80.

retired to Birstal, near his native place, where for thirteen years more he toiled in his Master's vineyard, as strength allowed, until he had reached his 78th year. He died with heaven beaming on his countenance, as he exclaimed, "It is finished! it is finished!" His brethren say of him that "he was a lively and zealous preacher," and that "his preaching was peculiar to himself."

Of Richard Cornish little is known; but of John Murlin, the "weeping prophet," many interesting facts have been preserved. Of him it has been aptly said, that he wept not for sorrow, but for joy. His style was plain, but an affectionate pathos attended his preaching, and his "tears were his chief eloquence." He was born in Cornwall in 1722, was early left an orphan, and, while yet a youth, became an adept at swearing, gaming, and drunkenness. In that state the Methodist ministry found him, and, while listening to a sermon, he was made to feel the pangs of a guilty conscience. Under the oppressive load of sin, he wept, fasted, and prayed often till the midnight hour; until, as he was hearing another sermon, he was able to say, "Behold God is my salvation, I will trust and not be afraid." Years afterwards he could bless God and say, "I have never lost my confidence."

Having quenched his burning thirst at the fountain of living waters, he longed to bring others to the same source of satisfying good. It is a peculiarity of experimental religion that it never fails to multiply itself. Every one who possesses a knowledge of it can teach it to others. This is one secret of the success of Methodism, for, while it urges all its members to grow in knowledge and in grace, it requires of them that they liberally distribute the bread of life bestowed on them.

Thus John Murlin soon found employment; first, as a class-leader and local preacher; and, in the autumn of 1754, he received a commission from Wesley to travel, and while he hesitated a second letter arrived, and, after a short struggle, he took horse, and rode away into the West of Cornwall,—"rather," says an historian, "he rode away into all England, for thenceforth, during half a century, John Murlin was one of the most devoted labourers of Methodism." In 1787 he sat down at High Wycombe, where he died, as he had lived, full of the "comfort of the Holy Ghost." His remains lie in the same tomb with those of Wesley, and a mural tablet in City Road Chapel commemorates his faithful and affectionate services.

There is a blank in the list of preachers, extending from 1758 until 1765. No minutes of Conference, taking the form of an annual record, were published after the year 1749, till 1765. Happily we are able, from other sources, to fill up the hiatus, as far as the Wiltshire Circuit is concerned. John Furz had occupied the field for thirteen years. He was followed by Thomas Johnson and his two colleagues, and they were succeeded at the Conference of 1759 by a staff of four men—Thomas Hanby, Thomas or Wm. Hitchings, Robert Roberts, and George Roe.

From an old Society book which lies before us, we gain the interesting information that the Newport Society was favoured with the services of the travelling preachers once a month, on the Sabbath day. They stayed two nights on the Island, and the Steward paid them 1s. per night for themselves, and 2*s.* for their horse, in all 6*s.* This, however, was not regular, as in some instances they received 1*s.* 6*d.* board, 1*s.* horse, and 2*s.* 6*d.* in cash.

The horse was an indispensible companion of the itinerant preacher in those days, when circuits embraced several counties. When Thomas Olivers, author of that justly admired hymn—full of rugged grandeur—beginning

"The God of Abraham praise,"

commenced his career as a Methodist preacher, he bought a colt, which, says Southey, was as well suited to him as Bucephalus to Alexander, for he was as tough and indefatigable as his master. "I have kept him," says Olivers, a quarter of a century afterwards, " to this day, and on him I have travelled comfortably not less than a hundred thousand miles." Sometimes, however, the horse was a difficulty, being found to be not a help on the way, but a hindrance. This was the case when the preacher had a long remove by water. Under those circumstances, it was more economical to sell, and buy again. Thus, one of the preachers, who at a subsequent period removed from this locality to West Cornwall, sold his mare previous to leaving the Circuit, but when he should have received the cash was mortified to find that the animal was thrown upon his hands.

From the beginning of the year to the Conference of 1760, Messrs. Hanby and Roberts were on the Island twice each, and their colleagues once each. During that period, the entire expenditure, which included preachers' pay, horse keep, rent of preaching-room, and lighting, was

£1 15*s.* 6½*d.* We will insert a copy of the account, as it appears in the Steward's book. It is a curiosity, and shows that a penny a week and a shilling a quarter was no part of Methodism in the Isle of Wight in the year 1760.

		£	s.	d.
Jan. 5. Collected at times in the Class . . .		0	9	7½
April. do. do. . . .		0	13	7
		1	3	2½
Balanced in April		1	0	6½
Remains in Stock		0	2	8
June. Collected at times in Class		0	6	3
July. do. do.		0	4	9
do. do.		0	2	9
		0	16	5
Balanced		0	15	0
		0	1	5

From the above it is evident that, as yet, there were no quarterly collections, and no contributions to the Quarter Board.

Thomas Hanby, who was the Assistant this year, was one of the most true-hearted, long-tried, and devoted servants Methodism possessed. The meekness and gentleness of his disposition were not more remarkable than his heroic courage when difficulty and danger beset his path. Possessing considerable ministerial ability, his labours were eminently successful in most of the circuits in which he travelled. During the space of forty-four years, often amid cruel persecution, did this zealous man pursue his ministerial course. He was elected President of the Conference in 1794. He maintained an unblemished reputation to the end of life, and in his dying moments could say, "I am departing, but I have fought a good fight." His death took place at Nottingham, on Thursday, December 29th, 1796, in the sixty-third year of his age. But few of his brethren have bequeathed a more fragrant memory than the amiable Thomas Hanby.

Robert Roberts owed his first religious impressions to Mr. Brisco, and in a short time entered into union with the Methodists. Wiltshire was his first circuit. His judgment was sound, his life irreproachable, and as a minister of the Gospel he was zealous and faithful. His death took place in Macclesfield in 1799.

The appointment for 1760 was James Morgan, Nicholas Gilbert, and Richard Lucas.

James Morgan was a man of superior ability and deep piety. He began to sigh after the peace of the Gospel at fourteen, and, having received the Saviour, he entered upon his pulpit labours before he was twenty, and took a circuit in 1750. Possessing a vigorous mind, which he had improved by extensive reading and thought, an agreeable person, and a pleasing address, he was a popular preacher. His delicate, nervous constitution, however, ill-fitted him for the hardships of an itinerant life, and he retired and took up his abode in Dublin, where his days were ended in 1774. He published the life of that intensely spiritually-minded and deeply-devoted man, Thomas Walsh. It was a high encomium paid to him by John Wesley, who said, when complaining of the Irish preachers—" there is scarce one of the spirit of Thomas Walsh; the nearest to it is James Morgan."

Nicholas Gilbert was a young man of high promise, but he was suddenly cut off by fever in the city of Bristol. Wesley pronounces him "a good man, and an excellent preacher."

Richard Lucas had been in the work eight years. He was clothed with humility, and manifested great zeal for the glory of God. But he quickly wore out a feeble frame, and was compelled to relinquish his work. His retirement was spent chiefly in London, where he died in great peace in 1774.

In May, 1761, John Furz paid a visit to the Island, and received from the Society at Newport 2s. 6d., and 2s. board. We presume the 2s. 6d. was for passage-money.

At the Conference of this year the ministerial staff was increased to four—Richard Henderson, Nicholas Manners, James Glasbrook, and John Heslop. It is a singular fact that this entire batch of preachers left the ranks of the itinerancy. Nor need it occasion surprise that so many of the first race of preachers forsook the work. Many causes led to this. The hardships to which they were exposed broke down the health of those whose constitution was not robust; the pressing claims of a growing family, change of opinions, and openings in other churches, induced others to retire. Those who remained in union with Methodism did good service in the localities where they became residents, and many of those who entered other churches were scarcely less useful in spreading the leaven of Methodism in them.

Few records are left of any of the above-named preachers, save Richard Henderson, who was a native of Ireland; he entered the ranks of the ministry in 1759, and came to England in 1762.   He was a gifted minister, deeply devout, with a constitutional tendency to melancholy, but tender and amiable.   Although possessed of strong sense, he was too apt to yield to false reasoning, which involved him in gloomy bewilderment, and at length drove him from the work of the ministry, but happily not from the cross. Strange to tell, he opened an asylum at Hanham, near Bristol, an employment every way calculated to make a man of his sensitive nature uncomfortable, if not miserable. His end, however, was remarkably peaceful.   "He seemed," said one, " to be let into the infinite love of God, and His mercy to him in particular, that awed both himself and all around him."   The eccentric but highly-gifted John Henderson, A.M., of the University of Oxford was his son.*

We now present a copy of a Society class-paper, which is valuable, not for its antiquity only, but also as the earliest register of the names of the female members of the little Methodist Church at Newport.

---

* This young man died at 32.   The Magazine for 1793 contains a brief memoir of him.   He taught the Latin tongue at eight years of age, and the Greek at twelve.   No bodily change was visible on his death, and he was kept from burial longer than usual. In consequence of certain impressions on his father's mind, he was thrice disinterred.   The last time he was found turned in his coffin, with a scratch on his face, from which the blood had oozed,— evidence that he had come to life again.   This deeply affected the father, though no one could be blamed.

COPY OF A SOCIETY CLASS-PAPER.

1762.	JULY 28.	AUGUST				SEPT 1.
		4.	11.	18.	25.	
Mrs. Pike	P	P	P	P	P	P
,, Nanny Perry .	P	P1	P1	P1		
,, Bevis . . .	P	P	P	P	P	P
,, Sanger . . .	P	P	P	P	P	P
,, French . . .	P	P	P	P	A	1
,, Barter . . .	P	P	P	P	P	
,, Denton . . .	B					
,, Perry · . . .	P1	P1	P1	B	P2	

The class-paper, of which the above is an exact copy, is ruled in pencil for the whole quarter, but it is filled up only to the first week in September. The mode in which the pence was collected throws light on the entry in the steward's book, where he says "collected *at times* in the class." Doubtless there was a men's class in addition to the above, which seems to have been composed of females only.

It is manifest that everything in connexion with the cause at Newport, at this time, was of a humble character, and such men as John Hanby, James Morgan, Alexander Mather, and Coates, must, as they came to and from this remote corner of their wide-spread circuit, have sighed over this day of "small and feeble things," but they were too much like their Lord and Master to despise it. To their self-denying perseverance it is that we owe the superior advantages which we enjoy this day in this highly-favoured island.

CHAPTER VI.

(1762—1768).

"A solemn, yet a joyful thing is life,
Which being full of duties, is for this
Of gladness full."

THE leaven of Methodism was now beginning to diffuse itself on the opposite coasts of Hampshire, especially in the important town of Portsmouth. The ground had been broken up, and a good deal of labour bestowed—as it has been already intimated—prior to Wesley's first visit, and a society had been formed, but it was blighted by the "itch" of disputation. This destructive infection was probably occasioned by the introduction of Calvinism by some of the members belonging to a society of Whitefield's, which was of older date still. John Cennick, who had gone over from Wesley to Whitefield, and had become a rigid Calvinist, came about the year 1746, and preached in the open air at Portsea. He was followed by Messrs. Adams, Meredith, and other of Whitefield's preachers, and in 1749 crowds stood in the fields to listen to the great orator himself, who thrice repeated his visits. The blessing of God attended these labours, and a society was gathered of persons drawn from the congregation of the Rev. Mr. Williams, of Gosport, faith began to show its fruit in the activities of a devoted life. He became a leader, and a local preacher. Feeling a strong desire to give himself up fully to the work of the Christian ministry, he opened his mind to Mr. Furz and other preachers. They advised him to "fight against God no more," and accordingly, at the Conference of 1764, after paying a short visit to the Isle of Wight in company with John Furz, they set out together for the York Circuit, to which they were both appointed. From that time, Mr. Mason continued zealously to discharge the duties of his high vocation with great success, until the year 1797, when increasing infirmities compelled him to seek a more contracted sphere of labour, and he came to reside at West Meon, near Portsmouth. A gracious unction still attended his ministry, which was made a great blessing to the people. The life of this venerable and highly-esteemed servant of Christ was brought to a close on the 27th of April, 1810. He is spoken of as a good man, studious in his habits, and the amenity and liberality of his spirit were not less remarkable than the soundness of his judgment, and the manliness of his Christian deportment.

Alexander Mather, Thomas Hanson, Thomas Mayer, and William Minethorpe were the next appointment. Mr. Mather had just come from the midst of an extensive revival which he had witnessed in the Staffordshire circuit. He came to the Island but twice, first in December and again in May. Alexander Mather was a man who occupied a position in Methodism too high to allow of his being hastily passed by in this history. Born in North Britain in 1733, religiously trained, and "sharing in the educational advantages which the piety and wisdom of John Knox insured as the birth-right of every Scotchman," he grew up "an utter stranger to the vices common among men." Out of a childish frolic he joined a party of rebels, and was present at the battle of Culloden. Flying home after the defeat, he met his mother, who was in search of him; but his father closed his door, and even informed against him. His youth no doubt saved him from punishment, and he was sent home, where he learned his father's trade—that of a baker. In 1752 he came to London, and in the following year married a fellow-townswoman, whom he had known as a child. Shortly after that, he entered into the service of Mr. Marriott, a zealous Methodist. Here, to his joy, he found what he had long desired—a family wherein was the worship of God. This acted as a stimulus. He gave himself to more earnest private prayer, and, at the same time, he reared his family altar. Notwithstanding, while his wife found a " degree of peace," he could find none: they seemed to put a keener edge upon his anguish, till his flesh wasted away like a garment fretted by the moth, and his bones were ready to start through his skin. The great hindrance was Sabbath baking. This he resolved to give up, even if it should cost him his place. Accordingly, on the Monday morning, he gave his master warning. The old Methodist "did not speak one word, but soon after came into the shop," and questioned him on the subject, and then waited upon "all of the trade in Shoreditch and Bishopsgate Without." All but two agreed to give up the evil practice. A meeting of master bakers, which he called, ended with no better result. Afterwards, he asked the advice of "our brethren at the Foundry," then the only Methodist Chapel in London. "After he had taken all these steps," proceeds Mather—"more than I could reasonably expect—he told me, 'I have done all I can, and now I hope you will be content.'" Mather thanked his master, and told him he could not stay in his service. "But I continued," he says, "in prayer, and on Sunday evening, after family prayer, he stopped me, and said, 'I have done to-day what will please you. I have stayed at home, and told all my customers I will no more bake on a Sunday.' I told him, 'If you have done this out of conscience toward God, be assured it will end well.'" And so it did. "Marriott became wealthy, lived to attend the ministry of his journeyman, changed into his Superintendent, and, for a long series of years, dispensed extensive charities. His son was one of Wesley's executors, and his grandson, Thomas Marriott—who died childless, and appointed" the late Dr. Bunting "one of his executors—bequeathed many thousands of pounds to Methodist objects."*

Under the first sermon which he heard Wesley preach, Mather was set at liberty, and soon after, with his wife, joined the Society. Then he entered upon the duties of band-leader, class-leader, and local preacher. His time was fully occupied. Long hours were given to trade, and his mornings and evenings to preaching, so that for some time he slept but eight hours a week.

Wesley's eye was upon this granite-framed and fervid Scotchman, and he proposed to take him to Ireland. Mather consented, on the condition that the Stewards would

* Life of Jabez Bunting, D.D., p. 77.

allow his wife four shillings a-week during his absence; but the funds of the Society were not equal to the demand. Another year passed before his wife's maintenance was secured, and then, in 1757, he entered upon his itinerant work by walking a hundred and fifty miles to his first circuit—Epworth, in Lincolnshire. He met with his full share of rough usage, but that was the common lot of all his brethren at that day. It was a severe ordeal through which they all had to pass. It tested and hardened their character, and helped to qualify them for the arduous duties of their peculiar work. It is a fact worthy of note that so few were recreant to their call. Mather was not more distinguished in the Connexion as a leading man and a preacher than for rich and deep Christian experience. His ministry was remarkable for unction, and the prominency which he gave to the doctrine of Christian perfection, or perfect love, of which he was a loving example. On his death-bed he poured forth many "heavenly breathings," one of the last of which was—"O Jesus, whom I have loved, whom I do love, in whom I delight, I surrender myself to thee."

Thomas Hanson was a native of Horbury, near Wakefield, to which place he returned after spending twenty years in the full work of the ministry. During the same term of years, he was a supernumerary. Copying the example of his Lord and Master, he went about doing good. He was 72 years of age when he departed to be with the Lord.

The name of Thomas Mayer was dropped from the Minutes in 1767, at least so says Mr. Myles.

William Minethorpe was a local preacher in the vicinity of York. He had entered the ranks of the ministry at the preceding Conference. The tenderest of all earthly ties was not to him a source of consolation, but of sorrow. He was a man of strict integrity and godly simplicity. Wesley commends him to Walter Sellon thus: "You will find Billy Minethorpe a right man. His resolution in the late affair was admirable. I have scarce seen another such an instance in the kingdom." His death, which took place at Dumbarton in 1776, was most affecting and joyous.

It seems to have been a very rare thing for the preachers to have stayed on the circuit more than one year,—hence there was an entirely new appointment in 1763. The senior of this new supply was a man of some note. Possessing extraordinary pulpit talent, he was exceedingly popular, and his great conversational powers rendered him a wonderfully pleasant and instructive companion. This was Alexander Coates. He had already travelled twenty-two years, and he lived to be the oldest lay preacher in the Connexion, although his death took place in the year following that in which he was in Wiltshire. When he was ceasing to breathe, he was asked if he had followed a "cunningly devised fable?" "No! no! no!" was his emphatic reply. "Do you see land?" "Yes, I do!" he said, and, after waiting at anchor a few minutes, he put into his quiet harbour. Christopher Hopper, one of his fellow labourers, alludes to his departure, and with deep emotion says, "I saw him fall asleep in the arms of our adorable Saviour without a doubt. Farewell, my brother, for a season, but we shall meet again to part no more."

John Shaw laboured for thirty years in the ministry, and was useful in all his circuits. He died with unshaken confidence in God.

Thomas Rourke left the work in 1770, and three years afterwards William Ellis followed his example.

Several of the preachers were now beginning to suffer from the physical effects of their incessant labours and exposure, and at the Conference of 1763 the question engaged the earnest attention of that assembly—"how may provision be made for old worn-out preachers ?" The answer was supplied by the institution of a general fund, to which each preacher was expected to subscribe ten shillings annually, and from which the needy were to receive a scanty relief. This fund, it would appear, did not, after a time, work well; at least, it did not meet the expectation of some of the preachers, and an attempt was made by them to form a separate institution, and a few subscriptions were actually sent in. The subjoined letter, from one of the chief promoters of the new scheme, will be read with interest. It was addressed to Mr. G. Lowe :—

" Bristol, Oct. 6, 1798.

" My dear Brother,

"I have received your five guineas, and placed them to your account, and entered your name among your right noble brethren. We have now nearly £150 in stock, and expect many more subscriptions. Now, as this is not to be touched for five years, and still the annual subscriptions will be going on, we shall have, by God's blessing, one of the best, most solid, and respectable funds (considering the number of members) perhaps in Europe. Messrs. M. and P. are highly offended at it, and are now publishing a pamphlet *against it!* What think you do they mean? Will they at last attempt to force us to do what *they please* with the little money that God sends us! I'll tell you a secret, which you should know: the old fund has not only not one sixpence in it, but is perfectly *illegal.* The Act of Parliament states that all funds of this kind that were instituted *prior* to the passing of the Act, should be deemed illegal if not registered (according to provisions made in said Act) before Michaelmas, 1796. Now this has never been done, therefore the fund is not only worth nothing, but is contrary to the British laws. We must be steady. God be with and prosper you!

"Yours in Christ,

"A. CLARKE."

Happily, at the next Conference the difficulty was met, when this important fund was reorganized, and based on sound principles, which have ensured its prosperity, and made it a source of help to a large number of worn-out ministers, who otherwise must have been left to struggle with straightened means, at a time of life when they more especially need all the comfort which freedom from worldly anxiety can impart.

It was during this year that Methodism found its way into the city of Winchester. The event produced a far greater and more permanent excitement than did the introduction of the gory body of the Red King, as it was borne along the streets of the city in the foresters' rude cart, six

and a-half centuries before. The curiosity of the citizens
was soon satisfied with gazing on those silent lips, which
could utter no more imperious mandates. Not so did they
feel in reference to Methodism. Here, thought the staunch
Churchmen, is a living, speaking, active enemy, who may
endanger our craft, and they began to cry aloud in favour
of their Diana. Various were the means which God
employed to advance his cause. The sacred fire was kindled
in this instance by a silent messenger. John Wesley's
writings had preceded his preachers. Some of the former
came into the possession of Mrs. Winscom, the wife of
Jasper Winscom, a name well known in the Isle of Wight,
and in the adjoining county, and to which frequent reference
will be made in subsequent pages of this book. Jasper read
Wesley's writings with a lively interest, and felt a strong
desire to invite the Methodist preachers to the city. Church
influence frustrated all his attempts till the year 1763,
when he fell in with William Minethorpe, at Romsey,
which was probably opened for preaching about that time.
At Winscom's invitation, he came the week following, and
preached in a summer-house belonging to the mother-in-law
of the former. These services were continued fortnightly,
until the May following. Four persons were formed into
a class, with Winscom at their head.

As yet, this little band of Methodists had no Sabbath
services of their own, and were invited by the Dissenters
to worship at their chapel on that day. This offer they
declined, prefering to adopt the course generally pursued
by the early Methodists—that was, to attend the church in
the morning, and to have a service of their own, of some

kind, in the evening. Winscom, who was an ironmonger, was now placed, as it were, between two fires. Discountenanced and opposed by both Churchmen and Dissenters, his business fell off, and he found himself in danger of being involved in difficulty. In the midst of his perplexity, a dissenter, who was in the same line of business, died, and he was enabled to unite the trade of the two establishments, and thus escaped from his threatened embarrassment. The growth of this little vine was slow; after two years' culture it numbered only twelve members, nor is there any evidence to show that there was any advance when John Wesley preached there in 1766.

Although the remark made in reference to the slow progress of Methodism in the city of Winchester is still applicable, and it will apply (with a few honourable exceptions) to all other cathedral towns in the kingdom,— yet the fact must not be forgotten that it was from Winchester that Methodism was carried to the Norman Isles and Gibraltar. This was effected by Methodist soldiers, who were removed from the city to those places, where, as from centres, the light has penetrated the adjacent countries of France and Spain. There is a powerful leaven of Methodism in the South of France, and a beautiful and commodious chapel has been recently opened in Paris. In connexion with the French Conference, there are 24 ministers and 1,645 members. The foundation-stone of a new chapel has just been laid in the city of Winchester.

Of the appointment for 1764, consisting of John Morley, Mark Davis, Isaac Brown, and William Minethorpe, the two former departed from the work. Isaac Brown was a native of Hawksworth, near Otley, in Yorkshire. He travelled forty-three years. The child-like innocency of his spirit won him many friends, and greatly endeared him to the generous heart of Wesley, who familiarly termed him "honest Isaac Brown." His last days were spent at Pontefract, where he died in 1815.

It is worthy of note that the Island Methodists were favoured in the spring with a visit from that somewhat unpolished but brave north-countryman William Darney. At the ensuing Conference his name appears amongst the London preachers. It has been supposed that he was "the first Scotchman who became a Methodist itinerant preacher." The "fire of his youth, re-kindled at the altar of the great revival, burned with a bright and steady flame during a long period of extensive labour."

John Furz and John Mason, as before stated, gave their old friends on the Island a call before they set out to York, to which circuit they were appointed. From these and other occasional visits, we infer that the Society at Newport, though poor, still manifested those attractive excellencies which had won the esteem of Wesley himself.

A new item now presents itself for the first time in the Newport Society Steward's book. The sum of 5s. 3d. was sent to the June Quarter Board. Exactly the same sum was remitted for twenty-three quarters in succession.

Now, too, another step in advance was taken, when the preachers doubled the amount of service hitherto given to the Island. It was not to be wondered at if the Society in Newport was low and feeble. Was it likely to be otherwise, when we reflect that they saw their preachers but once a month, and that on a week-night only? And it is probable that, as yet, they had little or no local help. From this date they had service every other week.

The publication of the annual Minutes of Conference was re-commenced in 1765. Wiltshire appears on the list as a separate circuit until 1768, when it was divided into South and North, names which were changed into Salisbury and Bradford in 1780.

It was resolved at the Conference of 1765 to furnish persons migrating from one part of the kingdom to another with a note of removal, and also to give a uniform ticket to all the members of Society throughout the Connexion. Previous to that, the Society ticket had been various in size, and were often adorned with an emblematical device.

	£	s.	d.
The income of the Society in the Island for the year 1766 was	2	9	0
The expenditure was	2	6	8
Balance in hand	0	2	4

Three years only had elapsed when Alexander Mather received a second appointment to his old circuit, and remained two years. John Haime was one of his colleagues during the second year,—a name which is familiar to every Wesleyan, for who has not read the thrilling story which this good soldier of Jesus Christ gives of the sanguinary fields of Dettingen and Fontenoy? After his discharge from the army in 1745, he entered upon the work of a circuit, and laboured in various parts of the kingdom. For some years a morbid state of mind caused him many painful exercises, but the latter part of his life was sunny and joyous. When he had reached extreme age, and the fever was wasting him to skin and bone, "his zeal for God," says George Story, "and concern for the salvation of souls abated not in the least." His last words were, " This is a good way." Oh that all may tread this path in the important hour! He died at Shaftesbury, his native place, on the 18th August, 1784, aged 77.

John Catermole came to this circuit in 1767. It was his last appointment. He was a deeply serious and devout man, but withal nervous, and too apt to look on the dark side of things. He opened a school at Portsmouth Common, and preached occasionally, as long as he was able. He retained his piety and integrity, and was very useful in his line of life to the last. He published several useful tracts. He died in peace, about the year 1799.

CHAPTER VII.

(1768.)

> " Through all her words, the soul within,
> The honest, artless soul, was seen,
> Ingenuous, pure, and free ;
> Candour and love were sweetly joined
> With easy nobleness of mind,
> And true simplicity."

ABOUT this date an incident occurred near Salisbury which is worthy of record as an illustration of Wesley's discernment of character, and solicitude for the spiritual welfare of the young. A little girl, nine years of age, named Elizabeth Bushell, resident at Wilton, a regular attendant at the means of grace, and on whose heart the divine Spirit had begun to work, expressed a desire to be admitted, with the other members of the Methodist Society, to the table of the Lord at the Established Church, but was refused on the ground of age. On Wesley's arrival, probably on the 24th of October, 1768, the case was named to him. He had Elizabeth brought to him, when he took her on his knee and conversed with her, and was so satisfied with her knowledge and experience that he then and there administered to her, in the most solemn manner, the memorials of the Saviour's dying love. And in no act of his life did that great man more resemble his divine Master, who took little children in his arms and blessed them, and who has said to all his under-shepherds, "Feed my lambs."

Wesley was not mistaken in his judgment of that remarkable young woman. She lived and died an ardent and truly consistent Christian. Her experience in the deep things of God, it will be seen, was of a very high order. She was highly esteemed by the preachers and their wives, some of whom kept up a correspondence with her long after they had removed from the circuit.

Her Journal and letters supply many valuable facts, and throw much light upon the progress of the cause both in Sarum and Newport. One of her earliest papers is a portion of a letter, in which she narrated the remarkable circumstances connected with her early union with the Methodists. Though but a fragment, its contents are too precious to be suffered to perish. It is dated July 3, 1779 :—

"Dear Friend,—As you seem so very desirous of knowing the dealings of God with me from the beginning, I will, as far as the Lord shall enable me, speak freely. From my very earliest days I had a great desire of being good,—so much so, that my mind was taken off from those things to which children are inclined, such as play, &c. My mother was constantly trying to teach me songs, but, with all her striving, I do not remember that I could ever say one. At the same time, she kept a strict watch over my morals, being what is called 'a good sort of a woman,' but a bitter enemy of the Methodists, and would have thought that she was doing God service if she could have destroyed every one of them.

' But oh the power of grace divine,
In her behalf and mine !'

I was now about five years old, when, one Sunday evening, our next-door neighbour's child, a few years older than myself, took me by the hand to the chapel. It was a new thing to me to hear the singing, and I was very much delighted indeed with it. I determined to go the next Sunday. Accordingly, after we had been at church morning and afternoon, my mother said to me, ' Come, Betty, we will go up to the castle along with the rest.' I answered directly, ' I won't, for I will go and hear the people sing,' upon which she struck me to the ground, and locked me in the house by myself, and went part of the way."

Here, unfortunately, this interesting narrative ends, and it is to be feared the remaining portion is now amongst the things that were. After carefully weighing the evidence bearing on the subject, and enquiring of a grandson, we are led to the conclusion that this bigoted woman was induced to accompany her daughter to the chapel, and that she became affected by what she saw and heard there.

The esteem in which Miss Bushell was held while yet young will appear from the following letter, which was penned by Mrs. Rodda:—

" High Wycomb, May 18, 1783.

" My dear Sister,—I received your kind and loving letter, and was very glad to hear of my friends at Sarum whom I love and esteem, such as Mr. and Mrs. Gifford, yourself, and many more. My dear, keep close to God. I would gladly hope you are rejoicing in redeeming love, and that you are a pattern to the young women in Sarum. We have many good people here, but some do not meet so well in class as we could wish. Mr. Rodda intended to be at Whitchurch, but was detained at Oxford by the new preaching-house which they are building. The Lord is reviving his work in many places in the round. Many are joining, and some are converted. My love to Mrs. Marsh, the Ingrams, Mr. and Mrs. Farr, and Jenny, Miss S. Brown, Mrs. Barnard, and all friends.

"Your sincere and affectionate friend,

"ELIZABETH RODDA.

"P.S.—Give my respects to Mr. Mason, and Mr. and Mrs. Moore."

Miss Bushell was united in marriage to Mr. J. Trimen about 1783, and came to reside at Newport. From this period she seems to have been a severe sufferer. A complication of diseases soon wore out her constitution, which was never strong. She was abundantly sustained by the consolations of the Spirit to the last, when in great peace she fell asleep in Jesus, on the 22nd March, 1803, aged 44.

The Rev. David Coe preached her funeral sermon at Newport, to an exceedingly crowded and deeply-affected audience, from Rev. vii., 14.

At the Conference of 1769, Wiltshire was divided into South and North. Out of 1,014 members, the North took 814, leaving but 200 for the South. Two preachers were sent to the South—John Mason and Thomas Briscoe. The latter was disabled by damp beds and hard fare while labouring in the country parts of Ireland. He was sensible, well read, a good preacher, and a decided Methodist.

The year 1770 witnessed the departure of Wesley's

early companion and friend, George Whitefield. He is said to have been the greatest orator of his age. The power of Whitefield's eloquence must not be sought in the strength and beauty of his diction, and the poetic brilliancy of his ideas, but in the deep and tender pathos which sprang from profound sympathy with the sublime theme of his ministry. His heart was a glowing fire of love, which kindled his words into a flame, and often made his impassioned appeals overwhelming and irresistible. He ceased at once to work and live on the 30th of September, in the 56th year of his age.

Passing on to the year 1770, we come across the name of Francis Asbury. It is an interesting fact that South Wiltshire was the last English ground occupied by this revered and apostolic man. Henceforth he must enter a more rugged field, and fill a much more responsible post in America, where he became the first bishop of the Methodist Episcopal Church.

During the preceding year, Wesley had received a call for preachers to go and take charge of the infant cause which had been originated in New York. The honour of transplanting Methodism into the new world belongs to a humble band of Irish emigrants, amongst whom were Philip Embury and Barbara Heck, who in 1766 laid the first stone of that grand ecclesiastical edifice which has since then been reared in that great country. Captain Webb, who was providentially present at the time, afforded valuable aid to the rising cause by his zealous preaching.

The application was brought before the Conference by John Wesley, and the question proposed, "Who will go to

America ?"　To this question there was no response.　The Conference was silent.　The following morning, as was his practice, he preached to the Conference at five o'clock, and took for his text, "I have nourished and brought up children, and they have rebelled against me;" and when the Conference re-assembled, he again proposed the question, and then Boardman and Pilmore rose up and offered to go. They sailed in September, 1769, and were followed by Asbury in the same month of 1771.　During the time Asbury was in this part of the kingdom, he felt the kindlings of the missionary fire, which glowed in him with an intensity and force that neither privation, toil, nor even affliction could damp.　He thus alludes to it:—"On the seventh of August, 1771, the Conference began at Bristol, in England.　Before this, I had felt for half a year strong intimations in my mind that I should visit America, which I laid before the Lord, being unwilling to do my own will, or to run before I was sent.　During this time my trials were very great, which the Lord I believe permitted to prove and try me, in order to prepare me for future useful- ness.　At the Conference, it was proposed that some preachers should go over to the American Continent.　I spoke my mind, and made an offer of myself.　I was accepted by Mr. Wesley and others who judged that I had a call."

Asbury visited the Island six times, stayed thirteen nights, and received 12s. for the whole.　If he fared no better elsewhere, we do not wonder that he should have to tell of "very great trials," and yet this good man found still greater trials awaiting him in the New World, and certainly greater triumphs.

Asbury was tall in person, but not robust. His features were expressive, his aspect grave, and his manner dignified. When his soul was moved with deep emotion, his piercing eyes shot from beneath overhanging shaggy brows, awakening glances to the sinner's heart, while his voice rose with the grandeur of his subject, and fell in tones like thunder on the ears of his appalled audience. And yet, like all noble natures, there was in him a gentleness that inspired the hearts of children with confidence, as they climbed his knee in the log-cabin, to receive lessons of wisdom and his benediction, the memory of which was fondly cherished as being amongst the brightest reminiscences of childhood and home. He was never married. Out of a scanty pittance, scarcely ever exceeding £20 per annum, he gave all he had, even to the shirt on his back. When called to the episcopal office, he made full proof of that high trust by an administration impartial, sagacious, and effective, which directed the ever-growing energies of the Methodist Communion in America towards those grand results with which his name will be enwreathed in all ages to come.*

William Ashman took the place of Asbury, and was the first preacher who had his passage to the Island paid, which was 3*s.* Henceforth this was an established practice. The Board money was also raised from 2*s.* to 5*s.*

Two fresh names of preachers present themselves at the Conference of 1772. The first is Richard Bourke, who saw much affliction, but patience had its perfect work. In him were united the wisdom and calmness of age with the simplicity of childhood. "I buried the remains," says

* Coke's Life, by Dr. Etheridge, p. 93.

Wesley, Feb. 15, 1778, " of Richard Bourke, a faithful labourer in our Lord's vineyard. A more unblamable character I have hardly known. In all the years that he has laboured with us, I do not remember that he ever gave me occasion to find fault with him in anything." He was a man of unwearied diligence and patience, and "his works do follow him."

His ministry during his stay in the Circuit, is referred to by one, who says: " Dec. 20th. I found the drawings of divine love under the word, when Mr. Bourke told how many he had united with us." Again, in the following March : "In the evening Mr. Bourke's sermon deeply humbled me, and caused me to cry unto the Lord."

This was William Eels' first year of travelling. He was a talented preacher, and much beloved by the people. But, because his name was not inserted in the deed of Declaration in 1784, and accidentally omitted at the Conference of 1788, he left the Connexion, and joined John Atley, who had espoused the cause of the trustees at Dewsbury. Five years after, he sought re-union with the Conference, but was suddenly removed by death. His end was peace. Miss Bushell makes frequent reference to him, and of his last service says, " The love-feast was sweet to my soul ; but when Mr. Eels gave out the parting hymn, I found my will not so resigned as it ought. The Lord has blessed him much to my soul."

Wesley's visit to Salisbury, in October of the same year, is noticed :—" Oct. 7. I have found much of the presence of God to-day. The way, as Mr. Wesley described it, seemed a delightful one, though it was narrow, and I longed to walk in it."

In 1774, James Barry came into Wiltshire. It was his first circuit. He was a zealous labourer, but exposed to much suffering, which he bore with resignation, and in death stole quietly away. His colleague, Thomas Westall, was one of the first lay preachers whom Wesley called to his aid. He began his ministry in 1740, and continued faithfully to discharge the duties of his high vocation for more than forty years. His retirement was spent in the city of Bristol, where his triumphant spirit returned to God in 1794, in the 75th year of his age. His life was a pattern of Christian humility and love.

In 1775 an important event took place in reference to the Isle of Wight—the introduction of the first Home Missionary. Several letters passed between John Wesley and Jasper Winscom on the subject. Wesley had met with James Skinner probably at Winchester, in October, and had commissioned him to go forth as an evangelist to the Island. For some reason or other, Winscom sought to have Skinner's appointment changed, but the application met with a decided negative, as the subjoined letter will show :—

"London, Oct. 20, 1775.

"Dear Brother,—I should have no objection at all to brother Skinner going into Kent, but that it would interfere with our making a fair trial of the Isle of Wight. I would have this done without delay, and I much approve of the method you propose. We will help you out (as I said) with regard to the expense. I hope you will be able to procure the meeting-house. Peace be with you and yours.

"I am, your affectionate friend and brother,

"JOHN WESLEY."

This was decisive, and accordingly we find Mr. Skinner on the Island by Saturday, the 11th of November, ready to commence his work on the Lord's day. It is curious to observe how powerful the principle of itinerancy was at that day. Mr. Skinner was sent to give the Island a "fair trial," yet he seems to have taken his turn with the other preachers, the only difference was he remained a longer time, and yet that never reached three weeks. To meet the extra expense, Mr. Winscom paid eleven shillings as the first instalment of the "help" promised by Wesley. The next sum was nineteen shillings, which, says the Steward, "made all even for the preachers."

No records survive by which we can judge of the spiritual results of this mission to the Island ; but whatever they might be, the financial state soon began to wear a threatening aspect. When the Steward came to settle with Mr. Rodda, at the Conference of 1777, he found himself minus to the serious amount of £4 19s. 4d. But immediately after the Conference, Wesley, true to his promise, sent through Joseph Bradford £4 16s., and the debt was discharged. And this is the last item in the interesting old Society book.

This financial difficulty seems to have had a discouraging effect on the circuit, as we find the number of preachers reduced at the next Conference to two.

The initials T. V., in the appointment of preachers to South Wiltshire for 1775, stand for Thomas Vasey. He was removed, after being in the Circuit only about one month. This information is derived from Miss Bushell's Journal. She says, " Mr. Vasey preached his first sermon

to-day. I hope we shall have reason to praise God for
sending him among us. He has been made a blessing to
me. 15th. This evening my mind was not so stayed as in
the morning, owing in some measure to Mr. Vasey being
so soon taken from us."

Out of a variety of allusions to the effective ministry of
Mr. Rodda which we have before us, the following will not
be unacceptable :—

"Dec. 2, 1777.—I have been," says one, "sorely tried
to-day with peevishness of temper. Oh what a burden
have I been to myself, and I suppose to all about me. I
went often to the throne of grace, but did not find it
removed, nor any answer from the Lord, so that I soon
gave way to reasoning, and became as miserable as a soul
could be in this world. My way appeared to be blocked
up, and I seemed to be forsaken of the Lord.

" 3.—I spent this day in fasting and prayer, and was
determined not to give the Lord any rest, or any food or
sleep to my body, till He had smiled on me again. I felt
willing to suffer anything at his hands, if I could but be
assured of his love, but the heavens were as brass to my
petitions. While at the preaching I was so painfully tried
and exercised, that I was obliged to stand up, and then to
leave, lest the Lord should make me a public monument of
his anger. I went back to the chapel just as Mr. Rodda
was going to meet the bands. I thought I would go in
and tell him the state of my mind. The devil told me I
should not, for it would only distress others, and increase
my own burden. I immediately threw myself on the
ground, and cried to the Lord for a few moments, got up

and went in just as Mr. Rodda was giving out those lines :

> ' Long my imprison'd spirit lay
>   Fast bound in sin and nature's night,
> Thine eye diffused a quick'ning ray,
>   I woke—the dungeon flamed with light ;
> My chains fell off, my heart was free,
> I rose, went forth, and followed thee.'

" The Lord applied them with power, and in a moment spoke peace to my soul, so that I could sing the next verse with joy :—

> ' No condemnation now I dread ;
>   Jesus, and all in him, is mine !
> Alive in him, my living Head,
>   And clothed in righteousness divine,
> Bold I approach th' eternal throne,
> And claim the crown, through Christ my own.'

" Oh what a change ! On the preceding night I could not sleep for sorrow ; last night I could not sleep for joy !"

The name of Richard Rodda retains its pleasant odour to this day. Two instances of the special interpositions of Providence in his behalf, are recorded in his life. Once, when a good Quaker rescued him from being impressed and sent to the Havannahs ; and again, while in the act of kneeling in prayer, he was preserved from being crushed to atoms in the mine. While yet a youth, in his native Cornwall, he began to make known the Saviour whom he himself had found. He commenced his self-denying and successful career as a Methodist preacher in 1770. " A long succession of damp beds " disabled him, and in 1802 he became a supernumerary in London, and on the 30th of

October, 1815, his useful life was crowned with a triumphant end. Feeling the power of the Saviour's love in his heart, he said with his last breath, "I could go to Smithfield and die for his cause. I know I could."

Miss Bushell makes frequent mention of him. "The morning preaching was sweet, and I found a cry in my heart that I might labour to enter into that rest which Mr. Rodda described. This morning, Mr. Rodda spoke from those words, 'If I wash thee not thou hast no part with me.' Oh cleanse me, Lord, from every sin, nor let one remain." Again, "I found much life under Mr. Rodda."

Wesley's annual visitation is thus described: "Oct. 7, 1776: Mr. Rodda preached this morning, and I found it a time of love. Mr. Wesley preached in the evening from 'Israel doth not know.' And, indeed, my God, how little do I know of thy power to what I might have known. Surely thou art able to save me from all sin.

"8.—Mr. Wesley met the classes, and I found my soul blessed under him. Also his morning sermon was a blessing to me, and especially the letter which he read.

"9.—I found much satisfaction this morning under Mr. Wesley's discourse. He cleared up many things which have been great hindrances to me at sundry times."

Of Thomas Newall she complains: "I have found much uneasiness in hearing Mr. Newall. To me he neither preaches truth nor experience. His sermons are made up of suppositions,—striving about words to no profit. He said he stood up not to please men, but God; but I am apt to think he is mistaken, for I am sure he takes care to avoid the name of Jesus, which cannot be pleasing to God, and he makes a greater saviour of opinions than he does of my blessed Redeemer. Lord, if I am wrong, shew me, and do not suffer me to have any prejudice against him."

Mr. Newall forsook the work very shortly afterwards.

Although a third preacher was granted to South Wiltshire in 1778, an application was made by Mr. Winscom for an additional man in order to give the Isle of Wight a second trial. Wesley's reply shows in what light he viewed the itinerancy at that day:—

"London, Jan. 14, 1779.

"My dear Brother,

"Ours are travelling preachers; therefore I can never consent that any of them should remain for a month together in the Island. If you can contrive that the additional preacher have full employment, then we can enquire where one can be found.

"It seems to me that you take the matter exactly right, with regard to the Portsmouth preaching-house, and that the only thing to be done is to get the mortgage out of Mr. Pike's hands.

"I am, your affectionate brother,
"JOHN WESLEY."

Notwithstanding the discouraging character of the above letter, Wesley was induced to yield to the wishes of the friends, and a fourth preacher was sent. How much of his time was devoted to the Island we have no means of knowing, but henceforward the cause prospered.

One of the staff of preachers in 1778 was Richard Whitecoat (or, as the Americans write his name, Whatcoat).

He remained two years, and four years afterwards followed Asbury to the New World, where he finished his self-denying·labours and his life on June 5th, 1806. He was the second bishop of the Methodist Episcopal Church. "This holy man," his brethren say, "was sent to the Church as a sample, to show to what a life of peace and holiness Christians may attain on earth, where sincerity, privation, love of divine communion, and humble and active faith, do meet and centre." . . . . "His personal appearance was interesting, and his whole deportment was so beautiful, and adorned with personal graces, that of him it may be said, 'He was made of love.'"

While in this circuit, he found some old disciples who were faithful followers of the Saviour, and adorned their Christian profession by a consistent and useful life. With these mature Christians Mr. Whatcoat took sweet counsel, and formed friendships which time and distance could not destroy.

William Tunney, who succeeded Whatcoat, left the ranks at the end of the year, and his example was soon after followed by John Walker, one of his colleagues. John Pool stood his ground, maintained an unblemished character thirty-one years, and then passed away on the wings of faith and hope.

William Green also retired, after travelling sixteen years.  He was born in London, Sept. 22, 1739. His mother heard John Wesley's first sermon at the "Foundry," and soon after joined the Society. He received his education at the Foundry School. His heart was touched under the preaching of John Murlin. By the persuasions of his mother, he joined a class, and, after suffering painful convictions for sin, he received "a full sense of the love of God." Soon after hearing Wesley preach on the subject, he was enabled to realize the perfect love of God, and rejoiced with "joy unspeakable and full of glory." "In that moment," he says, "I was as clearly saved from sin as ever I was justified." Salisbury was his first circuit. In referring to this appointment, he states :—"Many of my prudent friends blamed me for leaving a quiet, comfortable, business. But I had counted the cost. So on Monday, Sept. 11, I set out for Salisbury. When I left my wife and three children, I felt a mixture of joy and grief, but with a full resignation to the will of God. I have been more than three months in my circuit, and am more convinced that this is the pleasantest life under heaven. Though I have left my wife and children, and dearest friends, and house and business, and wander about, chiefly on foot, through cold and rain, I find my mind uninterruptedly happy ; I feel a constant witness of the work wrought in my heart by the Spirit of Holiness. I have received in this world a hundred-fold, and I know that when my ' earthly house of this tabernacle is dissolved, I have a building of God, a house not made with hands, eternal in the heavens.' "

At the end of the year, he removed to the adjoining circuit of Bradford. In a letter of his which has fallen into our hands, we gain a glimpse of both circuits :—

"Shaftesbury, Jan. 18th, 1782.

" Dear Sister,

"You are happy in God ; you find the name of Jesus as ointment poured forth, and you trust his blood to cleanse you from all sin. In reference to your wish to know what success I have in my labours, I cannot say much. I frequently think that I 'spend my strength for nought, and fight as one that beateth the air.' Our circuit is large, and the people are numerous, having about nine hundred in society, but our success is small. The members seem to be in a low dispensation of grace: very few know their sins forgiven. Coleford is an exception. The members there are alive, and there are many witnesses of both justifying and sanctifying grace, and their number is increasing.

"As to myself, I must confess I have been discouraged by the deadness of the people, which seems to be an insurmountable difficulty. My dear wife is at Bradford. She has a good house to live in, but very few take any notice of her; and, being separated from the children, and seeing me so seldom, she lives the life of a recluse, which, considering her lively turn of mind, renders her situation very exercising. But the word of the Lord stands fast, 'All things do work together for good to them that love God.' How are you getting on at Salisbury? I have the pleasure of seeing the spire once a month if the weather is clear, and I sometimes feel a secret desire to come and see you. The Salisbury and Portsmouth people in general are very dear to me. I owe them much for their kind treatment of me and my dear wife, and likewise for the veil of love which they cast over my infirmities. Would that I had been more faithful to God and to his people! I had much to humble me last year, but I have more this. I found Salisbury circuit much more agreeable than Bradford. I believe God has sent you preachers after his own heart. But we need all possible help : we have much to do, something to suffer, and nothing but divine grace can support us. Blessed be God for Jesus Christ. Let us believe, and bid the devil defiance. Let us look up, a crown awaits us !

"From your friend and brother in Christ,

"WILLIAM GREEN."

We deem it right, ere we close this chapter, to correct a two-fold error into which Dr. Smith has fallen in his valuable History of Methodism, in reference to the Isle of Wight. He states that the early efforts of Wesley and his preachers in the Island "perished for lack of regular preaching and pastoral attention." This, as we have seen, was not the case. The cause was feeble, but, amid alien influences and discouragement, it stood its ground, until it was favoured with home missionary labour, when it revived and spread. It is doubtless an oversight which led him to place Winchester at the head of the circuit.*

* Smith's History, vol. i., p. 438.

CHAPTER VIII.

(1780.)

"And I will make them, and the place round about my hill, a blessing ; and I will cause the shower to come down in his season : there shall be showers of blessing."—*Ezekiel* xxxiv., 26.

JUST at the close of Mr. Whatcoat's second year, an extensive revival of religion took place in the circuit. This gracious work was greatly promoted by the ministry of Captain Webb and Robert Carr Brackenbury. The revival began at Salisbury, and extended to Winchester, Southampton, the Isle of Wight, and other places. The first drops of the shower fell at Salisbury in July, 1780.

Wesley, in his annual visit, alludes to it in his Journal, where he says :—"Tuesday, October 3rd, 1780, I walked over to Wilton, and preached to a very serious congregation in the new preaching-house. I found at Sarum the fruit of Captain Webb's preaching; some were awakened, and one perfected in love. Yet, I was a little surprised at the remark of some of our eldest brethren, that they had never heard perfection preached before."

It will be gratifying to the Christian reader to know that we are able not only to supply the name of the "one perfected in love," but also to supply a deeply-interesting narration of the circumstance under which that rich but free grace was obtained. The individual so favoured was no other than Elizabeth Bushell. The following letter, addressed probably to one of the preachers, is remarkably clear, and shows her to have been a young woman of some ability. She was at the time residing with a relative who kept a ladies' school in Salisbury.

"1780.

"Dear Brother,

"Excuse the freedom, for I cannot refrain longer from telling you that my soul is brought into the glorious liberty of a full salvation. The last night you were with us you said,—'Betty, here is peace and courage to you.' My heart replied inwardly, 'I have it.' I felt such a power with the words, that I went home on full stretch for [entire] sanctification, and thought I could not rest unless the Lord made me a partaker of it. As soon as I reached home I cast myself down before the Lord, and wrestled with him some time, when I felt something behind pulled me back from the place where I was, which (though not present to my eyes), I believe, was the devil; but I felt not the least fear, though my earnestness was removed, and I gave up seeking the blessing. But all the next day it seemed near to me. In the afternoon I drank tea with Captain [Webb, doubtless], at Mr. ——. Mr. and Mrs. Lacey, Mr. Gifford [a local preacher], and Mrs. Wilder were there. I wanted to tell them all what I felt, but had not power to do it. We all went to the chapel, to the

prayer-meeting. The moment I entered, those words came
with power :—

> 'Now, O my Joshua, bring me in,
> Cast out thy foes ; the inbred sin,
> The carnal mind remove,' &c.

It seemed as if the Lord asked me if I was willing to give
up all. I replied, ' Yes, Lord, I am willing to be nothing.'
I went to my seat in the chapel, but, while three of our
friends gave out hymns and prayed, I was wholly taken up
with those words—

> ' The blessing is free,
> So Lord let it be ;
> I yield that thy love
> Should be given to me.'

The Captain then gave out a verse, and went to prayer,
and in a moment the Lord brought those words with power
to my heart, ' What things soever ye desire when ye pray,
believe that ye receive them, and ye shall have them,' and
I felt the sealing of the Spirit that very moment, and was
constrained to cry out, not before the Lord only, but all
present,

> ' 'Tis done ! thou dost this moment save,
> With full salvation bless ;
> Redemption through thy blood I have,
> And spotless love and peace !'

The Captain then gave out a verse to sing, and went to
prayer again; and oh, what I felt !—a 'joy unspeakable
and full of glory.' I went home, and fell down before my
God, when the enemy insinuated that the work was not
done, but my God answered for himself: ' Be not faithless,
but believing, for I have cast out thine enemy; the king of
Israel, even the Lord, is in the midst of thee, thou shalt
see evil no more.'

"From that time, which was Friday, 28th July, 1780, about nine o'clock in the evening, I can say with the poet:

> ' Not a cloud doth arise to darken the skies,
>   Nor hide for a moment my Lord from my eyes.'

My heart is now so overwhelmed with God's goodness, I can scarcely write.

"Yours, &c., E. BUSHELL."

This was no transient good. To another friend she says: "This state I have been in ever since, my happiness increasing more and more. Blessed be my adorable Redeemer! I have no complaints,—all is glory, happiness, and heaven! I have neither fear nor care, but how I may live unblamably in love. I every moment find, not only union, but also communion with the Father and the Son, through the Holy Spirit. Even now, while I am writing, my soul expands to grasp the Infinite. Oh, if we were now together, how should we extol, adore, and praise our ever-living, ever-loving Lord! But, alas! how barren is human language! Let silence speak his praise."

From Salisbury the revival spread to Winchester, where Captain Webb was joined by Robert C. Brackenbury. On the 5th Sept., "Mr. Brackenbury preached at the barracks to a large congregation, and on the 6th, in the room in the town usually occupied for preaching, when many soldiers attended. After service, Thomas Miller, a grenadier, who had met in Mr. Winscom's class, declared that he had found the Lord, a declaration fully sustained by his deportment. On Sunday, the 7th, the Captain preached in the room morning and afternoon, and in the evening at Corlock to a very large congregation in the square. Monday, the 8th, at six in the evening, he preached in the street; and at seven Mr. Brackenbury conducted service in the room ; and at nine the Captain did the same in the barracks, and the following day in the street. When he had done, Robert Brison, a soldier who met in Mr. Thomas's class, testified that the Lord had spoken peace to his soul. When the Captain heard this account, he requested the friends to unite in prayer, being then at Mr. Jasper Winscom's. While they were thus engaged, his daughter, a girl about thirteen years old, was seized with powerful convictions of sin. For her the persons assembled continued in supplication, and in about half-an-hour it pleased the Lord to speak peace to her soul. On Thursday, the 11th, the Captain preached at the barracks, and under his last prayer Mary Edridge Hayter was deeply convinced of sin, and cried aloud for mercy. She, with several others under strong conviction, followed the Captain to Mr. Winscom's house, when God was earnestly besought on their behalf; and, in a short time, E. Hayter broke out in a rapture, exclaiming, 'Christ is mine! he is mine!' At the same time, two others were enabled to rejoice in God their Saviour: one belonged to Mr. Thompson's class, and the other had previously been made acquainted with the pardoning love of God, but had lost her peace, and for a time became inclined to mysticism. On the 12th, the Captain again preached in the room, where several more attended who were seeking salvation; they prayed until another soldier, who had been some time in the Society, found peace.

"As Mr. Webb was returning home, after service at the

barracks on Thursday evening, he overtook a very trifling, gay young woman, whose name was Sarah Day, in company with an elderly lady; they were church people, and, as was too frequently the case at that day, rigid Pharisees. Both appeared much displeased with the Captain's preaching, who, hearing their objections, spoke to them very abruptly, telling them that if they did not experience in their hearts what he had been speaking about, they would certainly be lost for ever. The young woman replied, that for her part, ' she was sure of going to heaven, if she died that night.' The Captain answered, 'If you die in your present condition you will certainly be lost,' and, after exchanging a few more words to the same effect, he left them. On the Saturday following, the elderly woman, Mrs. Butts, enquired where the Captain could be seen ; and being informed where he intended to dine, they both came to him after dinner, and conversed with him some time; he then prayed with them, and left them both under deep conviction. On Sunday Mrs. Butts attended service, and the following morning Sarah Day had some further conversation with Mr. Webb before he left Winchester. In his last prayer on Saturday night, Sally King, a young woman who had been under conviction some months, found peace. On Monday evening Mr. Winscom preached at the room, when Mrs. Betts and Sarah Day were present, apparently in great distress. After worship on the following Wednesday, they met at the house of Mr. Bannister, when one of the Society asked Mrs. Butts if she was earnestly seeking salvation, and whether she felt something of the misery of the torments of hell. At the mention of that word, Sarah

Day broke out saying, 'Hell! here is hell! I have hell in my heart; and there is the devil,—do you not see him?' She then flew about the room raving like a maniac. After some time, she screamed aloud, calling upon Mr. Winscom to come and save her from the hands of Satan, for she imagined she saw him stand before her, ready to carry her away to eternal misery. A messenger was despatched for Mr. Winscom. In the meantime, Mrs. Butts was in great distress, though not so deep as Sarah Day. Some of the friends present then prayed; but they had not been engaged long, when Sarah Day broke out with rage and despair pictured in her countenance, when they pleaded the promises of God and the merits of Christ. 'Christ!' said she, 'you know he never died for me,' with many kindred expressions. When Mr. Winscom arrived, he gave out the verse beginning—

'Oh that my load of sin were gone!'

and afterwards cried to the Lord in her behalf, and in a few minutes the Lord spoke peace to her soul. They then wrestled on behalf of Mrs. Butts, but, finding no answer, they were constrained to leave her. The next morning, about two o'clock, the Lord graciously visited her soul, impressing deeply on her mind these words: 'Work out thy salvation with fear and trembling.' She knew not where to find the words, but, visiting one of the Society early the following morning, she was directed to the part of Scripture where they might be found. Both of them immediately joined the Society.

"The following Sunday two others found peace; one, an elderly woman, awakened under the preaching of Captain

Webb two years before. On Wednesday, the 24th, at a prayer-meeting, a young man belonging to the Society at Houghton was cut to the heart, and soon after set at liberty. The next day, William Harris, a soldier, who was convinced of his sinfulness eight weeks before, came to Mr. Winscom's in great distress, on account of a rash oath which he had taken two years and a-half ago, and which he broke soon after. He appeared exceedingly terrified. He went to the class, where he was favoured with some gleams of hope, and soon after rejoiced in a pardoning God. In a little while others tasted the good word of life, among whom was a soldier, who was brought into liberty while on guard.

"On Monday, October 20th, a love-feast was held for the soldiers, and many found it indeed a feast of love. Thomas Miller testified that the blood of Jesus Christ had then cleansed him. So strong were his feelings, that he was unable to stand, and was obliged to be supported by those near him. Several of those who had been brought into liberty were constrained to cry out, 'Lord, withhold thy hand, or enlarge my heart.' At the same time, a child six or seven years of age declared herself happy in the love of God. Such was the gracious manifestation of the Spirit of God to the Methodist Society in Winchester. The affectation of learning and philosophy may stigmatize such a work," says Dr. Smith, "as madness, while the Pharisaic and the formalist will call it 'rant and enthusiasm.' The Christian, however, will joyfully admit that the cases above described exhibit the enlightening and saving influences of the Holy Spirit as 'the power of God unto every one that believeth.'"

This chapter may be appropriately closed by a brief notice of the two devoted men whose names are so intimately associated with the revival, the incidents of which are therein narrated. Captain Webb was converted under John Wesley at Bristol, and shortly afterwards was licensed by him as a local preacher. He soon became distinguished for his zeal and success. He was one of the principal founders of American Methodism, and, partly through his labours, or rather through the success of his labours at Winchester, Methodism found its way to the Norman Isles. The holy flame glowed in him with undimmed brightness until he had passed his three-score years and ten, when the angel reapers came and found him like a shock of corn, fully ripe, and suddenly caught him up and bore him home, on Tuesday, Dec. 20th, 1796, aged 72. The Rev. C. Atmore bears the following testimony to his excellencies. He records, Dec. 8, 1796 : " I spent a profitable hour with that excellent man, Captain Webb, of Bristol. He is indeed truly devoted to God, and has maintained a consistent profession for many years. He is now in his seventy-second year, and as active as many who have only attained their fiftieth. He has no family, and gives to the cause of God, and to the poor of Christ's flock, the greater part of his income. He is waiting, with cheerful anticipation, for his great and full reward. Wednesday, Dec. 21. Last night, about eleven o'clock, Captain Webb suddenly entered into the joy of his Lord. He partook of his supper, and retired to rest about ten o'clock in his usual health. In less than an hour his spirit left the tenement of clay to enter the realms of eternal bliss. Dec. 24. This afternoon the remains of the good old captain were deposited in a vault under the communion table of Portland chapel. He was carried by six local preachers, and the pall was supported by the Rev. Messrs. Bradford, Pritchard, Roberts, Davis, Mayer, and M'Geary. I conducted the funeral service, and Mr. Pritchard preached from Acts xx., 24. It was a solemn season, and will long be remembered by those who were present."

"Brackenbury," says Mrs. Smith, "is a name that belongs to the annals of England. It has been chronicled by our historians, and sung by our poets; it has allied itself to rank, and it has patronized science, and in our own days it has given divines to our church, officers to our army, and consuls to foreign states." The branch of the ancestral stem from which the subject of this notice was derived has long been established in Lincolnshire. A thoughtful stranger, on entering the church at Raithby, "is arrested in his musings by the impressive mural monument near the communion rails, to the memory of Robert Carr Brackenbury, Esq.,—a monument raised by the genius of Chantrey, and inscribed by the muse of Montgomery, whose beautiful mortuary lines we here record :—

> " Silent be human praise !
> The solemn charge was thine ;
> A widowed love obeys,
> And here upon thy shrine
> Inscribes the monumental stone
> With—Glory be to God alone !"

Mr. Brackenbury was born at the family estate, Panton House, Lincolnshire, in the year 1752. With a view to enter the Established Church, he matriculated at St.

Catherine's Hall, Cambridge, but was early brought into contact with Methodism; he commenced lay preaching about 1776, and joined the ranks of the itinerancy in 1784, when he entered upon his successful labours in the Norman Isles. When no longer able to discharge the full duties of the ministry, he retired as a supernumerary to his estate, Raithby Hall, where, after faithfully preaching the Gospel for forty years, he suddenly closed a life of deep piety, extensive usefulness, and growing benevolence, on Tuesday, August 10, 1818.

Mrs. Brackenbury, who was his second wife, and much his junior, survived him many years. Her maiden name was Holland. She resided at Loughborough, in Leicestershire. She was the band-mate of a young lady with whom she had entered into solemn covenant never to marry. Some time afterwards, Mr. Brackenbury came on a visit to Loughborough, when his preaching and deportment made such a deep impression on Miss Holland that she came to her leader, Mr. John Rawson, and disclosed her feelings to him, and at the same time told him of her rash vow. Mr. Rawson procured her a private interview with Mr. Brackenbury, when it turned out that the esteem was mutual, and, ere long, led to their happy union. These facts were given to the writer by Mr. Rawson himself, then resident at Kegworth, six miles from Loughborough, where he died shortly afterwards, at an advanced age.

CHAPTER IX.

(1780—1785).

THE wisdom of Wesley's determination to give the Island a
"fair trial" was seen, notwithstanding some drawbacks, in
the success which followed the additional ministerial labour
bestowed upon it. The cause in Newport began to prosper,
the spirit of hearing was awakened, persons of a higher
social position were added to the Society, and the erection
of a chapel became necessary. The first preaching-place in
Newport of which there is any knowledge was a room in
Node Hill, adjoining the "Duke of York" Inn. Here the
little Society met, and strengthened each other's hands in
God, by prayer, exhortation, and Christian fellowship,
hailing with delight the week-evening visits of the preachers.
These were days of persecution. It is true the opposition
raised against this new thing was not, in the Island, of that

brutal and savage sort by which it was characterized in many other parts of the kingdom. It assumed a mischievous form chiefly, and aimed to make religion the subject of ridicule. Let it suffice to say that the opposition with which the early Methodists in the Island had to contend was, with the exception named, precisely the same as that which confronted them everywhere else. The carnal mind was aroused, and showed its bitter enmity in varied forms of mortifying, and sometimes severe persecution. Drums, tin-kettles, bells, horns, or any discordant thing was brought into requisition to drown the preacher's voice, while a shower of rotten eggs, sticks, stones, with now and then a live animal, or any other offensive missile, fell with annoying and dangerous effect on the preacher and his audience. The dresses of the congregation were fastened together, that they might be torn when they separated; ferocious animals were turned into the worshipping assemblies, and sparrows were let loose to put out the lights; the top of the chimney covered with a lid, and the door tied, to suffocate with smoke those who were thus imprisoned; while foul imputations were cast upon the attendants on the private society meetings.

In Newport the principal tools in this mischief—for they were instigated by others—were two youths of the name of Osmond and Barton. The former lived to see his eighty-fifth year, and, just before his death, some years ago, gave to Mr. H. Urry, who visited him, a detailed account of the active part which he had taken in persecuting the Methodists, and that the remembrance of it had been the burden of his life. Mr. Urry, to whom we are indebted for the above facts, was a useful local preacher, but was cut off in the prime of manhood, and left a widow and large family to mourn his loss.

At the time the chapel was erected, the society in Newport had been in existence nearly thirty years. During the whole of that period they had been put to various shifts, having to put up with the inconvenience of small rooms and an out-of-the-way loft, which had been used as an auction-room.

Henceforth a neat and commodious chapel is to receive them, and not only afford them increased privileges, but also place them in a better position among the other churches in the town. These were the Established Church, the Independent, and the Baptist.

The chapel was erected in Town Lane; the situation was central, and no doubt was at the time regarded as a good site.

A full account of the building and cost of the chapel, have been preserved in the hand-writing of John Mason, who became the Assistant or Superintendent of the Circuit the year after that in which the chapel was opened. Two pieces of land were purchased, at a cost respectively of £84 and £18 8s. 6d. The deeds were £2 15s. 6d., and the expense of removing an old building £2 7s. 6½d., making the entire cost of the site £107 11s. 6½d. The cost of the chapel was £465 1s. 10d., making a total outlay of £572 13s. 4½d. Towards this expenditure the sum of £129 15s. 2d. was raised thus:—

	£	s.	d.
By subscriptions in the Salisbury Circuit	57	18	6
„ Collections made at divers places by John Mason	63	7	0
„ Collections at the opening of the chapel	4	0	0
„ Mr. Whitehead	0	10	6
Returned by Mr. Wooldridge	0	4	2
By Mrs. Bradford	2	2	0
„ A Friend. J. C.	1	1	0
„ Seat money	0	6	0
„ Stairs left in the old room.	0	6	0
	£129	15	2

It will gratify the descendants of some of those persons whose names are found in the following list of subscribers to the new chapel, to see them in print, with John Wesley's name at the head :—

Name	£	s.	d.	Name	£	s.	d.
Mr. Wesley	10	0	0	Mr. Fays	0	10	6
„ Angel	5	5	0	„ Cheverton	1	1	0
„ Porter	2	2	0	Mrs. Hays	5	5	0
„ Newbury	2	12	6	Mr. Winscom	5	5	0
„ Cantelo	0	12	6	„ Catermole	0	10	6
„ Pratt	1	1	0	Mrs. Bevis	2	2	0
„ Cribb	0	3	0	„ Parleby	1	1	0
„ Jones	1	1	0	Miss Angel	0	10	6
„ Bray	2	2	0	Mrs. Taylor	1	1	0
„ Reese	1	1	0	A Friend	1	1	0
„ Price	0	10	6	„	1	1	0
„ Gain	0	10	6	„	1	1	0
Mrs. Jolliff	0	7	0	„	0	10	6
„ Denton	0	10	6	„	0	7	6
Mr. Whitehead	1	1	0	„	0	5	0
„ Dyer	0	10	6	„	0	5	0
„ Nobbs	1	1	0	„	1	1	0
„ Rogers	1	1	0	Miss G.	1	1	0
„ Crockford	1	1	0	Mr. Newbury	0	2	6
„ Norris	1	1	0	„ Bray	0	2	6
					£57	18	6

Mr. Mason seems to have had a roving commission, and collected in—

	£	s.	d.
Bradford Circuit	12	12	11
Bristol „	37	1	9½
Gloucester „	7	3	9½
By a note from Mr. Wesley	5	5	0
Of Farmer Ivemy	0	10	6
Two Friends	0	13	0
	63	7	0
Expenses	1	7	3
	£61	19	9

There are a few items which we cull for the curious. The window-shutters and pews of the old room were used in the new chapel. The sum of £6 16s. 5½d. was expended in malt and beer for the workmen. The boon of total abstinence had not reached the sons of toil in those days. A soldier was paid 2s. 8½d. for labour. During the summer they suffered from scarcity of water, and on the 16th of June no less a sum than 16s. was paid for that common but invaluable article. Wesley's and Coke's expenses from and to Winchester, on the occasion of opening, were 7s. 5d. Travelling must have been cheaper at that day, or money much more valuable than it is now.

Wednesday, October the 10th, 1781, was a " red-letter day" in the history of the Newport Society, and one to which they had looked forward with eager anticipation as being that on which their new and beautiful house was to be dedicated to the holy purpose for which it had been reared. Wesley conducted the opening services, being accompanied by Dr. Coke. We cite the brief passage from his Journal which relates to it :—"Wednesday, 10. I opened the new preaching-house just finished at Newport, in the Isle of Wight. After preaching, I explained the nature of a Methodist Society, of which few had before the least conception." The last clause is different to Wesley's usual strain when speaking of the Newport Society, and indicates that there had been neglect somewhere.

It is said that Wesley was entertained by Mr. Thomas Cook, a deacon amongst the Baptists, and that with the Society he received the sacrament from the hands of his guest. This was looked upon as the more remarkable, because Mr. Cook was a Calvinist of the high school.

The chapel was 36 feet long, and 24 broad. The singers' seat was, in the old style, fixed immediately under the pulpit, and a gallery was erected soon after the opening across the end. It would seat about three hundred and fifty. It was well attended. The choir had been at some pains to learn a piece of music, which was set to "How beautiful upon the mountains are the feet of him," &c., intending to sing it when Wesley should again visit them. The time arrived, and on his entering the chapel they commenced singing, but the venerable man looked up and said, "Stop friends! give God the glory!" It is needless to add the remainder of the piece was not sung.

In the same month that the ground was purchased for the chapel, James Trimen received his first ticket as a member of the Methodist Society. The ministry of Wm. Ashman and John Haime was made a great blessing to him. While yet young, he employed his talents in visiting the sick, conducting prayer-meetings, and occasionally reading a sermon to village congregations. He was united in marriage to Miss Bushell, of Salisbury. His integrity was proverbial, and his life consistent with his profession. In his last affliction he could say, "The Master is with me." He died in the 69th year of his age.

Here is a specimen of the practice of the early Methodists:—"Jan. 1, 1782. Rose at five, and spent a comfortable hour in private; went to chapel at six. Mr. Shaw, after a short time spent in singing and prayer, gave a very profitable exhortation." After such a beginning, can we wonder at what follows: "I have found it a sweet and solemn day, having had much of the presence of the Lord with me."

It will be matter of surprise to some to hear that one of the preachers was laid up in the sunny south with ague, and yet such was the fact, and that, too, in the Isle of Wight. Jonathan Cousens, at the time a young man, was prostrated by that painful disorder, which he had contracted in the Norwich circuit the preceding year. In a letter to a friend, which was dated from Newport, 6th March, 1782, he says:—

"I should have written sooner had not disease prevented. I suppose you will have heard of me by my fellow-labourers. I know not that I was ever under so sharp an affliction in all my life, but I am fully persuaded this also will be for my good. I am a little better, and hope to see you soon after brother Poole comes to Portsmouth. I trust your soul is still athirst for the living God, the fountain of happiness, who alone can satisfy the immortal spirit. Oh, my dear sister, live near to Him, who is able to support you amid all your trials. *Jesus* is a refuge for his people at all times. Give my love to the friends, and accept the same from

"Your affectionate brother,

"Jonathan Cousens."

In the interesting memoir of him, written by Richard Waddy, and inserted in the *Methodist Magazine* for 1806, there is this reference to his affliction:—"Upon his arrival there [Salisbury] he had a relapse, by which he was greatly reduced. This affliction confined him to the Isle of Wight for a considerable time; but, though exceedingly weak, he endeavoured to preach. Being carried to the chapel in a sedan, and placed in the pulpit, he addressed an auditory, who frequently invited each other to '*come and hear the ghost preach;*' and He who 'hath chosen the weak things of the world to confound the things which are mighty' glorified himself by rendering his feeble efforts successful. As his indisposition greatly increased, in the month of April he was obliged to return home to his mother, at Bristol Hot Wells, where the change of air had a very salutary effect, so that he soon recovered his health, and returned to his circuit."

The subjoined letter was written soon after he reached home. He says:—"April 24. I am under the disagreeable necessity of informing you that my ague has returned upon me so sharply that I am prevented from returning to my circuit to take my turn, as was my intention. It is my turn to be at Sarum next Sunday. I must beg of you to inform the people that I cannot be there, but they may expect a preacher from Bath. I have written to Mr. Wesley to send a supply, which I hope will be in the circuit by Sunday week. I purpose to stay at home until my health is perfectly restored. I have likewise written to brother Hayter at the chapel. Should he be gone before it arrives, send it after him directly. I suppose he will go to Houghton. The enclosed key belongs to my box. You are the only person in Sarum I can trust it with. Go to sister Poole's, and beg her to show it you ; it is a brown one, and stands just at the top of the garret stairs. Open it, and you will find two small white paper bags. One of them contains two small books, which belong to the Isle of Wight Society, and the other contains bills of work and receipt, also belonging to the Island. If you should see a third little bag, I believe it contains some hymns, &c., of mine, but you will easily distinguish, by looking at each bag, which belongs to the Isle of Wight. Be so good as to put the two bags belonging to the Island in a sheet of paper, and leave them in the preachers' room, and beg the first preacher that goes to Portsmouth to take them with him, and send them on to the Island." After requesting his friend to take out his pocket bible, Wesley's " Notes on the New Testament," and sundry other articles, which were to be well packed up, he adds, " beg brother Brigden to fasten a bit of soft leather over the sock of my saddle-bags, and send the bags and bundle by coach to Bath. Direct them to be left at Mr. John Peacock's, shoemaker, Green-street, Bath. I think I have given you work enough, but I am sure you are willing to do this and more. Pray for your poor afflicted brother, that he may not repine, but in all say, ' The will of the Lord be done.' " In a fortnight after, he writes,

"I am still very bad, being obliged to have a stick to help me upstairs." But in the early part of July he was so far recovered as to announce his intention to return to his loved employment of calling sinners to repentance: "The Lord has in mercy removed my affliction, and I hope to be in Salisbury on Tuesday next. I believe it is brother Wrigley's turn to be there on Sunday; give my love to him, and tell him I hope to meet him at Sarum on Tuesday."

Soon after his removal to the Gloucester circuit, Mr. Cousens was united in marriage to Miss Newman, a young lady who had been the means of leading him to the Saviour. She was a friend and correspondent of John Wesley. Mr. Cousens is said to have been a man of mild temper, clear experience, and sound doctrine. His life and ministry were brought to a close on the 31st October, 1805, in the 49th year of his age.

In less than two years after the chapel was opened, Wesley passed through the circuit, calling at the Island on the way. He found the cause in Newport in a much more healthy state. "This place," he writes, "is now ripe for the Gospel; opposition is at an end. Only let our preachers be men of faith and love, and they will see the fruit of their labours."

At the Conference of 1782 John Mason was appointed to the circuit. He remained two years, having William Moore, William Hoskins, Nathaniel Ward, George Story, and Joseph Jerom as his colleagues. The whole of these preachers desisted from travelling, except John Mason and George Story.

William Hoskins removed to Wales. A letter of his

which has come into our possession, gives an account of his journey, and his own state of mind :—

"Swansea, Sept. 1, 1783.

"Dear sister,—I take my pen to give you a little history of my travels, and of the dealings of God with my soul since I left. I had a pleasant ride to Bristol, where I found my old friend Mr. Green. We had some talk together, and then went to preaching at Guinea-street chapel, where we had indeed a visit from heaven : God be praised for it. The next day I set off for Monmouth, had a pleasant journey, and met with a kind reception. I have been almost round the circuit, and find the people athirst for the Word of God. May it come with power! May this be your prayer as well as mine. I have reason to believe that some of the people are alive to God. May you be amongst the few who walk with God, having Jesus as your companion. Let us take courage, and fight our passage through; the mansions of glory are before us. Although Satan is busy, I find a pleasure in the service of God which no tongue can express. Pray for your unworthy brother,

"WM. HOSKINS."

George Story is a name well known and honoured throughout the Connexion. He evinced the genuineness of his piety by a uniform life of holiness. He was editor of the *Magazine* for some years. His attachment to Methodism was enlightened and steadfast. His end, like his life, was peaceful. "I feel," said he, "when passing the vale, Christ more precious to my soul than ever." Southey, in his "Life of Wesley," gives a fine sketch of his life and character. Amongst other references to him, our papers supply the following coincidence in connection with his ministry in the Sarum circuit. "My soul," says one, "has been much blessed to-day by opening on Isaiah xxvi., 1—4, and in the evening when Mr. Story chose them for his text they were doubly sweet. Blessed be thy name, I do find that thou hast appointed 'salvation for walls and bulwarks.'"

The revival was still in progress in various parts of the circuit. Wesley again refers to it:—"Mon., 6th Oct., 1783. I preached in the Devizes about noon, and at Sarum in the evening. Captain Webb lately kindled a flame here, and it is not yet gone out. Several persons were still rejoicing in God, and the people in general were much quickened. Tues., 7. I found his preaching in the streets of Winchester had been blessed greatly. Many were more or less convinced of sin, and several had found peace with God. I never saw the preaching-house so crowded with serious and attentive hearers. So was that at Portsmouth also. Wed., 8. We took a wherry for the Isle of Wight. Before we were half over, the sea rose, and the water washed over us. However, we got safe to Wooton-bridge, and then walked on to Newport. There is much life among the people here, and they walk worthy of their profession. Thur. 9. I went to Newtown (five miles from Newport), supposed to be the oldest town in the isle; but its glory is past. The church lies in ruins, and the town has scarcely six houses remaining. However, the preaching-house was thoroughly filled; and the people appeared to be all of one rank,—none rich, and none extremely poor; but all were extremely serious and attentive." One feature of the Newtown congregation noticed above is still remarkably

characteristic of the Wesleyan congregations in the Island
—the absence of poor people. It is our impression that
the number of extremely poor persons is happily very small
in the Isle of Wight. Work seems plentiful, wages fair,
and masters complain of a paucity of hands. We think
the poor are as well off in the Island, if not better, than
in any other part of the kingdom. Many of their cottages
are substantial, and pleasantly situated, with gardens
attached; and generally in the country they stand in the
midst of beautiful gardens and orchards, the produce of
which is more than a family can consume in a year. At
the same time, we are bound to say that here, as well as on
the main land, the wages of the agricultural classes are
shamefully low.

Wesley proceeds : "Friday, 10. I crossed over to
Southampton, and found two or three there also who feared
and loved God." This is the first notice we have of a
society at Southampton. It is remarkable that, although
Wesley and his preachers had been passing through it for
at least forty years, yet it does not appear that any regular
attempt had been made to gain an entrance into that large
and thriving sea-port. Wesley had preached there once
only, and that was sixteen years before. It is true it was
under rather discouraging circumstances. His own account
is: "Wed., Oct. 14, 1767. Rode to Southampton, and,
the wind being so high that I could not well preach abroad,
I sent a line to the Mayor, requesting leave to preach in the
Town-hall. In an hour he sent me word I might ; but in
an hour more he retracted. Poor Mayor of Southampton !
So I preached in a small room, and did not repent my
labour."

The revival, which was the subject of the last chapter, and which was still in operation, was genuine and deep. We supply, in the experience of Mrs. Chiverton, the mother of the Rev. H. Chiverton, another example of its power. "God has wrought," she says, "a great salvation in my soul, and given me a larger measure of faith and love than I ever before experienced, and yet I am afraid to say that he has saved me from all sin. I am so ignorant that I know not how to judge of my state. When Dr. Coke was here he formed three bands, in one of which I met, and, blessed be God, it has proved a blessed means to my soul. I was led to discover the depravity of my heart, and to see the great privilege of being delivered from it. After Mr. Story preached at the quarterly meeting, and led the love-feast (at which I spoke, and felt happy in the love of God), a few of us went to prayer in our kitchen, and the power of God was soon felt amongst us. E. and I found a great blessing, I believe in the same moment. I had no particular promise applied, but cried out, 'O Lord, thy precious blood cleanseth from all sin,' and immediately I found what I cannot express—an overwhelming power of saving grace! In a few moments afterwards I had some doubts if the Lord had cleansed me from all sin, but the next day I found an amazing change in my soul. It seemed as though everything was become new. I felt an inexpressible union and communion with my blessed Redeemer, such as I never did before. I was filled with love and joy unspeakable, and full of glory,—I was lost in wonder, love, and praise. At times, I had no doubt that God had made an end of sin. I do not know that I have found any evil tempers, anything contrary to love ever since, but I have many fears whether such and such a motion of my heart is sin or not. I find it difficult to determine what is temptation and what is not. Tell me what you think of my state. —Your unworthy sister in Christ, A. CHIVERTON."

Meanwhile the work was advancing Westward. John Pritchard was able to report, after the Conference of 1784, "I came back to Wilts Circuit, where I am at present. The work which last year began has broke out into a glorious flame, so that before the year is out I expect to see some hundreds in connexion, and happy in the love of Jesus."

One of the young converts of the name of Thomas Cook, who had recently gone up to London, sends an interesting account of a service which he attended, probably in City Road Chapel, and which was conducted by Charles Wesley: "Since I came to town I have found the Lord abundantly precious to my soul, especially on Sunday last, under Mr. Charles Wesley, who preached from these words, 'Strive to enter in at the strait gate, for many I say unto you will seek to enter in and shall not be able.' It was a heart-searching discourse. A remark which he made had an overwhelming effect. He said, 'Many of you do a great deal to get to heaven, but you will go to hell after all.' I felt as if I was struck down. Such an awful sense of the majesty and power of God fell upon me. Oh, it was a solemn but a blessed time. After the public service, I, in company with about three hundred Christian brethren, received from him with comfort the memorials of redeeming love. In the evening, after service, I went with two friends to the Workhouse. One of them preached to those in health, while I and the other visited the sick wards. My soul was melted to see the poor dear creatures in the utmost pain, and yet rejoicing and giving thanks. I felt as if I could have stayed with them for ever."

Four years in succession did the apostle of Methodism visit the Island. Thus, on Thursday, 7th Oct., 1784, he says, " I crossed over to the Isle of Wight. In the afternoon I preached at Newtown, once the largest town in the Isle, but now not having six houses together. In the evening, all the ministers, and most of the gentry at Newport, attended the preaching. Who hath warned them to flee from the wrath to come? Oh, may many bring forth fruit with patience!"

In the following autumn he is once more on the Isle, and is cheered with the evident tokens of prosperity which were presented to his eye. He had seen the society in its infancy, watched its struggles with poverty and persecution, and now he beheld it in its vigorous youth putting forth decided and successful efforts to extend itself into other parts of the Island. After preaching at Portsmouth Common to a " lively, and consequently an increasing society," he adds, " I crossed over to the Isle of Wight. Here also the work of God prospers. We had a comfortable time at Newport, where is a very teachable, though uncommonly elegant congregation." On the following day he took a final peep at Carisbrook Castle, of which he says : " Wed. 10. We took a walk to the poor remains of Carisbrook Castle. It seems to have been once exceedingly strong, standing on a steep ascent. But even what little of it is left is now swiftly running to ruin.   The window, indeed, through which King Charles attempted to make his escape, is still in being, and brought to my mind that whole train of occurrences wherein the hand of God was so eminently seen."

Want of space permits us to glance at two only of the ministerial staff who were in the circuit during the above-named years.   The first is John Moon.   At fourteen he was brought to a knowledge of divine truth, and the whole of his subsequent deportment evinced the power of saving grace.   He was upright, holy, and patient in suffering. His end was characterized by deep peace and strong con-fidence in God.

John Wittam, was one of the seals of the zealous ministry of the Vicar of Howden.   He took his first circuit in 1767, and continued to travel in various parts of England and Ireland for forty-four years.   "In the extremity of his affliction, he said, 'Come, Lord Jesus, and take me to thyself,' and calmly resigned his spirit to God."

On Sabbath morning, April 2, 1786, Mr. Moon made a vigorous attempt to open West Cowes, by preaching there from "Wheresoever two or three are gathered together in my name, there am I in the midst."   On the 14th he again addressed the inhabitants of this busy sea-port on "Come unto me," &c., and again on the 14th on "For lo the winter is passed," &c.; and once more, on the 20th, from "Blessed are they that hear the word of God and keep it." These services were followed up by a Mr. Ley, but who he was, or from whence he came, we are unable to tell, nor can we say what permanent good resulted from these labours.

CHAPTER X.

(1785.)

> " It prospered strangely, and did soon disperse
>   Through all the earth ;
> For they that tried it did rehearse
>   What virtue lay therein,—
> A secret virtue, bringing peace and mirth
>   By flight of sin."

NEWPORT Society, viewed as the parent tree of Methodism in the Island, had now been planted more than thirty years. Its growth had been slow, but it never perished, as it has been asserted by Dr. Smith in his excellent "History of Methodism." The opening of the new chapel brought fresh strength. Better accommodation was afforded, and more of the middle class began to attend.

Meanwhile the Home Missionary labours were beginning to tell upon the rural population. Societies were formed first at Rookley, Godshill, and Merston, and then at Wooton-bridge, Haven-street, and West Cowes. The labours of a local preacher of the name of Hayter were made useful to some at Rookley. This good man comes upon the scene— to compare small things with great—like the Tishbite of old, but the dwelling-place of the modern evangelist is unrecorded.

One of the first converts at Rookley was Thomas White-wood, a youth whose parents resided at Bagwidge Farm, situated between that place and Godshill. Thomas had several brothers, who were as much opposed to religion as he was alive to its importance. Thomas's parents, though not members, yet were so far favourable to the cause as to entertain the preachers. On one occasion, when Mr. Hayter was spending the night at Bagwidge, the young men observed that he carried a book with him, a common practice with the early preachers; and, bent upon mischief, they took the book from his coat pocket, and replaced it with the under jaw of a pig, vulgarly called by the islanders a "chopperkin." In the morning, when the preacher was preparing to start on his way, the young men waggishly asked him what he carried in his pocket. He promptly replied, "The Practice of Piety." They expressed a wish to see it. He put his hand in his pocket to take out the book, when, to his dismay and their merriment, he drew forth the jaw-bone. The most serious part of the affair was they at once accused the good man of theft. The thing was noised abroad, and henceforth for many years every Methodist in those parts had to bear the odious name of "Chopperkin."

Thomas having the root of the matter in him, held steadily on his way. The higher the storm of persecution rose, the more closely did he and the little band of believers who had been united in class cleave to Jesus and each other. Young Whitewood was bidding fair to make a useful Christian. His gifts, burning zeal, and thorough decision seemed to mark him out as a youth of more than ordinary promise. But this burning and shining light was suddenly extinguished in death.

The following sketch is drawn from an account of him, and of the origin of the society at Rookley, which was found among the papers left by Jasper Winscom. Thomas Whitewood heard Mr. Hayter preach it is believed in his grandmother's house at Rookley, in the summer of 1785. He was then about fourteen years of age. He was affected under the word, and felt the powerful drawings of the Spirit of God. About the end of harvest he and one of his brothers were in the field at plough; a kind neighbour came and invited them to a harvest supper. The thought gladdened the heart of the brother, but Thomas remembered that it was preaching night, and after a little consideration he avowed his determination to forego the supper and hear the Word of God. His brother denounced him as a fool. This was received with meekness, and immediately Thomas received such an overflowing of the love of God as he had never before felt, and the Gospel that evening was as the bread of life to his soul. From that time he became a regular attendant on the means of grace. In December a society was formed, and Thomas had his name enrolled, and thenceforward till the day of his death he was never known to be absent from class except once when he was prevented by deep snow. In the spring of 1786 he received such a manifestation of the Spirit, that he was filled with zeal for the salvation of souls. Young as he was, he began to take a leading part in the means of grace, often praying with an unction and power that melted the hearts of those that heard him. He travelled many miles to assist at prayer-meetings, and sometimes led a class. His meekness and forbearance under provocation were as remarkable as his zeal for the glory of God was strong and his life consistent. He mourned in secret over the ungodliness of his relatives, and the inconsistencies of others, by which the cause of God was injured.

In the fall of 1788 these trials were in some degree mitigated, and the signs of the times were such as to inspire in him the hope that God was about to revive his work. He was not mistaken in his anticipations, but he little thought that his own death was to be a chief means of bringing it about. But so it was. On the 22nd of November, he rose as usual, and sung that solemn hymn, the first and last verses of which are :—

> " And am I only born to die ?
> And must I suddenly comply
>   With nature's stern decree ?
> What after death for me remains ?
> Celestial joy, or hellish pains,
>   To all eternity !
>
>   .   .   .   .   .   .
>
> " Jesus, vouchsafe a pitying ray :
> Be thou my Guide, be thou my Way
>   To glorious happiness !
> Ah, write the pardon on my heart,
> And whensoe'er I hence depart,
>   Let me depart in peace !"

After breakfast, of which he partook heartily, he went into the barn, and, taking the flail from the hand of the thrasher, he used it for some time, and then returned it and stood with his back to a ladder. Shortly after, he sank down, and never spoke or moved again. His morning prayer was answered ; he had departed in peace. But,

> " The actions of the just smell sweet,
> And like seed sown, bloom in the dust."

His death made a profound and lasting impression on the whole neighbourhood. Many dated their conversion from that day. Some of these are well known, and must now be placed on record. We commence with Robert Bull, who was an apprentice in the hamlet, and who, though young, was a bigoted Churchman, and had hitherto manifested a decided opposition to the Methodist innovation. On the morning of the day on which Thomas died he was from home, but was made sensible of his need of a Saviour, and when he returned in the evening, and heard what had happened, he was arrested by strong conviction. The question arose in his mind with startling effect, "Had I been called, what would have become of me?" No one could doubt concerning the deceased. Every one could believe that for him "sudden death was sudden glory;" but in the awful alternative "celestial joys or hellish pains" they were not so happily clear for themselves. From that time Robert found no rest to his troubled spirit until he entered into reconciliation with God through our Lord Jesus Christ. He seemed to have been "baptized for the dead," as he at once began to tread in the steps of young Whitewood. He began to preach while yet a youth, and long and faithfully did he serve his generation ere he fell asleep. We shall meet with him again as we proceed with our narrative.

John Philips, than whom there was not perhaps a more wicked man in the Island, had been convinced of sin five days before, while listening to Mr. Homes; and when the tidings of the alarming visitation reached him, he was led to apply with increased earnestness to the throne of mercy, when it pleased God to make known his pardoning grace in a very clear and satisfactory manner. He immediately united with the Society, and stood his ground well. Another, to whom this sudden death was the savour of life, was a daughter of John Philips. She was at the time living in service at a farm-house, and her mistress was so strongly opposed to the Methodists that she would not suffer her to attend the means of grace. The young woman cherished the incipient work, and when the end of her term of service arrived she left her persecuting employer, and then entered into union with the people of her choice, and, in a short time afterwards, received the Saviour, and was filled with peace and love. Not content to receive without giving, her pious efforts in the new situation on which she had entered began to tell upon the members of the family and household. Her master's son, a youth of sixteen, and several of the men servants, began to attend the cottage preaching. This awakened opposition. The father and an elder son opposed the youth, and forbade his attendance at the preaching, but one of the men joined the Society. Another fruit of this solemn warning was seen in the conversion of Jane Moses, who was so deeply affected that she began to attend the preaching, and shortly after, with her husband, gave herself to God and to his people.

Emmanuel Prangnell was also, it is probable, brought to a knowledge of the truth about this time. He was one of the first local preachers in the Island. He removed from Rookley to Loverstone, where preaching was established for some time, but he was not characterized by great stability. He died in the faith, at an advanced age.

From Rookley the cause spread to Godshill, which is two miles beyond, and is situated about half way between Newport and Ventnor. The most prominent object in this quiet village is the church, which crowns the summit of a high conical hill. One of the first members of Society in this village was a farmer of the name of Thomas Bull. He entertained the preachers, and gave the ground on which the first chapel stood.

Godshill chapel was the second Methodist chapel in the Island. It was built of wood purchased from a wreck, which took place on what is termed the "back" of the Island. It was opened by Jasper Winscom on the 30th of May, 1790. The Society was, for many years, in a very prosperous state, and in 1813 it contained thirty-one members, whose names were:—Robert Wheeler (leader), John Ingram, Isaac Saunders, Robert Scott, James Woods, J. King, J. Kingswell, Jane Wheeler, Ann Ingram, W. Ingram, S. Scott, M. King, Han. Cosh, J. Jones, J. Ingram, M. Ingram, M. Jones, Mary Bull (leader), Thomas Bull, W. Corney, M. Joblin, J. Gladesh, S. Bull, S. Bull, jun., Thessaly Jackman, Elizabeth Dore, Mary Young, A. Small, Jane Woods, M. Abraham, F. Jones.

Jonas Jackman was a member of this Society. He was an acceptable local preacher, and for some years led the class at Hale Common. Afterwards he removed to Ventnor, where his useful life and labours were brought to a close in February, 1852. His death was improved at the church by Dr. Blackwood, who had often met him in the sick chamber.

John and Ann Ingram, the parents of Mr. Henry Ingram, of Ventnor, were truly consistent members of this society.

Their house was a home for the preachers for many years. The Rev. Dr. Worsley, the clergyman of the village, used frequently to call at Mr. Ingram's to converse with him on spiritual subjects, and would frequently say that "Godshill owes a great deal to the weatherboard chapel."

We close this chapter with short sketches of a few of the preachers who were on the circuit about this date. William Ashman was born at Coleford, in Somerset, in 1734. His parents were amongst the first-fruits of Wesley's ministry in that village, and both lived and died well. Convinced under his father's prayers, while yet a lad he began to seek the Saviour, and joined with other youths in holding prayer-meetings in the corner of a field, or in a "stable, barn, or hay-loft." After his marriage, which took place when he was twenty-one, he became increasingly devoted to God, and found it to be his element to love him and delight in him. After filling various offices in his own circuit, and acting as a local preacher for three years, he took up his cross, and entered into the full work of the ministry in Cornwall, where he found it difficult to provide a place for his wife. He gratefully records several special interpositions of Providence, one of which occurred on Salisbury Plain :—" Once, between Sarum and Shaston, being quite out of my road, and in very great distress, I cried unto the Lord to direct me, for I was utterly at a loss which way to go. My strength failing, and night coming on, and being many miles from any town, I could see no house or place of shelter; and the snow falling very fast, so that it filled up my tracks after me, while a very strong, sharp, piercing, north-east wind blew, I thought it was no use to go any further; therefore I stood still, and rested myself by leaning on the horse's neck. I then said, 'Lord, what shall I do? —must I die here, or must I go to the right hand or the left?' It came into my mind to go to the right. I found some comfort with the impression, and my strength was renewed. I had not walked above a quarter of an hour before I saw smoke arise, and gladly made towards it. It proved to be a small cottage, where the woman had just put some wet straw on the fire, which caused a very great smoke. She told me I might come in, but said she had no place for my horse, nor anything for him to eat. She said there was a farm-house about two miles off, and gave me the best direction she could. I set out in the strength of the Lord, trusting in him to bring me thither, and I do not think I went a quarter of a mile out of the direct road, though I could see nothing but snow. The farmer gave me and my horse some refreshment, and sent a guide with me to put me in the way to Shaston. If Providence had not brought me to this poor woman's house, it is likely I should have died on the plain which is called Salisbury Plain, as many did that winter."

Mr. Ashman lived to be one of the oldest preachers in the Connexion. He spent a long and cloudless evening of life in his native village, to which he retired in 1798. Perfectly resigned and happy in God, he took his departure on the 9th of February, 1818, aged 83.

William Butterfield was a native of Halifax, in Yorkshire. Converted in his youth, he soon after began to warn sinners to flee from the wrath to come. His ministry was useful and acceptable, but of short duration. He was

cut off by brain fever, but was in his lucid moments able
to testify to the goodness of God.   Mr. Butterfield preached
his first sermon at Newport from Col. ii., 6, showing that
Christ is to be received in his teaching—offices—example.

Charles Kyte, like his colleague, was taken away in the
midst of his usefulness.   Though naturally reserved, yet,
when surrounded with friends, he was remarkably open and
communicative.   He was a good preacher, and fearlessly
pursued the path of duty.   After having travelled about
seventeen years, he sank under the wasting fire of consumption.   Shortly before his death he was heard to say,
with tears in his eyes, " I never weep for sorrow, but for
joy; Christ is everything ; I used to do his work with
pleasure."   His last words were, " Praise him ! praise him !
praise him !"

About the commencement of the year, Thomas Gain,
of Newport, an old disciple, departed to his heavenly rest.
Mr. Butterfield preached his funeral sermon from, " And
all Israel shall mourn for him," &c., 1 Kings, xiv., 13.

John Pritchard was a native of Ireland.   Soundly converted to God in his youth, while he possessed the clear
witness of the Spirit, he panted after full conformity to the
Divine image.   In 1771 Wesley sent him into Wiltshire.
At the Conference of 1802 he was appointed Governor of
Kingswood School, where he remained five years, and then
retired to Bristol.   His preaching was characterized by
earnest zeal, and by the offer of a free, full, and present
salvation.   He died aged 71.

William Hunter is the next name on the ministerial
roll.   Drawn by the Spirit from very childhood, at sixteen

his heart was softened into love while hearing Christopher Hopper, and a wonderful change was wrought in his life and conduct. This brought upon him the reproach of Christ. His old companions beset him like bees, and cursed and swore, and raged horribly, and the babe in Christ was overcome and led astray, until he heard another sermon, which pierced him as a two-edged sword, and, after wading through deep waters of sorrow, he was restored to the joy of salvation. Having tasted of the goodness of God he was constrained to speak of it to others, and in 1767 he joined the ranks of the itinerancy, where he remained until the year 1798, when he was called to his reward. His death was glorious. He cried out in an ecstacy, "O, precious Christ! precious Jesus! What a sight is this!— a poor unworthy creature dying full of faith and of the Holy Ghost," and added,

> "'A feeble saint shall win the day,
> Though death and hell obstruct the way.'"

William Hunter is spoken of as an "eminently holy man," grave in deportment, profoundly humble, embodying in his conduct the spirit of our Lord's words, "He that is greatest among you, let him be as the younger, and he that is chief as he that doth serve." As a preacher he was deliberate in manner, solid and weighty in matter, but withal energetic and deeply affecting. For deadness to the world, and uniform deep piety, he was a pattern to all. He was partial to children, and ever ready to promote their welfare. He came to the close of his useful and happy life at the house of Mr. Dodd, of Nanthead, Cumberland, in 1798.

CHAPTER XI.

(1785.)

. . "If friendship be formed with the virtuous,
It will increase like the shadow of the evening,
Till the sun of life shall set."

FOLLOWING the order in which the cause advanced, we now come to Merston, a scattered hamlet in the parish of Arreton. It is situated in the most central valley in the Island. It is about three and a half miles from Newport, and forms a triangle with Rookley and Godshill. This was one of the most luxuriant branches of the parent tree, and bore fruit of rare quality. Mary Prangnell, Robert and Elizabeth Wallbridge, Mary Ward, John Damp, and others, were members of this little church. These all possessed a character stamped with more or less of originality and high moral worth, while the inimitably touching narrative by which Legh Richmond has embalmed the memory of Elizabeth Wallbridge has rendered the place of her birth and burial more sacred than classic ground.

A brief sketch of some of these worthies will now be given. We commence with the leader, Mary Prangnell. This mother in Israel was born at Arreton in 1750. Neglected in early life, she was ignorant of the merest elements of learning, and was sent to service at the tender age of eleven. After her marriage she settled with her husband at Merston. About 1785 she was convinced of sin while listening to a dissenting minister, a visitor of the name of Curtis. At Mary's request this gentleman came to Merston, and preached in a barn belonging to her father-in-law. Mr. C. was a high Calvinist, and gave great prominence in his preaching to his favourite doctrines of election and reprobation. This kind of teaching brought no relief to Mary's troubled breast, but perplexed her mind, and drove her into reasonings which plunged her into deeper anguish.

The preaching soon ceased at the barn, and Mary opened her cottage for the Methodists, who were establishing preaching in the neighbouring villages, and had already begun to proclaim the gospel in the streets near her own house. That house still stands in the narrow lane not far from the present chapel. It is a humble thatched cottage, with a vine at the end and a garden in front.

Satan took the alarm, and, heading his furious subjects, assailed the preaching with his usual weapons—discordant music, stones, rotten eggs, &c. To the preachers this was nothing new, and Mary, regardless of the frowns and sneers of the ungodly, kept her house open for their reception, and the truth triumphed. Mary was one of the first to reap the benefits of the gospel. The way of salvation through the expiatory blood of Christ, was revealed to her, and she was filled with "joy and peace in believing." This is her own account of the gracious change: "One day, when busily employed in my domestic concerns, I felt my soul more distressed than ever on account of my sins. I prayed earnestly to the Lord, but still my anguish increased,

and my hope was almost gone, when at length the Sun of
Righteousness arose on me with healing in his wings. I
opened a hymn-book on these words,

> ‘ Peace, troubled soul, thou need'st not fear,
>   Thy Jesus cries ‘ Be of good cheer ! ’
>   Only on Jesu's blood rely,
>   He died that thou might'st never die.’

and was enabled to rely on him that justifieth the ungodly.
The Holy Spirit shed abroad the love of God in my heart,
and I knew that I was passed from death unto life.”

Mary possessed great energy of character, which, under
the stimulus of vital godliness, soon began to show itself.
Keenly alive to the disadvantages arising from the lack of
education, and feeling a strong desire to be able to peruse
the word of God, she determined to learn to read. By
diligent application her wish was gratified, and in a short
space of time she was able to read the Scriptures with ease
and fluency.

She now devoted herself to the work of God, and
zealously sought to promote the spiritual welfare of her
neighbours. She introduced in various parts meetings for
prayer and exhortation, in which exercises she often took a
leading part, and, undaunted by the persecution and
reproach by which she was assailed, persevered until she
had lived down all opposition. Possessing a large degree
of the shrewdness which often distinguishes the Saxon
character, her zeal was tempered with wisdom and prudence;
hence her reproofs were not only keen, but well-timed.
Thus, one market-day, at Newport, as Mary was passing a
butcher's shop in High-street, the owner, who stood at the

door, called to her, and said, "Mary, did you pray for me this morning?" "Yes, I did," she promptly replied. "That's a lie," said he. She stood still, and, turning to him, said in a very solemn and impressive manner, "I prayed this morning that God would have mercy on the worst of sinners, and I know you are one of them." Self-condemned, the man was silenced, and seemed but too glad to beat a retreat.

Mary Prangnell was a woman of prayer, and has been known to spend a greater part of the night in this holy exercise, pleading with God for her children, the members of her class, and for the salvation of souls. While she diligently attended to her domestic duties as a wife and mother, she bought up every spare moment, and devoted it to her Saviour's cause. The afflicted, the destitute, and the anxious enquirer, were alike the objects of her solicitude and attention, and not a few were ready to bear grateful testimony to the fact that her counsel and care had afforded them instruction and comfort.

Her residence was but little more than a mile from that of Elizabeth Wallbridge. Elizabeth was a member of Mary's class, and during her sickness was watched over by her with tenderest care. And it will be interesting to the reader to be informed that the "remarkably decent-looking woman" who addressed Legh Richmond as he stood gazing on the blanched features of the dairyman's daughter, as her remains lay in the coffin, was no other than her class-leader Mary Prangnell. The touching language, "Sir, this is rather a sight of joy than of sorrow; our dear friend Elizabeth finds it to be so, I have no doubt"—bespeak not only her intimate knowledge of the spiritual state of the deceased, but also the strong and joyous character of her own faith.

This excellent woman continued to adorn her Christian profession until she reached an advanced age. As the infirmities of years crept upon her, the flame of love seemed to gather strength ; and as the veil of mortality grew thinner, her spiritual vision became more vivid, yet the views she entertained of herself were more and more lowly.

Her last affliction was acute, and her sufferings severe. She was taken ill on Sabbath, Nov. 12th, and on the following day had a joyful manifestation of the love of God, and expressed a desire to depart and be with Christ. On another occasion, as her son entered her room, she exclaimed with uplifted eyes and hands, "My son, heaven is now open to receive me!" On the day on which she died, she said, "My prospects are brighter and brighter." To another who enquired how she did, she replied, "Happy! happy !—precious Jesus!" She added, "Mine is a blooming hope !" With the rapturous exclamation on her lips, "Heaven, heaven!" she breathed her triumphant soul away, on the 11th of December, 1826, in the 76th year of her age.

Robert Wallbridge was for many years a consistent and highly respected member of Society, and a useful local preacher. He was at first united with the class at Merston. Afterwards he came to reside in Newport, where he became foreman in a mercantile establishment. Robert Bull was the means in the divine hand of turning his attention to

the necessity and importance of personal religion. Prior
to young Bull's conversion, they were companions ; and
after that event Robert Wallbridge opposed him in the
capacity of a gainsayer, and earnestly sought to convince
him of his methodistical errors. Their trades—the one a
carpenter, and the other a bricklayer—brought them together
at a lady's house at Shide. At the usual hour for meals,
they retired to an out-house for the purpose of commencing
the contest. Being both well versed in certain parts of
Scripture, many passages were quoted in support of their
respective views. The conversation was from time to time
renewed. From the first interview, feeling the superior
force of his antagonist's weapons, Robert Wallbridge sus-
pected himself to be in the wrong, but would not give up
the contest until one evening, as he was walking homeward,
thinking on what had passed that day, the truth came home
with power to his heart. The road was low, and then
lined with trees, whose outspreading branches cast their
shadow over him. But dark and dreary as it was without,
it was still more so in his own soul; he feared, as he afterwards expressed himself, the judgments of heaven were
about to overtake him for his sins. This, and subsequently
hearing John Wesley preach at Newport, led to his conversion. Now these young converts were drawn together
by mutual sympathy, and their hearts became knit like
those of David and Jonathan. On Robert Bull's removal
from the Island, a correspondence was commenced between
them. From a specimen or two of their letters, it will be
apparent, we think, that the piety and intelligence of
the dairyman's son and his friend were not inferior to those
of his more famed daughter.

"Jan., 1792.

"Dear Brother,—Your letter* filled me with such gratitude that I could scarcely contain myself. The more I read the more my heart warmed with love. I am in health of body, and in regard to my soul I have good reason to bless God. Through faith in Christ Jesus my sins are pardoned, and I feel the love of God shed abroad in my heart. I believe that God is both able and willing to cleanse me thoroughly. I am labouring for purity, knowing that the pure in heart shall see God.

"My dear brother, I bless God on your behalf. God used you as the instrument in the conversion of my soul. May He make you useful in turning many more from the way to perdition. I little thought, the first time I conversed with you on the subject, that there was so much pleasure in religion. I now know that there is no permanent happiness without it. My desire is to have more of the Spirit to take down self and to set up Christ. My dear friend, I begin to feel more and more of the depravity of my nature, but, glory be to God, I have great power over it. I hope to be found growing in grace, and abounding in every good word and work. I would not hide, but improve my talent, and thereby glorify God.

"I am at work for Mr. Hollis, at Sir Richard Worsley's, St. Lawrence, so that I am quite driven from the means of grace, but not from God. Glory be to his holy name, I find his protecting hand over me to deliver me from the wicked. My dear brother, pray for me; the enemy strives hard, and 'there are many that fight against me without a cause,' but 'thanks be unto God that giveth me the victory.'

* Probably to some other friend.

"I bear you up at a throne of grace, praying that God would bless you in body and soul. May all things work together for your good, and the glory of God! May your eye be single, and may grace be continued to you to the end! 'May the God of peace sanctify you wholly, and preserve you blameless until his coming;' and then I hope we shall receive the 'crown that fadeth not away,' and 'the kingdom that cannot be moved.'

"Mr. Dap—r, R. Y., H. Y., M. W., T. B., S. N—ly, M. Pr—ll, and my wife send their love to you.

"I remain, your loving brother till death,

"R. WALLBRIDGE."

The following is the reply which he received from his friend :—

"Brierton, Feb. 17th, 1792.

"Dear Brother,—I was exceedingly glad to hear from you, the more so as it was voluntary on your part. I ought to have been the first to write, but my time is so fully occupied in preparing for the important work I am called to do. I see the importance and necessity of improving my spare moments by reading and other exercises, that I may be in some measure qualified to do the will of God. In writing to my friends I have mentioned your name. After all, these excuses do not satisfy me; I feel I ought to have written to you, if I had taken the time from sleep. But to turn to a more important subject. It is well with me both in the outward and inner man. I have reason to bless God for every degree of good, knowing that all comes from him. I believe I am justified by faith, and am accepted in the

Beloved. I trust also that I am making some progress in
the divine life; I have a greater victory over inbred sin (oh
that it were all destroyed). Still I have to mourn over my
unfruitfulness in the things of God. I find it needful to
cherish every seed of grace and to shut every avenue to
evil, in order that the one may grow and the other be cast
out, to the comfort of my own soul and to the glory of God.

"I have also to bless God for the situation in which I
am placed. I believe as a family we are all striving
together for the hope of the Gospel. I hope this will find
you rejoicing in spirit, knowing in whom you have believed.
You must not, however, be surprised if difficulties meet
you, for it is through much tribulation that we are to enter
the kingdom. At the same time, provided we live near to
God, the happiness that will accrue to us even in this life
will amply compensate for the opposition of the wicked,
and the pleasures (so-called) that we may lose by forsaking
the world. If God in Christ be our Friend, that is enough;
let us press through all opposition, afflictions, crosses, and
disappointments, perfectly resigned to the will of God.
Amid persecution be watchful against irritation: let no
anger be seen or felt. Let the persecutor be the object of
your pity, and be thankful that you are not as dark and
ignorant as they are. And if you are constrained to speak,
let your words be few, and delivered with judgment. Let
your zeal spring from love. If your opponents are not
convinced by argument you must have recourse to the
throne of grace.

"Let me urge you to live near to God, watch over yourself, and strive to bring your will into conformity to the

will of God, and keep watch over the heart, which is the fountain of sin, for 'out of it proceed evil thoughts,' &c. Keep this, and then you will have a continual victory over yourself, the world, and the devil. Keep an open access at the throne of grace.

"I hope you will be successful in winning your partner to Christ. This would afford you great satisfaction. May the Lord bless you both! When you go to Newport give my love to my sister and brother Morgan. Tell them to convey my duty to my father and mother, and my love to my brothers and sisters at Rookley. Be so kind also to give my love to all that shall ask after me, M. W., H. Y., R. Y., J. H., &c., to sister and brother Prangnell, and to all the friends at Merston and at Rookley, and especially to your wife. May the Lord bless you all with grace, and may you all live in love and peace. My dear brother, pray for me. Although we are at a great distance from each other, I find the same God in Buckinghamshire as in the Isle of Wight. Should Providence spare me to come again to the Island, I shall by some means, God willing, see you, and I hope we shall meet in 'the fulness of the gospel of peace.'

"And now, my brother, I commend you to God and to the word of his grace, which is able to build you up. Once more, 'give all diligence to make your calling and election sure, for if you do these things you will never fall.'— Farewell!   "Yours affectionately,

                                        "R. Bull."

Through the kindness of a friend, we are enabled to present the last letter ever penned by this highly respected and estimable man. It will be seen, that after the lapse of more than forty years, he was still breathing the same, if not a greater fervour of spirit than that which characterized his early correspondence.

"Jan. 24th, 1837.

"My dear Sister,—Not having heard from you this year, I have had some fears that you were not well. I thought I would write a few lines to enquire after your health, and how your soul prospers in the divine life. I hope you are striving after perfection. I hope my young friends also are growing in grace, and in the knowledge of our Lord Jesus Christ. I am always happy to hear of the prosperity of the Church of God, although I can now do but little towards it. I can only pray for prosperity, and that I do from the bottom of my heart. I hope this will be the best year that we have had, and that more souls will be converted to God than during any year since the death of our Redeemer. Oh, my dear Sister, pray earnestly for the prosperity of Zion. I hope all my dear friends are well, and going on hand in hand. Give my kind love to them all. Brother C. Hollis and partner, and the good old lady who was so kind to me when I was at your meeting in the Chapel, the Lord bless them all! Remember me to dear Eliza, and your little flock. It gladdens me to think that I have so many friends in Cowes. What a change has been wrought since I first entered the town! Then the greatest part of the inhabitants were standing about the streets on the Sabbath, but now you have a good chapel, and well filled, while not a few are true believers and belong to the family of God.

"I believe you wish well to my soul, and that I may be more useful. Well, I recollect an instance in which a woman was useful in teaching a man the more perfect way, and so he became a more excellent preacher. I hope your endeavours will prove beneficial to me, but I am such a dull scholar that I fear your labour will be in vain.

"But let that suffice; and now I enquire—is the work going on? have you heard of one converted on the right, and another on the left? My dear sister, it is pleasing to hear that your congregations increase, but it would be far more so to hear that you had the publican's cry amongst you, 'God be merciful to me a sinner!' Many persons go to church and chapel for years, and never get converted. They go full of the world, and leave it the same. I remember that in olden times our practice was very different. Ten or a dozen of us used to go about a mile from the preaching, and not a word was spoken of a worldly tendency. We endeavoured to apply the sermon, and make it tell upon our own conduct. I do not condemn any of you, but urge you to pray on your bended knees for God's blessing on your ministers, and on what you hear. I pray that God would bless you with his grace in this life, and with eternal happiness in the world to come.

"I remain, dear sister in the Lord,

"Your humble and unworthy friend,

"R. WALLBRIDGE."

During the space of forty-five years Mr. Wallbridge filled the office of a local preacher with acceptance and usefulness. The following honourable testimony, borne by Dr. Etheridge to the excellency of his character, will be read with pleasure. The Doctor says:—"When I joined the Society, in my eighteenth year, Robert—at that time an elderly man—was my class-mate; and my regard for him was of course not diminished by his near relationship to the saint of the dairyman's cottage. Though a dweller in the town, he never lost the air and manner of his rustic origin. He had the bearing of some farmer of the humbler class, of a middling stature, square set, and with a countenance of a sunny look, which beamed with honesty and benevolence. As a Christian, he was habitually meek and lowly. He had not the mental cultivation of the others [Robert Bull and Robert Yelf,] but he loved to read a good book, and was a hearty preacher of a heartfelt gospel." A touch of humour gave raciness to his speech, and he could say a keen thing; but so genial was his spirit, so thoroughly imbued with Christian charity, that he was a stranger to all gall of bitterness and slander, and he lived in the esteem and respect of the entire circuit. In advanced life he endured a long and painful affliction, with meek submission to the Divine appointment. Shortly before his death he was met by one of his brethren, who, looking on his disease —cancer in the face—said, " Robert, you must prepare for the worst!" "Prepare for the *worst!*" exclaimed the good old man, "nay, my brother, I will prepare for the *best!*" He did not die of cancer ; God spared him the suffering, and took him away by more gentle means, on Feb. 25, 1837, aged 71.

Another member of this favoured little church was Miss Mary Ward. She was awakened under the searching ministry of John Moon, who preached in the open air at Merston about the year 1784, and joined the Society on its formation, being then in the fifteenth year of her age. Her union with the Methodists was strongly opposed by her parents. Believing the favour of God to be better than life, she, with admirable meekness and fortitude, "held fast her profession." The fiery trial served only to give strength to her purpose to live to Christ. Having found the class-meeting to be an invaluable aid to Christian holiness, she prized it highly, and was a conscientious and persevering attendant to the end of her protracted life, often testifying that she never wilfully absented herself. When she was about thirty years of age, she became the housekeeper of the Rev. Legh Richmond. We must reserve any further notice of her till a future page.

Passing over for the present the name of Robert's sister, we come to that of John Damp, another sterling member of the Merston Class. John was a blacksmith, and resided at Arreton. In the old churchyard his remains rest, not far from those of the Dairyman's Daughter. This good man met with his full share of persecution. One of his employers, a farmer, tried hard and long to shake his constancy, but in vain. In the year 1793 he opened his house for preaching, and the villagers flocked to hear, but the storm of persecution rose to such a height that many quailed before it, and, after a time, for that or some other cause not now known, preaching ceased. John Damp, however, held on his way, though difficulties beset his path. He was the eldest of a family of twelve orphan children, who were left to his care. But remembering the apostolic injunction, that while he was "fervent in spirit" he must not be "slothful in business," by the blessing of God upon his industry he was enabled to "owe no man anything," and could call his little homestead his own. After preaching was commenced at a cottage at Hale Common, near to that of the Dairyman's, John joined the

class that was formed there.   Ardently did he desire to see
a little chapel erected, but years passed away ere that desire
was realised.   At length a site offered, directly opposite the
Dairyman's Cottage; and so strongly was John's heart set
upon the attainment of this object, which had been the
ambition of his life, that he not only walked through the
Island to beg money for it, but actually mortgaged his
small property for £70, and built the neat little chapel
which has been the scene of several gracious visitations of
the Spirit, and the birth-place of a goodly number of souls.
The chapel was opened on the 19th of May, 1837.   Shortly
after this noble act of liberality, to his great surprise John
received the sum of £75, which had been left him by one
from whom he had no expectations.   With this money he
was enabled to pay off the mortgage and the law expenses,
and thus his homestead was once more his own.

John had a neighbour for whose spiritual welfare he
felt deeply interested.   He had often invited him to preaching, but in vain.   One excuse was, "You have no chapel;
if you had a chapel I would attend."   John remembered
this, and when the chapel was to be opened he called and
reminded him of his promise.   "Ah," said he, "but I am
now so lame that I could not go unless you were to wheel
me in a barrow."   He little thought that the condition
would be met.   On the day of opening, John procured the
requisite vehicle, and actually wheeled his lame neighbour
to the chapel.   He did not lose his reward.   The sharp
arrows of Divine truth found their way into the heart of
this hoary-headed sinner, and he was led to seek the healing
balm of the gospel.

CHAPTER XII.

(1786—1790).

" I live for those who love me,
For those who know me true,
For the heaven that smiles above me,
And awaits my spirit too :
For the cause that lacks assistance,
For the wrong that needs resistance,
For the future in the distance,
And the good that I can do."

WE must now direct attention to the state of the work elsewhere. The subjoined letters, which are now published for the first time, were addressed to Jasper Winscom. They relate to the new chapel which Wesley had opened at Winchester, in November, 1785.

"London, Oct. 27, 1786.

" My dear brother,—The sooner the affair is settled the better. I desire, therefore, that Mr. Ashman will receive what is in Mr. Smith's hands. You say you can borrow as much more than Mr. Gifford's ten pounds as will make up the hundred. As soon as this is paid, the house may be transferred to five or more trustees on the Conference Plan. I forbid engaging any attorney. You have the form of conveyance in the Minutes, which any one may transcribe.

" I am, your affectionate brother,

" J. WESLEY."

Instead of the affairs of the chapel being promptly settled, they became more involved; as, from some cause or other, they got entangled in the meshes of a law-suit, which it would seem brought Mr. Winscom into some difficulty, and from which he was rescued by Wesley's prompt and generous aid. This will be made evident by the following highly characteristic letter:—

"Sept. 30, 1788.

"My dear brother,—The Conference cannot, and will not, bear the expense of that foolish law-suit. I can conceive but one way to pay it. The hundred pounds which you borrowed of me, you may pay to the attorney, and his receipt in full shall be your discharge.

"I am, your affectionate brother,

"J. WESLEY."

Surely this entire transaction shows the nobleness of Wesley's nature. He advises—nay, he uses his authority —to keep the chapel out of the hands of an attorney. They despised his authority, and did the very thing which he had forbidden,—foolishly did it, and thereby involved themselves in debt; yet he showed no resentment, but immediately came to their rescue, and by the generous gift of £100 delivered them from their difficulties.

At this period the preachers came from Salisbury by Lymington and Yarmouth to Chessel Farm, the residence of Mr. Hollis. They preached, and slept at the farm on Saturday evening, preparatory to their labours at Newport on the following day. Mr. H. afterwards removed to Shalfleet.

During the time of the Conference of 1787, Mr. John

Etheridge, the father of Dr. Etheridge—a name well known and honoured in Methodism—preached at Newport. This was probably the first time that he had made his appearance in the Newport pulpit, a place which he was afterwards often to fill. The Doctor has kindly supplied us with the subjoined brief but valuable memoir :—" My father was the son of William and Hannah Etheridge, of Youngwoods and Colemans, two small estates (in what was then called the Royal Forest of Parkhurst) which have long ago passed away from our family. He was their only child, and was born in 1765, at a somewhat advanced period of their life, —circumstances which rendered him the object of their strong and concentrated affection, the influence of which is not always propitious to the real welfare of either the parents or the child. He received his education at an academy in Newport, kept by a clergyman named Potecary ; and, designed for the hereditary employment of his fore-fathers, on leaving school was trained to the affairs of agriculture, and sought his recreations in hunting, fishing, and the sports of the field, and the homely intercourse of a few wide-scattered rustic families. These forest people lived at a long distance from their parish church, and had but scanty opportunities for hearing the gospel, till their slumberous condition as to eternal things was broken in upon by the coming of the Methodist preachers into the neighbourhood. It may be said that then ' a voice was heard crying in the wilderness.' Among those who were drawn to listen, was my father, and in it he discerned the voice of God. He was then about eighteen years of age. The first of the preachers he heard was Mr. Barber. The word came to him with saving effect. The Lord laid his hand on him, and found him willing in the day of his power. A great change unfolded itself in his life. He told his former companions that he had been constrained to give up his sins, and wished to know whether they would do the same, as otherwise he must consort with them no more. Already he felt the movements of the evangelist within him, and, beginning in this humble way, was made meet for greater things. His parents received the preachers, and Youngwoods became one of their welcome homes. My father entered on the regular work of a local preacher, and, having a good horse at his command traversed the length and breadth of the Island, and had honourable fellowship in the labours of those faithful men who laid the foundations of those now long-established Christian Societies which have been made such a blessing to its towns and hamlets. He applied himself with great diligence to the cultivation of his mind, was a close reader of well-chosen authors, as I gather from one of his old common-place books; and his manuscript sermons, written in a small elegant Italian hand, show by their clear statement of the great truths of the gospel, that he did not read in vain. He had not only the friendship of the preachers who itinerated in the Island, but the venerable founder of Methodism, on his visits to the Island, encouraged him by his kind and paternal words. Discerning in him a young man whose life should be devoted to the ministry, Mr. Wesley proposed to him to enter upon the full work of it. As nothing seemed to stand in the way, his name was set down at the following Conference for what was then called the Salisbury Circuit. But his aged mother shrank from the pain of losing him, and, whether right or wrong, he yielded to her distress, and declined to go. This he ever after regarded as an error which entailed upon him not a little providential chastisement. Nevertheless, he still continued the steady labour of preaching in all parts of the Island, as well as several stations on the other side of the water—at Portsmouth, Southampton, Romsey, the New Forest, Winchester, and away as far as Salisbury. He pursued this work many years, and did substantial service in the church in fulfilling the offices of leader and steward. In his declining years he lived in greater retirement, but walked humbly with God. His wife was Alley, the daughter of George Gray, an old officer in the navy, who had seen much battle-work under Nelson and Howe, and whose four sons attained commissions in the same service, the eldest dying flag-lieutenant at the bombardment of Copenhagen. My mother, who was a saint, took me when a child along with her to her class-meeting, where the earliest sound impressions I ever felt came upon my heart. She died, with the serene assurance of salvation, in 1835. My father survived her about three years, and died in solemn peace, with his soul, as he expressed it, 'full of prayer.' "

In the summer of 1787, Wesley and Coke were detained at Yarmouth by contrary winds as they were on their way to the Norman Isles, where Methodism was gaining a firm hold, under the effective ministry of Robert C. Brackenbury and Adam Clarke. After preaching at Southampton, Wesley records :—

"Aug., Sat. 11.—We went on board the 'Queen,' a

small sloop, and sailed eight or nine leagues with a tolerable wind. But it then grew foul, and blew a storm, so that we were all glad to put in at Yarmouth harbour. About six, Dr. Coke preached in the Market-house to a quiet and tolerably-attentive congregation. The storm continuing, at eight in the morning, Sun. 12, I preached to a much larger congregation. I had uncommon liberty of speech, and I believe that some of them felt that God was there. At eleven we went to church. There was a tolerable con-gregation, and all remarkably well behaved. The minister read prayers seriously, and preached on 'Blessed are the poor in spirit.' At four I preached again, on Luke xix., 42 (part of the second lesson in the morning): 'If thou hadst known, even thou,' &c. The Market-house was now more than filled, and not a few seemed to hear as for life. In the evening Dr. Coke preached again. We have now delivered our own souls at Yarmouth, and trust God will suffer us to go on to Guernsey."

It was about this date, at the small town of Blandford, that a good woman was often drawn to the Methodist chapel to quench her thirst at the streams of the water of life, as they flowed through the earnest ministry exercised there. That woman was the mother of John Angell James. His biographer says :—" Good Mrs. James was often weary of the coldness and formality of the services at the Independent meeting, and many a time on a winter evening she called one of her boys (she had two) to light the lantern and walk with her to the humble room where the Methodist preacher was stirring the blood and firing the devotion of the simple-hearted hearers. She found there less polish, but more

power, and believed that the dignified discourses of her own
minister were well exchanged for the rude eloquence of less
cultivated but more fervent men."

Although for a time she had no reason to suppose that
her eldest son was at all affected by what he heard, who
can venture to affirm that the stirring sermons he listened
to at his mother's side, in the Methodist conventicle, produced no impression on his boyish heart? At least they
must have helped to teach him that lesson which he often
and solemnly endeavoured to teach others—that the gospel,
though preached by unlearned men, is always and everywhere " the power of God unto salvation."

While reading these remarks, the question very naturally
arises, who were the men of " less polish" and " rude eloquence" to whom Mrs. James and her son John Angell
listened in the humble room at Blandford. They were such
men as Henry Moore, Joseph Alger, Robert C. Brackenbury,
T. Lessey, sen., Joseph Sutcliffe, and others of like stamp.
The first-named gentleman wrote a valuable, if not the best
Life of Wesley, and the last a very useful commentary on
the Holy Scriptures, and was not without academic honours.
In representing these Methodist preachers as being inferior
in " polish" and " rude in eloquence" as compared with the
" polished but cold and formal Independent preacher" deal-
ing out his dignified discourses, Mr. Dale, like some others
—for it is the fashion when touching on Methodism—wrote
without reference to the facts of the case, and therefore at
random. It is to be regretted that authors who professedly
write history, should draw on their imagination, when the
slightest investigation would enable them to give us fact
instead of fiction.

On the 29th of March, 1788, Charles Wesley departed this life in the eightieth year of his age. For more than fifty years he had been preaching Christ to a perishing world, and writing spiritual hymns; for while John Wesley gave form to the constitution of Methodism, and was its Divine and Lawgiver, Charles was its Bard. As an hymnist he has never been surpassed, and for deep and varied religious feeling never equalled.

It would be impossible to over-estimate the influence of the Wesleyan hymn-book, or to tell how much superior are the advantages of those tens of thousands of our country-men who are familiar with its rich treasures over their fore-fathers centuries back, who were for ages doomed to sing doggerel pæns full of popish superstition and error. We are indebted to Charles Wesley for this hymn-book, for, out of 766 hymns which it contains, 625 were composed by him. John wrote but 32 of the whole number. This hymn-book, which the Wesleys designed to be "a little body of divinity," is, in fact, an epitome of the doctrines, precepts, promises, and general teaching of the Word of God, or, as it has been said, "the Bible put into poetry." It is adapted to all ranks and conditions of men, and to all the phases of religious experience. It overtakes the sinner "greedy of eternal pain," and in pathetic strains expostu-lates, "Why will ye die?" It meets the sinner in his deepest despair, and bids him hear the speaking blood while "justice lingers into love." "It may be affirmed," says Isaac Taylor, "that there is no principal element of Christianity, no main article of belief as professed by Protestant churches,—that there is no moral, or ethical sentiment, peculiarly characteristic of the gospel,—no height or depth of feeling proper to the spiritual life,—that does not find itself emphatically, and pointedly, and clearly conveyed in some stanza of Charles Wesley's hymns."

In 1779 Wesley had refused to allow a preacher to stay a whole month on the Island at a time, but in 1787 he sent a missionary to reside at Newport, who was to devote nearly the whole of his time to the Island, being evidently determined to give it another "fair trial." This determination was doubtless strengthened by the fact already noticed, that several small Societies had sprung up in the rural parts of the Island, and other openings were presenting themselves. The name of this home missionary was Thomas Warrick. He is said to have been a man of solid piety, respectable talents, and great self-possession and intrepidity,—a faithful friend, and an agreeable companion. He was an acceptable preacher, and was owned of God in winning souls to Christ. When the billows of Jordan assailed him, he lifted up his hands in triumph and exclaimed "I am going to glory!"

Mr. Warrick's first sermon on entering on his labours at Newport, was founded on Phil. iii. 8, "I count all things but loss for the excellency of the knowledge of Christ Jesus my Lord."

On the 23rd of September, Joseph Bradford preached at Newport from Tit. iii., 8, showing: 1. What it was to believe in God; 2. What the good works were; and, 3. How reasonable it was that these good works should be maintained.

In the winter, Mr. Warrick paraphrased the seven epistles to the Asiatic churches, and the sermon on the mount, which seems to have made a good impression on the town Society. It appears that he occupied the pulpit in Newport nearly every Sabbath, making occasional visits to the country as opportunity served, and giving them their full share of labour during the week.

We now come to some curious but interesting correspondence respecting Mr. Warrick, and the division of the Portsmouth circuit. It enables us to see in what high esteem he was held. The first letter is addressed to Mr. Br—r—y, Portsmouth, and is dated—

" Newport, July 13, 1788.

" Dear brother,—Hearing that you are about to write to Mr. Warrick, and knowing that his character has been misrepresented, there are two motives which induce me to address you on this subject. I think you may depend upon the following points as plain matter-of-fact, viz.:—Do you wish for a preacher who observes Methodist discipline? Would you wish for one who deals faithfully and plainly? Above all, do you desire to have one who preaches Universal Redemption and Christian Perfection with that strength which overthrows his opponents? Then Mr. Warrick is the man. I trust you will pardon me for troubling you with a letter, and believe me to be,

"Your affectionate friend and humble srrvant,

" SIMPLISITAS."

During the same month two letters were written to John Wesley, relating to the state of the work in the Island, and to its minister.

"Newport, July 17, '88.

" Rev. Sir,—We whose names are undermentioned (being

the year 1788 they ventured to purchase a public-house which they transformed into a house of prayer. In Wesley's Journal, under date Aug. 11th, 1788, there is the subjoined statement in reference to it:—"They have lately built a neat preaching-house in the town, something larger than that at Deptford. It is well situated near the midst of the town, and has three well-constructed galleries." It is rather remarkable that Newport should have been in possession of a chapel eight years before Portsmouth was so favoured.

The quarterly income of the Portsmouth Circuit during the second year of its existence as a separate circuit was £16 3s. The contributions from each place were as follows: Portsmouth, £7 10s.; Crowdhill, 10s. 6d.; Timsbury, 15s. 6d.; Winchester, £1 10s.; Southampton, £1 1s.; Whitchurch, £1 1s.; Newport, £3; country places, £1. Exactly the same total amount was contributed for each quarter throughout the year. This was a prosperous year for both the new and the old circuit. Portsmouth returned 480 members, and Salisbury 282, being an increase of 50 in the former circuit, and of 44 in the latter.

From the interesting memoir in the *Methodist Magazine* for 1822, which the Rev. Theophilus Lessey, jun., has given of his esteemed and godly father, who was one of the last preachers stationed in the Salisbury Circuit, prior to the division just named, we find some brief but valuable information in relation to the extent and working of the circuit; and from which it will be seen that it was not divided before there was a needs-be. "The journey from St. Austle to Salisbury," says Mr. Lessey, "nearly proved fatal to my mother. It brought her into so dangerous a state that, for several months her life was despaired of. The work of the circuit was so extensive that my father could only be at home six days in six weeks. It reached to Portsmouth and Chichester in one direction, and to Blandford and Swanage, in the Isle of Purbeck, in the other. Notwithstanding the labour and suffering through which he was called to pass during this year, his mind was cheered by manifestaticns of the Divine favour, and by the most satisfactory proofs that the pleasure of the Lord was prospering in his hands."

If the question should be asked, "How could any man endure such privation and toil?" the answer will be found in the following statement respecting Mr. Lessey, and it is equally applicable to the bulk of Methodist preachers in those days: "The cause of God was so dear to his heart that his duty to his Heavenly Master weighed more power-fully with him than the strongest earthly tie or the greatest earthly comfort."

On Sabbath, Sept. 27, 1787, Wesley's Abridgement of the Church of England prayer-book, for the use of the Methodist Episcopal Church, America, was introduced into the Newport Chapel. It is not stated by whose authority this was done, but it is said that it met with decided opposition, and the reading was not repeated. "Either," said the Society, "give us the sacraments and service in church hours, or let things remain as they are, and save us the pain of discord and division." The controversy on this and kindred subjects had yet to come. Well was it for the Connexion that it possessed men at the head of affairs equal to the emergency. Newport was one of the places in which the Sacrament of the Lord's Supper was allowed to be administered by the Conference of 1794.

In December, 1789, Dr. Coke preached twice, and administered the sacrament of the Lord's Supper. His text in the evening was, "Who shall change our vile body," &c., Phil. iii. 21; and on the following morning, Matt. ii., 1 and 2. His subject was Divine Illumination: 1st, in its rise; 2nd, in its progress. As the wise men followed the star, so we must follow the direction of the Spirit of God, who shines within us, in order to find Christ.

CHAPTER XIII.

(1790—1794.)

. . . . "The autumnal year
Make mournful emblems. To me they show
The calm decay of nature, when the mind
Retains its strength, and in the languid eye
Religion's holy hopes kindle a joy
That makes old age look lovely."

In the autumn of 1790 John Wesley's foot pressed the shores of this Island for the tenth and last time. It was fifty-five years since he and his companions were detained in its coasts as they were on their way to America, and nearly forty since he came and found the first germ of Methodist life in Newport. Then he was in the prime of his vigorous manhood, but now he comes in "age and feebleness extreme," for he had entered upon his eighty-eighth year,—the last of his life. This venerable apostle of the greatest religious revival the world has seen, had outlived opposition, disarmed prejudice, and his old age resembled a long and serene evening of a summer day.

After preaching at Winchester and Portsmouth, he crossed in a wherry, on Thursday, 30th September, "through Cowes harbour to Newport," which, he says, is "one of the pleasantest, neatest, and most elegant towns in the King's dominions. Both the nights I preached here, the preaching-house would by no means contain the congregation. I was likewise well pleased with the poor, plain, artless Society. Here, at least, we have not lost our labour.

"Friday, Oct. 1. We purposed to return to Portsmouth (about twenty miles)—it being a calm sunshiny morning—in the wherry in which we came; but a friend offering us a kind of hoy, we willingly accepted his offer. It was well we did, for, as soon as we were out of the harbour, the wind rose, and the sea raged horribly. The wherry would have been swallowed up. The waves washed over us on both sides. Having no decks, we were soaked from head to foot; but before noon we got safe to Portsmouth."

Mrs. Yelf, of Freshwater, the widow of Mr. R. Yelf, remembers watching the venerable patriarch, accompanied by some half-dozen ministers, sail up the Medina to the quay, where they landed. The "friend" who offered his vessel to carry the party back, and to whom John Wesley possibly owed his life, was Captain Osborne, whose wife was a member of Society in Newport.

Those services left a vivid impression on the congregation,—an impression which was deepened five months after by the sad tidings of the death of the great man to whom they had then listened for the last time. That sanctuary never before or since presented so striking and memorable a scene. Seventy-four summers have come and gone since that day; yet some ancient ones linger in the vale, before whose memory those scenes, like dim shadows, still flit. No doubt every Methodist in the Island that could possibly attend would form a part of those congregations. A band of young men were there, including, as we know, Robert

Wallbridge ; and—who can tell ?—perhaps his light-hearted sister Elizabeth might that day sit by his side, and listen to the low and tremulous, but sweet and mellow tones of the venerable man, who, it is recorded by one of his hearers, "preached admirably well" to that "crowded auditory." His last sermon was on Christian perfection, founded on Heb. vi. 1. "It was a useful discourse," says the same witness, "in which he observed that the height and depth of Christian perfection consisted in "loving God with all the heart, and our neighbour as ourselves." There were a great number of people to hear him, to whom, after the sermon, he gave an affectionate exhortation, as one not likely to see them any more. He urged them to love one another, let their opinions be what they might, which had a good effect. Notwithstanding his great age, he was remarkably cheerful and lively."

Five months only had elapsed when the mournful intelligence arrived that the founder of Methodism was no more in this life. On the 2nd of March, 1791, in the 88th year of his age, with the song of praise on his lips, and in holy triumph, John Wesley reached the end of his marvellous earthly career, and the beginning of his heavenly reward.

John Wesley lived in an age of memorable men, but none were so memorable as he, for none has left his mark so deep. His life, it has been truly said, was manifold. His extraordinary travels—his voluminous writings—his incessant preaching, amounting to forty-two thousand sermons—were each alone sufficient to fill a life, and that no common one. And yet the whole was performed by him with ease, exemplifying his favourite maxim, "Always in haste, but never in a hurry." Action was his recreation and his strength.

Wesley's death produced a profound impression on the Connexion, and funeral sermons were preached in all the chapels. Two were preached at Newport; the first on the 13th March, by William Stephens, from "Some said he was a good man ; others said, Nay, but he deceiveth the people," John vii., 12; and the second on the 27th, by John Easton, from "He went about doing good."

So strongly was Wesley's mind fortified with the belief of the special providence of God in relation to Methodism, that he had no anxiety respecting the future. He felt assured that He who had cared for it in its infancy would still shape its course when he was taken from it. As he anticipated, so it has proved then and ever since. The crisis came, and Methodism had to pass through a fiery ordeal, but it came out with a character hardened and strengthened by the test; and it would be a sin of ingratitude not to note the fact that in every time of emergency the providence of God has raised up men of wisdom and learning, gifts and grace equal to the demand of the times.

There was a youth in that congregation which listened to the venerable apostle of Methodism in Newport, who was one of the last seals of his closing ministry. This was Edmund Wavel, then in his fifteenth year. His heart was touched under the word, and in the succeeding spring he joined the Society. His piety, like that of many of the young men whom we have had occasion to notice was of an active kind ; and it is refreshing to meet with so many

examples of the expansive power of the revival, as it was
so generally and often powerfully expressed in the activities
of its youthful converts. At that early period there were
no Sabbath schools where youth could find a suitable
sphere of labour. It was therefore a common practice for
young men to resort to the cottage prayer-meetings where
they could pour out their earnest supplications for sinners,
or by exhortation urge them to flee from the wrath to come.
To these means young Wavel had recourse, and opened
prayer-meetings in various country places. He was a
trustee of the new chapel, and a class-leader. For many
years he cherished a lively interest in the prosperity of the
work of God ; and then there stole over him the shadow of
a cloud, and his soul seemed to slumber as in the night;
but the voice of God in deep domestic affliction awoke him
from his sleep, and henceforth he gave diligence to make
his calling and election sure. After a lingering illness, he
peacefully fell asleep, on the 8th of September, 1846,
aged 71.

Mrs. Wavel was a Miss Tabitha Daniels. Her piety
was unobtrusive, but it shed a clear light over the family
circle, and exerted a benign influence which is felt to this
day. She was given to hospitality and deeds of charity.
In company with Mrs. Abraham, Miss Nicholson, and
some others, she wore the, at that time common and well-
known, scuttle bonnet. Miss Nicholson's parents were
strongly opposed to their daughter becoming a Methodist.
But so set was her heart on the house of God, that she could
not be hindered from uniting with the people of her
choice.

At the Conference immediately following the death of Wesley, the Connexion was divided into districts. This was done with a view to facilitate the multifarious business of the body, and to meet any emergency that might arise within the limits of those districts respectively,—all which cases had hitherto been disposed of by Wesley himself.

About this time, an interesting conversion took place under the ministry of Wm. Thom—that of Elizabeth Wickenden, of Newport, whose subsequent life was so truly Christian that she has been spoken of as a "star, if not of the first magnitude, yet the finest lustre." She sanctified the Lord of Hosts in her heart, and her life was "hid with Christ in God." She filled the office of class-leader with great acceptance and success. Actuated by Christian benevolence, it was her delight to gather together the poor of her own sex for instruction and prayer. She was a mature Christian. Her end was sudden, but welcome and joyous. She could say, "I have not a doubt, not a cloud, not a fear." And with an inexpressible rapture on her countenance, and her eyes and hands uplifted to heaven, she exclaimed, "Glory! glory! everlasting glory!" and then fell asleep in Jesus, December 18, 1808, aged 33.

Joseph Sutcliffe, M.A., who had been received into full Connexion at the preceding Conference, came to the Island in November, 1790. He was on his way to Jersey, but was detained at Newport until the end of January, 1791. He was not idle, as we hear of him frequently occupying the pulpit, to the delight of the congregation. On Sabbath, Jan. 20, a Mr. M——, a Swede, preached in the morning, and, though a foreigner, spoke in English "tolerably well."

Mr. Sutcliffe followed him in the evening, and preached from 2 Cor. v., 20, and, as an ambassador in Christ's stead, in "the most moving and pathetic manner, exhorted sinners to be reconciled to God." On the 25th he gave an affectionate farewell address, previous to setting sail for the Norman Isles.

Jasper Winscom was one of the two preachers granted to the Island when the attempt was made to form it into a separate circuit. He had left his shop and trade at Winchester, and had gone out at the preceding Conference to have the toils and privations of the itinerant life. For some reason or other, he remained in the work but four years. The subjoined letters may throw some light on the subject, and will at least serve to illustrate the character of the men and times in which they were penned :—

"Manchester, Aug. 5, 1791.

"My dear brother,—I have just time to inform you that you are to continue in the Oxford circuit another year; that your walking plan was laid before the Conference, but rejected by them; and I am desired by that body to inform you that they judge you to meddle with things that belong only to the Assistant, and that they recommend you to mind your own business only. I most cordially wish you every good; and am, with love to Mrs. Winscom and self,

"Yours, most affectionately,

"JOSEPH BRADFORD.

"P.S.—Since I wrote the above, I am informed you are stationed for Wells, near Lynn."

"Wycomb, Aug. 8, 1791.

"My dear brother,—I received yours of the 5th inst., this morning, for which I thank you; but as your is an alteration from the former part, I cannot possibly comply with it under three months at least, as my affairs must undergo a considerable alteration before I could go to so great a distance. I must beg you to inform the Conference I cannot comply with Wells, near Lynn. I will readily take any circuit within forty miles of Winton. Respecting the charge of ' meddling with things only belonging to the Assistant,' as it is a general charge, I cannot answer anything to it other than this, saying the information is false, unless the proposed plan of walking is such; and yet, that it is not, I prove by Brother Horner's letter of May 28, which justified me in that, excepting my laying the proposal of that plan before Mr. Wesley; and, I believe, you know I have had for years authority from him to lay any improvement before him I thought would be useful, and, therefore, I must be acquitted on that head. The change of circuit is from bad information, unless there is anything that has not come to my knowledge, which I am not conscious there is, as you, Dr. Coke, and Mr. Mather all know. I could not go so far. I hardly think the alteration for Wells can be the result of Conference deliberation, but from another cause.

" I am, yours,

" J. Winscom."

We must now follow the advancing cause in the Island, which had by this time effected an entrance into Wootton Bridge, half-way between Newport and Ryde. The village is situated pleasantly on the slopes of a deep hollow, the bottom of which is occupied by a broad arm of the sea, crossed by a causeway 905 feet in length. This inlet is about two miles in length, and the declivities on either side are adorned with fertile fields and woods.

Somewhere about the year 1790, a few persons in Wootton became impressed with religious truth, and were formed into a class. These earnest Christians were in the habit of collecting together at the end of the village, and walking in company to morning preaching at Newport. In 1794 a weather-board chapel was built. It stood on the right-hand side of the road, as you descend towards the water. This was the third Methodist chapel in the Island.

When service was introduced in an evening, several respectable families began to attend, and some members of those families united with the Society. In 1805, there were two classes, of ten members each. It will be gratifying to some to know their names, which were :—John Macket (leader), Jane Macket, George Cooper, Jane Young, Mary Cheverton, Mary Harbour, Mary Alford, Ann Alford, Hannah Alford.—William Alford (leader), John Alford, Jonathan Jolliffe, William Cheverton, William Barkham, Jane Barkham, Lydia Cooper, Ann Flux, John Harbour, Joseph Beard.

In 1815 the number in Society amounted to thirty-one. At this time Mr. Jonathan Jolliffe was appointed to take charge of a class. He was the maternal grandfather of Mrs. Charles Dore, of Newport. He received his first serious impressions of Divine truth at Haven Street. He resided first at Guildford farm, and then at that of Cumly Lynn. Afterwards he retired to Wootton Bridge. He was in the habit of passing through Haven Street on his way to church. Somewhere about the time when the cause was established at Wootton Bridge, preaching was begun in the open air at the " Corner," in Haven Street on the Sabbath. This greatly annoyed " Farmer Jolliffe," and on one occasion as he was passing with a companion, he sharply reproved him for stopping to listen. Very shortly, however, the temptation proved too strong for the " farmer," and he began to linger on the outskirts of the congregation, and at length·a barbed arrow smote his conscience, and he could not shake off conviction. This led to his sound conversion and union with the infant cause. He braved the scorn of the world by opening his house for the messenger of Christ, and taking charge of the class which was formed. This filled the minds of some of the members of his family with dismay, as they laboured under the impression that now the Methodists had got hold of their father nothing but ruin stared them in the face.

The following incident will illustrate the earnest and decided character of the early Methodists in these parts. Some time ago there was standing on the common near Blacklands an ancient oak, under the spreading branches of which Mr. Jolliffe, William Denham, William Taylor, and Reuben Russell used to meet in band on a Sabbath morning, previous to walking down to morning preaching at Newport. These noble-minded men have long since renewed their fellowship in a brighter clime.

John and William Alford were fellow-pilgrims. They walked by the same rule, and gave heed to the same thing. John Alford was the grandfather of Mrs. Henry S. Morris, of Kingston Farm. Mrs. M. remembers when she was but a little girl, making one of the family party who in the winter mornings went, guided by the light of a lanthorn, to the early meetings.

The surviving members, who knew those old disciples, bear testimony to their sterling worth, and with one voice declare that they were good men, true-hearted Methodists, and humble and consistent followers of the Lord Jesus.

Another individual who probably received his first knowledge of the gospel at Haven Street, and was in the habit of walking with his son Emmanuel from Bembridge to hear Methodist preaching in this village at an early date, was John Wheeler. John had to pursue his spiritual pilgrimage all alone for some years. Bembridge, lying at the eastern extremity of the Island, was too remote for the small staff of preachers at that time in the Island to supply it with preaching. This want was met to a great extent when Legh Richmond commenced his ministry at Brading and Yaverland, in 1797. This good man will come under our notice again as we advance with our history.

William Legg was a member of the Wootton Society for a period of several years. He was a valuable class-leader, and an acceptable local preacher. He was a native of Calbourne, and while yet a youth was deeply impressed with eternal things. These impressions were deepened by a dream, or vision of the night, when, apparently amid the thunders and terrors of dissolving nature, the Eternal Judge in appalling majesty was presented to his excited imagination, and intensely painful convictions were left on his wounded heart. The eternal world was unveiled; death and judgment, hell and heaven, seemed close at hand, pressing their momentous claims upon him. He poured out his soul to God in prayer, and not in vain, for while he was at work in the open air, God in his mercy turned his mourning into joy by bestowing upon him such an assurance of his love in Christ Jesus as banished all his guilty fears. He was at first a member of the memorable Merston Class, but soon after removed to Cosham, near Portsmouth. Both at this village, and also at Tipners, where he afterwards resided, he opened his house for preaching, and was the happy instrument of raising a Society in each place. He was a local preacher more than thirty years. He was endowed with a good understanding, unswerving integrity, and deep piety, and his memory is still cherished by many of the aged members of the Society by whom he was known. A circumstance which occurred in his declining years illustrates his character, and affords a fine example of christian integrity. When in advanced age he found it necessary for his support to apply to the parish officers at Arreton, and he was required to attend in the church vestry after divine service, to receive direction as to his employment during the succeeding week. He appeared before the bench of magistrates, appealed with great force against the requisition, and so effectually pleaded the rights of conscience, and the sanctity of the Sabbath, as to obtain the exemption which he desired. Seventeen of the last years of his useful life were spent at Wootton Bridge. He was poor, but his poverty neither shook his faith nor impaired the dignity of his mind. He felt he was a son of God, and an heir of an incorruptible inheritance. His last illness was protracted; but as the cords of life slackened the bounds of his spiritual vision were so enlarged, and his understanding so invigorated, that he was filled with astonishment and joy at the vividness and grandeur of his own conceptions of God, and the mediatorial work of the Reedeemer. "I beheld," says the Rev. B. Carvosso, "and was edified, and delighted; and had there been at hand another Legh Richmond, we might again have had 'apples of gold in pictures of silver,' and the whole world once more charmed and instructed by the sublimity and riches of christian piety, exemplified in a poor dying cottager in the Isle of Wight."

CHAPTER XIV.

(1794—1796).

"The world wants MEN—large-hearted manly men—
Men who shall join its chorus, and prolong
The psalm of labour and the psalm of love."

AMONG the names of ministers who were stationed in the
Portsmouth circuit in 1794-5 was that of James Crabb.
Like John Furz, the first evangelist of Methodism in these
parts, he was born at Wilton, near Salisbury. After quench-
ing the drawings of the Spirit in childhood, he was
awakened under the Wesleyan ministry to a discovery of
his lost condition as a sinner; and in January, 1791, being
seventeen years of age, he was admitted a member of Society.
Seven times a-day did he wait on the Lord in secret prayer,
faithfully reproved sin, diligently attended the means of
grace, while at the same time he walked in the fear of the
Lord and in the comfort of the Holy Ghost. Burning with
love to souls, he was constrained when he was yet but nineteen years of age to go out into the hedges and highways to
call sinners to repentance. From the first his preaching
was popular, and, many openings presenting themselves,
his Sabbaths were fully occupied. With bread and cheese
in his pocket, he would start before breakfast on a preaching
tour which extended from ten to thirty miles, usually
ending the day at his native village. His preaching

N

excited the displeasure of his father, but, on the other hand, he had the comfort of knowing that, under it, his mother had been led to a knowledge of Christ; and at length his father was brought to a better mind. After continuing these exercises for about two years, he offered himself to the Conference, and was appointed to the Portsmouth Circuit. The circuit at that time included what were called "two Missions,"—one of which comprised part of Sussex and Surrey, and the other large portions of the Isle of Wight. Mr. Crabb's journal throws important light on the extent and working of the circuit, which extended over ground now containing some nine or ten circuits. Mr. Crabb says:—"It embraced the whole of the Isle of Wight; extended into the Andover circuit, within nine miles of Newbury, in Berkshire, viz., at Baughurst; and within fifteen miles of Salisbury, to Timsbury. Then in the east of Portsmouth we had what was called a Mission, which ran up within little less than thirty miles of London. On this Mission, we had some tremendously long walks. We took in Chichester, Arundel, then struck across the Sussex downs to Storrington, where we had a kind of Irish cabin to rest in." The excessive labour required to work such an extensive circuit—at least, in the way he worked it—soon began to tell upon Mr. Crabb's constitution, which was said to be good. Look at his preaching work. He says: "I had one competent qualification for a minister, and that was the love of souls. I entered upon my work in the name of the Lord, and did not do it by halves. I preached every morning at five o'clock, and every evening in the week, besides five times on the Lord's-day when in Ports-

mouth, exclusive of the seven o'clock prayer-meeting, and
the meeting of the Society for wholesome advice, or a love-
feast. My times for preaching were three times in the
two chapels, and twice out of doors, one of the latter being
to seamen in Bath-square. I used to think of my dear
mother's words, which were, 'James, I wonder your tongue
does not ache,' and truly, after my Sunday's work in the
evening, my tongue has literally ached." Let us now
follow him through some of his wearisome journeys on foot,
for it was not Mr. Crabb's good fortune as yet to be
favoured with a horse. He had now been in the circuit
three months, when he makes the following entry in his
journal :—" Saturday, 20th June. Notwithstanding the
weak state of my body, I set out between seven and eight
in the morning, intending that day, if possible, to walk
near thirty miles. It was so cold a day (though the 20th
June), that I was obliged to put my hands in my bosom
many times to get heat. That day, owing to the cold,
scores of swallows were taken up dead, and hundreds of
sheep that had been shorn died with the cold. The wind
was so strong (though we had two days' rain successively,)
that in about ten hours it caused the dust to fly. The wind
being right against me, and I being weak, could at times
hardly creep along; once it was so powerful, it blew me
against some rails, by which I was alone saved from falling.
How good is the Lord! . . . The first mile I walked
I was very tired, but I soon got a little strength. When
I had walked about twelve miles, I was so tired and faint
that I hardly knew how I should get on. I seated myself
under a hedge, and having put up my umbrella to keep off

the wind, took out my bread and cheese (having bought a penny loaf in Chichester,) and prayed God to bless it to the strengthening of my body, and to feed my soul with hidden manna. Oh, how my soul was blessed! I was for a season as in heaven, though under a hedge." The young evangelist went the remainder of his journey "rejoicing and praising God." He spent a happy Sabbath in that extremity of the circuit, and on the following Tuesday he had to return from Hammer Ponds to Portsmouth, a distance of thirty-four miles. He says, " Twelve I rode, and twenty-two I walked. I filled my pockets with two penny loaves and two-penny-worth of cheese, and with these I marched on. I can truly say I fed on Jesus all the way."

Here is a specimen of the toils and privations which awaited him in the "Garden Isle :"—"Sunday, 28th. I arose this morning for the prayer-meeting, and it was a comfortable season to my soul. I felt a gracious time this morning in preaching. In the afternoon, I had to ride six miles, through heavy rain, to preach. I was importuned to stay at home, *but I remembered the* 19*th of June*"—when he had been induced to neglect a distant appointment, and had suffered grief in consequence—" and I ventured forth, and having got wet to my skin, I was obliged to remain until I went to bed, for I had no clothes for a change. I preached, and had a good time. I was very poorly and weak in body most of the day. In the morning, when I came from the prayer-meeting, I was obliged to go to bed again, and when I returned from the country I was so overpowered with fatigue (being so weak) that I laid myself down until preaching time in the evening. At six o'clock I preached in Newport Chapel, and my soul was watered from on high in a gracious manner."

At the end of the year, Mr. Crabb returned to his home, broken down in health ; but on his re-appointment by the Conference of 1795, and finding his strength in a measure restored, he returned to his circuit, where he was received "with open arms." But fresh trials taxed his strength, and tested his zeal. "Towards the middle of the day" (Oct. 21st) he says, "I set out for Freshwater. It was very wet and dirty all the way, and I was soon wet through. My boots and umbrella being almost worn out, made it disagreeable to flesh and blood. Though it was but a little way from Yarmouth to Freshwater, yet with the wind, rain, dirt, and want of food, I was so worn out with weakness that I was obliged to take rest by leaning against a gate. I searched the almost barren hedges for provision, and when I could find any it was very acceptable. . . . My soul at this time much rejoiced in God,— indeed, in winds and storms He is a sweet portion to my soul." This missionary tour terminated on Friday, when Mr. Crabb says, "I have been wet through every day since I set off, have not tasted a bit of meat since Tuesday, and sometimes hedge-fruit was a substitute for everything. Lord, what a mercy I could get this !"

By the end of the month he is on the Island again. "30th Nov. I this day went from Cowes to Newport, and from Newport to Youngwoods to see my brother Etheridge. Passing over the forest, I lost myself, but I was enabled to cast my care on the Lord. After tea, I walked to Shalfleet, where I preached. My road all the way from Newport was like a river, and I was generally half a leg high in water and dirt. I could bless the Lord that I was counted worthy to bear these little crosses, and I had a present reward in them. I preached after I got to the house, though I was very wet. I had a good time with the people, and I know the Lord was in our midst. After preaching, I had three miles to walk, and through water almost all the way. On the road I was so much fatigued with walking, preaching, and want of food, that I could hardly stand; once I fell down with weakness. Oh, my God, it is good to bear a little for thee! I am not worthy thus to be honoured! After a little refreshment, I recovered strength, and retired to bed." It would seem that Mr. Crabb took a day's rest at Youngwoods, and on the following morning set off for Newport, and could "bless God that he was not weary of the work to which the Lord had called him;" and adds, "I had to walk through wet and dirt, as usual, half a leg high, and sometimes higher, but I thought on the road I would not change my state with any person in England. . . This evening I felt myself quite ill, not having had any dry boots for three days; but my Lord satisfies me with his grace." After reading the above, it will occasion no surprise to learn that Mr. Crabb was compelled to leave the circuit before the end of the year, to recruit his health by a few weeks' rest; and although he returned in January, he was compelled reluctantly to leave it finally in April. A circumstance, which probably hastened his departure by still further taxing his already overwrought frame, was a sudden call which he received to occupy the post of a brother minister, whose health had failed, at Southampton. He was at the time at Portsmouth, and the whole distance, eighteen miles, was traversed on foot, but so weak was he that the journey occupied the whole day. It was during his visits to Southampton that he was permitted to reap the richest fruit of his ministry, in being made the honoured instrument in the conversion of the "Dairyman's Daughter."

After spending a year in the Salisbury circuit, Mr. Crabb was compelled to retire from the ranks of the Itinerancy, but continued to act as a local preacher. After passing through a chequered scene of business trials and losses, he finally settled in Southampton. When he was forty-nine years of age, he felt the stirrings of the old fire, and offered himself again to the Conference; but his age, and a large family, stood in the way of his acceptance. He then erected Zion chapel, in which he preached the doctrines and introduced the means of grace peculiar to the Wesleyans, with whom he had been united thirty years.

We cannot avoid the conviction that Mr. Crabb was sacrificed. During the former and harder part of his work as a travelling preacher, he had no horse; and if he had possessed the strength of that animal, he could not have sustained—to leave out of sight his preaching and pastoral work, for he tells of preaching nineteen times a week—the fatigue of such incessant walking. We most decidedly question the wisdom of weakening a circuit by taking in a number of places which were so small and extremely distant from the centre of action. If the time which he spent on the roads—a single journey often taking up a whole day—had been devoted to the masses which he left behind in Portsmouth, Southampton, Newport, and the population within reasonable distance,—in a word, if he had been instructed, as happily our home missionaries now are, to give concentrated labour, on the principle that the repeated blow breaks the stone, far greater results would doubtless have been realized, and a valuable and popular minister would have been saved to the Connexion.

The following brief but beautiful sketch of him has been kindly communicated by Dr. Etheridge :—" My father became acquainted with him when he was working as a Methodist missionary in the Island. Crabb was a man somewhat above the middle height, with a rather swarthy complexion, dark hair, and an eye flashing with the 'thoughts of eternity.' He had a very solemn look. I remember him from my childhood. When I saw and heard him converse I always felt I was in the presence of a man of God; and the observation of his good career, in after times, confirmed and sealed that conviction. His life was full of mercy and good works, and his name is to this day sacred in many a home in Southampton, where, as the exemplary minister of Zion Chapel, he died revered not only by Christians of all communions, but by a multitude of the strange outcast people called ' Gipsies,' among whom, in their haunts in the New Forest, he had acquired a religious influence never perhaps attained by any other minister of the Gospel." He died at Southampton in 1851, aged 77.

Out of a number of ministerial names which want of space compels us to pass over, we select that of John Cricket, who entered upon his work in the Portsmouth circuit in 1793. He was simple in his manners, unaffected in his piety, and of tried integrity. Though not brilliant, yet his style was lucid, and his ideas often striking and original. He was loyal as a subject, a hearty Methodist, and an agreeable colleague. Twenty-six years he toiled in his Master's service with general acceptance and success. He refused medical aid in his last sickness. "It is of no use," he said, "I tell you I am going home;" and soon after he fell asleep.

Our papers supply us with the following notice of Mr. Cricket's ministry in Newport. After giving the outlines of a sermon on 1 Cor., xiii., 13, it is observed that "Mr. C. seems to be much more esteemed than he was when he first came into the circuit, which goes to prove that contracted prejudices may be removed after a little acquaintance with each other's virtues as well as failings."

On the 18th November, 1795, there was a terrific storm of wind, which terminated towards evening in torrents of rain. Mr. Algar, the superintendent minister, in returning from Mr. Etheridge's, missed his way while crossing Parkhurst forest, fell into some water, and was in danger of being drowned. After struggling out of his perilous situation, and after wandering about several hours, he providentially found his road and thus escaped.

Events of such magnitude as the French Revolution, and the flames of war which it spread over Europe, could not fail to awaken the deepest interest in the Isle of Wight. That interest grew into intense excitement, when this country proclaimed war with France. Lying so contiguous to the French coast, and being so exposed to attack, the inhabitants were all on the alert.   Sermons were preached on the subject.   Volunteers enrolled themselves, and military men were poured into the Island, until it became like a vast fortress.   The evils of war but too speedily followed. The first note of alarm was sounded at Cowes when it was announced—"*The Press-gang is out!*"   Then followed dearness of provisions and other articles.   It was recorded first that bread was 1*s.* 3*d.* per gallon, then 1*s.* 5½*d.*, next 1*s.* 7½*d.*, and as the winter set in it reached 1*s.* 10*d.*   Then came the pestilence.   "Bad fever," writes one, "is spreading about the Island, and is very severe at East Cowes, where it is said ninety Hessians have been cut off by it."

Although the military brought much dissipation and immorality into the Island—choosing the Sabbath for fetes and reviews, so that in the afternoons and evenings of the day the streets were full of scenes of drunkenness and associate crime—still there was a set-off; and it is refreshing to read notices like these :—"On the 7th [Oct., 1793,] the North Hants Militia came to the Island, many of whom attended the chapel, and heard Mr. Bland preach an excellent sermon from 'And yet there is room.'

"Jan. 19th, 1794.   The chapel was not large enough to contain the people who crowded to hear a soldier preach, whose name is Hammond.   He belongs to the 28th Foot. He has many in Society in the Regiment, which, with several thousands of English and Hessians are on board transports at Cowes, waiting for an opportunity to make a descent on the French coast and join the Royalists.   He is likely to make a good preacher."

During the period now under review (1792) the cause

at Southampton passed through a severe ordeal. The spirit
of intolerance was exhibited in the vain endeavour to put
the Methodists down. The Society rented an auction-room
as a place of worship. "It happened that a Roman
Catholic lady offered to rent the dwelling-house adjoining;
but, on learning to what purpose this room was applied,
she refused to take the house, unless she could have the
room also, on which conditions she was willing to take the
whole on lease for twenty years. The landlord thought
this offer too good to be refused, so he gave the Methodists
notice to quit, and let the premises to the lady. For some
time this caused the Society some embarrassment. But
their trouble came to the knowledge of a bricklayer, who
lived on the opposite side of the street; he offered to fit up
a large loft in which he had been accustomed to store his
scaffolding, for their use, on the same terms as they had
held the former room. They gladly accepted this offer;
the loft was more commodious than the auction-room, and
made a better place of worship; while the lady who had
expelled them, as she supposed, from the neighbourhood,
found that she still had them, notwithstanding, in more
disagreeable proximity than ever. They were now immediately before her eyes, and, worse still, the windows of the
new place of worship completely overlooked her drawing-
room. But she had signed the lease, and could not escape
the consequences of her conduct. She endeavoured to
prejudice the bricklayer against his new tenants, but the
only answer she obtained was, 'My word is my bond: they
shall have it.'" From this time the cause seems to have
made steady progress, and, ere long, they found it necessary

to enlarge their borders by the erection of a chapel. This humble structure would contrast strangely with the commodious and tasteful edifice in which the present generation of Methodists worship in that town, as the contractors engaged to find ground and build a chapel and dwelling-house for the sum of 316 guineas. Yet this, at the time, was regarded as a sufficient establishment to justify a division of the Portsmouth circuit, which, in 1798, made Southampton the head of a new one, having two preachers, Robert Green and John Sydserff. At the end of the year they had 180 members.

Humble as that bricklayer's loft might be, it has acquired an imperishable fame as the spiritual birth-place of the " Dairyman's Daughter," whose history will occupy the pages of the next chapter.

CHAPTER XV.

(1796—1798.)

> " It is a lowly tomb.   No marble there
>   Or sculptor's art doth blazon forth high birth,
>   Or deeds of proud renown.   A simple stone,
>   In modest characters, reveals the spot
>   Where sleeps her precious dust, whose earnest faith
>   And humble love are registered on high.
>   Her name from records of the holy dead
>   Hath perished not ; and the ungarnished tale
>   Of her meek piety and fervent zeal
>   Hath found a listener in the lordly hall,
>   And by the cottage hearth.   Well I recall,
>   While bending o'er her dust, the days of yore,
>   When, in my far-off home—' a dreamy child '—
>   I conned the pages of that simple tale,
>   And in my nightly orisons, I prayed
>   That my young life might be as pure as hers."
>
> —Eliza Hessel.

We now approach a subject which has given an interest and attraction to the Isle of Wight, equal to that which it derives from the beauty of its scenery and the amenity of its winter climate—the conversion, life, and death of Elizabeth Wallbridge, the Dairyman's Daughter, the account of whose latter days has been recorded by the inimitable pen of Legh Richmond, and is familiar to every one, not only in this, but also in many foreign lands. Methodists have long since claimed the Dairyman's Daughter as a fruit of their ministry; and her " single character," says Dr.

Stephens, "has consecrated the Isle of Wight for ever in the history of Methodism, and the regards of the Christian world."   Millions of copies of Legh Richmond's tract have been circulated, and, thirty years ago, it was recorded as an ascertained fact that it had been the means of the conversion of three hundred and fifty persons.   Her conversion was the direct fruit of Methodist preaching.   This event, as before noted, took place in the bricklayer's loft, Hanover-buildings, Southampton.   Elizabeth Wallbridge, like her brother Robert, first saw the light in the parish of Arreton. She was born July 29, 1770.   The cottage is still standing in which she was born and died.   It is in much the same condition as it was sixty five years ago, when seen by Legh Richmond, and the description which he gave of it then will still apply, where he says, "I dismounted, and was conducted through a very neat little garden, part of which was shaded by two large over-spreading elm-trees, to the house.   Decency and cleanliness were manifest within and without."   Here, Elizabeth, a light haired, ruddy faced, and merry hearted girl, spent her childhood, amid rustic society, and rural scenery.   Of scholastic learning she had but a slender share, derived probably from the village dame. Like the children of her cottage neighbours, Elizabeth left home at a tender age, and lived in various respectable families in the capacity of a servant.   In these situations she conducted herself with propriety and application to her duties, and acquired the reputation of being a good servant, in command of high wages ; and, in time—notwithstanding her extravagance in dress, the love of which was her ruling passion—she managed to accumulate a small fund for future use. She was, at this period of her life, characterized by a high flow of spirits, vanity, and ready wit, so that she could hurl the shaft of raillery and bitter sarcasm with considerable force against those who provoked her ire. But the period now arrived when an important change was effected, —when she felt the breath of the life-giving Spirit, and the current of her after-life found a new and heavenly channel. She was at the time living in the service of Mr. Rolstone, a gentleman resident in Southampton. The Rev. James Crabb, as before stated, was the honoured instrument of bringing Elizabeth Wallbridge to God. He was a young minister, as we have seen, of great zeal, more than average ability, and popular in his style of preaching, so that his visits to Southampton were anticipated with delight by the crowds who thronged the loft.

In Mr. Rolstone's service there were, besides Elizabeth Wallbridge, Elizabeth Groves, Elizabeth Cox, and Robert Taylor. Elizabeth Cox had been a member of the Methodist Society, but her steps had faltered, and her lamp had become dark. The conversion and efforts of Elizabeth Wallbridge acted as a powerful stimulus, and, by the grace of God, she recovered her forfeited peace, and finished a consistent membership of forty years' duration with a triumphant death.

Robert Taylor was a pious Methodist, and was deeply concerned for the salvation of his fellow-servants. Elizabeth Groves and Elizabeth Wallbridge both attended the Established Church. The latter was bitterly prejudiced against the Methodists, a feeling which had been greatly strengthened since her brother Robert's union with so despised a people; while, at the same time, her pride was deeply wounded, and her anger inflamed, by a letter of warning and earnest expostulation which he had addressed to her. And we would here observe that sufficient prominence has not been given by preceding writers, who have touched on the facts connected with the conversion of the Dairyman's Daughter, to the influence which her brother's efforts had in bringing it about. The fact seems to have been unknown, or overlooked, that his conversion and union with the Methodists took place some years before she became a member. And from the well-known zeal and energy of his character, it is highly probable that he would address himself with most earnest solicitude to lead his vain and worldly-minded, but affectionate sister, to a knowledge of Christ; and that the letter which he addressed to her at Southampton was by no means a solitary attempt to accomplish the object of his ardent desire. His godly labours in her behalf were doubtless begun before she left the Island; and, although she met them much in the same spirit as that in which a younger sister afterwards received her own pious exhortations and warnings—with laughter and ridicule—yet who shall say that no seeds of truth were then sown, or impressions made, which contributed to the formation of that lovely character which has won such universal admiration.

It will scarcely be deemed irrelevant to our story to pause for a moment to notice Elizabeth Groves, especially as it was from her that the most important portions of this narrative were derived. She was a native of the Isle of Wight, to which she afterwards returned, and was united in marriage to Mr. John Yelf, of Brading. She was a devout Christian, much respected by her own people, with whom she remained in union from the period of her conversion—which took place at the same time as that of the Dairyman's Daughter—until her death in advanced age.

On one occasion, when Mr. Crabb was expected to preach at the little loft, Robert Taylor happening in the course of the day to enter the room where Elizabeth Wallbridge and Elizabeth Groves were at work, said to them, "Maids, will you go this evening, and hear preaching at the Methodist chapel ? Mr. Crabb, the missionary from the Isle of Wight, is to preach. He is very much liked as a preacher ; and I think, if you were to go and hear for yourselves, you would be pleased with him." To this request, Elizabeth Wallbridge, with her characteristic levity, returned such a reply as left Robert no ground to hope for a favourable result. But the Spirit was at work, and, as they discussed the invitation, a strong desire was felt to hear the popular young missionary.

That evening, to the surprise and joy of their fellow-servant, those two thoughtless young women formed a part of the congregation in that humble upper room, and, although no deep impressions were then produced, prejudice was disarmed, and they resolved to go again. As Mr. Crabb had a Sabbath appointment at Southampton shortly afterwards, the opportunity soon presented itself, and they went. But Elizabeth Wallbridge was at this time, by her own confession, a captive, enslaved by the sins of pride and vanity. She thus describes the motives which influenced her to go : " Curiosity, and an opportunity of appearing in a new gown, which I was very proud of, induced me to ask leave to go. For a while, regardless of the worship of God, I looked around me, and was anxious to attract notice myself. My dress, like too many gay, vain, and silly girls, was much above my station, and very different from that which becomes a humble sinner, who has a modest sense of propriety and decency. The state of my mind was visible enough, from the foolish finery of my apparel."

Mr. Crabb's sermon was founded on 1 Peter v., 5, "Be clothed with humility." A divine unction attended the word, especially when the preacher began, in searching language, to expose the sins of vanity and worldly-mindedness. The wandering eye of Elizabeth now became fixed on the preacher, her conscience was reached, new light burst upon her, and she had such a humiliating discovery of the selfishness, the ingratitude, and the pride of her heart, as overwhelmed her with shame and confusion of face. She says, "I looked at my gay dress, and blushed for shame on account of my pride; I looked at the minister, and he seemed as a messenger sent from heaven to open my eyes; I looked at the congregation, and wondered whether any one felt as I did; I looked at my heart, and it appeared full of iniquity. I trembled as he spoke, and yet I felt a great drawing of heart to the words he uttered."

Elizabeth returned home, pondering silently, but with trembling anxiety, the grand problem of personal salvation. The change in her outward deportment astonished her fellow servants, who as yet knew not the cause, and could not help expressing their wonder that the " giddy, trifling, and talkative 'Betty Wallbridge' had become serious, and 'slow to speak;' but their astonishment was greater when they saw her sit down in a chair, and actually tear off those parts of her dress which she deemed most expressive of her vain and wicked heart. Suffering too deeply from a wounded spirit to relish food, she refused the ordinary meal, and retired to her own room to complete the demolition of her idols, and to seek, in godly sorrow and prayer, reconciliation and peace with God. "In the evening, divested of her foolish and outward adorning, but full of eagerness for the ornament of a meek and quiet spirit, she once more appeared among the hearers of this heart-searching preacher. This contempt and dread of everything in dress unsanctioned by Christian propriety, she retained to the end of life without change."

From that memorable Sabbath, a divine life was commenced in her soul, and

> " It was here that she began to fulfil
> The ' woman's mission ' of a woman's heart,—
> A model of devotedness to Him
> Who wore the platted thorn with bleeding brow."

The conversion of the Dairyman's Daughter was truly of the New Testament type, and, like those of many of the early Methodists—sudden, sharply defined, thorough, blissful, and abiding. The great change from the bondage of sin to the glorious liberty of the gospel, seems all to have been effected on that memorable Sabbath. Mrs. Yelf, who was at the time her fellow servant, stated to the Rev. B. Carvosso, that "she had no recollection of anything but gratitude and praise proceeding from Elizabeth's lips, from that decisive day when the truth of God reached her heart."

Thenceforth Jesus·was her all in all; she "felt the heaven of loving him alone," and was one of the happy few who "rejoice evermore, pray without ceasing, and in everything give thanks."

"One of her earlier spiritual letters was addressed to her brother Robert. It was written at Southampton soon after she had embraced the gospel. It was given to the late Mr. Claxton," then of Cowes, "who had it put into a valuable frame, between two plates of glass, and suspended it amongst the ornaments of his own parlour." It is now in the possession of Mrs. Fidler, of Ventnor, and will doubtless descend as an heir-loom to succeeding generations. "The handwriting and orthography are just such as might have been expected from an uneducated servant girl; but it contains the genuine effusions of a heart overflowing with love to God and man. Even did it partake less of excellence than it does, yet as it is an original letter from one so celebrated as the 'Dairyman's Daughter,' and was written three or four years prior to the date of those which have already been published, there is sufficient reason for giving it a place in this account; but I think the reader will see that, throughout the whole, an elevated and admirable spirit continually breathes. I give it entire, with the exception of a piece of doggerel poetry, which she had picked up somewhere, and the mere alteration of slight and common grammatical errors. Seeing that she had but just begun to read the Bible attentively, and with a warm heart, her inaccurate quotations from Scripture are quite natural, and only what was to be expected. I subjoin it as nearly as possible verbatim, as I think it will in that state be more interesting, and will, at the same time, fully relieve Mr. Richmond from the charge of having himself written the other letters which are published in her name."

"Southampton, March 3rd, 1797.

"My dear brother,—I received your kind letter the 2nd inst., and you may think what a transport of joy I felt to receive such an affectionate letter from a brother I had so little regarded since he had left the world and me. You may well say what great joy it gave you to hear I was converted to God. But are you the only one? No, my dear brother; think what shouting and rejoicing there was with the angels of God in heaven, that are around the throne, and continually cry, 'Worthy the Lamb of God that was slain, to receive all glory, and honour, and praise!' And, blessed be God, who hath showed strength with his hand, and with his holy arm hath gotten himself the victory! Yes, and he hath scattered all the proud imaginations of my heart, the great enemies of my soul's salvation. Oh, how true are those words of my Redeemer, that 'whosoever is in me is a new creature,'—'for, behold, old things are passed away, and all things are become new.' Oh, how often would the Lamb have gathered me unto himself, as a hen doth gather her chickens, and I would not! And how often hath he stretched out his arm, and I have not regarded it! But how shall I ever praise my God enough! To think how long he hath spared a wretch like me, who drank in iniquities like water, and followed after the vanity of my own deceitful heart, which was wicked above all things! It was when I was sitting under that delightful man, Mr. Crabb, that the Lord opened my eyes. It was the second time that I heard him. And on Sunday last, in the morning, I was standing, at the window, and he came past, and when I saw him my heart leaped within me for joy ; for I believe him to be commissioned from the most high God to preach the gospel of salvation and peace to all that will hear it. My dear brother, I know it is not good to be partial to any of God's creatures, but I liken him to St. Paul, for he seems to labour more than they all; yet not he, but the grace of God which is in him, and that is extended to all that hear him speak. It seems as if I could say with David, when he is there, ' O, that I could dwell in the house of my God for ever !' I shall ever have the highest esteem for him as a minister of God and Christ. And now, my dear brother, as I have no money with me, I beg you will apply to my dear mother for six guineas of my money, and give them to Mr. Crabb, and tell him it is a free gift of a poor needy creature, who has been to the Lamb of God naked and destitute of everything ; and then, when he saw my wretched condition, with what tender compassion did he look down upon me, and sprinkle me with his blood, and give me the whole armour of God, the shield of faith, the helmet of salvation, and the breastplate of righteousness. And now his sweet voice still whispers in my heart, ' I counsel, thee, my child, to buy of me gold tried in the fire.' What then would be the dominion of the whole world to me, and what indeed to the love of God that He hath been pleased to shed abroad in my heart ? My dear brother, praise God for it ! Buy Mr. Crabb a very large Bible, that when he looks upon it he may bless his God, and think what good he hath done for my poor soul, through the gracious influence of the Spirit of God; and the rest he may dispose of to the glory of God and the good of poor souls. And what is between you and me think no more of; and pray, my dear brother, send your children to school, and I will pay for them as long as I am able. And do see that our dear brother is not in want of anything that I can do for him. I hope that God will be merciful to all my dear friends who are yet in darkness. May they be filled with the Spirit of God, and may they feel the pardoning love of God shed abroad in their hearts! Do, my dear brother, if possible, assemble them together, and prevail on that good man, Mr. Crabb, to be with them, if possible (I know he is a dear lover of souls) that he may assist them in turning to God. I fear what you can say to them will be of no great use; for, remember the words of our Saviour, that a 'prophet hath no honour in his own country.' My dear brother, how can you rest, seeing any so nearly related to you so far from God? O, when will God cease to be merciful! It is said when the tide ceases to ebb and flow, then God may cease to be merciful. See them—

> ' Lo, on a narrow neck of land,
> 'Twixt two unbounded seas they stand! . .
> ' O God, their inmost soul convert!'

Be sure you do as I have desired, in the name of the Lord, and for the glory of his holy name; and my love to all that are in him, and that are wanting to turn to him. Pray excuse this, and write as soon as you conveniently can. Adieu, dear brother!

.   "ELIZABETH WALLBRIDGE."

A letter, in which she gave an interesting account of the manner in which she received the blessing of entire sanctification, was unfortunately lost or destroyed, before its preservation was deemed a matter of any special moment. We are able, however, to insert two additional letters, which were addressed to her father, while she was still resident in Southampton. They breathe the same ardent spirit of devotion to the Saviour. Those passages which are strictly personal and private are omitted.

"Southampton, Feb. 23, 1797.

"My dear and honoured father,

. . . . "And now, my father, I do not know what to say, to change the scene. I suppose you were a little alarmed the other day, when the fleet of colliers came in, and they were taken for French. It was reported here that they were landed at several places; and we should soon have been over in the Island for shelter from them,—as if by that means we could 'flee from the wrath to come,' or stay the hand of an almighty and justly avenging God, who, for the sins of mankind has sent his judgments abroad in the earth. And even now, we are ready to say to that God who hath so long withheld the sword of vengeance from destroying us, and still extends his everlasting arms of mercy to save us, 'Depart from us,' for we desire not the knowledge of him. But I hope, my dear father, that the Lord will have mercy on us, and bring us out of that gross darkness into his marvellous light, and set our feet on a Rock that is higher than we are. But we are informed by the Word of God, that if we would have all these blessings bestowed on us we must fix all our hopes and our faith on the blessed Lamb of God that was slain to redeem the fallen children of Adam. For, ' as in Adam all died, so shall all' true believers 'in Christ be made alive' to God; and then, my dear father, we may say—

> ' Prisoners of hope, lift up your heads,
>   The day of liberty draws near ;
> Jesus, who on the serpent treads,
>   Shall soon in your behalf appear :
> The Lord will to his temple come,
> Prepare your hearts to make him room.'

My dear father, I hope that God will not suffer sickness or death ever to surprise us unawares, or find us in a state unprepared.

" .   .   .   . Please to give my duty to my dear and tender mother, and accept the same yourself, and love to dear brothers and sisters; and may the blessed Spirit of God be very powerful in all your hearts to root out every evil !"

" Southampton, April 11, 1797.

" My dear father,—I have been silent longer than I should, had my dear sister written before; but as I know all things are guided and governed by Him whom my soul loveth, I wait patiently his appointed time. O, my dear father, it is good to trust in him, to call upon him, to honour his holy name. O, if you have not, then, turn and seek him while he may be found. None ever sought his glorious face in vain; and those ' that come unto me (saith the dear Lamb of God) I will in no wise cast out.' No ! his tender love, pity, and compassion, never fail to poor sinners. No ! though my dear mother and father have lived near to the time that my God hath said shall be the age of man, ye

have still been sinning, and grieving, and hiding as it were
your faces from that God who is still pursuing you with his
love and mercy,—yea, even the blessed Jesus, who is still
making intercession for sinners at his Father's right hand; and

> ' When Justice bared the sword
>   To cut the fig-tree down,
> The pity of my Lord
>   Cried, Let it still alone :
> The Father mild inclined his ear,
> And spares us yet another year."

But remember, my dear friends, his blessed words, ' My
Spirit shall not always strive with man ;' and ' except you
are born again ye cannot inherit the kingdom of God ;' and
if you are not washed in the precious blood of that dear
Lamb of God, you can have no part with him ; and if his
Spirit does not ' bear witness with your Spirit' that you are
born of God, you are still in your sins, and strangers to the
blood that bought you on the tree. O, my daily prayer to
God is, that he will turn you, and so shall you be turned.
O, the dear Redeemer waits to be gracious ; he is ever ready
to pardon your sins, and seal it with his precious blood ; he
is ever calling, ' Come unto me all ye that do labour and
are heavy laden' with the burden of your sins, ' and I will
give you rest.' Then, I entreat you my dear friends, in the
name of the most high God, that ye turn and lay hold of
the ever-blessed Jesus as your shield of faith, and he will
arm you with the whole armour of God. But remember
this : though God is full of love and mercy, yet he will be
sought unto. Then draw nigh unto God in secret prayer,
and God will draw nigh unto your precious souls, and that
to bless them, and will say unto you, Believe on me, ' my

gracc is sufficient for you,'—I will cleanse you in my precious blood, and then shall your leprosy be healed, and you shall return without spot. And then you must watch and pray to him continually to keep you clean. O, he is always more ready to hear than we are to pray, and more ready to give than we are to ask. Remember, my dear father, that the language of every prayerless and unconverted soul is, ' Depart from me, O God, for I desire not the knowledge of the Most High. Then put off the evil day no longer, lest you should hear him say (who is willing and able to save to the utmost those that come unto him), 'I have stretched out my hand all the day long, and no man regarded.' And 'behold I knock at the door of every man's heart, and to him that openeth unto me I will come in, and sup with him, and he with me.' My dear father, these are blessed and comfortable words, and I am his living witness, and I ' set to my seal' that Jesus is true. O, the happy state of the children of God ! Now I ask and receive, I seek and I find him whom my soul loveth ; yea, I always find I have a very near access, through his blessed intercession, to supplicate the throne of grace ; and now I can say,

> ' Before the throne my Surety stands,
> My name is written on his hands ;'

and now I am so filled with the peace and love of God, that I can lift up my soul and say,

> ' My God, I know, I feel thee mine,
> And will not quit my claim,
> Till all I have is lost in thine,
> And all renew'd I am ;'

and

> ' Where'er I am, where'er I move,
> I meet the object of my love.'

The Lord doth so strengthen my faith in him, that I find all his promises stand engaged to make me blessed. O, may God pardon what his poor unworthy dust has written through ignorance, which is not agreeable to his most blessed will, which I will ever seek to fulfil. . . . I have so little taste for the conversation of this world, that it is very unpleasant to think on it. My sister's love and duty to all. Mrs. B. will be in the Island soon, please God, and then you are to write to and direct her to the house of God in Bath, for she is still walking in darkness, and is ignorant of it. O, may the Lord be graciously pleased to bring you all into his marvellous light, that you may praise him in time and eternity; then strive to enter in at the strait gate. . . . . If the Lord shall please to spare me, I hope to see you ere long,—if not in this world, in that where we shall bask in unutterable bliss. My dear friends, take not this advice amiss from your unworthy child; it is the command of my blessed Lord, 'When thou art converted, remember thy brethren,' and I daily take up my cross, and follow him whithersoever he goeth; and I pray God enable you to do the same. O, how should I rejoice and praise my God to see you enabled, through the inspiration of the Spirit of the Most High, to answer this ill-written letter! Farewell, in the Lord, dear friends!"

Shortly after writing the above, declining health compelled her to remove from Southampton, and she came and took up her abode with her parents at Hale Common. With the blessing of God, rest and the balmy air of the Island so far restored her health that she was able to leave home and become a resident in a Wesleyan family at West Cowes.

While resident in this town, she penned the subjoined letter to her only sister:—

> "Cowes, Oct. 14, 1798.

"My dear sister,—I have not had a convenient opportunity to write till now. I hope you have not been unhappy at my long silence. Consider that God is my keeper, therefore 'I shall lack no manner of thing that is good.' I entreat you to commend the keeping of your soul, spirit, and body to the Lord, for he is a promise-making, and a true and faithful promise-keeping God.

> 'Then let me commend my Saviour to you,
> The publican's friend and advocate too.'

My dear, I say that God is my keeper. You will say, he is yours. It is true, for 'in him we all live, and move, and have our being.' But I can say with Job, 'I know that my Redeemer liveth,' and

> 'Now he is pleading his merits and death,
> And still interceding for sinners beneath.'

He is waiting to be gracious to you, for he is long-suffering and kind, plenteous in goodness; his love and mercy know no end nor bounds, and his compassions fail not. Now, my dear,

> 'Ready for you the angels wait,
> To triumph in your blest estate ;
> Tuning their harps, they long to praise,
> The wonders of redeeming grace.'

O, my dear sister, search the Scriptures diligently; pray to God earnestly; for in so doing you will find that he is a God 'nigh at hand, and not afar off.' He has promised to be found of those that seek him; for none ever sought his face in vain, neither did ever any trust in him, and was deceived. O, my dear sister, if you did but believe how willing God is to reveal his Son in your heart, the hope of glory! O, how would your soul be ravished, if Christ would appear to you, the altogether lovely, and the first among ten thousand! Then could you say those blessed words,

> ' My soul, through my Redeemer's love,
>   Saved from the second death I feel ;
> My eyes from tears of dark despair,
>   My feet from falling into hell.

> ' Wherefore to him my feet shall run,
>   My eyes on his perfections gaze,
> My soul shall live for God alone,
>   And all within me shout his praise.'

I entreat you to read the Word of God carefully, for in it is eternal life. All the promises there stand engaged to make you blessed, if you truly repent, and forsake your sins, and turn to God with full purpose of heart, and fully believe on the Lord Jesus Christ, that he will save you from your sins with a present and everlasting salvation; for he says, only believe, and thou shalt be saved. We should receive the word of God as if it were the awful voice of God from heaven. It will be awful to the wicked and un-converted. . . O may the Lord quicken your dead soul

> . . . . ' With life divine,
> And make you in his image shine !'

O may you feel the kindlings of love divine shed abroad in your heart! Farewell in the Lord, my dear sister."

On leaving Cowes, her health being still in a precarious state, and having a small fund of savings laid by for future need, she did not again enter upon regular service. Limited engagements in respectable families in the Island, and the demands of affliction in the domestic circle in her own home occupied her time. From this period she seems to have lived a life of rigid self-denial in relation to both diet and dress. A few facts, which have been placed on record by the Rev. B. Carvosso, will best illustrate these traits in Elizabeth's character. "As an instance," says Mr C., "of her mortified spirit and self-annihilation, a friend of hers (who has just now [1837] gone to join her above) informed me that she dined with him, he believed, the last time she was at Newport; and when they sat down to partake of the humble meal provided for them, she abstained from the use of anything but potatoes, declaring that so deeply was she penetrated with a sense of her own unworthiness in the sight of God, that she felt that only the meanest fare was fit for the use of such a sinner as she was; exemplifying the feeling of the patriarch when he exclaimed, 'I am not worthy of the least of all thy mercies.'" Mr. Carvosso supplies another striking instance, showing that, however self-denying she might be in relation to herself, she was large-hearted and generously disposed towards others. "There was in the Newport Society a pious and a very afflicted man of the name of William Adey, well-known and much esteemed; but at this time he and his wife were poor and much distressed. The charitable Dairyman's Daughter, now residing at Cowes, heard of his case, and forwarded for him a small parcel to a mutual friend residing at Newport, who took it at once to his needy brother, and, carelessly throwing it on the table, said, with apparent unconcern, 'I wish you may find a guinea in it.' On opening its careful foldings, to their agreeable and grateful surprise, it did contain "a guinea for William

Adey, presented to him by Elizabeth Wallbridge.' William told me this himself, with much emotion, on his dying bed, on my incidentally asking him if he knew anything of her. He added, 'O she was a good creature ! and at another time, when she knew I was in want, she kindly sent me half-a-guinea.'

"She lived in the spirit of obedience to that useful direction of Methodism, 'Exhort, instruct, reprove, all you have any intercourse with.' None were spared, not even old professors, when she saw any hope of being useful. And a word of exhortation or reproof was sometimes followed by an act of kindness in reference to temporal circumstances, in order to enforce attention to matters of higher moment. A little before her death, happening to be at a house in Newport, a neighbour stepped in, a poor woman, and destitute of religion. Elizabeth seized the opportunity of conversing with her very closely about her soul, and the affairs of another world; and that she might fasten the words of holy counsel on the heart of the poor woman, she immediately afterwards sent her one of her own gowns, of some value."

CHAPTER XVI.

(1798—1800).

SUCH, as we have seen in the last chapter, was the Dairyman's Daughter when she became known to the Rev. Legh Richmond. He found her a decided Methodist, and such she remained to the end of life ; indeed, the Methodists were the only Christians with whom she lived in fellowship; they were her spiritual counsellors, and it was they who visited and watched over her in her affliction, and followed her remains to their last resting-place. The open air singing, which took Legh Richmond by surprise, and afforded him so much delight, and the account of which he has drawn with such graphic power, was led by Mr. Isaac Atkey, who then, and up to the time of his death, was a much-respected and useful member of the Wesleyan Society at Newport. And yet Legh Richmond, as Mr. Carvosso observes, "not only gives no hint of the fact that the Dairyman's Daughter was a Methodist—this might have been very proper, circumstanced as he was—but he conducts the reader to the full impression that she was indebted to a clergyman of the Established Church for the instrumentality

P

of her conversion.   By this means, not only are those
deprived of the honour which is their due, but it is ascribed
to a quarter to which it does not belong.   On this account,
the author of that perhaps unequalled tract has been even
severely censured,—not, indeed, by those who had the
privilege of knowing his character, and his truly catholic
and most affectionate spirit, but by those who have been
imperfectly informed of the facts of the case. . . . .
Whether Mr. Richmond did or did not know that Elizabeth
Wallbridge was a member of the Methodist Society, I
cannot learn; but I have a full conviction that, when he
represents her as informing him that she was awakened in
the Established Church by a sermon from a missionary
clergyman, it was a mere mistake, very naturally resulting
from the imperfect recollection he would have of the terms
which she employed.   Mr. Crabb would, at that time, be
called a missionary, as the tract of country over which his
labours were spread would then be called a home mission
among us; and, as Mr. Richmond wrote from memory,
some years after the events had occurred, and when he was
resident in another part of the kingdom, he might easily
confound the words which were floating in his memory,
and suppose it was some wind-bound missionary who had
come ashore at the Island, while the vessel was detained on

the coast.   As the Rev. J. Crabb is still living [1837,] now
a venerable and highly respected minister of a congregation
at Southampton, and has very kindly furnished the writer
of this account with a letter on the subject, an extract from
it will set the matter in a clear and candid light.   Mr.
Crabb says :—' You request me to give you some informa-

tion relating to the conversion of the late Elizabeth Wallbridge, known by the name of the 'Dairyman's Daughter.'
Perhaps it is known to thousands that I was the honoured,
though unworthy instrument of leading her to Christ
Jesus, her only and dearest friend. Several friends have
urged me many times publicly to correct the little in-
accuracies in Mr. Richmond's narrative; but I have felt
very unwilling to do it, lest I should in any measure lessen
the importance and value of the tract; especially as these
little mistakes no more affect the truth of the facts stated,
than if a man were, through forgetfulness, to make a
mistake as to the right name of the person by whom a very
fruitful vineyard had been planted. What does that signify
when it is seen that the trees live and bear fruit? And no
one doubts the fact that it is the supreme Ruler of the
universe who gave life to the trees, and who preserves them
in life. I was well acquainted with that highly and
deservedly beloved servant of Christ, who visited that
interesting family in their affliction; and I once ventured
to ask him, at his own house, 'Pray, did you know the
instrument of Elizabeth's conversion?' 'No,' was the
answer, 'but I expect it was under the ministry of a missionary who was going abroad to New South Wales,—I
think it must have been Mr. Marsden.' The remark
evidently showed how he had misunderstood Elizabeth's
reference to a missionary. I said no more, only rejoicing
that the Holy Spirit had converted her. Mr. Richmond
must have fallen into the mistake by only writing from his
memory some years after the events had occurred, and not
having understood at the time the exact import of the words

which fell from the dying lips of Elizabeth. I lost sight of her myself for several years, being obliged to retire from my public duties on account of ill health ; but one day a friend came to me and said, 'I have a guinea sent to me by the brother of Elizabeth Wallbridge for you. It comes from her death-bed, and she desires your acceptance of it as a small token of Christian love to you as the instrument of her conversion. I valued the manner in which it was done, and received the token as the grateful gift of a dying Christian. I love her memory, and rejoice that the memoir has been the instrument of converting and comforting thousands of my poor fellow sinners, and I most fervently pray that it may long continue to be a blessing to the church and to the world. And I trust, also, that your account of dear Elizabeth may satisfy all who have heard imperfect statements of the business. May all the glory be given to God for all his grace bestowed on us mortals !'

"This sainted young woman, the influence of whose fervent and consistent piety has been so extensively diffused, and is still operating on so large a scale, died at Hale Common, in the parish of Arreton, in the full triumph of faith and hope, May 30th, 1801, in the 31st year of her age. On this interesting spot, where the Dairyman's Daughter breathed forth her dying prayers, and where 'the chariot of Israel and the horsemen thereof' rested for a moment to receive her happy spirit, as it was delivered from the burden of the flesh, a very neat little Methodist chapel has recently been opened." [See p. 148.]

The following letters were addressed to the Dairyman's Daughter by Legh Richmond, and will be welcomed as

illustrative of the style in which he addressed her. The
first is a short note, and was probably written in answer to
her second letter which he has inserted in his tract.   He
says :—

"It has pleased God, my Christian sister, for several
weeks past, to keep me in a state of sickness, from which
soon, by his goodness, I hope to be relieved. I am at
present unable to say half what I wish to you ; but, lest
you should suspect me of inattention to your friendly and
welcome letter, I write these few lines to say that you shall
either hear from me at length, or see me shortly. May
God support you through your trial of ill health ; and the
nearer you approach the other world, whenever it be God's
appointed time, may you be more and more heavenly-
minded. Peace be multiplied to you. I pray for you, and
beg you to know how faithfully I am,

"Yours in Christ,

"LEGH RICHMOND."

The second letter is evidently a reply to the one which
Elizabeth's aged father carried to Brading church, when
the author of it overheard him speaking in such high
terms of his "precious Betsy." It commences thus :—

"You may be assured, upon the faith of one who loves
God, and would fain serve and obey him, that you are not
out of my mind, though I have been prevented from doing
myself the pleasure of calling upon you. I have also
delayed writing till now, from an almost daily expectation
of coming your way; but it has happened otherwise. I
now acknowledge the receipt of your last letter, and rejoice
at the sight of words dictated by a spirit of godliness,

humility, and love. In a perverse and adulterous generation like the present one, what can be so cheering to the soul as converse with those who really know the Lord, and love him because he hath first loved them? I am well convinced of the propriety and force of your advice with respect to my conduct, and that of ministers of the Gospel in general. God grant such a weak and unprofitable servant as I am may find grace and ability to conduct myself as becomes a faithful labourer in the vineyard! For who can do it of his own strength? What are the natural powers of sinful man to work out the righteousness of God? To the Spirit of Christ, which changeth and strengtheneth the inner man, we must attribute all: to him be honour, glory, and praise, in all the churches, now and evermore!

" I have read your two books, and find much profit in them both. It appears that the life of Madame Guion should be attended to with some caution, which Mr. Wesley very frequently draws our observation to in his short notes at the bottom of the pages. She was sometimes influenced by notions which had not a sufficiently strong scriptural foundation, and therefore in these things should not be set as a pattern; but her love of God, and her anxiety to be for ever joined to him, are lovely and interesting. The true rule for discerning the motions and operations of the blessed Spirit within us, is to compare our feelings with those ways of holiness—happy fruits of the Spirit—which the apostle describes. Let everything be referred to this as a standard, and we never shall be mistaken. May God so guide and direct you and me to all goodness, that our works may glorify—not ourselves, none but Jesus can do that, but—our Father which is in heaven! May numbers have reason, through the mercy of God, to bless our memory! and may the seed which, in my ministerial capacity, I am commissioned to sow, to plant, and to water, receive its due increase from God! I assure you this is much at my heart, and occupies much of my thoughts. Seeing and 'knowing the terrors of the Lord,' I would 'persuade men,' with all truth, earnestness, and sincerity, to flee from the wrath to come, and throw themselves and their sins at the foot of the cross, with true repentance and faith. Faith is the hand which we stretch forth to receive the benefits of Christ's blood; it is the soul of the spiritual life, and the grand distinguishing characteristic of the true Christian from the false; it is the touchstone of Christianity; the burning coal which sets fire to the sacrifice on the altar; the sun which enlightens the wilderness of the world; the lantern which guides our feet through the valley of the shadow of death. True faith never can be separated from hope and love; they are three lovely sisters, who take up their dwelling in the heart when it becomes the temple of the Holy Ghost; their parent is God, and their offspring righteous works: how do they shine forth in the midst of a vain and wicked world, like a candle set upon a hill in a dark and gloomy night! May their operations spread wider and wider over the face of the world, and may the church of God increase in their fruits, till at length the happy time shall arrive when the kingdoms of this world shall become the kingdom of the Lord and his Anointed! God hasten so blessed a period!

"I was much shocked at the sudden death of my

neighbour ———. Such unprepared calls ought to operate upon those that are left behind as salutary warnings. Alive and healthy this morning, who knoweth that this very night our souls shall not be required of us ? Let us be on the watch, and endeavour to make others so, for we 'know neither the day nor the hour' of our Master's coming. I am told that his successor has given some strong calls to duty and attentiveness in religion, which I hope in God will prove efficacious. He appears in conversation very much in earnest, and seems steady and persevering; but I have only seen him twice. In that parish you well know how much reformation is wanted. Alas! into what place can we go where it is not wanting ? Iniquity triumphs, and presumption darkens the very heavens with her wide-spreading wings; blasphemy, covetousness, and uncleanness, abound and prosper; men are lovers of pleasure rather than lovers of God. Does not the world go just as Satan would have it ? Sometimes he will even suggest to the faithful that their endeavours are in vain, and he tempts to inactivity and sloth; but, blessed be God, the Bible is in our hands, and there we find arguments, and strength, and consolation, and admonition, and precept, and commandment, and encouragement to proceed in the mighty task of beating down the strongholds of iniquity, and destroying the works of the devil. Even though ' the overflowings of ungodliness may make us afraid,' God worketh the good cause, and in the end it shall prosper. The church shall never fail, nor shall the gates of hell prevail against it. Your health, I hear, is weak; may God strengthen the inner man, as he thinks fit to weaken the outer ! may his kingdom rule in your heart, though the outward fortifications crumble to dust! If it please God to shorten the span of your life, I trust you will meet your Redeemer with peace and joy, and that you will employ the rest of that time which is appointed you on earth in promoting the cause of righteousness, in combating the artifices of Satan, resisting the ways of ungodliness, conversing with God in fervent prayer and holy meditation, contemplating his redeeming love, and hungering after higher and higher degrees of virtue. May the prospect of a heavenly inheritance keep you alive to holiness and gratitude! and, in looking upon the world around, remember that the true spirit of the Gospel teaches us to love the sinner, while we hate the sin.

"Grace, mercy, and peace, be multiplied upon you from God, and the Lord Jesus Christ.

"Believe me to be, yours with Christian regard,

"LEGH RICHMOND."

The following unfinished narrative was doubtless intended for her own private use. It seems to have been written just six months before her decease, and at the time when her strength was fast failing :—

"Nov. 30th, 1800.

"Elizabeth Wallbridge, born July 29, 1770.

"I feel my mind more composed when writing, and more free from wandering thoughts, than at any other time; for I have little retirement, and, when I have, it is seldom free from disturbances, so that I am almost continually conversant with the world. The Lord knoweth what a burden it is to my mind, and how impatient I have been. May the Lord pardon his unfaithful, unprofitable servant,

and sanctify me throughout soul, spirit, and body, and
plunge me in the Godhead's deepest sea, that I may be lost
in his immensity! O glorious hope of perfect love! may
it ever fill and lift my ravished spirit up to things above!
—there I shall for ever love. I thought I would just set
down, as the Lord is pleased to give me time and strength,
a few of his particular mercies and favours as I can recollect. He has abounded in love and mercy to me : O that I
had made him all the returns that love could make by
giving myself a sacrifice daily unto him! But now I have
to lament my shortcomings, and to apply to the 'blood of
sprinkling,' which speaks my sins forgiven, and purifies my
soul, and makes it meet for heaven. O what a precious
Saviour have I found! O that I could make him known to
all mankind, that all may turn and taste the riches of his
grace! At present, I am so very weak in body and mind
that I can recollect but very little. They have been decay-
ing near four years ; but in the Lord Jehovah is my everlasting strength, and whoever relies on him shall never be
ashamed, and shall be freed from all slavish fears. I
seemed to have some fear of God, and love to him from my
childhood. His restraining grace kept me from falling into
great and open sin, and gave me such a love of truth and
uprightness, that I seemed to hate every false way, word,
and work, in myself and others. I remember, when I went
to school, one of my playmates, that I was very fond of,
used to take every opportunity to get money from her
mother unknown to her, and bring to school, and buy all
kinds of little toys, and then freely give me and another or
two an equal share with herself. But oh, how did the

Spirit of the Lord strive with me at that time, and convince me of the evil! so that I had no peace of mind while I partook of the sin, and yet I had not strength to resist it. It was so on my mind that I ought to make her fault known,—not to conceal it and partake of part. I could see it a great evil in the person that sold her the things, whose daughter took part, and, I believe, knew as well as I did how she came by it; but I never revealed it, though I always bore it on my mind with abhorrence. What a sad thing to yield to sin against such clear convictions! I was early taught a form of prayer, which I continued to repeat in a careless manner when I was laid down in my bed; but very often I fell asleep before I said them half. But, blessed be God, he still spared me, and often drew me to himself by the cords of love, for at an early age he drew me to secret prayer, where I often felt the kindlings of his love, but had none to set me forward, so that I often neglected this duty; but, when alone, I have often felt great sweetness in it. I believe if I had heard the gospel preached, I should have been very early devoted to that God I now love and adore. But I do not yet love him as he has promised I shall, with all my loving heart, when sin is all destroyed. O happy moment, how I long for it!"

Another document of deep interest is her WILL:—

"My dear father, and mother, and brothers,—If it should please the Lord to spare you all till after my decease, I take this opportunity to set down what I simply desire, if it be the Lord's will, and agreeable to you all. If I die under this roof, it will be best, as soon as I am dead, to have my coffin made. Let Mr. —— make it, if it is quite agreeable; and then I can be carried down stairs, and not disturb you or break your rest. And there the angels of my covenant-making and promise-keeping God will watch over me, and protect my sleeping dust; so that you need not fear evil spirits, for they will have done with me for ever; they will never assault me any more. I shall then, through Christ, who hath loved me with an everlasting love, gain the glorious victory over all the principalities and powers of darkness; for they know that I. am a redeemed captive from their power, though they cease not to tempt me to return to my former customs, that I may be again in bondage to fear. But glory be given to God, his grace is sufficient for me; hitherto he hath brought me safe through, and I know he will save to the end. May I lift up my heart to him, and cry, O thou,

> ' Fairer than the sons of men,
> Do not let me turn again ! '

Let my coffin be very plain, neat, and strong, made to cover very close. Let it be made white inside and out, if no trouble; and for my shroud a little wool will do, if you like it; it will be less expense; for it will all turn to dust. I care not who you ask to my funeral; I want no form of young people; I had rather have those that love God, that they may rejoice over me with angels above, and praise a God of love. [She then names several friends whom she desired to be present, and proceeds:] Let them all meet together that can or will come; . . . and I trust they will feel the Lord powerfully present in the midst to bless every waiting soul, and reveal the secrets of his love. Mr. Richmond, or the minister at Newchurch, which you please. I love them both, because they love God; for 'God is love,' and his love constrains us to love one another. . . . Do not be afraid of disturbing the peaceful dead in singing praises to God and the Lamb, who hath redeemed me from sin. It may be, my happy spirit may be permitted to join with listening angels who catch the approving sound, while all heaven's host cry, 'A child is born into our world above.' Let these hymns be sung:—the 37th, 'Hosanna to Jesus on high;' the 35th, ''Tis finished, 'tis done;' the 33rd, 'Ah, lovely appearance of death;' the 50th, in the large book, 'Hark, a voice divides the sky.' If the preacher please, for the glory of God and the good of the living, let him preach a sermon from Psalm cxvi., 15, 'Precious in the sight of the Lord is the death of his saints;' and may the Word be attended with power, a divine energy, and the quickening influence of the Spirit of God, rest upon the minister and the hearers! that glory may be given to God, and great good done in his precious name; that his saints that love him may be strengthened and refreshed, and built up in their most holy faith; that they may go on their way, rejoicing in the strength of the Lord, from grace to grace, till glory end what grace begun; that they may be fully prepared to meet death with Christian courage. And may all my dear friends follow on to know the Lord, and experimentally to feel the saving power of divine grace in each of their hearts, that they may give glory to God, and triumphantly quit the stage of mortality, shouting, 'Victory through the blood of the Lamb that was slain, who is now ascended on high for ever to reign.' But I would have all remember, if they have never yet been convinced of their lost and miserable state by nature, that it is high time for them to awake out of sleep, and cry mightily to God to show them their danger and save them from destruction; for without faith and prayer you cannot be saved. Then come like the humble publican, with a feeling sense of your sins, and true faith in his merits to atone for your sins and cleanse your guilty souls, and you will be sure to find mercy, pardon, and peace, and grace to help you in every time of need. When I was brought home, I was in great hopes I should see a great change; but I have been painfully disappointed to the present moment, which often fills my heart with grief and sorrow, to see sinners so unconcerned upon the brink of death. But if I am never permitted to see that happy change, I hope you will experience it, and meet me in glory: there we shall part no more." [The remainder is occupied with the distribution of her little property, consisting almost entirely of wearing apparel, among her relatives.]

In a friend's house recently we took up the life of the Rev. Samuel Marsden, Church of England Missionary to New Zealand, and casually opened on the following statement :—"While she [the ship] lay off Portsmouth, Mr. Marsden went on shore in the Isle of Wight, and on Sunday asked and obtained permission to preach in the parish church at Brading. His text was, ' Be clothed with humility,' 1 Peter, v., 5 ; and amongst the congregation was a young woman, to whom the Word preached was ' quick and powerful,' being carried home by the Spirit of the living God. To that sermon the ' Dairyman's Daughter' owed her conversion, and the church of Christ her bright example, as depicted by the loving heart and pen of Legh Richmond." * We were delighted, and thought—Here then, at last, we have discovered the solution of the mystery. Here is a remarkable coincident on which Legh Richmond's mistake was founded. He had the impression that the Dairyman's Daughter told him that she was converted under a sermon preached by a missionary from the text, " Be clothed with humility." Mr. Marsden was a Missionary, and while detained on the Island preached at Brading on that text. How easy for Mr. Richmond—who wrote his narrative some years after from memory—to confound Mr. Marsden, the foreign missionary, with Mr. Crabb, the home missionary!

Deep was our disappointment when we afterwards learnt that this part of Mr. Marsden's life was mere fiction, being founded on Mr. Richmond's mistake.

In the second edition of Mr. Marsden's life, there is the following note :—" Some doubt having been thrown on this interesting fact, it was omitted in the first edition. We have since ascertained from Mr. Marsden's family its perfect truth and accuracy."

The foregoing letter of Elizabeth Wallbridge, which may still be seen, in which she expressly states, " It was when I was sitting under that delightful man, Mr. Crabb, that the Lord opened my eyes," will show that Mr. Marsden's family are mistaken, and that the " interesting fact" ought to be omitted in the next edition of Mr. Marsden's life. Besides, the dates do not agree. If Mr. Marsden preached at Brading at all, it was in 1793, whereas

* " Life of Rev. H. Marsden," 2nd Ed., p. 6.

His house-keeper, Mary Ward, was a Methodist, and one who loved the peculiar ordinances of her own church so well, that she would only enter on the duties of her vocation in his household on the stipulated condition that she might be allowed to attend her weekly class and the other means of grace among her own people.

The nature of his strong attachment to the Wesleyans will be best shown in his own words. A large number of his letters, which have never been published, lie before us. In one of the first which he wrote after he left the Island, he enquires, "How is my excellent friend John Wheeler and his family?" and then, evidently from a full heart, exclaims, "That man will be dear to me as long as I have life." And surely it is worthy of note, that that eminent young clergyman should have found himself surrounded, and in daily contact with such thorough Methodists, and at the same time such devoted Christians as were his clerk and housekeeper, at the very moment when his own heart was beginning to pant after the waters of life. How much the relation of their Christian experience and their example assisted him in his early struggles after salvation we may not be able to tell; but that he greatly relished the one, and profited by the other, is abundantly evident from his own testimony.

The high esteem in which John Wheeler was held by him was warmly reciprocated. It arose from a kindred feeling which subsisted between them as Christians. They were both young in the way. Legh Richmond had discovered and embraced the truth as it is in Jesus while reading Wilberforce's " Practical View of Christianity," and his clerk had made the same grand discovery while listening to the Methodists in the open air, or under some lowly roof. They were drawn together by the instincts and yearnings of the renewed heart, which, true to the social character of experimental religion, seeks for fellowship, and in the neglect of which it cannot thrive. A few extracts from Legh Richmond's published life will confirm these views, and will not prove unacceptable to the reader: " Jan. 15, 1804. Went to Arreton. My excellent though humble friend, J. W., was there. I pray God I may sit at his feet in the kingdom of heaven ; I know of no such Christian here. Would to God I were like him ! Found much comfort with my Society." Again, " Had some interesting conversation with J. W. once more." " Drank tea at John Wheeler's ; his cottage is God's palace." If the grateful tone of these records are considered, it will appear evident, we think, to every candid reader, that, on the subject of experimental religion, Legh Richmond was to some extent disciple to his humble clerk.

Scarcely less strong was the esteem and Christian affection which he cherished towards his housekeeper, with whom, and her husband, Mr. Harry Caws, Mr. and Mrs. Richmond kept up a correspondence until death. Mr. Caws was a pilot residing at Bembridge. He became an early fruit of Mr. Richmond's ministry, and so high an opinion did he entertain of the pilot's piety, intelligence, and thrift, that he recommended him to his housekeeper, and soon after Mr. Richmond's removal from Brading they were united in marriage. We insert the first letter which he wrote him after he had reached London :—

"Lock Hospital, Aug. 17, 1805.

"My much respected Friend,—I write a few lines, in the midst of haste and business to enquire how you and all our friends are. You lie near my heart, and have my prayers for your present and eternal welfare. I shall be glad to hear from you. I sincerely hope your prospects are those of peace and comfort in your proposed union with our sister Ward, to whom remember us most affectionately. Tell me how our friends go on. Most especially give my kind love to John Wheeler. I am deeply engaged in God's labour, and have an amazing load on my mind arising from it. But all is for the best, and souls are evidently coming to God, and strengthening in the knowledge of the truth. This short letter is more to convince you that I am thinking of you than to afford you much information. Salute the Society with Christian love and blessing from

"Your affectionate pastor and friend,

"LEGH RICHMOND."

His next letter is long and deeply interesting, but our space forbids us to give more than an extract or two. It was addressed to Mr. Caws, from Turvey, Bucks:—"I want to know how John Wheeler's business goes on. I wrote to Mr. Jacob, of Shide, immediately on hearing of the illness of Mr. Kent, to remind him of the promise which he gave to John, but have heard nothing since. God continues to prosper my ministry much. For ever blessed be His adorable name! Our congregations increase fast; people flock for miles around. . . . How does Mr. Broadhurst go on? Any particulars of the parish and people will be acceptable. I hope God prospers you in your own soul.

' Seek and you shall find.' I shall be glad to hear a good account of your wife, for whom I entertain a very great and particular regard in the Lord. Tell John Wheeler that if anything is wanting to be done on my part respecting Mr. Jacobs I shall do it with pleasure. What is become of Ann Cantelo? I heard lately from James Weston, who seems to be in a very happy state. To our brethren and sisters, who remember me and their own souls, communicate my love and affectionate blessing. Pray for me. Mrs. R. sends her kind regards to you and your partner. May the Lord of glory give you grace," &c. James Weston, it is said, became a local preacher.

As soon as Mr. Richmond had left Brading, John Wheeler and Harry Caws united in the attempt to place Methodism on a better foundation at Bembridge; but its remote situation, and being difficult of access, no doubt proved a barrier, and the supply of preaching was inadequate and often precarious. And we may observe that the same obstacles lie in the way of its temporal prosperity, or, so lovely is the situation of this rustic hamlet, that it would long ere this have become a place of general resort.

So earnestly did Mr. and Mrs. Caws desire to enjoy a full supply of Methodist ordinances, that, induced by this sole motive, they removed to Portsmouth. Here they lived an exemplary and useful life, and glorified God in death. Mrs. Caws sustained the office of class-leader for the space of forty years with distinguished fidelity. Although moving in a comparatively humble sphere, and possessing no splendid gifts, she had great influence, which was sanctified to the benefit of her numerous kindred and connexions.

During her last illness her mind was not only happy, but exultant in the sublime prospect which faith opened to her view. She died in the 86th year of her age, and the 71st of her membership.

John Wheeler, who was a local preacher, bravely stood his ground. The Society of which he was the leader, consisting of some half-dozen persons beside himself, met in his own house. It is universally affirmed that he was a local preacher at the same time that he acted as clerk to Legh Richmond. If this were the case, we are inclined to think that his labours were confined chiefly to his own cottage, as his name is not found on the Portsmouth Plan before the division of the circuit, but it appears on the first Plan that was issued after the Island became a circuit. John afterwards removed to Ryde, and thence to Gunville, where he finished his long and useful life in peace. His remains rest in Carisbrook churchyard. His brother left the preaching-room at Gunville for the use of the Wesleyans.

The Rev. Robert Ferguson bears testimony to his excellencies, when he says of him that "he was a man of eminent piety, and of earnest devotedness. If neither profoundly read nor learned, he had no common knowledge of the deep things of God. He had graduated in the school in which apostles had been taught, and he was deeply read in their writings of Him who was their Master and his."

"A good man," says Solomon, "leaveth an inheritance to his children's children." A large number of Mr. Wheeler's descendants became members of the Wesleyan or other Christian communions, and some of them sustained with honour the ministerial office. One of these, the late

Rev. J. W. Wheeler, missionary in Jamaica, under the auspices of the London Missionary Society, was a grandson of John Wheeler, to whom young Wheeler was indebted for some of his first lessons in sacred things. Mr. Henry James, son of Emmanuel Wheeler, was another grandson, who, had health permitted, would no doubt have entered the Wesleyan ministry, but he was cut off at Ryde, in the autumn of 1836, by consumption, in the height of promise and usefulness. In the succeeding spring his sainted spirit was joined by that of his sister Jane, who had been united in marriage to Mr. Woods, his friend and neighbour. She was remarkable for her love to the Word of God and secret prayer.

In 1811 Bembridge returned ten members. A small chapel was built in 1826, and was the only place of worship in the hamlet. It was replaced by a larger one in 1844. At the time the church was erected James and William Goodall were the leading members of Society. They were gardeners—one in the employ of Lord —— and the other in that of Lady D—e. When the church was ready for use, his Lordship proposed to his gardener that now they had got the church opened the Methodists should give up their morning services and attend. "But," said the staunch Methodist, "that would not be fair; we are the mother church in Bembridge." On another occasion, Lady D—e summoned James into the drawing-room, and rather abruptly accosted him with, "Why, Goodall, they tell me that you Methodists teach that people are to get to heaven by their good works." "Don't believe them, Ma'am," said the gardener quaintly, " this is our creed—

> " Thou all our works in us hast wrought ;
>   Our good is all divine ;
>   The praise of every virtuous thought,
>   And righteous word is thine !"

It was in the summer of one of these years, which he spent in the Isle of Wight, that Mr. Richmond met the " negro servant," of whom he has given such a touching tale.   It will be remembered that in one place he describes an interview which took place between the negro and a number of Christians.   John Wheeler informed Mr. Bustard (who at the time was stationed on the Island) that it was to his own cottage at Bembridge—while they were holding, it is believed by Mr. B., a class-meeting—that this sable son of Ham was brought by his spiritual guide.

During a visit which Mr. Richmond paid to the Isle of Wight in the summer of 1822, we find him making himself at home with his old Wesleyan friends.   Thus, August 30, he records in his journal:—" Met R. Wallbridge, and talked about his sister and father.   Attended the Bible Meeting.   Entered at large into the Isle of Wight feelings. Much affection manifested.   A number of persons came in the evening, and joined us in family prayer.   Dear John W. and his wife were full of kindness and holy affections. I expounded and prayed.   Mr. Butterworth was there.   It was an affecting season.

" Sept. 5.—After breakfast went with Mr. B., &c., to distribute tracts at Bembridge Point.   The most affecting and affectionate scene ever witnessed."

Mr. Richmond's companion was Joseph Butterworth, Esq., M.P., brother-in-law to Dr. Adam Clarke, a well-known and firmly-attached member of the Methodist Society.

" 6th.—Visited Robert Wallbridge and Mrs. A. Had much useful conversation about the Dairyman's Daughter. She gave me a lock of her hair. We went to Arreton Church, and visited her grave.

" 18th.—A stone was this day put up for the Dairyman's Daughter at Arreton churchyard. To God be all the praise ! "

The female referred to was Mrs. Atkey, of Newport. She was cousin to Elizabeth Wallbridge ; and she and her husband were highly respected members of Society at Newport. We have had a lock of Elizabeth's hair in our hand. It was presented by the above-named relative to the friend in whose possession it now is. We were struck with its delicate flaxen texture and light auburn shade.

After his return to Turvey, Mr. Richmond addressed the following letter to his old friend, Mr. Wheeler :—

" The remembrance of the days and hours which we spent together in the Isle of Wight is very refreshing to me. I hope that the numerous meetings which we enjoyed have been profitable to not a few of those who assembled together. My daughter and I frequently look back upon the two days passed at Bembridge and Brading, while the tracts were distributed and the grave-stones were set up, with much affectionate gratitude, that I think they will never be forgotten by many. I did feel a lively hope that so much seed would not be sown in vain, and that the Lord would give his blessing to such means as I trusted he had put it into our hearts to employ. My affections for the Island are founded upon many of those circumstances which you will remember in our younger days. It was then that my own heart was first made acquainted with the infinite value of immortal souls, and of the difficult office of a Christian minister. It was there that those means of grace were enjoyed which have been since felt and remembered by me as 'times of refreshing from the presence of the Lord.' It was there I met with the Dairyman's Daughter, the Negro Servant, and the Young Cottager, and with my respected friend John Wheeler. These, and many more events, betwined my heart to the place with very tender ties. When you see our friends at Bembridge, tell them how much I feel towards them. Some of them are the children of my early ministry; others are their children; and others, again, have been brought to a knowledge of the truth through the Lord's blessing upon instruction established and blessed when I first knew them. These are strong ties for spiritual regard. I pray, my dear friend, that you may grow in grace and in the knowledge of the Lord. He that has accompanied you thus far in your way, will not leave nor forsake you. 'He is the same yesterday, to-day, and for ever;' 'Cast your care upon him,' &c. 'The promise is to you and your children.' Let me hear from you soon. May grace, peace, and mercy be with you and yours. Pray for me and mine, and believe me, faithfully and affectionately,

"Your friend in Christ, LEGH RICHMOND.

"Mr. John Wheeler, Ryde, Isle of Wight."

The "instruction established and blessed when he first knew them," refers, in all probability, to the Methodist preaching, and their other means of grace.

One additional and brief citation must bring our remarks

in relation to Mr. Richmond and his connections with Methodism in the Island to a close. It is taken from a letter which he addressed from Cowes to Mr. and Mrs. Caws, and contains the only reference to Methodism through the whole of his correspondence. With this exception, there is not the slightest allusion that would lead us to suppose that such a religious system was in existence, or that the people with whom he was corresponding had the slightest connection with it. We can scarcely conceive of such a fact on any other supposition than that his reticence was designed. This single reference will prove that he perfectly understood to what branch of the church his old friends in the Island belonged. He says:—"I have seen our friends in Bembridge, and rejoiced to find many old ones going on well. But I feel much more satisfied with those who keep to your own old respectable Connexion of the Wesleyans, than to the violent, eccentric, and disorderly habits (as they are related to me) of the B——tes. And many seem to feel the same also who at first were affected by their zeal. I have generally found that great and disorderly vehemence and departure from the sobrieties of Christian worship, beget evils, and produce uncomfortable divisions. Your brother and sister Hale see this clearly. May God keep us all in much lively religion, but preserve us from all error."

We would observe, in conclusion, that Mr. Richmond's ministry during the time that he resided at Brading, though popular, does not seem to have been so remarkable in its effects as it afterwards was at Turvey. He had a few interesting seals, such as little Jane and Mr. Caws, but there was no wide-spread excitement, resulting in anything like a powerful revival of religion. It is our impression that Legh Richmond's writings have been more extensively useful than his ministry, though many for that will have cause to bless God through eternity.

Our space will allow us to glance at two only of the staff of ministers who were on the ground at this period.

Robert Smith spent three years in the Portsmouth circuit. From the time of his conversion to God, which took place when he was about fifteen, his Christian course was marked by great decision and diligence ; and for the maturing of these qualities he was greatly indebted to the fostering care of Richard Rodda. He entered upon his ministerial labours in the St. Austle Circuit in 1792. His ministry, throughout its protracted duration, was both acceptable and useful, and in some instances in an eminent degree. The estimation in which he was held by his brethren, was shown by the posts of special responsibility in which he was repeatedly placed by them. For two years he discharged the onerous duties of Secretary to our Missions with great fidelity. For twenty-three years he sustained the office of Governor of Kingswood School, with a paternal solicitude and care which met the entire approval of Conference. The amiability and spirituality by which his character was distinguished became more conspicuous as he advanced in life. He was an ardent lover of Methodism, and ever jealous for its efficiency. Full of confidence, love, and peace, his death was truly patriarchal. He entered into rest Dec. 19th, 1847, aged 77.

John Burdsall was one of Mr. Smith's colleagues during

his third year. He was a son of the excellent Richard Burdsall of York. Enjoying the invaluable blessing of christian nurture, he was led in early life to embrace the Saviour; and at twenty-one was called to the christian ministry, in which he laboured with success more than forty years. The excellent quality of his mind was more remarkable for acuteness and balance than for brilliancy and depth. He was in the main a self-taught scholar, and was well read in theology. His amiable and genial temper endeared him to the people of his charge, whose salvation he sought with ardent desire. He was sound in judgment, fluent in speech, and pointed in his application. The failure of mental and bodily vigour withdrew him from scenes of activity into great privacy; but the ruling passion was strong in death. It is reported of Garrick, that when a doubt arose as to whether he had actually departed this life, a purse of guineas was jingled in his ears, upon which he instantly shewed signs of vitality. In like manner, it is said, that when the friends who stood round the death-bed of Euler were in doubt whether they had finally lost him or not, one whispered in his ear, "What is the cube root of ——?" naming a pretty large number; and the expiring calculator almost instantly faltered out the answer. So, when John Burdsall had sunk into apparent unconsciousness, the name of Christ wakened his slumbering spirit, and brightened his countenance with joy. He peacefully passed away at the advanced age of 85, on Feb. 7, 1861.

CHAPTER XVIII.

(1800—1810).

FOLLOWING the thread of our history, we are brought down to the close of the eighteenth century, and may pause to enquire into the civil and religious condition of the Island at that comparatively modern period. It has been seen that Methodism had but recently begun to extend itself beyond the central and chief town, where it had been so long cradled. One writer informs us that the Island at this era was a century behind England. Newport contained a population of not more than 2,500; Cowes, with all its advantages of a fine harbour and ship-building yards, was but 1,660; while Ryde could boast of but a few rude huts on the hill, having about 500 inhabitants; Ventnor had not half-a-dozen dwelling-houses; and the population of Chale did not reach 300; while that of the whole Island was not more than 20,000. The ministry of the Island, as a whole, was lamentably destitute of evangelical point and power, and consequently the churches were neglected. Dissent was almost unknown in the rural districts. The Sabbath was profaned, and brutal sports were the delight of the multitude; while highway robbery and other crimes were more common than happily they now are. The improved moral state of the Island—and it is our conviction that it will compare favourably with any other part of Great Britain—is greatly owing to the spread of religion by Methodist agency. With a slight exception, there is not a town or village, or scarcely a hamlet where the influence of Methodism is not felt, either through the parent society, or some of its branches, by whom the doctrines of revealed truth are preached, and the young taught in Sabbath schools.

That part of the Island which was least affected by the revival was the south-western coast. Excepting Chale, scarcely any other portion of this sea-board, extending from Blackgang to Freshwater Gate, some ten or twelve miles, has been reached even now by Methodism, save by one of its modern offshoots. When other parts of the Island were brought under the influence of the Gospel, that remote and sparse population seem to have been neglected, or, being out of reach, were left behind in the march of improvement. They were notorious for their smuggling propensities, and the barbarous practice of plundering any ill-fated vessel that might be driven on to their treacherous shores. Many, at least, seemed not only to have imbibed the spirit of those lines, but also to have stoutly practised what they called—

> " The good old rule, the simple plan,
>   That they shall keep who have the power,
>   And they shall get who can."

R

So late as the autumn of 1862 such a disgraceful scene was witnessed on this coast, as we are glad to believe no other part of the Island could possibly have exhibited. During the equinoctial gales, on a dismally dark night in October of that year, a fine West Indiaman was driven into the dangerous bay, some distance west of Blackgang. She was caught on the shingle of the "trough," where the terrific rollers rise into a wall of waters many feet in perpendicular height, and burst with a force that nothing can resist. The vessel was torn to pieces like a match-box, and her cargo, consisting of sugar and rum, was strewed along the shore, and her crew of thirteen hands all found a watery grave save two, who, after being knocked about and badly bruised, gained the land. The darkness of the night prevented the ship from being seen, and the howling of the wind drowned every cry for help. In the morning the news quickly spread, and scores of the peasantry flocked down to the sad scene of devastation and death. Some were impelled by feelings of humanity; others by curiosity; but more, we regret to say, by a baser motive. A scene was exhibited on that day, on those dreary shores, never to be forgotten, and let us hope never to be repeated. On the road leading to the cliff, persons were met whose unsteady step on the one hand, and the awkward attempts to conceal suspicious-looking vessels on the other, too plainly told that the rum puncheons had been tapped. This was still more painfully evident, when the chine was reached, by which access was gained from the cliff to the shore. Up this steep ascent men dead drunk were being carried by their neighbours; while lower down, in a boat-house, a shocking sight met the eye—a number of men lay stretched along the bare floor, so utterly insensible that others were endeavouring to restore animation by rubbing and other means. But a few moments before, those wretches had been joint occupants with the dead and mangled bodies of the poor sailors, which had been washed on shore. The life of one was despaired of; he was swollen in every part, and of a livid hue, while the froth oozing from his mouth rendered him an object too horrid to gaze upon.

On reaching the shore another marvellous scene revealed itself. All along the shingle, in strange confusion, lay spars, cordage, splintered timbers, &c., with here and there a puncheon of the fiery liquid which had unmanned so many unwary ones, as well as those who were more addicted to drink. The stem of the ship almost in shore, but deeply imbedded in the ground, rose above the waters, and was all that remained of the vessel to show the fatal spot where she had struck. The Coast Guards—that is, those of them who had not yielded to the temptation—were taking charge of the property, or knocking out the ends of the casks, and pouring out their fiery contents; while the crowd was as busy in tapping others, and carrying off the spirit in every kind of vessel on which they could lay their hands, or gulping it down as though it were the elixir of life. A dealer was already on the cliff driving his nefarious trade at 10s. per gallon; on the following day the price rose to 20s.

At the distance of a mile and a-half lay another wreck; and on the way to it a drunken man was seen lying with his body half in and half out of the water, utterly un-

conscious of the peril of his position. Another poor sot
sat swigging away at a bottle in a corner, which he had
selected perhaps for concealment, and in which he was
apparently destined to find a night's lodging ; while many
more were fast losing the power of self-government. As
these sad objects were gazed upon, it was impossible to
repress the feeling of gladness that every wreck did not let
loose so potent a foe.

It has been said in palliation that the spirit was
plentiful and accessible, and that the country people were
not aware of its strength until they were overcome by it.
The fact is they had timely warning in seeing those who
were its first victims on the one hand, and the example of
those who were under the restraints of religion on the other,
—who, while they were ready to afford help, neither tasted
nor handled the forbidden thing.

At the Coroner's Inquest, held four days afterwards,
when all the bodies had been recovered, a man who had
found one of them on the day of the wreck, and soon after
drank away his consciousness, gave evidence that he picked
up the body *that morning !* The truth was he had but just
then come to himself.

The facts narrated above show what man would be if
left to himself, and also how much we owe to the civilizing
and elevating influence of our holy religion for the improved
morality which now happily prevails, more or less, over all
our coasts.

We must now turn to what has been termed "the
entrance to the Isle of Wight"—West and East Cowes.
As you enter this fine harbour, which is formed by the

mouth of the Medina, East Cowes lines the shores of the river on the left. Its houses and villas are widely ranged, and prettily grouped along the gently rising slope, which terminates in a thickly wooded ridge, from amid the dense foliage of which peep out the mansions of Osborne, and Norris and East Cowes Castle, with numerous villas, the whole presenting a picture of rural beauty and loveliness. The Island does not, perhaps, present a finer situation than that which is occupied by the royal mansion. The name is said to be derived from "Austerbourne [Oysterbourne], from the oyster-beds of the Medina, the denizens of which, though rather large and coarse, still enjoy local celebrity." We shall be pardoned if we tarry a moment in this interesting locality. It will interest all loyal hearts—and Wesleyans possess no other—to know something of Osborne and its Royal occupants. The estate contains about 5,000 acres. The model farm, in which the late Prince Consort took so lively an interest, is still carefully cultivated. The superior model cottages which dot the estate, the new church at Whippingham, and the excellent day schools for the children of the poor, are a pleasing evidence that the Queen and the late Prince were mindful of the intellectual and moral welfare of both old and young; and it is a well known and delightful fact that royal hands often minister to the needs of the infirm and afflicted, and that at the same time the throne of grace is devoutly approached in their behalf.

A Sabbath-school was opened at East Cowes by Mr. James Pinhorn and others at the beginning of the present century. This was followed by preaching, and there is now a small Society, but not in a thriving state.

West Cowes, with its terraces of streets rising one above another, its villas deeply embosomed in lofty trees, and its spacious harbour, crowded with craft of every size, presents a very fine and exciting scene when approached from the sea.   It was, it is said, this view, on a more extended scale, that woke the sacred muse in the breast of Dr. Watts, and moved him to pen that beautiful hymn on Heaven, beginning

> " There is a land of pure delight,
> Where saints immortal reign ;
> Infinite day excludes the night,
> And pleasures banish pain."

It has been seen that several attempts had been made to effect an entrance into this thriving port.   It lay in the way of the preachers.   Indeed, after the union of the Island with Portsmouth, it lay in the direct, and, at that time, the almost exclusive route.   The "hoy" or "wherry" sailed daily, wind and weather permitting, between Portsmouth and Cowes.   So early as 1785, John Moon, a Mr. Ley, and others, preached there, as already noticed.   The subjoined account was penned by one who was a temporary sojourner there in June, 1786 :—"My situation is pleasant, but expensive ; and I might take up the language of the Psalmist, and say, 'Woe is me, that I sojourn in Mesech, that I dwell in the tents of Kedar !' for a place more devoted to the prince of the power of the air I never saw or heard of.   As to Christian fellowship, I have not one to converse with who has any experience beyond slight conviction.   Neither have we met in class but twice since we came here, and then we walked ten miles for it.   Sometimes we have preaching once a week, and sometimes not.   When I reason about it, I am ready to faint, but the Lord does graciously revive my sinking spirits, and strengthen me with might in my inmost soul."

If, during this early period any were savingly affected by the gospel, they were few, and if a Society was formed, it was feeble and poor. And after it is known that a Society was actually gathered, it was fluctuating,—now strengthened by the addition of a member or two, and then weakened by their removal to other parts. Various places were occupied by the Society, until a small loft was fitted up for its use on Sun-hill. Five persons were all this little church could muster so late as the beginning of the present century. Their names were William Hillyer, Jane Hillyer, James Alford, Sarah Alford, and Sarah White. About this time the Society entered with a Mr. Walker into the joint occupancy of a room over a lath manufactory, about half way up Sun-hill. This room had been fitted up by Mr. Walker, who was a Congregationalist, for religious service, which he conducted on a Sabbath evening. It was afterwards supplied by students from the Gosport Academy, among whom were Morrison, the well known missionary to China, John Angel James, and John (afterwards Dr.) Stiles, who became the pastor of the first Independent Chapel which was erected at Cowes.

The Methodists occupied the room at first on week evenings only. The preachers came to Cowes on Friday, preached in the evening, and then walked down to Newport on the Saturday to be ready for their work on the Sabbath. When the Independents removed to their new chapel, the Methodists took sole possession of the upper room, and introduced preaching on the Lord's day. And now Jacob, though small, began to arise. The word came with power, and several important additions were made to the Society. Messrs. James and Charles Pinhorn, with their sister and others, were induced to cast in their lot with this persecuted little flock, and in a short time the number amounted to sixteen. This sudden accession of strength, with other signs of prosperity, emboldened these young Christians to venture upon the erection of a house for God. This project was carried into effect in 1804, when a small chapel was built in Bath-road. It was, like its predecessors in the country, a very unpretending structure, and, for some cause or other, was vulgarly called the "Salt-box."

The cause still prospered, in the face of much opposition, and the chapel underwent no less than three enlargements; while the Society, in ten years after the chapel was opened, contained forty members, and ranked second to Newport, which had ninety-six, Ryde only thirteen, and Sandown seven; while Ventnor, Freshwater, Yarmouth, and some other places, were unknown to Methodism. Passing through another decade, and the Cowes Society contains sixty-four names on its register. One of the main causes which gave the first impulse that led to this result, was the appointment of the Rev. William Baker as a home missionary to the Island. He was stationed at Cowes in 1809, to give the people there a more regular supply of preaching on Sundays and week nights, while the rest of his time was to be devoted to the breaking up of fresh ground. The Sunday-school was commenced by Messrs. Pinhorn and Hollis in 1813. The latter gentleman is still the Superintendent.

The head of the circuit was now making, if not rapid,

yet steady progress. The number of members in Society had reached seventy, and the congregations were often overflowing ; the demand for additional accommodation became pressing, and, the old chapel not admitting of enlargement, it was resolved to erect a new and more commodious sanctuary. Land was purchased in Pyle-street, and the present plain but substantial building was erected. It was opened on the 28th of February, 1804. Stormy weather, it is said, prevented the minister, who was invited for the occasion, from reaching the Island, and the Revds. W. Aver and G. Gellard, the circuit ministers, had to conduct the opening services. The Rev. Dr. Winter, pastor of the Independent Church, St. James's-street, engaged in prayer, and the Rev. W. Aver preached from "How dreadful is this place," &c., Gen. xxviii., 17 ; and in the evening he was followed by his colleague, who preached from "He shall have dominion from sea to sea, and from the river unto the ends of the earth." Ps. lxxii., 8. The concluding prayer was offered by the Rev. John Stiles, Independent Minister of Node-hill Chapel. The chapel was enlarged in 1834, and will now seat from seven to eight hundred persons.

Meanwhile the cause was being extended along the east coast of the Island, and found its way into Ryde, St. Helens, and Nettlestone, or, as it is now called, Sea View. One hundred years ago, Ryde, now one of the most populous and fashionable places of resort in the Island, consisted of two detached hamlets, known as Upper and Lower Ryde. Lower Ryde was a straggling village lying along the shore. Its name is derived from the Normans, by whom it was called "La Rye." So late as 1793 it is spoken of as a populous village, but difficult of access. It had but two inns, a few chaise and wiskies, and there were some "decked boats for those who love the sea." From this time, a rapid change came over the place ; as houses sprang up, spacious streets were formed, beautiful shops opened, and thousands of visitors poured into it from year to year. In 1815 the noble pier was constructed, and, in ten years more, the slow and uncertain wherry gave place to the swift and commodious steam-boat.

A favourite resort of visitors is the Marine promenade called the Strand, formerly the Dover. Few of those gay throngs know or think, as they step lightly along its paths, that underneath and around them lie the victims of that terrible catastrophe, the loss of the Royal George. On a summer day, the 19th of August, 1793, that noble vessel, the pride of old England, lay moored, with apparent security, off Spithead. The Admiral is in his cabin, and crowds of sailors and visitors throng the decks. The noble ship is undergoing some repairs, and is heeled too deeply on her larboard side ; the waves find a ready entrance,— now a gentle stream, then a rush of waters ; alarm comes too late ; the vessel heels deeper and deeper ; confusion and despair seize the multitude. The shouts of the officers and men, and the shrieks of the women, rend the air. All is in vain !—the ship takes one deep plunge, and eight hundred souls find a watery grave. In a few days the bodies were washed up by the score on the Ryde shore, and buried on the "Dover," in rude graves, which remained for years to tell the sad tale of woe.

Like most other places in the Island, Methodism was very small and feeble in its origin at Ryde. While tracing the rise and progress of the work in the Island, we have been struck with one of its peculiar features—the absence of extensive revivals. There have been no sudden outbursts of religious feeling,—no deep and wide-spread excitement, so characteristic of Cornish Methodism. From small beginnings there has been in almost all cases a gradual growth. The native Islanders are not so excitable and impulsive as the Cornish, nor do they possess the same energy and decision of character as the Yorkshire Methodists. They are more even, but possess less fire and originality. These remarks apply to the country more than to the present town population, where society is more mixed, persons having been drawn to these flourishing localities from all parts of the kingdom, and of course there is greater variety of character.

One of the first Methodists in Ryde was a gardener in the employ of Sir John Simeon, uncle of the Rev. Charles Simeon, of Cambridge. At first there was no one to take the preachers in, and afford them the hospitalities of a temporary home. One tells of taking his dinner with him, and eating it under the shelter of a tree, which is still standing. After a time, an old woman was induced to open her door and provide them a dinner, which consisted of a mutton pudding, which was the only and never-failing dish.

Mrs. Dore, a member of Society, removed from Newport to Ryde about this time, and her house became the preachers' home. That the Wesleyans did not go to Ryde before there was a needs-be, this one fact may suffice in proof—there was but one religious service a week, and that was on the Sabbath afternoon at church.

In 1810 a class was in existence, composed of seven members. John Whitehorn, who was also a local preacher, was at its head as leader. When Mr. Withers removed to Ryde, a more commodious room was opened for preaching. The cause at Portsmouth was now in a prosperous condition, and its leading and most active members being wishful to see the Island formed into a separate circuit, laboured diligently to promote the growth of the, as yet, feeble cause on its eastern coast, which was chiefly supplied with preachers from the head of the circuit. They came over in parties in a boat on the Sabbath morning, and, landing at a convenient point, dispersed to their respective appointments at Ryde, St. Helens, Bembridge, &c., or broke up new ground, as the case might be.

When a minister was appointed to reside at Ryde, a second class was raised and met by him; and at the Conference of 1813, twenty-three members were returned, whose names were John and Mary Whitehorn, John Brown, Mary Binston, John and Catherine Rook, James Hunt, Isaac Stevens, William Mundell, Hannah Dyer, C. Greves, David Richards; 2nd class—W. and S. Austin, Mary Dore, E. Chiverton, John and Mary Southcote, John and Louisa Cook, Mary Spark, Martha Mundell, and — Henderson.

A new chapel was erected in Ryde in 1811. The day was exceedingly unpropitious. The Rev. Jonathan Barker laid the foundation-stone amid torrents of rain. Being war time, building material was extremely high in price ; and little effort being made at the time to meet the expense of the erection, the consequence was that the chapel was left heavily burdened with debt. The difficulty of meeting the interest of borrowed moneys pressed heavily on the trustees at the outset, most of whom resided in Portsmouth. The congregations were thin, most of the pews unlet, the Society poor, and, as we have seen, small in number; and the trustees became impressed with the idea that their speculation was a bad one, and that it would be their safest and wisest course to dispose of the chapel (which had been opened but twelve months) by sale. With this object in view, they called a meeting at Portsmouth; and it was only by the earnest pleading of the Rev. John Bustard, who was sent as a deputation from the Island, that the chapel was saved to the cause at Ryde and to the Connexion.

As a matter of course, when the Island was made a separate circuit, the larger Societies would claim their full share of ministerial labour, and Ryde, being small, would suffer. This was especially the case after the Conference of 1813, when the ministerial staff was reduced to two. This reduction seems to have been so severely felt at Ryde, that it became difficult for the Society to maintain its ground,—indeed, it was a struggle for existence. In two years it was reduced from twenty-three to thirteen members. The incubus of debt grew year by year until it assumed frightful dimensions, and pressed with crushing weight upon the people, crippling all their efforts. The debt reached £1,600; the ground-rent was £1 10s.; while the income was only £10. During this time of discouragement, the resident minister had been withdrawn, but "light is sown for the righteous, and gladness for the upright in heart." In 1832 application was made to Conference for the appointment of a minister to Ryde to be renewed. The request was granted, and from that time things took a favourable turn. A genial spring suddenly burst upon the wintry season through which they had passed, and the "wilderness was made to rejoice and blossom as the rose." The Society shared largely in the times of refreshing, which came from the presence of the Lord immediately afterwards on the whole circuit; so that there were in 1834 in Ryde no fewer than six classes, containing 104 members, while Cowes numbered only 112, and Newport 230. In 1830 the Ryde Society sustained loss by the removal by death of Mr. George Kilpin, a promising local preacher, who was cut off in his thirtieth year in the midst of his usefulness. Standing on the Rock of Ages, he saw the approaching waves of dissolution, but felt no dismay.

The flame of the revival in Ryde was fanned by the visit of a band of Missionaries, who were delayed by contrary winds as they were on their way to the West Indies. The Rev. William Moister, in his interesting "Missionary Memorials," records :—"We came to anchor on the Mother-bank, on Saturday, the 1st of February, [1834,] with the beautiful town of Ryde, in the Isle of Wight, full in view. About ten o'clock a.m. we went on shore, and were delighted to meet with six missionaries—the Rev. Messrs. Pilcher, Cheesborough, Gordon, Cameron, Osborne, and Nun—who were bound for Antigua, by the "Glaphora," which had been detained there by contrary winds for several weeks. The friends in Ryde received and entertained us most cordially, and the kindness of Messrs. Woods,

Wedgwood, and Wheeler, and their families, espccially, will never be forgotten. Little did I think that four of the above-named honoured missionaries would so soon afterwards be called to their eternal reward! But so it was. The ways of God are a great deep which we cannot fathom! And still less did I think, at the time alluded to, that we should be spared to return to our dear native country, and have the pleasure of labouring in the same beautiful Isle of Wight, where I now write, and commit to press these humble records of my missionary labours!" We may here add that the rev. gentleman is once more a resident in the Island, and our prayer is that he and his partner, the sharer of his toils, may be spared to spend a long and useful evening of life.

Mr. Moister continues: "On Sunday morning, the 2nd, at seven o'clock, I attended an excellent prayer-meeting in the chapel at Ryde; and immediately after breakfast we were all summoned on board the vessel, the wind having become fair. We weighed anchor, and proceeded as far as the Needles, when the wind veered round, and we were obliged to return. We came to anchor again on the Motherbank, about six in the evening, having spent an uncomfortable Sabbath in thus attempting to get out to sea. The following morning we went on shore again, and the friends in Ryde hailed our return with every expression of joy, for, during the stay of the missionaries in this place, many delightful meetings had been held, the Holy Spirit was poured out, and much good was done through their instrumentality. We now resumed our meetings, and the chapel was crowded with attentive congregations. On

Wednesday night I preached from Daniel vii., 18, and we had a most delightful prayer-meeting afterwards. On Thursday evening we took tea with the Rev. Messrs. Phillippo and Coultart (Baptist missionaries, bound for Jamaica) at the residence of the late Rev. T. S. Guyer; and on Saturday, the 8th, the wind being favourable, we took leave of our dear friends at Ryde, and proceeded on our voyage."

Another happy event followed this blessed revival— an event which exceeded the hope of the most sanguine— the effectual relief of the chapel from its embarrassment. The following account was written at the time :—"A grant from the Loan Fund of £600 was offered, on condition that £600 were raised by the trustees and their friends. The trustees offered to give £300, if the friends in the Island would give £300. But this would never have been raised, but for a providential occurrence. James Heald, Esq., one of the treasurers of that most important fund, then a visitor at Ryde, was the honoured instrument of inspiring hope where desponding fears had predominated, and his kind promise of a liberal subscription gave the needful impulse. Four members of the Ryde Society, not affluent, but diligent in business, contributed one half of the amount. Other subscriptions, several of which were from members, and one from a minister of the Established Church, and a public collection throughout the Island, with some additional aid from the trustees, made up the remainder. On Friday, May 22nd, 1835, the chapel, having been repaired, was re-opened by the Rev. Messrs. Burgess and Sherwell, of Portsmouth, and a good collection was made to assist in defraying the expense of repairs. This, it is anticipated, will form a new era in the history of Methodism in that beautiful and rapidly-increasing town. Our Society at Ryde—who are strongly attached to Methodism as it is, and not as some would make it—relieved from the overwhelming burden by which they have been so long depressed, are now disposed to thank God and take courage."

Leaving Ryde, the next place on our route is Nettlestone or Sea View,—a quiet and pleasant watering-place, rendered more attractive by the extent and firmness of its sands. We meet with the first notice of a Society in 1813, when there were eleven members, and two on trial. It is probable that a cause existed some two or three years before this date. A chapel was erected in 1828, and re-built in 1845.

Mr. John Matthews was one of the oldest and most steadfast members of this Society. He was enlightened under the Wesleyan Ministry, and joined the class at St. Helens about 1810. When a class was formed at Sea View he transferred his membership to it. From that period until his death, in the year 1845, his life and conversation were such as becometh the Gospel of Christ. His end was sudden : while attempting to remove a bathing-machine, he fell down and expired. The Rev. S. Lucas (1st) says of him that " he greatly rejoiced to see a permanent provision for the preaching of the truth, in the erection of a small chapel ; and that he should not soon forget the manner in which he laid the foundation-stone of a more commodious one, which he was not permitted to see opened. He was greatly beloved as a class-leader, of which his members are giving evidence in erecting a stone to his memory. How many fall as sudden, not so safe!"

St. Helens lies to the south of Sea View, and to the north of Brading Haven. Anciently, it was more noted than it is now. The sea encroached so much upon the land that a portion of the churchyard was swept away, and a new church was built at the opposite end of the village. This place was once notorious for its smuggling propensities, and the improved state of morals is mainly owing to the influence of the religious element which the Gospel has infused into the circles of its social life. In 1809, under the home missionary labours of the Rev. W. Baker, a gracious revival of religion took place, and the little Society increased to twenty members, and in three years they were able to build a house for the Lord. In 1813 there were two classes led by Charles Stamp and Robert Woodford.

In the spring of 1818, when the Rev. John Geden— then a young minister, now the Chairman of the Portsmouth District—was stationed in the Island, Olinthus Gregory was staying as a visitor at Ryde, the Methodists at St. Helens, mistaking him for a minister, invited him to preach their chapel sermons. The deputation were somewhat disconcerted when they discovered their error; but that excellent gentleman showed his appreciation of their good-will by walking down, in company with a member of his family, to St. Helens, to hear Mr. Geden, and to worship in the sanctuary to aid which his services had been solicited.

Mr. John Burden, who married a daughter of Mr. Harry Caws, was a member of this Society, and stood firm while the surging waves of agitation were sweeping many of his old companions into its vortex. His death was pre-eminently happy and triumphant.

The Rev. David M'Nicoll was stationed in the Island in 1808. To a man of his poetical genius, and with his exquisite love of Nature, it must have been a spot just suited to his taste. And doubtless many a time, as he has traversed its valleys, and roamed over its downs, his soul has been raised to an ecstacy, the like of which he felt when he gazed on the Cambrian vale Clywd, and exclaimed, " It is like a fragment broken off Paradise, and preserved as a specimen of the residence enjoyed by our first parents." We can gather no reminiscences of this gifted minister, whose stay terminated at the succeeding Conference.

CHAPTER XIX.

(1810—1820).

"Take heed that ye despise not one of these little ones."
—MATT. xviii., 10.

"Even so it is not the will of your Father which is in
heaven, *that one of these little ones should perish.*"—MATT.
xviii., 14.

WE now approach the period when Sabbath-schools were
first opened by the Wesleyans in this Island. Nothing can
be more clear than that it is the will of God that man
should "multiply, and replenish the earth;" and that if he
multiply the nations without "increasing the joy," the
cause must be sought in the wickedness of the people. And,
without doubt, one chief cause of that wickedness will be
found to be ignorance,—that "lack of knowledge" which
is the alleged reason why the people "perish." If all
true religion is founded on knowledge, then to expect
religion to flourish in its absence, is as vain as the hope of
reaping a harvest on ground which has never been sown
with seed. "The genial fount of maternal nourishment,"
as Dr. Hamilton expresses it, "supplies the babe, and
deeply-seated parental love provides for the bodily needs of
children until they can shift for themselves." But there is
not the same universal and natural provision for their
intellectual and spiritual necessities. The pressing instant
demands of the animal man are met, but the higher hidden

man of the heart and intellect is too often neglected, and suffered to run wild in ignorance and sin. In thousands of instances parents were—and still are, alas!—incapacitated to meet these demands of their offspring. This was too generally the case with the poorer classes, and where they were massed together in crowded cities and towns, revolting scenes of ignorance, poverty, and squalid wretchedness, crime, and woe, met the eye. These frightful evils were beginning to create alarm in thoughtful minds: they beheld them growing with the rapid increase of the population, and the conviction could not be resisted that these degraded multitudes were on an inclined plane, and were slowly but surely gliding down to deeper depths of infamy, misery, and ruin.

To cope with these evils,—to overtake these outspreading waves of depraved social life,—to arrest the progress of ignorance and crime, and to impart the knowledge of divine truth, and thus lay the foundation of religion and morality —was, and still is, the object and design of Sabbath-schools. That these valuable institutions have not accomplished all that was fondly hoped, is admitted,—and this admission will apply to other philanthropic agencies,—yet their utility and importance cannot be over-estimated.

To the Wesleyans belong the honour of establishing one of the first Sabbath-schools in the Isle of Wight. They are now found in almost every village in the Island. The first Wesleyan Sabbath-school was commenced in Newport in 1810. It was organized at a meeting held on the 29th of November. It consisted of the following office-bearers and teachers:—Mr. Yelf, Superintendent; Mr. Wavell, treasurer. Committee: Messrs. R. Yelf, R. Bull, and T. Trimen, with the Superintendent Minister. Teachers: Male—Messrs. James Cass, H. Haydon, John Trimen, and Timothy Trimen ; females—Mrs. Cardy, Mesdames Sophia Denton, — Matthews, Sarah Denton, M. Salter, E. Taylor, and M. Denton.

Ninety children were received at the opening of the school—50 boys and 40 girls. A library was opened at an early period for the use of teachers and scholars. The school was at first conducted in the new chapel, Pyle-street, then in the old chapel, Town Lane, which, having been sold, was at first rented, and finally re-purchased and fitted up for more convenient use. During the time that it was out of the hands of the Wesleyans, it was used for various purposes. For a while it was occupied by the Baptists, and the baptistry which they constructed in front of the pulpit remains concealed by a trap-door to this day.

In 1834 Messrs. W. B. and Joseph Groves were elected to the offices of Superintendents of the School, which they filled with credit to themselves and advantage to the Institution for many years. On their recent retirement a very handsome copy of the Word of God was presented to each of them by the teachers, as a memento of the affectionate esteem in which they were held. Messrs. J. Deacon and J. Camp are the present Superintendents; and Mr. Robert Bull, the grandson of Mr. Robert Bull so often named in our history, is its efficient secretary and librarian.

Other schools have been opened at successive dates, in various parts of the Island, and there are now in the two circuits about 800 scholars and 150 teachers.

The Rev. William Baker—who, it will be remembered, was stationed at Cowes—was followed by the Rev. Jonathan Roberts, who was appointed to the Island as its Home Missionary in 1810. On entering on his work he seems to have adopted a method very similar to that which is practised by our present noble staff of Home Missionaries. He drew out a Plan which took in a new field of labour; and, at the same time, engaged a fresh band of spiritual husbandmen, in the form of exhorters. The subjoined are the names of the places and the persons entered on the first Plan :—

PLACES.	HOURS.	EXHORTERS.
Winston	2½	J. Roberts, Missionary.
Brading	2½ & 5½	J. Wickenden.
Forest Side	2½	R. Shepherd.
Haven Street	2½	B. Exton.
Sandown	2½	J. Pinhorn.
Nettlecomb		C. Stamp.
		J. Wheeler. T. Trimen.

Such of these as can are desired to meet at 7 o'clock in the morning at Capt. Drake's.

Such is the request placed at the foot of the Plan. This early meeting was held daily, the time being occupied in prayer, consultation, and reporting progress. Capt. Drake resided in the old chapel-house, Town Lane. His widow is still living at Winchester, and is now in her 90th year.

Out of the above-named places, Winston, Brading, Forest-side, and Nettlecomb, proved failures. It is true that at Brading there was a Society in 1815 of ten members, but in the following year it was, for some cause or other, abandoned. At Nettlecomb also there was a class of thirteen members, which were under the care of James

Wood, of Godshill, but this place was likewise given up. If chapels had been erected in these villages, it is probable we should have been able to chronicle a widely different result.

While one of the new band of exhorters was addressing his congregation at the latter-named place, a number of persons came from the adjoining village of Whitwell, and fastened the door on the outside, while one of them climbed on to the roof and stopped the chimney, so that the congregation were nearly suffocated with smoke before they could make their escape. J. Kirkpatrick, Esq., of Newport, banker and magistrate, took the case up, and compelled the offenders to ask pardon and engage to keep the peace in future, which they accordingly did.

Haven Street was permanently occupied, and is now a part of the Ryde Circuit. In 1813 there was a Society consisting of seven members : William Denham, Hannah Denham, James Barlow, J. Broomfield, M. Broomfield, A. Griffin, and J. Griffin. The preaching was at the cottage of James Broomfield.

A new chapel was opened in 1833. The total cost was £160, and the subscriptions and collections £70. It was said at the time that the inhabitants, "who are generally poor, were liberally assisted by several members of the Established Church, who followed the noble example set them by their excellent clergyman." This little church was afterwards, for some years, under the care of Mr. Wm. B. Groves, of Newport, who showed his love to the good cause by going weekly a distance of five miles to meet the class there.

The next name on the Home Mission Plan is Sandown, which has since risen into considerable importance as a watering-place. The completion of the railways from Newport and Ryde to Ventnor will yield advantages and give an additional stimulus to this rapidly improving place. The town is exposed in winter, but as a summer residence it has many advantages. It is pleasantly situated in the deepest part of a fine semi-circular bay, which stretches from Luccombe Chine to Culver Cliffs; while

> " The gentle South, with kisses smooth and soft,
> Doth in her bosom breathe, and seems to court her oft."

Its extensive sands afford delightful facilities for bathers, and a healthy play-ground for the young. Twenty-five years ago the population amounted to but a few hundreds; now it is but little short of 2,000.

No sooner was preaching commenced than a blessed work of grace broke out, and eighteen persons were united in Church fellowship. Their names were William Mundell (leader), Mary Gilchrist, Hannah Stimbleton, Mary Milbourne, John Collins, Grace Gilchrist, Elizabeth Gray, Joseph Milbourne, Elizabeth Oubridge, John King, Mary Boyce, Sarah Pridmore, Elizabeth Walker, John Ward, John Lambert, Ann Lambert, Mary Ward, and William Knapp. For some years the Society held its meetings in a cottage; but in the year 1816 they were, by the favour of Divine Providence, placed in more comfortable circumstances. During that year Mr. William Thompson, of London, who was studying for clerical orders, came to recruit his health on the Island, and took up his abode at Sandown. Piously disposed, and there being no services connected with the Established Church in the place, he found his way to the Methodist meeting. He seems to have been both delighted and profited, and he soon threw his heart and soul into the promotion of the Methodist cause in Sandown. He was not only a diligent attendant on the public and private means of grace, but he also sought to extend the work of God by his example and large liberality. By his personal efforts the Sabbath-school was originated and supported, and the school-room built, towards which he subscribed the handsome sum of £50. This school-room was also used for preaching. Mr. Trimen was the Superintendent of the School for many years. For a series of those years he walked every Sabbath-day from Newport to Sandown and back, a distance of at least sixteen miles, to discharge the duties of his office. One of the early and principal members of Society was the wife of one of the men belonging to the Royal Artillery, and who, by the permission of Sir William Wynn, had the privilege of entertaining the preachers at the Castle.

Henry Jackman, who succeeded W. Mundell in the office of class-leader, was a highly respected local preacher. Henry was an original both in style and manner. He was a servant, and had the charge of his master's horses, and was allowed to leave home but once a fortnight on the Sabbath. His master, who was a rigid churchman, was induced by some means to become a hearer of the despised Methodists. On entering the chapel he found, to his great surprise, his own carter in the pulpit. The word found its way to his heart, and the master became like-minded with his servant. He joined the Society, and henceforth they walked to the house of God in company. Henry could now not only go out every Sabbath, but when his preaching duties called him far from home a horse was provided for his use. He was preaching at Ventnor on one occasion, and had to make a collection for Bembridge chapel, when he observed, in his own peculiar way, "I am not much of a beggar, that is for money; I can better beg for grace." Messrs. Chapel and Westhead, from Manchester, were among his hearers, and it is said liberally aided the collection.

A comparatively new chapel has been erected in Sandown, but it is not, in more respects than one, suitable to the place. There is a demand for a new one which, for architectural design, accommodation, and situation, shall be better adapted to the claims of this beautiful watering-place. We are glad to hear, as we write, that these objects are likely to be accomplished. The importance of this will appear when it is known that Sandown is a favourite resort of foreigners of rank, especially Russians, Poles, and Germans, and who sometimes find their way into the Wesleyan chapel. Let us record an instance: it will encourage those who are making watering-places an object of special attention; and will shew that their liberality has not been barren of results. Shortly after last Conference, a German lady found her way, on the Sabbath evening, to the little Methodist chapel, and was deeply affected under the word. On the following day, as she was standing on the platform, waiting to take her departure by the train, she observed the Rev. J. M. Morrill, to whom, at first in broken English, and then—on finding that Mr. M. under-

stood her—in her own native German, with deep emotion
told him how her heart was broken under the word preached
by him on the preceding evening. She told him that she
was a countess, residing at L——, and how gladly she
would, on her return, open her house for preaching by the
Wesleyan missionaries in that country. It is remarkable
that our missionaries there have been endeavouring, for
years past, to effect an entrance into that very town, but in
vain. We trust we shall hear of this hopeful convert
again.

At the Conference of 1811, the Isle of Wight was once
more enrolled on the list of circuits. It was thus thrown
on its own resources, and had thenceforward to maintain an
independent position. Previous to the division, the ministers who resided at Portsmouth were one fortnight a month
on the Island. They came to Newport on the Saturday,
preached there on the Sabbath and on the Monday evening,
at Cowes on Tuesday, Wootton on Wednesday, Rookley on
Thursday, and Godshill on Friday; returning to Newport
on Saturday, where they preached on the second Sabbath
and again on Monday, at Cowes on Tuesday, and at Ryde
on Thursday. "This," says Jonathan Barker, in his instructions to his successor, "is the plan for the present.
If the circuit should be divided, the plan must be altered,
and several of the places must have preaching once a-week
instead of once a fortnight, and the mission ground must,
in part, be taken into the regular circuit. Mr. Roberts will
leave a plan of the mission ground."

In the same instructions there is a statement of the
amount of Wesleyan literature in monthly circulation in

the circuit, which is highly suggestive:—"About one hundred take the sixpenny Magazine, and about the same take the shilling number. I publish them in the chapel, and they come for them into the vestries." Seventy-five of the above periodicals were sent to the Island. At the same time there were twenty-four subscribers for Wesley's Works, twenty-three for Dr. Clarke's Bible, and twenty-five for Joseph Benson's Commentary on the Old and New Testament.

It is our impression, that not one-third of the above periodical literature would be found in circulation on the same ground at this day; while scarcely a fraction of Wesley's, Clarke's, and Benson's works are called for; but the place of this sound, healthy, religious literature is supplied by publications of a far lighter and unsubstantial nature, in which there is a large mixture of Calvinism on the one hand, and a loose sort of teaching on the other,—a northern importation, which makes no account of that "godly sorrow unto repentance which needeth not to be repented of." This is a serious evil, and we fear it will be difficult to supply an antidote.

There were more than eighty subscribers to the Preachers' Fund, whose various subscriptions amounted to £42 3s. 6d. Owing to the fact, of which Mr. Henshaw complains, that Mr. Barker did not insert any of his collections in the proper circuit-book, we are unable to give the amount of the other circuit contributions to the various Connexional Funds for that year; but for the preceding year (1809) they stand thus:—Missions, £50 7s.; Kingswood, £35 9s.; yearly collection, £32 12s.

There was no difficulty in dividing the circuit. This was already done geographically by the Solent Sea. By this division, ten places remained in the parent circuit, and fourteen in the Island. The former were Portsea, Portsmouth, Gosport, Fratton, Tipner, Stamshaw, Portchester, Hardway, Stubbington, and Funtly. In the Island there were Newport, Cowes, St. Helens, Ryde, Wootton-bridge, Rookley, Godshill, Bembridge, Sandown, Merston, Winston, Forest-side, Haven Street, and Nettlestone.

The following was the division of the local preachers. There remained on the Portsmouth Plan, Messrs. Etheridge, Thompson, Taylor, Whiston, Legg, Silk, Dorey, Kilpin, Johnson, Leggatt, Knight, Mead, and King. On the Newport Plan there were Messrs. Bull, Yelf, Wallbridge, Hill, Whitehorn, Shepherd, Exton, Pinhorn, Trimen, Stamp, Wheeler, and Wadmore.

It is worthy of remark that out of the above names two still remain—Messrs. James Pinhorn and Timothy Trimen—the former in his eighty-fourth year, and the latter nearly four-score. They are both remarkably hale and active, being able to take two full services on the Lord's day, and walk several miles to and from their appointments.

The cottage now standing on the South side of the old chapel was the preacher's house. It was part of the Trust property, and was furnished for the Superintendent, at a cost of £47 17s. 6d. Portsmouth contributed £21 2s. 4d., and Newport the remainder.

At the September Quarterly Meeting, held immediately after the division of the Circuit, the number and income of each place in the Island was as subjoined :—

PLACES.	NUMBERS.	INCOME.
Newport	98	£4 18 0
Cowes	32	1 12 0
Wootton	29	1 9 0
Rookley	10	10 0
Godshill	20	15 0
Ryde	10	10 0
St. Helens	20	1 0 0
Bembridge	10	10 0
Sandown	16	11 0
	245	£11 15 0

The Superintendent received £7 12s. 9d., and his colleague, £5 11s. 7d. At the December Quarterly Meeting, Richard Shepherd was passed, and recomended as a suitable candidate for the Wesleyan Ministry. At the ensuing Conference he was appointed to the Norwich Circuit; he discharged his ministerial duties with acceptance for a period of thirty-three years, and then departed to be with Christ.

It is rather singular that the first three christian names on the new plan should be the same, Robert Bull, Robert Yelf, and Robert Wallbridge; their excellent characters, and the good service which they most cheerfully rendered for a long series of years to the cause of God, are too important to allow them to be passed over with only a cursory glance, their names must be written for ever amongst the pioneers and founders of our churches in this Island; the latter has been noticed in a preceding page, the two former may find a not unsuitable niche here.

Robert Bull was converted while yet a youth at Rookley. The circumstances have been already narrated. Shortly after that event he began to give a word of exhortation. Possessing

a good understanding and a ready utterance, he met
with encouragement, and soon became an accredited local
preacher. The firmness of moral principle by which his
whole life was characterised, was evinced by him at the very
onset. He was a carpenter by trade, and was at the time
working at the house of a lady at Shide. It is well known
that it used to be the custom at a certain stage of a building
to dispense intoxicating liquors freely, and many yielded
to intemperance. Without the slightest hesitation, and in de-
spite of the boisterous taunts, and ridicule of his fellow-
workmen, he declined joining in the festivity, fearing to
give countenance to other men's sins. The satisfaction which
he felt in having gained a moral victory was afterwards
disconcerted, at least for a moment, when as he was on his
way home he unexpectedly met the lady of the house who
had provided the sumptuous feast, and who, surprised at his
strange conduct in leaving it, promptly demanded the reason.
Young Bull felt he was doing right, and neither his fortitude
nor his good sense forsook him. His modest, but firm and
sensible answers, not only satisfied the lady, but drew forth
her full commendation.

Shortly after the termination of his apprenticeship he
removed to Brierton, then in the Oxford circuit. Here he
found himself almost alone, and there was no public service
of the Methodists in the neighbourhood. He at once
opened a room, and commenced preaching on a Sabbath
evening. It speaks well for the native talent and zeal of
this raw country youth—for such he was at that time—to
find that the place was crowded, and that the Baptist and
Independent Ministers were at times among his hearers.

He was encouraged by the counsel and approval of the Rev. Richard Reece, who was then a young man travelling in the Oxford circuit. Mr. Bull's labours were extended to the surrounding villages, and he was cheered by seeing sinners converted to God. During his stay at Brierton, he married Miss Durley, his master's sister, who had given herself to God and to his people at the age of seventeen. It is said of her that, for the space of thirty-five years, she adorned her Christian profession by "walking within her house with a perfect heart," by attending upon the Lord in the ordinances of his Church, and by a constant exercise of benevolence towards the sick and the poor. She died in peace, Oct. 1st, 1827.

In 1795 the Society at Rookley were rejoiced to receive Mr. Bull once more as a resident amongst them. At that time, it will be remembered, the circuit was wide, and many places were remote from Rookley, and much pioneering work had to be done in breaking up new ground. From this toil Mr. Bull did not shrink, and had his full share of long walks and hard fare, having, in some of the more distant places, neither a crust of bread nor a drink of water offered him, so that he and his brethren were compelled to wander fasting in the fields and lanes, and sometimes they were more roughly handled by the baser sort.

About 1800 Mr. Bull removed to Newport, where he found a large field for usefulness. He was appointed general Society Steward for the Island; and, up to the time when the Isle of Wight became a circuit, he was in all weathers found at the Portsmouth Quarterly Meeting, the esteemed and faithful representative of this part of the circuit. On the division of the circuit, he was chosen as one of its Stewards, an office which he continued to fill until 1831.

In the winter of 1828 he caught a severe cold, while taking an appointment in the country, from which his hitherto vigourous constitution never fully rallied. His ardour carried him through his public duties, but amid much pain and suffering, until the year 1833, when he was again prostrated by affliction; and although he so far rallied as to be able to preach, yet his strength was evidently failing, and his work nearly done. He preached his last sermon at Cowes, 14th Feb., 1836, from that appropriate text, Heb. iv., 9. He entered the pulpit to preach again in the evening, but he could not go through the service, and was led with difficulty to the house of his youngest daughter, Mrs. C. Pinhorn, where he lingered five or six weeks, a great sufferer, but peacefully resting on Jesus. An interesting interview took place at this time. His old friend and fellow-labourer Robert Wallbridge called to see him. For nearly 50 years they had travelled together in the way to Zion, and for more than 46 years they had laboured together for the glory of God, and the weal of their fellow Islanders. They had been permitted to witness great conflicts, and now these two veterans meet once more as they stand on the verge of the battle-field. The shades of evening are thickening around them both; the valley is at their feet, and the land of promise and rest is right a-head in full view. Listen! Rejoicing in hope of the glory of God, his friend said, "You are going home before me." "Brother Wallbridge," rejoined the dying veteran, "you must not envy me my happiness." That happiness was consummated on the 25th March, 1836, when he departed this life in his 67th year.

The esteem in which Mr. Bull was held was shown by the respect which was paid him by persons of every Christian denomination and rank of life. His intellect was vigorous, and his mind well stored with religious knowledge. His Christian course was undeviating. Like Paul he could say, " This *one* thing I do." He was one that ruled well his own house, and had the happiness of seeing his four children united with the church of his choice, and his two sons leaders and local preachers. Possessing a sound judgment, and great urbanity of spirit, he filled various offices in the Church with great acceptance and success, and was ever looked upon as a pillar in the house of God.

He was a superior class-leader, and a useful visitor of the sick, but it was as a local preacher that he excelled most. He stood at the head of that very useful body of men, whose self-denying labours so greatly contributed to the spread of the rising cause in these parts. When it is remembered that for 49 years he laboured without intermission, walked thousands of miles, and maintained an unblemished character; and that his preaching and conversation were the means of good to many, both saint and sinner, it will be seen that the high commendation awarded him was not undeserved. The memory of this good man is fragrant with the manifold virtues of a long and useful life; and, though he has long slept in the grave, still—

> " The sweet remembrance of the just,
>   Like a green root, revives and bears
>   A train of blessings for their heirs,
> When dying nature sleeps in dust."

His widow (he was twice married) survived him eleven years, except one day, when she died in the rapturous hope of joining her friends above.

This good man's character is thus briefly but ably drawn by Dr. Etheridge, who had every opportunity of forming a true judgment, having met in his class for a number of years :—" This well-tried servant of Jesus Christ was a pillar and ornament in the church. He knew and made known the saving and elevating power of divine grace, and showed in his own example how practicable and pleasant it is, when faithful to it, to be not slothful in business, yet fervent in spirit, serving the Lord. As a leader, he had one of the most choice and amiable classes I ever met with. I had the privilege of being a member of it some years, and shall retain evermore the memory of the good lessons we used to derive from his sagacious and faithful counsels. But it was as a preacher he was best known and respected in the Island. His well-tried character, his somewhat clerical appearance, and, shall I say, gentlemanly deportment, contributed to give him weight as a public teacher. He was a man of extensive reading, a healthy, clear thinker, gifted with a good address, and, above all, with the unction of the Holy Spirit of God. So, though he never sought ' popularity,' he was always ' popular,'—not for a transient hour, but for the lapse of numerous years. This was the case, not only in the rural congregations, but in the towns of the Island. I remember ' when Mr. Bull preached' in

Newport the congregation was generally larger than at other times, and sometimes attended by persons who belonged to the aristocracy of the town, including gentlemen of the medical and legal professions. But none of these flattering circumstances disturbed the uniform sobriety and meekness of his temper, for God had given him not only the spirit of power, but of love and a sound mind.

Of Robert Yelf our notice, for want of material, must necessarily be more brief. He wrote much, but, unfortunately, for some reason or other, he destroyed his numerous papers and diary. It is said that he preached his first sermon at Haven Street about 1790, and his last at Freshwater in 1855. He came to his grave in a full age, like a shock of corn cometh in his season, being summoned to his reward in his eighty-fifth year.

Happily we are able to present an exceedingly graphic sketch of this venerable man, from the pen of Dr. Etheridge, who, as it will be seen, knew him well, and says of him that he was "a man of similar temper" to Messrs. Bull and Wallbridge, "though he excelled his companions in literary acquisitions. The greater part of his long life was devoted to the attainment and communication of knowledge, as a teacher of the young, and an able preacher of the Word of God. When I first became intimate with him, he was a bachelor approaching sixty years of age, with white short-cut hair, a shaven face which wore the physiognomy of a Roman Catholic Abbé, and a long brown surtout, his invariable garb. He lived aloft, in a remote room of a large old-fashioned house, near the church. The apartment was lined with books, about one-

half of them in the French language. He could read the
Greek Testament, and had some acquaintance with Hebrew
and Latin; but his great delight was to explore the treasures
of French theological literature, both Catholic and Protestant. I spent two afternoons a-week with him steadily
for four years, in the course of which we read the works of
some of our great English Divines, among whom I remember Stillingfleet's ' Origines,' Gale's ' Court of the
Gentiles,' and Cudworth's 'Intellectual System of the
Universe;' and these were intermitted with the choicest
pieces of Bourdalone, Masillon, Bossuet, and that too little
known, but magnificent Protestant preacher, Du Bose. I
possess, as a purchase from Mr. Yelf, the works of the Port
Royalist Nicolle, in twenty delicious little volumes, in old
dark gilded calf. He made me, too, some costly presents,
among which I prize Du Pin's 'Library of Ecclesiastical
Authors,' in 16 volumes quarto. Next to Adam Clarke's
work, his favourite commentary was that of Calmet, of
which he had a fine copy in nine tall folios. Mr. Yelf was
a purely extempore preacher, having written scarcely a
sermon in his life; but his discourses were rich in material,
and delivered with a tone of authority which bespoke the
strength of his own convictions, and often brought the
truth with greater power to the minds of his hearers. When
a middle-aged man, Dr. Coke set his eyes upon him as a
desirable missionary for Gibraltar; but he preferred to live
and labour on in the sphere in which Heaven had first cast
his lot. He worthily fulfilled the task, and went to his
reward."

Two years after the Isle of Wight was made a circuit, the ministerial staff was reduced to two. It seems difficult to account for this reduction. It is true there had been a decrease of twenty-eight members during the year, still, the circuit was twelve in advance of what it was at the start. The ministers in the circuit this year were Josiah Goodwin and John Rigg, both men of "superior intelligence and information." Mr. Rigg was appointed to the Island for the benefit of his health, which had been severely tried by a bronchial affection which had laid him aside during a considerable part of the preceding year. In an edifying memoir of him, inserted in the *Methodist Magazine* for 1859, by his son, the Rev. J. H. Rigg, it is said that "he passed a very happy year in this lovely island, which, as he once wrote to one of his sons, 'seemed at that time, to his young eyes, an earthly Paradise.'" Mr. Rigg's health was established, and he lived to labour in many of the most important circuits in our Connexion.

During one of the years passing under review in this chapter, the Rev. E. B. Lloyd was stationed in the Isle of Wight. He was then a young man, but his ministry was weighty and effective. But his career was short, being brought to a sudden and painful termination by the upsetting of the coach by which he was travelling from Halifax, in company with several other ministers, to the Sheffield Conference in 1823. This melancholy event took place on Monday, Aug. 23, at Shelly Bank, six miles from Huddersfield, when "the coach was overturned, and the passengers were laid prostrate on the ground in awful and agonizing confusion." Many were severely hurt, and the injuries sustained by Mr. Lloyd and the Rev. G. Sargent proved fatal. The latter died on the Wednesday, and the former, after lingering another week in great bodily pain, but joyous in spirit, followed his fellow-sufferer to that better land where there is no physical or moral ill. *

In 1814-15, Carisbrook and Shalfleet were taken on the Circuit Plan, and Societies were raised in each of them. At the Conference of 1815 there were ten members returned for Carisbrook. Carisbrook was transferred to Gunville. At first, Mr. Wickenden, of Newport, led the class; then William Salter; and, when John Wheeler came to reside at Gunville, it was placed under his care. A chapel was erected in 1816.

The cause at Shalfleet owes its origin to Mr. Hollis, the father of Mr. James Hollis, of Cowes, and Mrs. James Bull, of Newport. On his removal from Chessel Farm to Shalfleet, he opened his house for preaching, and a small Society was gathered into church fellowship. The first recorded names were William Cotton, Leader, George Arnold, Ann Hollis, Thomas Gill, and James Gubbins. In 1860 Sir John Simeon generously gave a piece of ground, in a very eligible situation, for a new chapel. The foundation-stone was laid by Mrs. C. Dore, of Newport, and an exceedingly pretty little Gothic building was erected. It was opened by the Rev. John Rattenbury. The chapel is too slightly built, and does not stand the action of the weather well.

In the year 1818, Messrs. Charles Pinhorn and James Hollis established a Sabbath School at Northwood. At

* See Wes. Meth. Mag., 1824, pp. 73—78.

first they rented a cottage ; but this was so crowded with children that they found it necessary to secure better accommodation. It was therefore resolved to build a chapel, that, while the youth of the place were taught to read the Word of God, the adults might also hear the Gospel. The chapel was opened in 1820, and in 1822 there was one member in Society and six " on trial."

During the time that the Rev. Robert Wheeler was the Superintendent of the Circuit, Mr. William Galpine joined the Society in Newport, and became a member of Mr. Wittington's class. He was remarkable for his attachment to the means of grace, especially the 7 o'clock prayer-meeting on the Lord's-day morning ; and it was while he was in the act of preparing for this early meeting, that he was suddenly called to enter the heavenly Sabbath and join in nobler praise.

CHAPTER XX.

(1820—1825.)

> " The genial showers those spiritual clouds do yield
>   Enrich them with new beauty, like a field
>   Which God hath blessed,—oh ! 'tis exceeding sweet
>   When humble hearts and heavenly truths do meet."

In noting the different stages of progress which the cause
has made in the Island, we are struck with the fact that,
for the first thirty years, it was confined exclusively to the
town of Newport. Up to that time the Society was poor
and feeble, kind and loving, but destitute of men of gifted
mind and enterprise; or, so expansive was the revival, that
it must have radiated to surrounding places at an earlier
period. But, if we come down the stream of our history,
and allow a still longer space to pass under review, we
shall meet with what may seem, at first sight, a startling
fact—that, after Methodism had been in the Island more
than seventy years, with one solitary exception, it had not
made a single permanent conquest west of Newport. That
exception was Shalfleet. It is true there had been an
attempt to establish a cause both at Newtown and Youngwoods, but preaching had not, from different reasons, been
continued in either. Two things may partly account for
this. The first is, the connection of Newport with Portsmouth necessarily brought the preachers into contact with

the population to the east of the Island, which lies between those two places, and would, at the same time, take off their attention from the population lying westward. Another reason will be found in the distance between the villages in that direction, and the state of the roads. Long after John Wesley and his preachers first came to the Isle of Wight, the highways were in a very primitive state, and the passage of a four-wheel carriage through a village was quite an event. Historians tell us that little more than a century ago there was but one four-wheel chaise kept at Newport for the whole Island, and that the owner walked at his horse's head, leading it by a leather strap attached to the bridle. It will occasion no surprise that, years afterwards, such vehicles were few in number, when we learn that the roads were obstructed by an almost innumerable number of gates, there being, according to the testimony of Hassell, " 52 between Newport and Yarmouth, 50 between Freshwater and St. Catherine's, and 35 between Ryde and Ventnor;" at the same time we have seen what a wretched plight they were in when Mr. Crabb was prosecuting his laborious mission close upon the beginning of the present century.

The Revds. James Sydserff and John Brown were the first to occupy this new ground permanently. For this purpose the circuit provided a horse and gig. Five new places were opened to the west—Yarmouth, Freshwater, Calbourne, Yafford, and Brixton ; and three to the eastward—Newchurch, Hale Common, and Wroxall.

Yarmouth—or "Eremouth" as it was called in days of yore—is situated at the mouth of the river Yar. It is ten miles west of Newport, and five east of the Needles. It was twice reduced to ashes by the French. Before that time, it derived considerable importance from the number of coasting vessels by which it was frequented ; but since then it has had to yield the palm to Cowes, which has risen to a more important position. Although it enjoyed the privilege of returning two members to Parliament, from the reign of Edward I. down to the time when the Reform Bill came into operation, it is doubtful whether the population ever exceeded 600 ; and even now, notwithstanding many improvements, it does not reach 700.

At the time when our history commences—now about half-a-century ago—the population consisted mainly, as it had for ages back, of sea-faring people, said to be a "hardy, skilful set of seamen, not surpassed in these qualities by any of the sons of Neptune who live in this sea-girt Isle." They are found in command of noble merchant ships, and many of the white winged fleets of yachts for which the Solent is so celebrated have won their fame under the guidance of Yarmouth men. But at the time when Methodism secured a hold in the town, many of its inhabitants, in common with their fellow Islanders, followed the hazardous employment of smuggling. Many a thrilling narrative of hair-breadth escapes from dangers by land and perils on the deep, are still told by grey-haired veterans, who have since then sought the true riches, and who, embarked in the Gospel ship, are steadily sailing towards their "desired haven."

Yarmouth, as we have seen, was favoured for a brief space with the ministry of those two distinguished men—

John Wesley and Thomas Coke. "It is an ill wind that blows no man favour:" the unpropitious winds detained them in Yarmouth Roads as they were on their way to Guernsey, and the Islanders reaped the benefit, for, during the delay, they preached four times. What results followed those powerful appeals, the great day alone will reveal. It was thirty-five years before the inhabitants of Yarmouth were again favoured with the regular ministry of the Wesleyan Methodists.

Some six or seven years previous to the introduction of regular preaching, a solitary light had been shining in this dark and spiritually destitute place. Mrs. Mary Coward, an old Methodist who had been residing in the chapel-house at Bristol, and had often waited on John Wesley, and knew well the old preachers who were stationed in that city, came to reside at Yarmouth. On her arrival, she found no dissenting place of worship, and only one service on the Sabbath at church. This good woman resolved not to hide her light under a bushel, and, having by diligent search found out those who had a desire for salvation, began a prayer-meeting at the cottage of Mrs. Kent, High-street. These sheep were as yet without a shepherd: still they were not altogether destitute of the word of life, for a local preacher of the name of Whitehorn, who travelled with books, on his periodical calls at Yarmouth, preached at Mrs. Kent's. Persecution raged, but Mrs. Coward held on her way, and soon met with encouragement. Amongst the few who attended the meetings at the cottage, might have been seen a youth of tender frame, but serious in his deportment. George Arnold—a name intimately associated with

the foaming waves below, which rush, as if in maddened anger, against the mighty cliffs which for ages past have stood like majestic bulwarks to defend the shores of the "Garden Isle." It is a grand sight to stand in the fort directly over the Needles, at an elevation of 240 feet, and gaze upon the noble vessels as they dash full sail through the narrow and dangerous opening beneath. Freshwater contains a numerous but very scattered population. The church, which from days of yore was the only place of worship, is situated at one extremity of the parish, and is inconveniently distant from the principal portion of the inhabitants, who were, within the memory of the living, as low in their morals and as much addicted to smuggling and kindred vices as those of any other part of the Island.

Some years before Methodism became established in Freshwater—for its early efforts had left no trace behind—a burning and shining light had been seen, like a solitary star in the darkness of night. This was Mrs. Mitchell, of Norton Cottage. This excellent lady was a member of the Established Church. She was piously disposed, and was deeply affected at the spiritual destitution of the neighbourhood. Extremely diffident and retiring in her disposition, she began her philanthropic efforts by collecting the children of the poor for instruction. This excellent lady thus took the first step in a path of usefulness, the length and breadth of which she had not then the faintest idea. The mothers of the children begged to attend with an importunity that she could not withstand, and an afternoon was set apart for them weekly : thus did Mrs. Mitchell actually begin a "Mother's Meeting" before the recent efforts which have made them so popular. While visiting Bath for the benefit of her failing health, she, with her husband, entered Argyle Chapel by mistake, and, although their church prejudices were at first shocked by the absence of the prayer-book, yet the service left a deep impression on their minds. Afterwards they heard Dr. Styles, of Brighton, and Mrs. Mitchell was recommended by him to call upon the Rev. Daniel Tyerman, minister of the Independent Chapel, Node-hill, Newport. By his recommendation, and for their own protection, they licensed their house for preaching. Results followed, such as Mrs. Mitchell had never anticipated, and from which, could she have foreseen them, her sensitive nature would have shrunk. Hitherto she had conducted her meetings in a way which was strictly private; indeed she had locked the door of the hall, and steadily refused admission to the members of her own family. Now, to her dismay, she saw the hall, drawing-room, parlour, kitchen, and every available spot crowded with people who had come from far and near. To attempt to speak to such a multitude seemed impossible ; and she would probably have shrunk from the cross but for her husband, who encouraged her, and promised to stand by her and give out the hymns. This devoted woman believed the call to be providential, and with much trembling, but humble dependence on Divine help, obeyed. God blessed her efforts; crowds continued to come, and not a few found the word as expounded by her to be the "power of God unto salvation." At the same time, while she believed that the extreme ignorance and the spiritual famine which her neighbours were suffering justified this attempt to deal out the bread of life, she often remarked that she was no precedent for others. This extraordinary conduct alarmed the genteel circles with which Mr. and Mrs. Mitchell had hitherto lived on terms of intimacy, and he was warned by them that if he did not put a veto upon the actions of his wife they would "cut" them both. To his honour be it recorded that he nobly stood by his lady, and bravely bore the obloquy and insult which his firmness brought upon him. For seven years the threat was carried out, and their old friends passed them by without the slightest recognition. It is a pleasant thing, however, to be able to state that Mr. and Mrs. Mitchell outlived prejudice without the sacrifice of Christian principle, and regained universal respect and esteem.

Mrs. Mitchell soon discovered the Christian worth of Mrs. Coward, of Yarmouth, and received her into her own household, where she became her almoner to the poor, and daily gave out medicine from the Dispensary which Mrs. Mitchell had opened, for, at that time, there was not a medical man in the whole of that part of the Island. Although their circumstances were so different, yet in spirit were they so truly one that those godly women met in "band" daily, and, by exhortation and prayer fanned the flame of love in each other's hearts. They reached a patriarchal age, and died in great peace.

The Wesleyan ministers found the heartiest co-operation from Mr. and Mrs. Mitchell. Their house was always open to them; and Mr. Mitchell gave a suitable site and £10 towards a new chapel, and Mrs. Curry (Mrs. Mitchell's sister) gave the liberal sum of £70. This truly venerable lady still survives, and is just verging on the hundredth year of her age. Her cheerful piety falls like sunlight over the domestic circle, which forms a little church in her own house.

The first cottage in which the Wesleyans preached the Gospel at this period was that of a Mrs. Parkes, an old lady who lived on School Green, not far from the present chapel. The room was small and inconvenient, and the necessity of a larger place of worship was soon felt. Through the liberal gifts already named, and other contributions, a small chapel was erected in 1824. Mr. Arnold acted as the class-leader for some years, and, after his death, Mr. Robert Yelf, of Newport, came to reside at Freshwater, and most efficiently sustained the office till his own decease.

There was a debt of £40 left on the chapel, due to Mrs. Mitchell, which in course of time accumulated to £56, when she and her sister, Mrs. Curry, generously offered £36, if the circuit would raise the remainder, but on the express condition that the surplus income of the chapel be paid every three months to the quarterly meeting. This arrangement is in accordance with the tenure of the trust-deed.

The chapel was re-built in 1860 at a cost of £327, and the entire debt was liquidated at the anniversary in 1864. This important result was greatly aided by the Rev. J. Corbin, of London, who at the preceding annual meeting liberally offered £5, on the condition that the entire debt should be paid in twelve months. The chapel is plain Gothic in style. It is neat and commodious in its arrangement, being capable of seating about 230 persons. At the Conference of 1863 a junior minister was appointed to reside in this populous locality, which presents one of the finest fields in the Island for moral culture.

Chale is a long straggling village, eight miles south of Newport, and the same distance west of Ventnor. Like Gunville and Chillerton, it lies on the old road, along which it is said the ancient tin trade was carried. It is supposed that the ore was brought from Cornwall and North Wales to a point on the coast of Hampshire, and thence in carts across the Solent at low water to the Island, which was crossed by a road leading from Gurnard Bay, through Rew-street, Gunville, Chillerton, and Chale, to Puckaster, whence it was shipped to Marseilles in Gaul.

The village of Chale commences at Blackgang Chine, and extends in a north-westerly direction, a distance of two miles. We must not, however, pass on to our more immediate object without a passing glance at the celebrated Chine which attracts so many visitors to this part of the coast. Blackgang (the *black way*) is said to be the most famous curiosity in the Island ; but we cannot help thinking it is somewhat over-done in the "Guide books." It is a bare bleak cavity, cut by the action of two streams deep into St. Catherine's Hill. Perhaps the best view is about half-way down, where you stand amid bare and bleak chasms of dark-brown rock and sand, with the boundless ocean in front. "There is neither tree nor shrub ; no bright masses of foliage relieve its sombre sides ; and on a breezy day, when the south wind brings up the foaming waters with a ' thud ' upon the shore, filling the dark hollow with its echoes, anything more desolate or sorrowful it is impossible to conceive." Blackgang, however, can be seen to perfection only in a storm, when the winds howl up its gaunt sides, and the immense waves, peculiar to this bay, fall on the foot of the cliffs with a roar that can be heard to the very heart of the Island.

William Wheeler, the modest and sensible guide who lives in the "Gang," is a respected member of the Wesleyan Society, and is noted for his humane, brave, and successful endeavours to rescue from a watery grave the numerous persons who have been wrecked in this dangerous spot.

While touching on the natural scenery of the Island there is one of its physical features to which we must give a brief space—its landslips. We cannot enter at length into the subject, and our object will be best served by an abridged description of one which occurred near Blackgang. The whole of a farm called "Pitlands," consisting of 100 acres, was observed to be in motion, and continued so during two days, directing its course towards the sea. The changes which took place on the surface were extremely curious, as there was scarcely a square yard which had not altered its appearance, while rocks and trees were shifted into strange positions, and the whole presented a mass of confusion as great as though it had been convulsed by an earthquake. In one place the fissures nearly swallowed up a beautiful summer cottage, and in others the ground sunk to a depth of over 30 feet. It is supposed that this landslip was caused by the formation of ice in the chasms of the hills, the expansive power of which caused a separation at the base of the cliffs, and consequently the ground above began to move by the force of its own weight, and was only arrested in its further progress by the " stability of a range of hills, which prevented the dreary mass from rushing headlong into the sea." One of our respected local preachers—Mr. Wickens, of Ventnor—on his way to his appointment at Chale, passed over the scene of the above landslip, and found the road all sound and right as he went in the morning, but on his return it had disappeared, and he found great difficulty in picking his way over the broken ground. Another of his brethren was driving over the same spot at the moment when the ground began to give way under him; he struck the horse, and drove for his life. At the distance of a few hundred yards he found the ground firm, and turned to gaze on the scene of ruin which he had left behind; at that moment he beheld an enormous block of solid rock bound from the cliff across the road along which he had come, and imbed itself in an upright position, where it now stands, close by the side of the road from Chale to Niton. It has been computed to weigh 300 tons.

About the year 1822, Mr. Reuben Russell, a member of Society at Newport, but resident at Whippingham, removed to Chale. Here, with the exception of his wife, he was alone, and far from the means of grace. In a short time preaching was commenced at Brixton, four miles distant. Thither he repaired, and as a few began to feel under the Word, they were formed into a class, and placed under his care. Preaching was afterwards given up at Brixton, and Mr. Russell opened his house at Chale about the year 1831. At the same time his hands were strengthened by the union and co-operation of Mr. Henry Morris, of Kingston Farm.

By their joint efforts a second cottage was opened near the green. For some time the Society was stationary, and did not number more than from six to seven persons. It was resolved, however, to erect a chapel, but great difficulties were experienced in the attempt to secure a suitable piece of ground. At length a plot was offered, and the bargain was eagerly struck. The then resident clergyman, who was strongly opposed to the Wesleyans, went the day following to purchase this same piece of ground, but, to his mortification, found that he was one day too late. The chapel was erected in 1833, and opened by the Rev. B. Carvosso. From this time a good work commenced, and in two years the Society increased to twenty-six. Then there was a gradual decline, and in 1840 they were reduced to eight, at which figure they stood for several quarters. But in the spring of 1842 a gracious outpouring of the Spirit took place, and there was a sudden accession of between thirty and forty members. Mr. Henry Morris and Mr. Charles Morris were appointed new leaders, and by the end of the year 1844 they had, including six on trial, no fewer than fifty-five persons in church-fellowship. The chapel has been enlarged, and an adjoining plot of land, with a cottage, has been secured to the trust.

A romantic incident occurred to an inhabitant of this village, which, although it may not strictly belong to the subject of our history, yet we feel sure every loyal-hearted person will pardon us for presenting a fact which is so full of interest, and which reflects the highest honour on the noble personage who acted so prominent a part in it. A poor woman was returning from Newport, carrying her

well-stored market basket and a bundle of birch brooms.
Toiling on beneath her burden, she had nearly reached
Blackwater, when a splendid carriage drawn by four superb
greys, with postillions and footmen in richest livery, overtook her.   The carriage stopped, the footman alighted, and,
opening the carriage door, to her astonishment bade her
enter.   Two ladies occupied the carriage,—one was elderly,
the other was a young and blooming girl.   The poor woman
drew back in bewilderment, but the affable manners of the
ladies, and their kind words, banished her fears, and she
stepped up and took her seat, and the market basket and
the brooms were handed into the carriage after her, and
away the whole party whirled over the hills to Chale, and
quickly reached the market woman's humble dwelling, at
the door of which she and her treasures were set down, and
the carriage soon vanished out of view.   You very naturally
ask, And who were those ladies who stooped to do so rare
an act of kindness ?   It was the late Duchess of Kent,
and her daughter our beloved Queen Victoria.   With such
a training, can we wonder that the Sovereign of these
realms should present so fine an example of domestic
excellencies and practical benevolence, and that she should
always have paid such special attention to the poor ?

In the summer of 1823 the Bryanites—or, as they call
themselves, the "Bible Christians"—found their way to
the Isle of Wight.   This offshoot of Methodism took root
in the West of England, to which it is chiefly confined,
although they have missionaries in Canada, &c.   The
mission to the Island was opened by a Mary Toms, and the
wife of the founder of the Society.   Female preaching

being a novelty, immediately attracted attention, and, after
struggling with some difficulties, they gradually gained
ground.   They were countenanced, entertained, and assisted by members belonging to the Parent Society, until
they began to form societies of their own.   At the end of
two years they reported two hundred persons in membership with them.   According to the report of their last
year's minutes of Conference, they now have in the Island
one circuit (Shanklin), and two Home Mission Stations
(Newport and Ryde, and Yarmouth.)   Their numbers stand
thus :—7 ministers, 23 chapels, 775 members, and 993
Sabbath-school children.   The Primitive Methodists have a
small interest in the Island, but they have been forestalled
by the Bryanites.

The Rev. Thomas Binney was exercising his luminous
ministry in the Independent old Meeting-house, St. James's
Street, Newport, at this period.   His ministry does not,
however, seem to have awakened more than ordinary
interest ; nor did his congregation appear to be aware that
there was in him any very striking indication of future
greatness.   Mr. Binney's stay at Newport was but short.

CHAPTER XXI.

(1825—1835.)

"A story in which native humour reigns,
Is often useful, always entertains."

"The path of bliss abounds with many a snare,
Learning is one, and wit however rare."

THE ministerial staff on the Island for the year 1825 were the Revds. Isaac Phenix, William Hicks, and James Kendall (1st.) The last-named gentleman has given us his impressions of both his circuits and his colleagues, with a humourous description of an adventure in which he himself acted a ludicrous and unministerial part. He says :—
"This charming little island, so deservedly celebrated for its natural beauties and loveliness, was my first circuit. Here I enjoyed myself. Religion flourished among the Wesleyans. No Connexional controversy existed. Ministers and people were of one heart and soul. I walked to the extremities of the Island, in its length and breadth, nine times during the year, in fulfilling my preaching appointments. The Rev. Isaac Phenix was my superintendent; the Rev. William Hicks, my senior colleague. This good man was an amiable curiosity,—singular in his dress and conversation, but a faithful and efficient labourer. In the summer season he would often be attired in nankeen

breeches and sky-blue stockings, a quaker-like coat and waistcoat, straight hair over his forehead, and his countenance betokening a singular mixture of gravity and jocoseness. His preaching was colloquial, and somewhat humourous, but solidly instructive. English grammar, and the niceties of pulpit diction, he seemed to set at defiance. He often quoted blank verse from Young or Milton, or some other of our English poets, but made sad havoc of the quotations by his blundering accent, pronunciation, and emphasis. He was, nevertheless, tolerably popular. He was a working preacher ; no weather, however bad, ever kept him from his appointment. In excessive winter cold and storms he wore an old rough cape coat, exactly like the coats worn by our primitive London watchmen. Studying his own comfort and convenience, he was utterly heedless of the jokes passed upon his dress and appearance. He seemed to have accumulated a good stock of sermons, as he produced considerable variety. Instead of troubling his head with different languages, which so very few preachers learn sufficiently well to turn to any good account in their proper work, he read and studied English divinity, and had evidently well read his bible. Even good scholars, fond of carefulness, accuracy, and elegance in the composition and delivery of sermons, cheerfully put up with the want of these recommendations in the sermons of William Hicks, because they always contained much sound sense, much originality of illustration, and much of direct reference and appeal to the Holy Scriptures. He was a good old man, and has long since gone to his reward.

"In this circuit we had abundance of work, and did it

cheerfully. Very long walks, and very frequent preaching, and a few little hardships now and then in the way of foul weather, and studying in a cold garret without a fire, did us no harm. I found all the people kind, and I love to think of them to this day. Although at that time Methodism and its peculiarities were not so much before the public as they are now, and we had happily less fuss in placarding for anniversary sermons, and almost nothing was said about us in newspapers, and we were content to go on our way unostentatiously; yet we were not altogether despised, even by rank and title. I remember, one lovely afternoon, sitting down to tea on a beautiful lawn at Cowes, in company with the Right Honourable Lady R——, the Right Honourable Mr. R——, and two daughters of Lord O—n, at a Wesleyan Sabbath-school Anniversary Meeting, of which I was chairman. At that time, however, public speech-making was a task and a difficulty, and few excelled in it. My own performance I utterly despised, both at the time and ever after. At that time—oh, happy time!— there was so far from being any restlessness and anxiety to get invitations to public honours in the way of anniversary sermons and addressing public meetings, that we rather shunned and avoided them. We had so much of the regular and ordinary work of an itinerant preaching life to do, and we were so cheerful and happy in doing it, that we had neither inclination nor time for any great and extra doings.

"A good deal of our theological reading and study was carried on in a peripatetic way. We read much in walking; and, as we often went out early on Sunday morning, and did not return till the following Friday night, and could not carry our libraries on our backs, we took one substantial volume—sometimes two—which we could manage to get carefully through before we reached home. I used to rise early, and read and study before breakfast in every place on the circuit as well as at home. At the time I read much, studied hard, walked long journeys, and preached often, I was ever cheerful, but sometimes too frolicsome to please grave people. I could relate several instances of my departure from official gravity; one, however, shall suffice. It refers to the country, at St. Helen's, where there is a harbour for small ships. One morning I was awakened by a loud thump at my bed-room door. 'What's the matter?' said I. 'Cum and zee zum porpoises,' said the good man who awoke me. As soon as I could, I dressed and went down to the harbour. A singular scene presented itself. Three large fish—not porpoises, as the men supposed, but grampuses, or young whales as some thought—had got into the harbour at full tide, and had proceeded so far that on the ebbing of the tide, on their return to the sea which was just at hand, they found their passage intercepted by sand-banks, over which they had floated when the tide was at the full. I witnessed a regular battle. Men fighting with fish in their own watery element. One man stood near the shore, in water about two feet deep, fighting one of the fish with an adze. He chopped away lustily, inflicting terrible gashes, while the fish whirled round him, snapping with its frightful jaws, and flacking with its huge tail. The water was covered with foam, and froth, and blood. Men in boats

were firing musket balls into the other two fishes, and
making great efforts to capture them. After a good deal of
chasing, and loss of blood from about twenty bullets, the
poor things became dreadfully weak. Being anxious to
obtain a near view, I got into a boat loaded with seamen
and shipwrights, with guns and boat-hooks to carry on the
attack. We proceeded a little way: our boat upset. Here
was a double danger,—that of being beaten by the fish,
and losing an arm or a leg, or a head, or being carried by
the current into the sea. After awhile the boat was recovered, and all got in but myself. In the struggle, and
confusion, and floundering, the men and boat got separated
from me, and I was left to my meditations standing on a
sand-bank up to my breast in water. I was in danger
every moment of being carried off into the sea. I was
about to attempt to swim across the deep water of the
middle of the harbour to reach the opposite bank, but a
loud shout of warning prevented me. While I was wondering what to do, I perceived that the men in the boat had
captured the largest fish. They had fastened the prongs of
some boat-hooks in the top of his head, one of them in the
hole whence these creatures spout out the water. By long
and strong ropes attached to the boat-hooks, they were
pulling the poor bleeding victim to the shore. Seeing the
head of the fish so secure that he could not turn it, and
having no other mode of conveyance, I climbed on his
back! This produced a roar of laughter ; but I kept my
seat. My saddle was fearfully slippery, and the fish
thwacked me with his tail ; but I kept tight hold of a
large fin, having no bridle ; and after the brave men with

the ropes had given some long and strong pulls, the fish with its rider was brought to the shore. The poor animal lay gasping and groaning, and snapping its huge jaws, lined with double rows of terrible teeth, with great violence. Its eyes resembled a man's, and seemed to look reproaches into us for our consummate cruelty. I could not endure this. To see blood streaming from its numerous wounds, to hear groans like human, to witness agonies insufferable, moved me even to tears. I borrowed a loaded gun. "Stand off, men!" said I, "never let us be amused with sufferings." And, I might have added—men are sometimes like devils; they are pleased when they can lacerate your feelings, and torment you; they think nothing of breaking your rest, or of breaking your heart, if they do not like you, or if you, however innocently, thwart them in their purposes and designs. I might have continued— Could that poor fish speak—a creature that has done not a man of us the slightest injury—would it not say, ' When I came up your harbour, I did not meddle with you; I gave you no disturbance; you were welcome to look at my gambols; and, had you let me alone, though I had my difficulties in the shallows, yet I could easily have lived till the time of high water, and then bid you. farewell, and gone out to sea. But you fiercely assailed me,—you stabbed me and chopped me,—you fired into me twenty bullets, and made me bleed dreadfully,—you have me now out of the water,—all hope of my life is gone for ever,— oh, pray, if you have any tender mercies left, do dispatch me—my agonies are insupportable.' ' Now, men,' said I, ' let me show mercy, if you won't.' With that, I fired right between the eyes. The blood spouted from the orifice in a full stream;—another heart-rending groan—the fish turned on its side, and instantly expired. He measured eleven feet. The other two were also captured and killed."

The following tabular view, which is said to have been compiled with care, gives the population, number of parishes, Roman Catholic congregations, Presbyterians and Unitarians united, Wesleyan Methodist chapels, Baptist churches, chapels in the Countess of Huntingdon's Connexion, Independent congregations, and the total dissenters from the Established Church, in Hampshire, for the year 1827 :—

Population of Hampshire	283,298
Parishes	293
Roman Catholic Congregations . . .	11
Presbyterian and Unitarian	4
Wesleyan Chapels	26
Baptist	25
Countess of Huntingdon's Chapels . .	1
Independent	30
Total Protestant Dissenting Congregations.	86

The Wesleyans have now as many chapels in the Isle of Wight alone, as there were at the above date in the entire county, while the number of those which belong to its different offshoots is perhaps nearly equal. In some instances in the country, chapel building has been carried to an extreme. In Gunville Lane, for instance, where there are perhaps some twenty cottages, we come first to the old Wesleyan chapel, and a few yards lower down we are surprised to see two new buildings standing within a few feet of each other, respectively designated Bethel and

Bethesda, the one belonging to the Bryanites, and the other to the Primitives.

During the year 1831 the cause in West Cowes was greatly advanced by the erection of a new chapel and minister's house. The chapel stands in an excellent situation, and its neat front of Portland stone, having a light pediment and cornice, give it an extremely chaste and pleasing effect. The entire cost of the whole, including an organ for the chapel, and furniture for the house, was £2,757. It was opened for Divine worship on the 29th of September of that year. Dr. Adam Clarke preached in the morning, the Rev. R. Martin in the afternoon, and the Rev. Josiah Hill in the evening. The collections amounted to £100. Altogether the sum of £349 6s. 7d. was raised, thus leaving a heavy debt. The above sum included a donation of £25 from the Duchess of Kent. Mr. White, the eminent ship-builder, presented the pulpit. It is due to this gentleman to state that this was his general practice, for, whenever the Wesleyans built a chapel, Mr. White gave the pulpit, and hence they are found all over the Island. They are most substantial structures, being made of the very best material, generally mahogany, teak, and yellow wood, with ebony, satin, and other fancy wood mouldings, exhibiting superior workmanship. Some are ornamented with pillars, and all are capacious, and would be found strong enough to do war with Neptune. The chapel filled so well that in little more than twelve months after the opening it became necessary to enlarge it by the erection of side galleries. Since then, a large portion has been added to the end of the chapel; and, notwithstanding this additional expense, the debt is now greatly reduced. Great praise is due to Mr. James Hollis, who has been long known as a loyal and liberal-hearted Wesleyan in West Cowes; and his worth was never more truly felt than at the time when disaffection and desertion had nearly emptied the house of God.

In the year 1831, the Rev. (now Dr.) John W. Etheridge left his Island home to enter upon the duties of the Wesleyan Ministry, having been appointed by the Conference to the Hull Circuit. After labouring in many of our most important circuits, this excellent minister is still in the full work, and gathering honours with advancing years.

The first Branch Wesleyan Missionary Society for the Isle of Wight was formed in 1832. Mr. W. B. Groves was appointed Secretary; Messrs. W. and R. Yelf, Treasurers; and the following, additional members of the Committee: Messrs. J. Abraham, jun., J. Atkey, T. Atkey, W. Booth, R. Bull, W. Burt, W. Galpin, jun., J. Groves, W. Rider, A. Trimen, T. Trimen, W. Whittington. At their first anniversary they were greatly favoured in having the Rev. Robert Newton and the Rev. W. Atherton as their deputation, whose stirring eloquence gave a powerful impulse to the cause of Missions in Newport. An incident, which occurred to another deputation is too rich in its way to be lost. As the Rev. Henry Davis (now the venerable Superintendent of the Southampton Circuit) and the Rev. James Cox were crossing in a steamer from Ryde to Portsmouth, in course of discharging their deputation duties, Mr. Cox observing a venerable-looking gentleman standing on a distant part of the deck, remarked, "That is a minister.

I will go and introduce myself to him." Mr. Davis replied, "That may be your practice abroad, but our sense of propriety would not allow us to do it in this country." Mr. Cox, however, walked up to the gentleman, and introduced himself by saying, "I am a Wesleyan Missionary from the West Indies." The gentleman received him very affably, and at once questioned him on the marked difference there was in the moral and religious condition of some of those Islands. The answers which he received were so pertinent and satisfactory that a very close conversation followed, and was kept up until they neared the land, when he expressed the deep interest which he had felt in the statements made by Mr. Cox, and then added, " And now I think it right to inform you who you have been conversing with : I am the Bishop of Winchester." Mr. Cox immediately took off his hat, and begged his Lordship's blessing, when the venerable Prelate solemnly implored the Divine benediction on the head of this open-hearted missionary. After cordially shaking hands, they parted.

In 1834 the Quarterly Meeting, by a unanimous vote, raised the Minister's stipend to £125 per annum. At that period this was a bold and liberal act. In consequence of the Reform agitation it was reduced far below that standard.

The efforts of Mr. John Bull, the younger son of Robert Bull—who at the time was a member of the Wesleyan Society—greatly conduced, about this period, to the establishment of the cause in Noke Common. A small boarded chapel was put up in 1836. Land has been secured, and it is hoped that a more substantial sanctuary will ere long ornament this locality. Noke Common lies conveniently near Parkhurst Barracks and Prisons, and persons from those places attend, and some, both soldiers and civilians, belong to the Society.

Rookley, it will be remembered, was the eldest daughter of the mother Church at Newport. We regret to say that it is no longer a member of the Wesleyan family. Some years after the time to which our previous notice referred, the ark of the Gospel was removed to a farm-house, still standing on the hill-side, a little way out of the village. An ungodly young man was paying his addresses to the only daughter of the persons who lived at the farm. His companions twitted him on the prospect of becoming connected with the Methodists. With profane language he swore that when he gained possession he would make the place too hot for the Methodists. That young woman, though a member, disregarded the authority of God's Word, which positively forbids the being unequally yoked with unbelievers, and married him. Some time after that event he came into possession of the farm, and at once carried out his wicked threat by closing his door against the Society; and, although another cottage was opened, the occupants dying the Wesleyans were shut out of this the first place in which a Society was raised out of Newport. The Bryanites effected an opening, built a chapel, and are the sole occupants of the hamlet.

We have now a story to tell which ought to act as a warning to persecutors, and to those professors of religion who are forming matrimonial alliances without due regard to the Divine limitation, "Only in the Lord."

This persecutor had not been in the possession of his

farm long before a quarrel with another farmer involved
him in a law-suit, and, after taking the case from one Court
to another, judgment was given against him, and he had to
pay the heavy costs. A short time only had elapsed ere he
was engaged in a second law-suit, and again he was cast;
and to pay the costs this time, he was under the necessity
of mortgaging his farm. This was followed by other losses
and difficulties, which came thick upon him, and at length
he had to quit the farm ; and now all he, his wife, and
family of three children, had to subsist upon, was the small
pittance which he could squeeze out of the mortgagee.
To add to his troubles, a severe nervous affliction seized him,
and he sank into a state of melancholy dejection. Heavier
sorrows followed. A daughter manifested signs of mental
disorder, which rendered it necessary, after a time, to
remove her to the Union ; and death struck down his almost
famished wife, who had long ceased to enjoy the consolations
of religion. These complicated afflictions seemed to have
no other effect on the heart of this man than to sink him
into deeper dejection, and greater estrangement from God ;
and at length, after suffering great destitution, he was taken
to the Union, where, amid extreme mental and bodily
suffering, he died as he had lived, a hardened rejecter of
the Gospel. His only son was heir to the property, but was
induced, under flattering promises from the lawyers, to sign
a deed of transfer, when they at once turned him adrift on
the world, and he was soon reduced to a penniless condition.
After filling a situation for a short time, he was again reduced to want, and came to the workhouse, where he died
in a wretched state of both body and mind. Some zealous

Wesleyans visited him, as they had done his father and sister; and when one of them spoke to him of the mercy of God, he said, with a look of horror, "Don't talk to me of *that;* I'm going to hell!" Strange to tell, his sister, the only remaining member of the family, also died in the Union, and in as hopeless a state of mind. The only thing she seemed to feel was the fall in life which she and the family had sustained.

At the Conference of 1835 the Rev. Benjamin Carvosso —son of the devoted William Carvosso, and editor of his useful life—was appointed to the Superintendency of the Isle of Wight Circuit. This proved to be a happy event. At that time the peace of the Connexion was endangered by evil disposed men. The unholy leaven had found its way into the Island, and, like poison in the physical system, was producing deranged action. This evil he sought to counteract and overcome by a zealous and persistent endeavour to promote the kingdom of God and the prosperity of the entire circuit. Nor were his efforts in vain. After preaching to the people in Newport on two Sabbaths, and visiting four or five country places, he was able to say, "The Spirit of the Lord was with us, and I had much gracious liberty. Indeed, since I came to the Circuit, I have mostly felt uncommon Divine assistance, so that now the adversary would harass me by the suggestion that I have no means of supporting such expectations as are raised among the people." At the end of the year he could rear his stone of grateful remembrance, and inscribe his Ebenezer upon it. He says, "We have commenced a prayer-meeting at four o'clock a.m., which has been well attended.

We have also begun the band meetings with a hopeful prospect. On the 20th of January, 1836, about 250 members of Society took tea together in the Choral Room of Newport. Five hours were occupied in agreeable conversation, singing, prayer, and in listening to addresses on various topics, interesting and important to those who cherish a love for Methodism. The object of this meeting was to promote unity and brotherly love, an increase of personal piety, and more zealous efforts to overtake the spiritual wants of the growing population." These means were not without effect, and, though the leaven of evil was latent, and sought to show itself, especially at the September Quarterly Meeting, yet sinners were converted, and, although others left the ranks of Israel, these filled their place, and the numbers were kept up.

In the spring of 1835 morning preaching was begun at Skinner's Farm, the residence of Mr. William Booth, a warm-hearted Yorkshire Methodist, who, having married a native of the Island, came to reside there. He was a good man and true, and cherished a lively interest for the cause of Christ, especially in its missionary department, his love for which was shown both in life and in death.

Early in the year 1835, Captain John Matthews, of Wootton Bridge, died suddenly, being seized with paralysis on board his vessel. He was a true son of Neptune, and a loyal, thorough-hearted Methodist. It is said of him that he lived for seven years in the enjoyment of perfect love, and was a faithful witness of this privilege both in private and public. Walking in the full light of the Divine favour, he was a stranger to doubt and fear, and the joy of the

Lord was his strength. His activity was incessant. On board ship—on quay—in the busy crowds of London—he was in labours more abundant. As a local preacher, the originality of his style—abounding, as did also his conversation, in nautical phrases—gained him the willing ear of the seafaring congregations which he was often called to address. The ruling passion was strong in death. " Tell them [his Christian friends at Wootton] I am entering the port, with a good breeze, a full sail, and flying colours." At another time he said, " I am lying to; the colours are flying; all is clear; I am waiting for the signal." His last words were, " It is all well. It is quite calm." He died in his fortieth year. He left a large young family, and the Wesleyan Islanders, with their wonted good feeling, made a liberal subscription for them in this hour of need.

Mr. Joseph Taylor, a native of Carisbrook, was a useful member of Society. While yet a lad, he was deeply impressed under a sermon of Wesley's preached in the open air; and he used to tell with delight, in after life, how he himself supplied the place of a pulpit on the occasion, the venerable preacher resting the bible on his youthful head. For his unshaken attachment to Methodism his father banished him from home. His steps were directed to Portsmouth, where he found sympathizing friends. Some years before his death, he came to reside in Newport, and, being released from the cares of business, he devoted himself to the duties of his offices as a local preacher, class-leader, and visitor of the sick. A holy triumph marked his passage through the valley, which took place in the 81st year of his age.

CHAPTER XXII.

> "There all the ship's company meet,
>   Who sail'd with the Saviour beneath;
> With shouting each other they greet,
>   And triumph o'er trouble and death."

WE must now climb the downs which lie on the southern limits of the Island. On reaching the summit, a fine view bursts upon us. The English Channel, it may be studded with vessels, stretches away before us, until it is lost in the distant horizon; while a panorama of varied beauty is spread over a strip of ground far below our feet, and which runs for miles along the "Undercliff," both east and west. That new and clean-looking town immediately beneath us, partly nestling among the thickly-wooded groves which run up the sides of the downs, and partly spread over the cliffs extending along the shore, is Ventnor. Yonder to the left, peeping out of that luxuriant vegetation, is the romantic village of Bonchurch; and beyond that, lies the great and most beautiful landslip. The scenery especially in this locality presents the perfection of beauty. Perched amid jutting and ragged pyramids and walls of rock, or peeping out of their bowers of fadeless and varied shades of green, are the villas and mansions of wealth and nobility. New forms of beauty charm the eye at every turn, as some lovely nook, or a wider and more varied landscape exhibits itself to the delighted spectator. Viewed from the shore, the scenery is equally unique and lovely. The downs rise almost perpendicularly behind the houses to an elevation of some seven hundred feet, and form a fine back-ground to the picture, and make Ventnor what it is. They not only shelter it from the north and north-east winds, but are powerful generators of heat. During winter and spring the beams of the sun fall directly upon them, and the heat which they reflect creates a climate so mild and genial, that Ventnor has become famed as the resort of invalids at these seasons of the year. The healthiness of this locality is placed beyond all doubt, by the returns of the Registrar-General, from which it appears that the rate of mortality is lower at Ventnor than in any other part of the kingdom. That rate would be still lower, were it not for the deaths of those who are brought thither in the last stage of pulmonary disease.

Not forty years ago, Ventnor was a tiny hamlet. At the foot of the cliff—now the " Esplanade "—lay a number of low thatched fishermen's huts clustered together in the deep hollow. To the east, an old mill was perched on a high crag, down the moss and ivy-fringed sides of which, tumbling and foaming, rushed the noisy stream which gave the mill its motive power, and was, at that time, it is said, a pretty cascade. A small inn, which is still standing, and another house or two, made up the whole of Ventnor. It now contains a population of about 3,500.

In the year 1824, there was an attempt made to introduce Wesleyan Methodism into Ventnor. There were a few resident Members of Society, who were in the habit of walking over to Wroxall to attend preaching and class, there being a small Methodist cause in this hamlet at the time. At the request of the Ventnor Members, Mr. Rider went over and preached there on the Sabbath morning, taking it in connection with Wroxall. In the December following, the time of service was changed to the afternoon; but in little more than twelve months Ventnor disappeared from the plan, and was not restored for the long period of ten years, when fortnightly service was re-commenced. The elements of discouragement were still at work, and the place was again abandoned for at least six quarters. Then a third attempt was made, and certainly in a way more fraught with the probabilities of success. Hitherto the preaching had been chiefly once a-fortnight, and that in the sleepy afternoon. This time, they are favoured with service twice a-day, every Sabbath. A small class was already in existence. It was formed in the summer of 1836, and contained seven Members, and one on trial. James Herridge was the leader in this day of small things. They remained about the same figure until after the Conference of 1839, when the tide of prosperity set in, and the number in Society, including five on trial, rose in two years to fifty-seven. At the end of this period, there were three classes, which were met by Richard Cue, Henry Ingram, and John Alford. To these were added, in the succeeding year, William Herbert, and E. Goddard.

It was at the commencement of this gracious visitation,

that the project for a new chapel was mooted.   The Society
at the time held its meetings at the house of John West-
wood, known as " Sea-weed Cottage."   John was a Quaker,
but a lover of all good men.   He sometimes held forth for
the Wesleyans, and evidently enjoyed their services, and
furthered their interests.   He presented them with a piece
of ground for a place of worship, and on this site, which
was near " High-bank Cottage," a chapel was actually commenced, and the walls had been carried up a considerable
height, when, from some cause or other, the whole building
suddenly fell to the ground, and it was abandoned. ` The
preaching was removed to Albert-street; and soon after,
Mr. T. Claxton, brother of the Rev. M. Claxton, gave a
piece of ground adjoining the preaching-house.   Here a
very humble sanctuary was reared, capable of holding a
little over a hundred persons, at a cost of £250.   The
chapel was opened by the Rev. James Goulding.   During
the following year, a gallery was erected, and the chapel
was re-opened by the Rev. James Crabb, of Southampton.
It is now occupied by the Primitive Methodists, who purchased it when the Wesleyans removed to their present
place of worship.

During the year 1861, the position of Methodism was
greatly improved in Ventnor, by the completion and opening
of a new chapel in the High-street.   It is, like most of the
new chapels in the Circuit, plain Gothic, and substantially
built of stone, with school-rooms and vestries at the back,
and with land on the west side sufficient for a minister's
house.   The interior has a light and cheerful aspect, and
has been made exceedingly comfortable, especially for

invalids during the winter, by the introduction of a good stove, the gift of T. Laycock, Esq., of Keighley, Yorkshire, and is a luxury which but few chapels in the Isle of Wight can boast. The chapel cost £1,320, and it is to the credit of the friends in Ventnor that we are able to state that the debt is now reduced to £200. A superior house has been furnished for the resident minister. It is in an open situation, commanding a fine view of the cliffs and the sea. The aspect of things at Ventnor is encouraging. The Rev. W..P. Johns, with his characteristic zeal, is throwing all his energies into the attempt to extend the cause of God, and heartily do the friends co-operate with him in these laudable endeavours.

We have an excellent class of warm-hearted Members at Bonchurch. They form a part of the Ventnor Society.

The Rev. Zephaniah Job was appointed to the Isle of Wight at the Conference of 1837. Being the junior minister, he resided at Ryde. A letter which he wrote to a friend, immediately after his arrival, throws some light on the then state of the circuit:—

"Ryde, Aug. 31, 1837.

"I am now comfortably settled in my new Circuit. I preached here on Sunday, and felt it to be a day of much pleasure and profit. Ryde is a clean, pretty town, very healthy. In the summer months the town is thronged with visitors, who come from various places, some for health and some for pleasure. The surrounding scenery is lovely. The people in Ryde, I think, are very affectionate. I hope to spend a profitable and comfortable year. I saw yesterday my Superintendent and his wife, who came to Ryde. He is, I think, an affectionate and pious man. Our work is very regular. We reside, as you are aware, at three distant places—Mr. Bentham at Newport, Mr. Walker at Cowes, and myself at Ryde. We are on Sundays at each place in succession, except about one Sabbath in the quarter, when I am at Wootton-bridge, between Ryde and Newport. On the week evenings each supplies his own place, and the surrounding places; so there are some parts of the Circuit which I shall never visit. Monday evenings I meet a class. I am glad that I have a class. May God give me wisdom and grace to watch over them, so that both they and myself may go forward in the way of holiness. I have entered upon my new scene of labour with new resolutions, and I have felt much nearness to God,—an increasing union. My last year's observation and experience have shown me the necessity of walking with entire circumspection. I wish, therefore, to live to God only. I determine also to seek more earnestly the anointing of the Holy Ghost, and for a blessing on my labours." Again, in the following March he writes:—"In the Circuit we have peace. There are a few added to the Lord. The members, I trust, are growing in grace. We are now engaged in visiting the classes. In this work I intend to pay particular attention to the experience of the Members. There is pretty generally an expectation of a shower of Divine influence."

In May, Mr. Job continues the hopeful strain:—"I hope good is doing in the circuit. I think that God will send prosperity. Hindrances appear to be moving. At each of our Missionary meetings, held during the past week, there was a gracious influence resting on the people;

and I have not been without some proofs lately that God has been pleased to make me an instrument of good to some souls. But that I may be an instrument fully prepared, I need much more holiness." Nearly the last letter which he wrote to his friend during his stay in this Circuit is full of holy aspirations. "Onward," he says, "should be the Christian's motto! Retreat should never be mentioned. Oh, I must plead fervently for a richer baptism of the Holy Ghost. I was preaching on Sunday morning at Cowes on the promise, 'He shall baptize you with the Holy Ghost and with fire' (Matt. iii., 11.) This great promise I want much more completely fulfilled in my experience. The need is seen, but not sufficiently felt. . . The day of the Coronation was with you, as it was here, a day of much gaiety and dissipation. The children of the different schools in the town took dinner in the Market-house, which was decorated so as to appear like one large arbour. There were, I think, about 800. There were flags and laurels in various parts of the town; a sailing-match, and various amusements, some of which were very foolish and wicked. Shows of this description, which do no more than please the eye or the ear, have for me scarcely any charms. I shall leave some very kind friends in this Circuit." Mr. Job left at the end of the year by his own choice, and not by the wish of the Circuit.

Returning from Ventnor along the Newport Road, the pedestrian will find it a pleasant walk through Appuldurcombe Park; the foot-path passes along the front of the fine old mansion, formerly a seat of the Earl of Yarborough; the road comes out at Godshill. Dr. Cole, dean of St.

Paul's, was a native of this village.   He gained notoriety
by his vacillating conduct during the Reformation.   At
first he was a staunch opponent, both from the pulpit and
the press; but when his royal master Henry VIII. cast off
the yoke of Rome, he veered round, and joined the
Reformers.   When Mary ascended the throne, he returned
to his old friends, and, after disputing with Ridley and
Cranmer, was appointed to preach the execution sermon of
the latter.   Having obtained a commission, he was on his
way to Ireland, inflamed with a desire to crush the
Reformation there.   Unfortunately for him, he could not
keep his own counsel, and, while divulging the object he
had in view to the Mayor of Chester, he was overheard by
his hostess, who had a brother in Dublin, a clergyman.
She contrived to substitute a pack of cards for the commission, which was carried in a little box for the purpose.
On his arrival in Dublin he was introduced to the Lord
Lieutenant, and with due formality presented the box,
when the mortifying discovery was made.   The trick of
which he was the dupe exposed him to the keen sarcasms
of the Governor, and rendered it absolutely necessary for
him to return for a new commission.   In the meantime the
Queen died, and thus terminated his ambitious and cruel
schemes.   Elizabeth rewarded the clever hostess with a
pension of £40 a year.

The Wesleyan chapel at Godshill was erected in 1838;
it stands on a fine piece of ground, which was given by the
late Earl of Yarborough.   It is worthy of being told of
this liberal-minded nobleman, that on one occasion, when
requested by a dignitary of the Establishment to put down
the Wesleyans on a certain part of his estates, promptly

met the request by the somewhat posing question, "But, my Lord, what if the Methodists are right?" The Bishop not being prepared with an answer, the matter dropped. (Matt. xxi., 25, 26.) One of Mr. White's substantial pulpits adorns this sanctuary. This, and other work done gratis by Mr. Hollis, the builder, and others, reduced the entire cost of £364 to £306. About four years after the chapel was opened, the junior minister was appointed to reside at Godshill, where he remained until the growing claims of Ventnor rendered his removal thither necessary. The Rev. T. Leach, who was sent out from this circuit, was the first resident minister in Godshill.

In the year 1840 Mr. W. Dawson, of Barnbow, near Leeds, opened a very excellent chapel at Wootton-bridge. A very serious debt, however, amounting to £1,050 was left upon it, and greatly impeded the cause of God in this village for some years afterwards. By the praiseworthy efforts of the Rev. James Taylor, and the liberality of the friends, this heavy burden was greatly lightened. Soon after, a gracious revival broke out, and a number of young persons, several of them members of Mr. Cooper's family, were brought to Christ, who remain steadfast to this day.

Under Mr. Dawson's morning sermon Miss Ellen Roach, of Newport, received the remission of sins, and became a consistent member of Society. She was afterwards united in marriage to Mr. W. B. Groves. During her last sickness, the enemy was permitted to assail her with distressing doubts. She keenly felt parting with her family, the children of which were young ; but grace triumphed over fond nature, and, being "filled with all joy and peace in believing," she could say, "To die is gain." She sank to sleep on the bosom of Jesus, on the 29th of October, 1853, aged 32.

Mr. and Mrs. Groves were, during the evening of life, associated with the Society in this village. They were the parents of the family of that name so well known and respected in the Island and at Portsmouth. Mr. Groves was a native of Freshwater, and Mrs. Groves, whose maiden name was Barton, of Haven-street. Training up their large family in the way they should go, it was their happiness to see all of them who reached maturity not depart from it. Henry entered the Wesleyan ministry, and laboured with zeal and acceptance in various parts of the Connexion until the Conference of 1848, when he was suddenly called to his reward. Three years of his ministerial career were spent in the Isle of Wight. Josiah, who was united in marriage to Miss Keet, of Portsmouth, was an acceptable local preacher, and died in that town. Mrs. Groves reached the end of her Christian pilgrimage in peace, November, 1838, and in 1844 her sainted spirit was rejoined by that of her beloved husband.

The cause at Blackwater originated in 1842. Mr. W. Rider—now one of the oldest local preachers in the Island —went to reside at Blackwater farm, and opened his house for preaching, and soon had the happiness of seeing a few rally round him whose hearts had been touched by the truth. On Mr. Rider's removal to Newport, a chapel was erected at a cost of £270. It was opened by the Revds. Dr. Andrews, J. Phenix, jun., and J. Mole. With subscriptions and collections the sum of £170 was obtained, thus leaving a debt of £100. That debt is now discharged, and Blackwater chapel is one among several in the Newport

Circuit which is free from such encumbrance. The effort commenced in 1860, and was completed in three years, thus: A grant of £12 was obtained from the Chapel Building Committee; a legacy of £16 13*s*. 4*d*. by the late Mr. Booth, of Skinner's Farm; and £70 16*s*. 8*d*. was raised by quarterly subscriptions and donations,—total, £99 9*s*. 4*d*.

Mr. James King was one of the first-fruits of the Gospel in Blackwater. He was a man of few words, but highly respected for his integrity and consistency. He took a severe cold, and his strong frame gradually gave way under the fatal inroads of consumption. He died resting on the atonement of Christ, on May 27, 1863.

We must now return to a familiar name and a conse-crated spot—Merston—where a new chapel was built in 1848. It stands near to the cottage of Mary Prangnell. During the preceding twenty years, this desirable object had been eagerly sought, but every previous attempt to procure ground had failed. Now, however, the very field on the corner of which the friends had often cast a longing eye, was offered for sale, and readily purchased by Mr. Thomas Tharle, who at once made over the coveted spot, and a very pretty chapel was erected upon it. It cost £204, and is out of debt. The air of tastefulness and cleanliness which this cheerful sanctuary wears reflects credit on those who have it in charge.

Mr. Tharle, named above, was a decided Methodist, and a sincere and blameless Christian. He was exceedingly retiring in his habits, but strongly attached to the preachers, whom he delighted to entertain under his own roof, and was a liberal supporter of the cause. He died of paralysis January 18, 1860. His last words were, "It is light."

Mr. James Bull, of Newport, son of Robert Bull, was appointed as the leader of the Merston class in 1835, and this important relation he sustained until the autumn of 1864, when the distance (seven miles to and fro) compelled him to relinquish the post, which he had filled with great acceptance and success. The Society presented him with a handsomely-bound copy of Wesley's hymns as a small token of their affectionate esteem. He was succeeded by Mr. James Linington, of Newport. Merston has been celebrated for its liberal doings for Foreign Missions, its annual income having reached the noble sum of £20.

A deeply affecting and painful occurrence happened to a member of the family of Mr. B. Tharle, of Little Budbridge Farm, where the preachers ever find a hospitable entertainment. Clement, a noble but modest youth of 17, was out with an elder brother rook shooting, and, while in the act of leaning on his gun it went off, and the contents tore away a portion of the upper part of his head, and so injured him that in about two hours he expired. How loud the call, "Be ye also ready!"

In the above year, a room was fitted up for preaching, and a Society formed at Red Hill, the residence of Mr. Morris. A wealthy gentleman in the neighbourhood was so annoyed at this, that he offered Mr. Morris £200 to take down the room. On a subsequent occasion, when applied to for a piece of ground for a chapel at Niton, among other things this gentleman observed "that as for himself he had no time to go to a place of worship on a Sunday, it was all taken up in looking after his hares." In a few days afterwards the final summons reached him in the midst of his pleasures, and he was suddenly called to give an account of his stewardship. "What shall a man give in exchange for his soul?" On the removal of Mr. Morris, the cause languished, and, after a time, failed entirely. Last year, however, a pretty little chapel was opened in the neighbouring village of Niton. The Watering Places Chapel Building Committee have kindly offered the trustees £150 towards the reduction of the debt of £605 on the chapels in our three watering-places in this Circuit, provided the whole be extinguished within a given period; which offer the trustees have accepted, and hope soon to accomplish.

The agitation, which had been smouldering for some years before, broke out in 1850, and carried destruction over the Connexion like a flood of lava. The Island did not escape. Several chapels were nearly emptied, and others were taken away. Four hundred and eleven members were lost to the Parent Society in two years. How many of these were lost to Christ the great day alone will reveal. The reduction of members went on until, in seven years, the Society contained only half as many members as it did at the commencement of that period. The tide now turned; some retraced their steps, others were added, and, in 1861, 830 members were returned. At the Conference of that year the Island was divided, and Ryde was made the head of a Circuit.

Shorwell lies in a valley greatly enriched by cultivation. It is almost buried amid giant elms, beech, and other lofty trees. On the 4th of October, John Wesley preached (as already noted) to the wondering villagers, who all flocked to hear, excepting a few rich ones, who, it seems, preferred a dinner to an open-air sermon. There is no record of any second attempt to preach the Gospel by the Wesleyans in this village until the year 1809, when the Rev. William Baker, then labouring as a Home Missionary on the Island, took Shorwell on his Mission list. He was stationed at Cowes, to give the people there a more regular supply of preaching on Sundays and week-nights; the rest of his time was devoted to the breaking up of fresh ground. He visited several places in the Island, but did not always succeed. Amongst others he made an attempt at Shorwell, for which he was threatened with imprisonment, but was fortunate enough to escape. Afterwards he got a house licensed, and continued the preaching. After a time the cause became extinct at Shorwell, and, although preaching was afterwards resumed at Yafford, it did not become established until the year 1860. Mr. Henry Morris, of Kingston Farm, had long had it in his heart to introduce Wesleyan Methodism into Shorwell, but every attempt had been baffled by High Church influence. At length this desirable object was gained. Some land coming into the market, it was secured by Mr. Morris, and a portion set apart for the Lord, and mainly through his liberality a neat and substantial chapel was built and opened in that year. During the last spring a gracious revival of the work of God took place in this village, and more than twenty persons were brought under conviction for sin, and many of them are now rejoicing in the salvation of God.

It was once our lot in this locality to witness one of the finest sunsets ever beheld in these Islands. Local scenery greatly heightened the effect. It was in the early part of the month of April. Accompanied by an American minister, we were on our way to the little chapel, and as we were descending the hill, towards the foot of which it stands, our attention was arrested by the setting sun, which was going down like a ball of molten steel. Wishful to obtain a better view, we climbed to the summit of a neighbouring hill, and here one of the sublimest scenes in Creation burst upon us. The atmosphere was peculiarly pure, and transparent as crystal, causing objects to appear not only remarkably distinct but surprisingly near. Freshwater Cliffs lay directly in front, stretching away from the Gate to the Needles, and rising out of the sea like an immense wall to a perpendicular height of nearly eight hundred feet, and, although some dozen miles distant, the very lines on the rocks were distinctly traced.

The descending sun now threw up such a flood of beams from behind the cliffs that the whole country beyond seemed like one vast furnace of fire, while those upturned rays were caught by the clouds, which at a high altitude stretched out in narrow strata far over land and sea. Immediately over the cliffs they hung in isolated patches, and were so permeated with beams of light that, as they slowly glided on, they resembled nothing so much as islands of burnished gold floating on a sea of glory. Above these were wide-spread masses of cumuli, the edges of which, with those of the still higher and extended strata, were fringed with a silvery light so intense and dazzling as to rival the brilliancy of a diamond, while the great body of the clouds wore a deep rich purple crimson, which softened down in the distance into rose, amber, and buff; and yet this gorgeous scene, like the dying dolphin, was changing colour every moment, and gave out almost all the varied tints of the rainbow. A little to the left of the Needles, Portland Bill, although nearly forty miles away, stood out in bold outline, and seemed like some huge sea monster sleeping on the placid waters. Beyond this the horizon-line, where sea and sky met, was as finely drawn as though it had been done with a pencil, and yet so distant that the numerous ships by which it was dotted were reduced to merest specks. This line swept far out towards the coast of France, and away to the left, until it was lost behind the crags which crown the eastern flank of Blackgang Chine. The sea was smooth, and looked like polished glass, and every vessel could be seen with surprising distinctness of detail—masts, sails, and cordage,—while the Island itself was bathed in a faint amber light, and its beautiful downs and valleys looked like some fairy land. The whole scene was one of indescribable beauty, rarely witnessed in these latitudes, and never to be effaced from the memory of those who were permitted to gaze upon it.

Carisbrook—hoary with age, and around which rarest associations thickly cluster—is probably the most ancient town in the Isle of Wight, and was at one time its capital. The castle stood on a commanding site, and was the strongest place of security and defence in the Island. It has been rendered famous as the prison of the unhappy Charles I.; and thousands come to view what Wesley calls the "poor remains of the room where the king was con-fined, and the window through which he tried to escape." The ruins of a fine Roman villa have been discovered in the valley between the castle and the village. It is sup-posed to have been the residence of the Military Governor of the Island during the Roman occupation. One cannot visit this interesting relic of antiquity, and walk over its beautifully tesselated pavement, without having the imagination carried back to that remote period when, untouched by decay, it was occupied by those lordly conquerors who slept securely beneath its shadow, protected by the encampment on the hill, strongly fortified and defended by veteran legions. Might not one of these be another Cornelius? and who shall say that it was not he who sent messengers, and gave the call to the Apostle of the Gentiles to visit these " distant Isles of the West?" And it is not impossible but that the Apostle Paul may have stood on that very spot, while, side by side, the blue-eyed Briton and the swarthy Italian may have listened to the Gospel as it was proclaimed by apostolic lips.

From the journal of Mr. James Trimen, we learn that Methodist preaching was commenced in Carisbrook more than seventy-five years ago. He states :—" May 31, 1789. Mr. Holmes preached at Carisbrook from 'If any man have not the spirit of Christ he is none of his.' They have a very neat convenient preaching-room. But few attended, while Mr. H. enlarged on the necessity of the Spirit of God to convince and convert the soul, man being morally helpless without it." This and other early attempts did not, it would seem, succeed. In 1861, Miss Spickernell, a liberal-minded lady belonging to another branch of Christ's Church, offered the Wesleyans the free use of an upper room for preaching. It was already furnished with pulpit and seats, and, through the kindness of the Rev. Calvert Spensley—who had recently come to reside in this lovely retreat, in quest of health—the room was put in order, preaching established, and a small Society sprang into being. We close our brief notice of the cause in this ancient village with a sketch of the above-named highly respected minister, who spent the evening of his days at Glenfield Cottage, which lies ensconsed in one of its most sheltered nooks. Love to the mission work, and the hope that a Southern climate might prove beneficial to his health, induced Mr. Spensley to offer himself as a Missionary to South Africa; and accordingly, at the Conference of 1850 he was appointed to Kuangubeni, in the rising colony of Port Natal. After seven years of arduous and successful labour, failing health compelled him to return home, a circumstance which was deeply deplored by all classes in the colony. His native air, and rest, proved so far beneficial as to excite the hope that he might take an easy station, and at the Conference of 1859 he was appointed to the Carmarthen Circuit, South Wales, and took up his abode at Llanelly. Here he devoted himself to the duties of his high vocation with his characteristic energy, and soon overtaxed his strength. It was the writer's happiness to have him as his colleague for that year, and well does he remember the raw October morning on which he took cold, and was so prostrated as to be unable again to resume his regular work. In the following spring he was compelled to leave the Circuit, to the great grief of the friends, in whose affectionate remembrance he will ever live, and, after visiting various places, came by medical advice to the Isle of Wight. Possessing vigorous intellectual powers, and untiring energy, his close application to study and reading enriched his mind with varied and most valuable information and knowledge. His preaching was argumentative and lucid, his language terse, and his sermons were attended with a Divine power which carried conviction to the hearts of his hearers. During his last affliction the flame of life trembled long in the socket, and was alone preserved by the Divine blessing on the unwearied devotion of his wife and niece, who day and night anticipated his every want. But as his physical strength gradually failed, the vigour of the inner man grew stronger and stronger. Prayer and praise were his daily employment, and he designated his room the porch of Paradise. His patience and submission to the will of God were perfect, his trust in Jesus implicit, and his views of Divine things were vivid and at times unspeakably joyous. On the 20th of February, 1863, he calmly fell asleep, in the 45th year of his age and the 20th of his ministry. A beautiful tomb marks the spot where his remains rest, beneath the shade of a venerable elm in Whippingham churchyard.

On the morning of Christmas-day, 1863, the Rev. Joseph Thorpe Milner left the militant to join the triumphant church above. Mr. Milner entered the Wesleyan Ministry in 1825, and laboured with great acceptance in various Circuits until 1861, when he became a supernumerary. In the spring of the following year he took up his abode at Elm Grove, Newport, Isle of Wight. Here, as health permitted, it was his delight to proclaim to others that Gospel which had been to him, especially in times of great physical suffering, his richest source of consolation and strength. During his last affliction, his sufferings were extreme, but faith gave him the victory, and he now sleeps with those who wait the resurrection of the just. With great natural sensitiveness, there was combined in Mr. Milner's character a noble Christian dignity of deportment, a frank and generous disposition, large liberality and benevolence of heart, and an unswerving maintenance of truth and rectitude. As a minister, Mr. Milner was a diligent student, an energetic preacher, and, to the intelligent portion of his congregations especially, highly acceptable. In listening to his richly evangelical and well-digested discourses, delivered in plain but strong Saxon language, and especially his powerful appeals to the conscience, one could not but feel that the Psalmist's declaration was applicable to the preacher, where he says, " I believed, therefore have I spoken ;" and it is not surprising that many of his vivid and striking utterances should have been caught and treasured up by those who love to cherish the memory of his heart-stirring sermons. A chaste tomb, reared by the fond affection of his sorrowing widow, marks the place—chosen by himself—where his mortal remains lie, near the chief entrance of Carisbrook Cemetery. In this famed village Mr. Milner closed his ministry by preaching from that appropriate text, Dan. xii., 3.

In 1859 an important movement was commenced in Newport, when the scheme was originated which contemplated the extinction of the oppressive debt on the chapel, amounting to £1,370. Application was made to the Chapel Building Committee, who liberally engaged that, provided the trustees would raise £1,000, they would extinguish the remaining £370 by a loan of £270 and a grant of £100. The friends, both rich and poor, entered heartily into the project, and Mr. W. B. Groves headed the subscription-list with £100, a noble example, which was promptly followed by others in various sums. These subscriptions were to be paid within a period of five years by quarterly instalments. Some preferred to pay their subscriptions at once, and at the end of three years the sum of £600 was realized, and half the loan and £65 of the grant were advanced by the Committee, so that £800 of the debt was discharged. Since then, £300 more has been contributed, thus leaving £100 still to be raised towards the £1,000.

In the summer of 1862 Mr. J. Cooper, a respected local preacher, was suddenly called to his reward; he has left a widow and large family to mourn his loss.

Last year a Juvenile Home and Foreign Missionary Society was organized in Newport, an example which was followed by Ryde, and in both cases the first year has proved a success, and our young friends will be encouraged to go on and prosper. The advantages which we believe will accrue from this source, especially to our young men, is great. When it is remembered that these Societies take hold upon them at that critical and momentous period when youth terminates in manhood, and they must go forth and meet the stern realities of life, and wage war with the thousand evils that will beset their path, the value of these institutions cannot be over-estimated. To pre-occupy the mind with good is half the battle won. Our churches have yet to awake to a sense of their importance and worth.

The Missionary Jubilee Meeting was held in Newport in the early part of the spring of 1864, when the sum of £150 17s. 4d. was promised. The amount in the Ryde Circuit was rather above that figure, so that over £300 will be obtained from the Island for this important object. The sum raised during the Centenary year was £387 12s. 10d.

In the autumn of last year Mrs. Jones, of Blacklands, entered into rest. She was brought to God under the ministry of the Rev. B. Carvosso. In her last affliction she was called to endure extreme suffering, but faith grew, and hope brightened, until she was raised into an ecstacy of joy, which rendered her superior to all the pains and weakness of the failing flesh. She went to be with Christ in the 53rd year of her age. Her sister, Mrs. G. Snellgrove, was a member of Society, and also died in the Lord.

In the autumn of 1862, Mr. Joseph Groves, jun., a medical student, and his sister—two members of Society— were walking up the Ryde Old Road, when the report reached them of an accident which had just taken place round the bend of the road before them. Mr. Groves ran forward, and soon came up to a carriage which had come in contact with a cart and was upset; two ladies were lying near it, entangled in the carriage furniture, which had been thrown out. The elder lady was quickly released, and had sustained no further injury than a few bruises and a rather deep cut on the hand. The other, who was much younger, had, beside a severe shock, suffered injury in the ankle, and was unable to rise. Mr. Groves raised her from the ground, and assisted her to a house on the road-side, where he dressed their wounds; and here, to his great surprise, he learned that his timely assistance had been given to no less a personage than her Royal Highness Princess Alice, who was accompanied by the Hon. Mrs. Bruce. It was pleasing to hear the grateful acknowledgment made by these ladies of the remarkable interposition of Divine Providence, by which their lives had been preserved in so great a danger. The attendance of Mr. Groves was required at Osborne, but on his arrival he was glad to find that no serious con- sequences had ensued to the Royal party.

A scheme, fraught with many advantages to the Ryde Circuit, has been introduced by its excellent Superintendent the Rev. Thomas Osborn, and is heartily supported by his colleagues the Rev. Charles Willis, of Cowes, and the Rev. J. M. Morrill, of Sandown. It embraces the erection of a new chapel at Shanklin, costing £300; the erection of side galleries in the Ryde chapel, the large influx of visitors in the season rendering this necessary; and a new chapel, with school-rooms, at Sandown, costing £1,000. The whole £1,500, with the aid of £300 from the Watering Places Chapel Building Committee, to be accomplished free from debt. The chapel at Shanklin has been opened, and has a congregation exceeding the expectations of many. Land sufficient for chapel, school-rooms, and minister's house, at Sandown, has been purchased in an eligible site.

We now come to notice a recent movement by which the cause of Christ has been advanced in Newport—the renovation of the chapel, which had become dirty and dilapidated, and was very badly lighted, while many of the seats were so narrow that they could not be let. After mature consideration important alterations were begun and completed during the last summer. The organ gallery, with two unsightly windows at the end of the chapel, have been removed, and a capacious pulpit platform, with a projecting circular front, has been placed in a semi-circular moulded and pannelled recess, the whole having a very chaste and pleasing effect. The front of the gallery has been lowered, and relieved with ornamental bronzed iron-work, and the lower part is flatted white and gold. The whole of the body of the chapel has been repewed, stained, and varnished; and new lobbies, with eight doors, four on patent hinges, have been introduced. A gaselier of fifty-four burners throws a flood of light into every part of the chapel. The whole of these alterations were effected for less than £400. Nearly £300 has been realised, and it is hoped the remainder will be obtained in a few weeks. A very large proportion of the pews are let, and both the income and congregation of the chapel are greatly improved. A series of special services recently held in it have brought an addition of some thirty persons to the Society. After a week of noon-day and evening prayer-meetings, a backslider found peace on the Sabbath morning while the Rev. Charles Bradley was preaching; and under the powerful appeals of the Rev. W. P. Johns, who preached several times during the succeeding week, followed by the Rev. C. Willis, of Cowes, many reached the crisis of their being, and became decided, and all, so far, hold on their way.

A measure was proposed at our last Quarterly Meeting which will place the finances of the Newport Circuit on a more solid basis. It was unanimously resolved that a combined and vigorous effort be made to extinguish the whole of the remaining chapel debts, and that the surplus income of each chapel should be regularly paid to the Quarter Board for the support and extension of the cause of God in the circuit. The first of the services (which are to be held throughout the Circuit) took place at Newport on the 5th and 6th Feb., 1865, when the list of promises was raised to £170, which the friends regard as an earnest and pledge of complete success.

We are glad to hear that very eligible School Rooms have been purchased at West Cowes, which no doubt will ere long be opened as a Day School,—an example which Newport and other towns in the Island will not, we hope, be slow to follow.

What a contrast—we may observe in conclusion—does the present moral and religious condition of the Island present to what it was at the time when the Methodist preachers first cast their eyes and bent their steps towards its shores. Somewhat above twenty churches were then scattered over the Island, but their pulpits were as destitute of attraction as they were of evangelical power. The Island was sleeping, with the rest of the nation, through that long night of spiritual darkness and insensibility which had overtaken it during the preceding century. But the morning was near, and the day broke when Wesley and his " helpers" lifted up their voice in the streets and lanes of its towns and villages, and woke those slumberers, some to a joyous reception of the Gospel, and others to a fierce opposition to it ; and yet not a few of these even were subdued by its power. Through its instrumentality many hundreds of persons in this Island have been made meet for the heavenly inheritance, into the possession of which they have entered, and hundreds more are now the subjects of a preparatory work of grace ; while Churchmen and Dissenters have kindled the flame of their zeal at its altar, and not a few of their pulpits have been supplied from its ranks. Of the Societies themselves we can truly say that we have seldom or never known a more willing and liberal people than the Wesleyan Methodists of the Isle of Wight.

CHAPELS.	BUILT.	COST.	SEATS.	DEBT.
Newport	1803	£2280	700	£250
Ventnor	1861	1320	370	200
Freshwater	1861	328	230	None
Yarmouth	1824	180	100	None
Chale	1836	300	130	None
Shorwell	1860	200	120	50
Blackwater	1845	270	100	None
Merston	1848	204	80	None
Godshill	1838	374	150	100
Shalfleet	1861	224	110	50
Gunville	1815	Given	50	None
Carisbrook		Lent	60	None
Niton	1864	327	110	114
Total..		5907	2310	764

H. S. MORRIS, Kingston,
C. DORE, Newport,   *Circuit Stewards.*

PLACES.	L. PREACHERS.	LEADERS AND STEWARDS.
NEWPORT ..	J. Pinhorn J. Bull W. Rider T. Trimen J. Linington W. H. Day T. Cann E. H. F. Payn J. Camp W. Garland G. Young J. Blackmore	Rev. W. Moister J. Pinhorn M. Pinhorn E. Bull J. Groves S. Groves C. Dore A. Dore L. Dyson J. Linington W. H. Day J. Punch M. Deacon J. Bull, G. Snellgrove, } *Stewards* J. Groves,
VENTNOR	H. Ingram W. Wickens H. Ingram, jun R. Medley G. Gilbert	H. Ingram W. Wickens G. Gilbert R. Saunders G. M. Burt } *Stewards* H. Ingram, jun.
FRESHWATER ..		J. Webb, T. H. Moody, } *Stewards*
YARMOUTH ..	J. A. Cole R. Down	J. Webb H. Warder J. A. Cole, *Steward*
CHALE	W. Spanner J. Linington G. Lowe	H. S. Morris J. Linington G. Lowe, *Steward*
SHORWELL ..	H. Brown	H. Brown
BLACKWATER ..		W. Rider
MERSTON ..		J. Linington J. Baker, *Steward*
GODSHILL ..		M. Morris J. Thomas, *Steward*
SHALFLEET ..		W. Fiander
GUNVILLE ..		J. Underwood
CARISBROOK ..		J. Linington
NITON		W. Spanner

CHAPELS.					BUILT.	COST.	SEATS.	DEBT.
Ryde ..	..	..	..	..	1841	£2000	450	£900
Cowes	..	..	..	..	1831	2757	600	450
Sandown	..	..	..	..	1860	310	150	80
Wootton	..	..	..	..	1840	1050	300	120
Sea View	..	..	..	..	1845	250	120	150
Saint Helens	..	..	..	..	1807	220	150	None
Bembridge ..	..	..	..	..	1844	200	150	60
Haven Street	..	..	..	..	1833	200	120	None
Noke Common	..	..	..	..		120	60	None
Northwood ..	..	..	..	..	1823	200	120	40
East Cowes (Rented Room)		..	..					None
Hale Common	..	..	..	..	1837	120	100	None
Shanklin	..	..	..	..	1864	320	120	None
Total..		..	..			7747	2440	1800

W. C. WOODS, Ryde, } *Circuit Stewards.*
A. HEWITT, Cowes,

PLACES.	LOCAL PREACHERS.	LEADERS AND STEWARDS.
RYDE	J. Jeffery	J. Withers
	E. K. Minter	J. Groves
	J. Withers	E. Groves
	G. Harber	J. Jeffery
	J. Osborn	W. Storey
	G. Godfrey	E. K. Minter
	W. Allen	W. Denham
	.. .. ..	W. Williams
	.. .. ..	M. A. Harmsworth
	.. .. ..	J. Bevins
	.. .. ..	Drew Osborn } *Stewards*
	.. .. ..	W. C. Woods,
COWES	J. Dauber	James Hollis
	.. .. ..	John Goffe
	.. .. ..	Mary Francis
	.. .. ..	John Dauber
	.. .. ..	Alfred Hewitt
	.. .. ..	James Hatch
	.. .. ..	Thomas Brown
SANDOWN ..	J. Mew	James Boyce
	.. .. ..	John Mew
	.. .. ..	J. Whittington
	.. .. ..	J. Bunt
WOOTTON ..	W. Hobbs	John Mew
	J. Cotton	William Hobbs
	J. Burden	Caroline Hobbs
	W. Thompson	Richard Patey
	.. .. ..	John Burden
SEA VIEW ..	J. Matthews	J. Matthews
	W. Matthews	
NOKE COMMON	G. Burgess	George Burgess
	G. Heal	Eliza Jupe
	.. .. ..	Isaac Flux
BEMBRIDGE ..	.. .. ..	J. Goodall
HALE COMMON	.. .. ..	T. Hawkins
NORTHWOOD ..	.. .. ..	—. Gubbins
EAST COWES ..	.. .. ..	—. Gough
HAVEN STREET	.. .. ..	W. Hobbs
ST. HELENS ..	.. .. ..	—. James

A LIST OF MINISTERS

WHO HAVE TRAVELLED IN THE ISLE OF WIGHT, COMMENCING WITH WILTSHIRE.

Date	No. in Society	Ministers.
1758		Thomas Johnson, Richard Cornish, John Murlin.
1759		Thomas Hanby, Robert Roberts, George Roe, — Hitchings.
1760		James Morgan, Nicholas Gilbert, Richard Lucas.
1761		Richard Henderson, John Heslop, Nicholas Manners, J. Glasbrook.
1762		Alexander Mather, Thos. Hanson, Thos. Mayor, Wm. Mincthorpe.
1763		Alexander Coates, John Ellis, Thomas Bourke, Wm. Mincthorpe.
1764		John Moorley, Mark Davis, Isaac Brown, Wm. Mincthorpe.
1765		Richard Henderson, John Slocomb, Richard Walsh, Thos. Simpson.
1766	941	Alexander Mather, Thos. Dancer, James Stephens, John Oldham.
1767	840	A. Mather, John Catermole, William Orpe, John Haime.
1768	956	N. Manners, William Barker.

Wiltshire divided into North and South—South Wiltshire.

Date	No. in Society	Ministers.
1769	200	John Mason, Thomas Brisco.
1770	323	John Catermole, Francis Asbury.
1771	277	William Pitt, William Ashman.
1772	278	Richard Bourke, William Eels.
1773	340	William Collins, John Crowle.
1774	330	James Barry, John Undrell, Thomas Westall.
1775	315	Francis Wolfe, Thomas Vasey, J. Undrell, James Skinner (Missionary to the Isle of Wight.)
1776	317	Richard Rodda, James Colley, Thomas Newall, John Pescod.
1777	309	R. Rodda, James Watson.
1778	301	Richard Whatcoat, William Barker, James Perfect.
1779		R. Whatcoat, David Evans, John Wittam, Richard Seed.
1780	331	W. Tunney, John Poole, John Walker, William Green.
1781	346	Francis Wrigley, Thomas Shaw, Jonathan Cousins, J. Poole.
1782	373	John Mason, William Moore, William Hoskins, Nathaniel Ward.
1783	386	John Mason, George Story, Joseph Jerom.
1784	385	J. Moon, G. Story, George Wadsworth.
1785	380	J. Moon, John Wittam, Robert Empringham.
1786	430	William Ashman, William Butterfield, Charles Kyte.
1787	593	W. Ashman, John Pritchard, William Hunter, Thomas Warwick (Missionary to the Isle of Wight.)
1788	464	William Thorn, William Holmes, Richard Cornish, J. Winscom, Thomas Allen.
1789	636	William Thorn, Theophilus Lessey, Richard Marshall; Jasper Winscom, H. Saunders (Missionaries to the Isle of Wight.)

Date	No. in Society	Ministers.
	Sarum 556 I.W.	*Portsmouth made the Head of a Circuit.*
1790	150	John Easton, William Stephens, Henry Saunders.
1791	430	John Easton, Michael Marshall, Thomas Dobson.
1792	480	John Easton, George Button, Thomas Tretheway.
1793	500	Charles Bland, John Cricket, Henry Saunders.
1794	550	Charles Bland, Thomas Simmonite, James Crabb, Wm. Howarth.
1795	500	Joseph Algar, George Deverell, James Crabb, John Jones, Joseph Brookhouse.
1796	540	Joseph Algar, Thos. Rought, Joseph Brookhouse, Charles Greenley.
1797	670	J. Algar, William Ashman, John Clarke, Thomas Stanton, John Sydserf; John Mason, Supernumerary.
1798	745	Robert Smith, jun., Thomas Stanton, William Johnson, J. Mason, Supernumerary.
1799	510	R. Smith, jun., Humphrey Parsons, John Rossell, J. Mason, Super.
1800	560	R. Smith, jun., James Alexander, John Burdsall; J. Mason, Supernumerary.
1801	625	William Horner, J. Burdsall, David Coe.
1802	518	W. Horner, George Gellard, D. Coe.
1803	491	William Avir, John Walmsley, G. Gellard.
1804		W. Avir, J. Walmsley, William Fowler; J. Mason, Supernumerary.
1805	535	Joseph Cole, Mark Daniel, Samuel Sewel.
1806	588	J. Cole, Mark Daniel, William Pearson, jun.
1807	593	James M'Byron, John Knowles, sen., Edward Roberts.
1808	683	J. M'Byron, Samuel Woolmer, David M'Nichol.
1809	800	Jonathan Barker, S. Woolmer, Thos. Twiddy, Frederick Calder; J. M., Super.; Wm. Baker, sen. (Isle of Wight.)
1810	930	J. Barker, William Henshaw, Joseph Wilson, Jonathan Williams, Jonathan Roberts (Isle of Wight).
		The Isle of Wight Circuit.
1811	260	Richard Moodey, John Smith, jun., Thomas Key.
1812	300	Henry Cheverton, John Bustard, Thomas Newton.
1813	272	Josiah Goodwin, John Rigg.
1814	250	J. Goodwin, George Banwell; Benjamin Hiley, Missionary.
1815	265	Francis B. Potts, B. Hiley, Edward B. Lloyd (Ryde).
1816	283	F. B. Potts, John Willis, John Coates (Ryde).
1817	300	F. B. Potts, Edward Batty, John Geden (Ryde).
1818	310	E. Batty, William Constable.
1819	316	E. Batty, W. Constable.
1820	320	Robert Wheeler, Robert Mack.
1821	308	R. Wheeler, R. Mack.
1822	291	James Sydserf, John Brown (2nd).
1823	320	J. Sydserf, John Brown (2nd), John Cropp.
1824	400	Isaac Phenix, sen., Jeremiah Pentefract, John H. Faull.
1825	390	Isaac Phenix, William Hicks, James Kendall.
1826	430	Anthony B. Seckerson, William Kelk, John Gick.
1827	430	Daniel Osborne, Robert Manwaring, John Cotton.
1828	440	D. Osborne, Thomas Moxon.
1829	450	William Griffith, sen., Solomon Whitworth.
1830	410	W. Griffith, sen., John Wesley Button, Charles Westlake.
1831	418	J. Hawtrey, J. W. Button, Charles Currelly; Samuel Simmons, supply.
1832	500	William Worth, William Tarr, William H. Sargent.
1833	671	W. Worth, W. Tarr, W. H. Sargent.